# KNIFE

EDGE

FERGUS MCNEILL

HODDER

McNeill

A chilling game of cat and mouse that should keep you awake long after bedtime. DI Harland is a welcome addition to the growing ranks of British detectives.'
Peter Robinson

Let's welcome Fergus McNeill to the ranks of British crime fiction innovators; he has found a darker shade of noir'
Quintin Jardine

'A gripping first novel'
*Irish Independent*

'Creepy, compelling and completely convincing'
Erin Kelly

great read and a chillingly clever insight into the mind and motives a killer. Harland is a welcome new addition to the force of fictional oppers and McNeill a refreshing new voice in crime fiction; on the idence of *Eye Contact*, we'll be hearing a lot more from them both.'
Brian McGilloway

'[A] cracking story, set in and around the Winchester/Salisbury rea and has a cliff hanger ending which will, I hope, lead on to the next from this author. Great stuff.'
*www.randomjottings.typepad.com*

A] confident debut from Fergus McNeill, mixing thriller with police rocedural . . . to create a tense, compelling and truly unputdownable read . . . *Eye Contact* is a novel that will have the reader losing track of time. It also ends on an atypical note, adding to its originality.'
*www.itsacrimeuk.wordpress.com*

'A tense police procedural from a new author with a promising future in crime fiction'
*Choice*

'A very impressive debut novel'
**** *Star*

*Praise for Eye Contact and Fergus*

*Also by Fergus McNeill*

Eye Contact

*About the Author*

Fergus McNeill has been creating computer games since the early eighties, writing his first interactive fiction titles while still at school. Over the years he has designed, directed and illustrated games for all sorts of systems, including the BBC Micro, the Apple iPad, and almost everything in between. Now running an app development studio, Fergus lives in Hampshire with his wife and teenage son.

To find out more about this and upcoming books by Fergus, you can visit www.fergusmcneill.blogspot.co.uk, like his Facebook page at www.facebook.com/fergusmcneillauthor or follow him on Twitter at twitter.com/fergusmcneill.

For Andrea & John:
friends & family.

It had started as a fleeting suspicion – the ghost of an idea. Where once the game had been so gratifying, now there was a faint shadow – the vague sense that something might be missing, that somehow it wasn't so sweet as once it was. For a long while, he couldn't put his finger on what was lacking . . . just a lingering sense of doubt that grew stronger each time, until finally he knew what was troubling him.

*Recognition.*

At first he had told himself that it didn't matter – that greatness wasn't dependent on other people, and he didn't need them to validate what he did. But more and more, he began to wonder.

He wasn't an artist – he didn't put his name to his work, and its worth didn't come from the perception of others. He didn't crave recognition from every person he met . . .

. . . *just from her.*

# part 1
# SUBMISSION

# I

*Sunday, 25 May*

Robert Naysmith padded silently through the unfamiliar cottage to the bedroom. The carpet felt like hotel carpets do, hard-wearing and frequently cleaned, but it was warm beneath his feet where the morning sun had touched it. Yawning, he leaned forward, carefully moving the make-up bag and wrist-watch to one side, making space for the mug of coffee, which he placed carefully on the bedside table. Straightening up, he paused to look at Kim as she slept, and wondered if this would be their last day together.

She looked so peaceful, her long dark hair spread out across the oversized pillows, her unconscious face calm, like a porcelain doll. Other women frowned in their sleep, or their faces blackened into dull, vacant expressions, but Kim was serene, her full lips slightly parted, one deli~~----~~ ~~----~~ulder showing bare above the d~~---- ----~~*ue longer.*

~~----~~er to the window. The curtains were tied back – it was the same all through the cottage – but the place was so remote that there was little need for privacy, even in the bedroom. And it was uplifting to wake up and see the rugged coastline outside. There were clouds on the horizon now but the sun was climbing higher in the sky, casting a long glittering reflection across the waves that crashed against the cliffs below. Gulls wheeled over the path that led up along the headland to the old lighthouse, riding the blustery wind that whipped through the coarse grass.

He sighed and stretched, forcing his broad shoulders back as he tensed his muscles, closing his eyes and enjoying the warmth of the sunlight on his chest. Limbering up, loosening his tall frame, shaking off the last of his drowsiness, his body feeling awake, ready.

*Ready.*

He bowed his head and frowned, one hand reaching up to toy with the simple gold chain around his neck. How had it happened? He'd never meant for things to turn out this way. Kim had always been special, but so were most of the women, at least for a while. He could have enjoyed her and moved on – *should* have done so – but somehow he'd never quite got her out of his mind. And moving in together – the last thing he needed was someone living with him. In his position, that could be a fatal liability. And yet, he'd found himself adapting, making allowances. In some ways, the difficulty of protecting her from the truth had become part of the challenge, part of the game.

But he couldn't hide the truth from himself: somehow, he'd let down his guard, let her get too close to him. Somewhere along the line, he'd started comparing the other women to her, and found they weren't enough. Kim mattered to him, and she was beginning to matter too much.

She'd always had a submissive streak running through her. He'd sensed that from the beginning and had steadily liberated her until she'd abandoned herself to him physically, emotionally, totally. And yet the more she gave in to him, the more he wanted her, needed her. A subtle bond was forming around them and he knew that it would eventually be too strong for him to break.

He turned and gazed across the room at her slender form, curled up in the huge duvet. So fragile, so perfect. He hoped he wouldn't have to kill her.

The cotton sheets were cool on his skin as he sat down on the bed. He felt her stirring beside him, watched as her small hand reached out and touched his, her brown eyes blinked open and her mouth turned into a sleepy smile.

'Hey you,' she murmured.

'Coffee's there beside you,' he pointed, but his eyes stayed on her.

She twisted around, struggling free of the duvet, wriggling backwards to prop herself up against the headboard. He watched her yawn, her small breasts rising and falling as she closed her eyes for a moment, then looked around and reached for her mug.

'Mmmm, you think of everything.' She smiled as she raised the drink and inhaled the steam.

Naysmith looked away.

'I try to,' he said quietly.

And he had. Careful preparations: taking her mobile phone and the car keys, and hiding them both in the bottom of his bag. The cottage was booked for a week, and it was just as isolated as he'd hoped – no neighbours and no interruptions. Everything was in place, everything was ready.

*Ready.*

'Kim . . .'

'What is it?'

He looked across at her, naked and vulnerable, her large eyes watching him. He turned away, worried that she might see the conflict that raged inside. Everything was ready except him.

'Nothing.' He paused. 'Let's go and see about breakfast.'

★   ★   ★

They went for a walk later that morning, following the faintly worn footpath that meandered along the clifftops and up to the point. Naysmith was quiet, staring out at the sea, while Kim was content to match his pace, linking her arm through his as the wind buffeted them.

'Thanks for booking this,' she said as they paused at a place where the path had fallen away, revealing the bay below them. 'It's so wild and beautiful here.'

Naysmith glanced up at the clouds, pale grey with bright silver edges, and nodded slowly.

'It is.'

White water swirled between the rocks, and he could taste the tang of salt on his lips.

'Rob?' Kim hesitated, then moved around to look up at his face. 'Are you happy?'

'Of course,' he shrugged. 'A week away with you, and the cottage is great—'

'Yes, but I meant . . .' She paused, then quietly asked, 'Are *you* happy?'

Naysmith gazed into her eyes for a moment, watching as the wind blew strands of hair across her upturned face, then turned and looked out past the whitewashed stone lighthouse towards the distant horizon.

'I have everything I could ever want . . . why wouldn't I be happy?'

Kim stared at him thoughtfully, then moved closer, slipping her small hand into his.

'I don't know . . . it's just that you looked so far away.' She sighed. 'I like having you close.'

Naysmith put his arm around her shoulders. They were only a few feet from the cliff edge, and her slight frame was resting against him . . .

*No!*

He pushed the thought away, and pulled her close, as the gentle roar of the surf in the rocks drifted up from below.

'That's what I want too,' he whispered, screwing his eyes shut for a moment. 'For us to be close. As close as two people can be.'

They stood there for a time, watching the endless wash of the waves that crawled in from the grey sea, then turned and made their way back from the precipice.

After lunch, they settled down to watch an old film on the cottage's one, elderly television set. Kim cuddled up to him on the large sofa while he absently stroked her hair. She had put her hand in his lap when they first sat down, but he'd gently moved it away, putting an arm around her and resting her on his chest so that he could kiss the top of her head, smell the scent that calmed him. Somehow, he couldn't – *wouldn't* – take advantage of her. He thought too much of her for that, no matter how things turned out later.

He knew now that he had to tell her. The thought of doing so, once a foolish whim to be dismissed as soon as it arose, had grown in his mind until it drove out everything else.

*As close as two people can be.*

He couldn't keep it from her any more. He wanted her to know who he really was, wanted her to understand what he could do. He wanted to take her with him. But was she ready?

*Ready.*

'Rob?'

The credits were rolling and Kim was looking up at him, her eyes searching his face for something.

'Is everything all right?'

He nodded, not trusting himself to speak.

'Rob?'

He gently untangled himself from her arms and got to his feet, pulse quickening. This was it. He had to do it now, take the risk of losing her while he still could. And hope that he knew her well enough to bring her through it all.

'Rob?' She was gazing up at him, a small figure in the corner of the sofa, questions in her eyes.

He moved over to the door, gently pushed it until he heard it click shut, then leaned back against it, studying her.

'What's going on, Rob? Talk to me, please.' She sounded concerned. Bless her, *she* was concerned for *him*.

If only he could spare her . . .

'Some things are difficult to say,' he sighed.

'It's OK, you can tell me.' She began to get to her feet, but he shook his head abruptly, pointing at the sofa. She faltered, and sat down again.

They looked at each other for a moment, then he turned his gaze to the floor, rubbing the back of his neck. It had to be said carefully.

'Rob?' She spoke in a small voice but it cut across the silence that had fallen on the room. 'What's wrong?'

He looked up at her, and again she seemed to flinch slightly. As though she could already see a glimmer of the secret in his eyes, as though she was suddenly worried by what he might say.

*She had no idea.*

'Kim . . .' He had to tell her. There was no other way. Maybe not everything, maybe not all at once, but he had to know if she could take it. 'I really care for you, Kim.'

The right words, but something about the way he'd said them unsettled her. Her eyes widened just a little as she stared up at him.

'I want us to be open with each other.' Again, calming words, but her expression didn't relax.

'I'm always open with you,' she said, then hesitated, realising that it wasn't her he was talking about.

He saw the understanding on her face, the worry, and nodded very slightly.

'Rob?' She bit her lip then watched him carefully as she whispered, 'Is there someone else?'

Always that same question: her greatest fear. At least, it had been until today.

He shook his head, and for a moment she seemed relieved. But he didn't smile. He didn't reassure her. Didn't tell her there was nothing to worry about. He stood silently, leaning against the closed door, allowing her to grasp that it was something else. Something worse.

He could hear her breathing, delicate and close over the distant roar of the sea. Her eyes began to glisten and she hugged her knees, pulling them up to her chin, but never taking her gaze off him.

'You're scaring me, Rob.'

There was power in this. Part of him exulted in a glimpse of the future, where she both feared and loved him, recognising his true abilities, knowing what no one else knew about him. It was a sensation that almost overwhelmed him, and the possibility that he might taste it gave him strength and drove him on.

If she could cope with the truth. If she could survive being told.

Oddly, she didn't ask if he was leaving her – her mind had already raced ahead to darker possibilities. He watched her shrinking into the corner of the sofa, saying nothing to her, forcing her to break the silence first.

'Are you in trouble, Rob?'

She said it almost hopefully, as though it might be something she could deal with, something she could help with.

'No . . .' He said it carefully, leading her towards the next question.

'Have you done something?' Her eyes widened as different fears flitted across her mind. 'Something bad?'

He stared at her, feeling an overwhelming release wash over him – and slowly nodded.

'Oh!' She put her hand across her mouth, her eyes staring. 'Nothing . . . sick? Nothing with children . . . ?'

'Of course not!' He leaned back against the door, shaking his head.

*How could she even say something like that?*

'I would *never* harm a child . . .' He frowned at her. 'And it's nothing . . . sexual.'

There was a momentary flicker of relief in her eyes, but then her face fell as it dawned on her what remained.

'Have you . . .' She couldn't say the word. 'Hurt someone?'

Unblinking, he held her gaze for a moment, then nodded.

'Oh God. Rob, you haven't killed someone, have you?'

She was looking at him, the first tears running down her cheeks, her eyes imploring him to deny it, but he just stared back at her.

'Oh God!' She bit her lip, her hand quivering in front of her mouth, wide eyes blinking, not knowing what to do.

He waited for as long as he could, trying to give her a moment, a chance to take it in, but he could see she was about to crack.

'Kim?'

She was trembling, breathing too quickly.

'I'm the same person now that I was yesterday,' he said, softly.

Kim looked at him, tears streaming now, shaking.

'Nothing's changed,' he told her. He could feel tears of his own forming. 'Not unless *you* feel it has.'

For a long moment their eyes were locked, each trying to read the other. He desperately wanted her to get through this. She *had* to. He didn't want to lose her, but he had to know, had to be sure. And if she couldn't accept it, he wouldn't let her know what was coming. He wanted it to be quick for her.

Kim blinked, wiping her eyes.

'Was it an accident?' She had to ask, but he could see she already knew. He could tell her in stages, cushion the blow a little, but he wouldn't lie to her.

He shook his head.

'No.'

She started to say something, but the words wouldn't come. Her breathing became erratic, her trembling more pronounced as she pressed her palms against the side of her face. This was the moment. If she could just keep it together . . .

'Oh Rob! What happened? *Why?*'

Fresh tears, her voice catching, and then it was finally too much to hold in and she hid her face, weeping desperately into her hands.

*So beautiful.*

He moved closer, instinctively wanting to console her, to soothe her.

'Kim . . .'

She flinched from his touch, and for a sickening moment he thought he had lost her.

But it was anger. Her tear-streaked face, eyes screwed-up, peering out between long strands of dark hair. She jerked herself back from him, then stood shaking, her hands clenched into fists at her side.

'Why? Why would you do something like that?' Her voice choked as she gulped down ragged breaths. 'What the fuck have you done?'

He stood in silence, letting her yell and hit him until she was spent, then gently put his arms around her as she finally buried her face in his chest, still sobbing quietly.

And held her close.

# 2

*Monday, 26 May*

The sun was shining, but not for her. Sitting on the cushioned window seat of the cottage bedroom, Kim toyed absently with a strand of her hair. She felt numb, and there was a terrible weariness that she couldn't shake off, despite crying herself to sleep early and getting up late. In those first cruel moments after waking she hadn't remembered their talk, or what he'd told her. For a few blissful heartbeats everything had been just like it was before. But then it had all come crashing back in on her, and suddenly she was so very tired.

*It wasn't true. Couldn't be.*

But somehow she knew he wouldn't lie to her. Not about this. She caressed the fabric of the cushion, then dug her fingernails into it, watching her knuckles whiten with effort.

*Oh God. Rob . . .*

Her thoughts were vague now, distracted. What was wrong with her? She should have said more, last night, this morning. She should have walked out, but somehow she didn't have the energy. Upset and anger had carried her through the first few hours, but now she felt detached from it all, as though it was happening to someone else, someone she didn't really care that much about.

*She cared about Rob . . .*

. . . about the person she'd thought he was. But what if that person didn't exist?

Her eyes were dry, sore from staring too long at the sea. She blinked, then rubbed them carefully. Where were the tears when she needed them?

*She needed him.*

But he was different now. It was as though there were two separate people, twisted together inside the same body. Two of them sharing her life, sharing her bed, for all that time. She shuddered. All that time, and until yesterday she'd only noticed one of them.

She drew her feet in close on the broad seat, pulling up her knees and resting her chin on them. Her fingers traced the line of the pattern woven into the fabric of the cushion and she listened intently for a moment, but there was no sound except the distant roar of the sea. She wondered where he was, what he was doing, pictured his face.

When she'd looked at him this morning, and he'd smiled back, had that been *her* Rob?

*Or was it the stranger?*

The sunlight was warm on her leg, but she still felt cold inside.

*It was too much to take in.*

And he'd only just begun to tell her about it. No details, no excuses, no answers to her sobbing questions. How much was he holding back, and what was still to come?

He'd always been so confident, right from that first evening back in Taunton. She'd gone out with a few colleagues from work – somebody's birthday probably. Not her usual group of girls, and definitely not one of her usual places – crowded together under a haze of stale beer and supermarket after-shave. A stray elbow had spilled her drink and she'd pushed her way towards the bar for another, jostled and groped by

'Kim!'

She tore her gaze away from the drop. Rob had turned back, his eyes full of care, his arm outstretched towards her. For a moment, she remained pressed against the cliff, but she knew that turning back would be impossible. Slowly, carefully, she reached out and took his hand. As his fingers clasped hers, his grip definite and firm, she glanced downward – suddenly the drop didn't look so terrifying, but there was still a cold knot in her stomach.

'You're OK,' he said softly. 'I've got you.'

The beach curved away in a long tapering arc, smoothly encircling the bay and funnelling the waves so that they crashed and tumbled through the jutting rocks at the far end. From down here she could see the stripes and creases on the cliffs, great folds of ancient stone twisted into eerie shapes. The path they'd followed was a thin scar against the strata of the rock face. It didn't look as though they'd come that far until she spotted the tiny dark smudges – a line of over-grown gorse bushes they'd walked around – and realised the scale of it, how far down they were.

She moved slowly now, smooth stones and shingle crunching underfoot as they made their way out from the shadow of the cliffs and down towards the water. He matched her languid pace, walking at her side, his hand almost brushing against hers . . .

. . . *in case she wanted to hold it.*

They clambered over long fingers of water-worn rock, continuations of a seam from the cliff that cut across the beach, and stepped across the line of slick dark seaweed that marked the tide's reach. The steady wash of the waves was soothing, and the smell of the beach recalled childhood holidays and stories of smugglers.

Kim turned her head away from Rob to stare out at the
sea, her pace slowing as she watched the dark green water
catch the light. A ribbon of bubbles slid towards her feet,
slowing and stretching as the water lost its way among the
pebbles, lingering for a moment before the undercurrent drew
it back. She watched it gently pick up speed, accelerating as
though falling away from her until it was lost in the swell of
another wave. Impossible to hold on to, like the thoughts that
swirled and eddied in her mind.

She heard the crunch of Rob's footsteps as he slowly started
to move on, but stood a moment longer, staring down at the
waves.

'Kim?'

She looked up and gave him a faint nod, before turning
to follow him. They meandered along the wet shingle, out of
reach of most of the waves, sidestepping the bigger ones as
they came.

At the far end of the bay, the cliffs marched down towards
the water. Rob jogged down to a huge, flat-topped rock, its
sides dark and wet, a skirt of seaweed about its base. Shrugging
off the rucksack, he hefted it up and pushed it onto the smooth
stone surface. Then, putting one hand on the rock, he vaulted
up onto it himself, before the next wave could touch his feet.
Steadying himself, he turned back to her.

'Come here,' he called. 'Quick, before the next wave.'

'What is it?' she replied, scampering over the slippery
pebbles to join him.

'Give me your hand,' he smiled, his strong grip quickly
settling on her wrist. 'And up you come!'

'Rob!' She squealed with surprise as her feet left the
ground. He lifted her up and round, straining to be gentle
as he placed her on the stone beside him. She grabbed him as
she regained her balance, then stood up straight.

'You could have warned me,' she protested. It had been oddly exhilarating, and she forgot herself for a moment, grinning foolishly as she gave him a playful thump on his arm.

He was staring at her thoughtfully as they caught their breath.

'It's good to see you smiling,' he said softly.

The top of the rock was smooth and cool, dark grey with thin veins of silver and brown. A small bowl-shaped depression retained a mirror of seawater, spray collected at the last high tide, but the rest was dry.

Rob sat down, cross-legged, and began to unzip the rucksack.

'What about the tide?' Kim asked, looking at the waves that licked up against the seaward base of the rock. 'We don't want to get caught here.'

He squinted up at her, shielding his eyes against the light, and shook his head slightly.

'We won't,' he smiled. 'Tide's on its way out.'

She peered back along the beach, wondering how he knew, then shrugged to herself.

*Somehow he always knew.*

She sat down opposite him, tucking her feet under her as he placed a pair of plastic glasses between them and opened the wine. Her fingers trailed through the cold water in the depression, rippling it then watching it settle again. She brought a finger to her lips, tasting the salt as a droplet touched her tongue.

'This might be better.' Rob was looking at her, a glass o wine in his outstretched hand. She took it from him, holdi it by the stem as she tilted it this way and that to catch light. He reached across with his own glass, tapping it a hers before drinking, but today there was no toast, r words.

*He was better than that.*

She glanced across, her eyes resting on him while he stared out at the waves. He was taking things easy with her, she realised. Giving her time – some breathing space – while she dealt with what he'd told her. So patient, so intense. Looking at him, she was struck by the *presence* that seemed to emanate from him.

*And now she was beginning to understand why.*

She wasn't really hungry, but she didn't refuse the food he offered. There was crusty bread, and French Brie, and grapes – his idea of her favourites – and the sea air made everything taste good. She poured them both another glass of wine and ate in silence, her eyes drawn to the distant horizon and upwards to where small clouds drifted across the sky, mottling the rippling water with shadows. Gulls were wheeling above them, riding a fresh breeze that had crept in from the sea, harsh cries echoing back off the cliffs behind her. She watched them circling, silhouetted shapes against the clouds, wondering how they could appear so dark when she knew they were white.

'Are you cold?'

Rob was looking at her, and she realised that she had been hugging her arms about herself.

'I'm OK,' she replied.

He got up onto his knees and leaned across to touch her bare forearm, his fingers brushing her skin.

'You're shivering.' He rolled back onto his feet and stood up, another silhouette against the sky, quickly slipping off his ⸱cket and stepping round to drape it over her shoulders. '⸱ere you are.'

⸱m reached up and drew the jacket around her, welcoming ⸱rmth of his body still held in the material.

⸱s *thinking of her.*

She watched him as he sat down again, catching his eye as he reached over to retrieve his glass. He looked at her quizzically, reading something in her face.

'What is it?' he asked.

She looked down, frowning slightly, trying to clarify her own thoughts.

'You really *do* care for me, don't you?' Watching him now, half questioning, half believing.

He stared back at her for a moment, then set down his glass and reached out to take her hands gently in his own. His eyes were close to hers, clear, unblinking.

'I do,' he said softly. 'More than you could ever guess.'

She forced herself to return his smile until he looked away, then continued toying with her glass as she tried to make sense of everything.

Had she been stupid? Given herself to a man she didn't know? No, it wasn't possible – what she'd felt must have been real, at least in some part. And she was sure, even now, that it wasn't just her – he felt something for her too. Nobody could fake that, not long-term – she'd have seen through it.

And yet, he'd hidden something so terrible from her. And she'd had no idea . . .

She bit her lip again, small fingers reaching up to twirl a strand of hair.

. . . or had she? Had she been so preoccupied about him cheating on her that she'd missed everything else? So busy telling herself that he wouldn't be unfaithful that she'd drowned out the other warnings?

Kim closed her eyes.

Perhaps he'd been more honest than she had. Perhaps she'd always suspected, but had pushed it all under the carpet, lying to herself. What did that make her?

'Hey.' His voice seemed calm, but he was looking at her intently, his head inclined. 'Did you want to talk?'

Caught off guard, she could only stare at him blankly.

*How was she meant to respond to this? Where did she even begin?*

He nodded and looked down.

'Sorry. I didn't mean to . . .' He trailed off, his hand drifting up to rub absently at his jaw.

Kim blinked and breathed. His silence cried out for her to say something.

'Are you going to tell me . . . what happened?' she managed.

His eyes flickered up to hers for a second, then down again.

'I don't want to lie to you, Kim.' It was strange to hear that tentative note in his voice, as though he was wary of each word. 'I want you to know, I need you to *understand*, but . . .'

He shook his head, frowning, considering how to proceed.

'. . . not details. Not yet, anyway.' His eyes found hers. 'Let me tell you about that in my own time, OK?'

She found herself nodding. There was an unfamiliar vulnerability in his expression that touched something inside her – his determination to share something so secret with her spoke of profound closeness and staggering trust. For a moment, she was overwhelmed by how hard it must be for him, and what it meant. And yet, it was impossible not to ask him.

'Can you tell me why?'

She watched as he wrestled with the question, his brows tightening to a pained frown. Finally, his shoulders dropped and he sighed.

'It's . . . complicated. I want to share everything with you, really, but it's not easy to explain . . .'

He looked at her for a moment, frustration tugging the corner of his mouth down, then lapsed into silence.

Kim nodded again, sensing the turmoil that he was in, but more desperate than ever to know something, anything. Anything that could help her to try and make sense of things. She had to ask him a question that he could answer. Nothing too specific, not yet, but something that would open the door a little wider.

'Rob . . . ?'

He waited, staring down at his glass, one finger tracing a slow circuit around the rim. She hesitated, then spoke the words.

'What was it like?'

Now it was his turn to be caught off balance. Something in his expression seemed to come alive as he looked at her, took a deep breath, then turned his head towards the sea. When he finally spoke, his voice had a soft, almost reverent tone.

'It's . . . incredible. You have no idea.'

She watched him, fascinated, unable to look away as that light came into his eyes. What was he reliving? In that moment, for the first time, she wondered if she should be afraid of him – properly afraid. How strange that the idea hadn't occurred to her before. But as he turned back to her, his face softened, intensity giving way to peace. He wasn't going to hurt her.

As if by some unspoken agreement, they slid closer together, moving simultaneously like a normal couple would. He put his arm around her shoulder, nuzzling her hair as she rested her head against him, and stared out at the sea. His chest felt warm against her cheek, and she could hear his heartbeat, steady and calm, as his hand stroked her arm.

*He cared for her. She mustn't lose him.*

Anything was better than being alone. Even this.


She came out of the bathroom and padded through to the bedroom. He was already in bed, his broad chest bare above the duvet. His eyes followed her for a moment, then turned away as she made her way across to the tiny dressing table.

From the beginning, he'd always encouraged her to sleep without clothes. He'd ignored her self-conscious nature, seeming to delight in her naked form. At first, she'd felt terribly exposed, though in time she began to find his attention gratifying and there was a strange thrill in submitting to him. But tonight, she felt different, oddly uncomfortable, as she had done back when they'd first met.

She placed her make-up bag on the table, looking at her reflection in the mirror – so ordinary, so *plain*. Was he watching her now, his eyes on her back as she hesitated? She bit her lip and her shoulders dropped a little. She found herself hoping that he was.

Slowly, she pulled her top up and over her head, and began to undress.

She just wanted the thoughts to stop, wanted to push all the confusion out of her head.

Stepping out of her underwear, she could feel her heart racing. Slowly, deliberately not covering herself, she turned around.

He was gazing at her, his eyes intense, thoughtful. He pulled the duvet aside for her and she walked across to the bed. It was all too much.

As she lay down, his strong arm enfolded her and pulled her against him. The last of her reluctance melted away, and she gratefully allowed his touch to push her objections aside. Closing her eyes, she welcomed the inevitable movements that brought them back together and drove out her fears. For tonight, that would be enough.

# 4

*Saturday, 31 May*

It was raining as they turned off the main road, a mournful shower that drizzled down through the open archway of trees lining the lane. The bowling green slid past, a perfect square of unnatural colour, lush in the wet behind its tidy box hedges, and the dark water of the river surged beneath the low bridge. Kim looked up at the grey sky and sighed.

*Nearly home.*

It felt strange, driving back into the village, as though she'd been away for years. Everything from before he'd told her seemed such a long time ago now. They slowed as the road swept around to the right, past the Pembroke Arms, then turned off as they reached the grassy square, the indicator clicking in time with the raindrops that pattered on the windscreen. Rob found a space just beyond the house and parked the car.

She sat for a moment while he got out and grabbed the cases from the boot. One final deep breath, oddly loud in the quiet of the car, and then she made herself open the door. The rain was cold on her face as she emerged and she drew her jacket collar about her throat. Everything looked the same but it felt different as she stepped around the puddles, following him to the house.

'Got your keys?' He indicated the cases, one in each hand, and looked towards her expectantly.

She nodded and reached into her handbag, fishing out the keys, which had somehow worked their way into a side pocket, and moving beside him to unlock the door. As it swung open, she stepped into the quiet stillness, aware of his footsteps behind her as she walked into the hallway and shrugged her bag from her shoulder.

Who was this man standing behind her, putting down her case? She caught her breath as the front door shut behind her, confused by such a familiar sound making her jump.

'Coffee?' He was beside her now, his voice close to her ear. 'The milk will be out of date but I'm sure there's some creamer in the cupboard.'

She turned her face towards him but kept her eyes downward.

'Thanks.' Her voice wavered slightly, as the tightness in her throat stole her breath. She needed some space, a moment to think. 'I'm just popping up to the loo.'

Kim could feel his eyes following her as she climbed the stairs, willing herself not to panic, not to run. What was the matter with her? How could she feel so unsettled in her own home?

She hurried into the bathroom and closed the door behind her, her fingers moving to slide the bolt across – a strangely unfamiliar motion. Rob had routinely walked in on her, gently teasing her for her shyness, doing so until she had abandoned her modesty and accepted him being in there with her. She never locked the door now . . . unless they had someone else staying with them.

She walked over to the small white basin and splashed some water on her face. There was someone else now. Here, in their home, her awareness of the stranger was suddenly heightened. The other man who stared out of her lover's eyes.

★   ★   ★

The house seemed quiet the following evening. At another time, the subdued atmosphere might have seemed like the natural comedown after a week away, but Kim was disturbed by it as she made her way through to the kitchen. Her initial panic was gone now but she remained on edge, unable to settle back into the normal routine of the weekend.

*She needed to calm down, get her head together before she ruined everything.*

Rob had disappeared upstairs to do some work and she moved restlessly between rooms, looking for something to distract her. Pouring herself a glass of wine, she picked up a magazine from the worktop and sat down at the kitchen table, flicking through the pages.

The phone startled her when it rang.

Kim twisted around to retrieve it from her pocket, then peered down at the screen to see who was calling.

*Sarah.*

Normally a phone call from her big sister was something she looked forward to. True, they hadn't always been close, but in recent years things had improved between them and they'd begun to confide in each other once again, whether the news was good or bad.

Kim hesitated, a sudden doubt gnawing at her as she let the phone ring in her hand. She wanted to tell Sarah everything, but this was no petty regret or bedroom confession, to be whispered into the microphone and absolved by a gasp and a squeal of suppressed laughter. What was she going to do?

Her sigh was drowned out by the ringtone as she resigned herself and answered it.

'Hello?' Trying to sound cheerful, as she propped her forehead on her free hand.

'Hey, sis!' On another day, Sarah's bubbly, high-pitched

voice might have made her smile. 'So, how was your little holiday?'

Kim shut her eyes. She'd been dreading this, on some subconscious level, ever since the night he'd told her. Keeping secrets was alien to her, especially keeping someone else's.

'It was fine.' Her own voice sounded so flat.

'Was the cottage nice?'

'Yes, lovely.' She needed to say more, anything. 'It was this really remote place, miles from the nearest village. And it was right on the cliffs. You could look out of the windows and see the sea.'

'Mmm, sounds very Daphne du Maurier. Did it rain much? It was bloody awful here.'

'Once or twice. But it wasn't too bad.'

Her sister gave a dirty laugh.

'Yeah, well I'm sure you and Rob found ways to entertain each other. Remember that time when Simon and I were in Italy and we had that downpour that lasted three days . . . ?'

Her voice babbled on, but Kim couldn't follow her. She wanted to say something, but every sentence threatened to get away from her, to reveal what Rob had told her, and she knew now that she couldn't tell anyone about that. Not her sister, not anyone. And yet, how could she keep something so awful to herself?

'Hello? Kim?' Her sister's voice was calling to her impatiently.

'Sorry, Sarah. What were you saying?'

'It doesn't matter. Are you OK? You don't sound like your usual self.'

She couldn't tell Sarah, could she? Sarah wouldn't understand. But then, she didn't understand herself . . .

'Kim?'

'I'm just tired,' she managed, painfully aware of the weariness she felt. That much was true at least.

'Have you and Rob had a fight?'

For a moment, she was surprised by the notion. But it was a natural assumption for her sister to make, so much easier to accept than the truth. Should she take refuge in that idea? Use it as a cover, to deflect more difficult questions? No, she didn't want Sarah asking Rob what was wrong.

'Kim, tell me . . . What's the matter? Have you guys had a fight?'

It was the whole truth or nothing. Kim bowed her head in frustration, rubbing her eyes with her free hand. If she told Sarah, she could never take it back, never unsay it. She'd be stepping beyond the point of no return, turning her back on Rob—

'No,' she said, straightening. 'I'm just exhausted. Too much fresh air and a lot of late nights – you know what I mean.'

She felt the moment slipping away, and then it was gone. 'Anyway, how's Simon liking his new job?'

She had committed herself to Rob, to keeping a secret that she didn't know the end of. She prayed she was doing the right thing.

They made love again that night. It was like make-up sex, but laced with an almost desperate intensity – this was no petty argument to be brushed aside after all. She welcomed him into her eagerly, finding comfort in his touch, a reassuring recognition in his eyes. The sensations in her body drove out the disquiet, and afterwards, exhausted, she slipped away into sleep before her doubts could creep back.

In the morning, as she looked over at Rob, with his hair untidy and his limbs sprawled across their bed, it was hard to believe what he'd told her. She watched the gentle rise and fall of his shoulder blades, the calm abandon of his expression as he slept. Someone so perfect, and he'd chosen her . . .

*But what had he done?*

She sighed, pushing away the thoughts as she pushed back her hair, then slid her legs out from the warmth of the duvet, tentatively pressing her toes into the carpet. Now, as the Monday-morning routine kicked in, the drama of the last week seemed distant, uncertain. She yawned, waiting for the digits on the bedside clock to tick over. 6.59 . . .

. . . 7.00.

The alarm came to life, an insistent buzzing tone that cut through the quiet of the bedroom. She watched him stirring, saw his face crumple into a frown as he turned his head away, one arm lifting slowly as though suspended by a puppet string, searching for the snooze button.

'Seven o'clock,' she murmured to him, just as she always did when she woke first. There was comfort in routine. Leaving him to bury his face in the pillow, she stood up and walked through to the bathroom.

*Had he really killed someone?*

Somehow, the question didn't seem quite so awful this morning. How could that be? Was it wrong that her horror was being diluted by curiosity? Leaning forward over the sink, she studied herself in the mirror, wondering all the while how it might have happened.

*Maybe it was self-defence . . .*

Perhaps he had been in a situation where he'd had no choice – kill or be killed.

She carefully applied a squeeze of toothpaste to the brush and glanced back up at her reflection.

*Was it a woman or a man . . . ?*

A man, almost certainly. He had told her it wasn't sexual, after all.

In the mirror her face looked calm. Thoughtful maybe, but strangely untroubled by the questions that occupied her mind.

Perhaps it had all happened a long time ago – something from his past, from before they met. A fight that got out of hand, or a terrible mistake? She visualised a number of different scenarios, trying to justify each notion to herself, wondering if any of her theories might be true. All the time being careful not to let her imagination roam too far.

She saw him appear behind her, movements still weary from sleep, eyes half closed as he drew close to plant a kiss on her bare shoulder.

'Morning.'

She reached up, caressing his head with her hand as he put his arms around her, his hands clasped over her stomach.

'Morning,' she replied. Was she being naive about things, or bravely fighting to hold on to the relationship she'd always wanted? Whatever had happened in the past, it didn't change how she felt about him right now. Cradling his head, she leaned it against her own, and watched as the couple in the mirror smiled back at her.

Despite waking second, he was out of the bathroom quickly and left the house before her. A meeting in Swindon or somewhere – she hadn't really heard all the details as he'd called up to her from downstairs – so she'd have to drive herself to work today. It was as though nothing had happened, life was returning to normal.

*Normal.*

She'd chosen a smart navy jacket, but the matching skirt left her legs feeling cold as she stepped outside, pulled the front door shut and locked it. The sky was a sullen grey.

There had been more rain in the night – a dry patch of tarmac indicated where Rob's car had been – and she kept off the grass verge, walking around the side of the house to where her own car was parked. The seat felt cold against the back of her legs when she got in, but she turned the heater up to full, and the radio on, to make things more comfortable.

*He was the same person he'd always been.*

There had to be a reason for it all, some hidden truth that would make sense of the little she knew. He would open up to her in time, tell her what had happened, help her to understand. It would be all right. He loved her and she loved him. For now, she just had to be patient, not do anything stupid, not drive him away.

The main road wasn't too busy as she turned out of the lane – she had missed the worst of the traffic. On the outskirts of Salisbury, a good song on the radio caught her attention, and she turned up the volume, singing along as she approached the city centre.

The car park was almost full when she bumped up onto the entrance ramp, but she threaded her way round to a narrow space and manoeuvred in between the white lines. The music died as she switched off the ignition and she sat for a moment, her hand on the door handle.

Rob had been honest with her. However bad it was, however difficult it had been to hear, he had respected her too much to lie.

*All she had to do was keep the secret.*

She stepped out into the cool morning, locking the car before hurrying out onto the pavement to join the stream of people, all on their way to a normal Monday at the office.

*She could do this. She would make it work.*

A breeze squalled along the street behind her, whipping

strands of her hair around into her face as she stopped outside the familiar white-brick building.

*She wouldn't let him down.*

The reception door was sticking as usual, but she gave it a good push and felt it open. Taking a deep breath and sighing out a false smile for her colleagues, she went inside.

# 5

Naysmith stood with his back to the street, studying the reflection in the window. Across the road, he could see Kim pause, a diminutive figure in navy blue, thrown into sharp contrast against the white-brick exterior of the building. He watched as she pushed back her hair, then stepped up to the reception door and passed inside.

As the door closed, he bowed his head and allowed himself a small smile.

It had been a curious experience, following someone he knew so well – and, more importantly, someone who knew *him*. A very different feeling from the usual pursuit of strangers, a different kind of challenge. But stimulating nonetheless.

With a final glance up at the building, he turned and strode back down the street, weaving his way between the other pedestrians on the narrow pavements. He wasn't really surprised she'd gone straight to work, but this would be their first full day apart since he'd told her, and it was reassuring to see that she hadn't tried anything, hadn't panicked. It couldn't have been easy for her – there had been so much for her to take in over the past week – but he was encouraged that his trust in her looked to be well placed.

*So far.*

His car was tucked away down a side street, but thankfully it hadn't been there long enough to get a parking ticket. There had been no opportunity to find anywhere better during his pursuit, and he couldn't have risked Kim seeing him or the car. He got in and settled back into the seat, allowing his body to relax a little as he shut his eyes.

What would he have done if she'd gone somewhere else? If she'd turned left at the end of the lane instead of right? His pulse had certainly quickened as they'd approached the main police station on Wilton Road, but she hadn't slowed, or pulled over. His brave and beautiful girl had driven straight on. She had overcome her fear and accepted what he'd started to tell her.

He opened his eyes and stared out at the people hurrying along the street, anxious about getting to work, unaware of who was in their midst. They were all blind, unable to see who he was, what he was capable of.

*But Kim would see.*

Slowly, he would reveal the truth to her, a little at a time, so that she could deal with it. He had to tread carefully of course. He didn't want to overwhelm her, and it would be easy to do that, as there was so much to tell. But he would give her the time she needed, gently leading her into the light so that she could see him as he truly was, and understand all that he'd accomplished.

He started the engine, and sat for a moment, his hand reaching up absently to toy with the gold chain at his neck, his mind wandering to a different time and place . . .

It had been a cool Hampshire evening in April, and he'd slowed his steps, turning his face away from the road to gaze across the fields as the car sped past. He'd glanced back over his shoulder, watching it pass under the narrow arch of the bridge and disappear up the road, waiting until the sound of it faded back into the quiet stillness of the rolling countryside. Then, once he was certain that nothing else was coming, he'd turned and walked quickly back to the bridge.

Green moss felt soft against the clamminess of the ancient brickwork as he placed a steadying hand on the wall and squeezed through a gap in the loose wire fencing. Leaves and twigs crunched and crackled under his feet as he slipped into the gloom beneath the canopy of the trees and began scrambling up the steep slope. He paused once to listen, but there were no more passing cars and a moment later he gained the top of the embankment. Straightening up, he brushed aside a tangle of brambles, then stepped out onto the railway line.

A few yards away, a lonely signal stood watch, its baleful red glare reflected on the polished metal of the rails. For a moment, there was no sound – as though the landscape all around were holding its breath – and then a gentle sigh of wind touched the trees, rustling the leaves high above him.

He adjusted the straps of the small backpack he was wearing, then climbed up onto the track bed, picking his way over the loose ballast and making sure not to touch the live third rail. Stepping carefully onto one of the huge concrete sleepers, he crossed over to the far side of the line and started walking. He made his way along the rough ground, staying close to the edge of the track where the weeds were withered and yellow. Absently, he wondered if they sprayed something on the railways to keep the plants down – an endless swathe of death meandering through the green landscape – and found himself smiling at the thought.

It wasn't far now. His car was safely hidden away down a quiet lane, far enough from where he was going that nobody would give it a second thought. And even if someone did remember it, the number plates he'd put on belonged to someone else.

Ahead of him, a large metal structure stood tall and dark against the evening sky – some sort of cellular phone mast, jutting up above the surrounding trees. There was a small grey building at its base, and the low whir of cooling fans grew louder as he approached. Beyond it was a broad metal gate and a narrow service road – little more than a gravel track lined by bushes – and he made his way over to it. Reaching out, he was about to place his hand on the top bar when he paused, then pulled the sleeve of his sweatshirt down and used it to grip the gate as he climbed over.

*You could never be too careful.*

The gravel track appeared to be seldom used – heavily overgrown in places, and separated from the railway line by a barbed-wire fence – but he was more alert now, moving carefully, watchful. Down on his left, the first houses of the village could be glimpsed through the bushes. He kept to the grass at the edge of the track, stepping quietly, listening for voices, but there was no one.

He could see the station now, with its weathered grey footbridge and its small red-brick buildings. Reaching the end of the gravel track, he stepped out onto the tarmac of the silent station car park – a long line of spaces, half of them empty, that stretched out along the edge of the railway line.

Quickly, his eyes sought out the vehicle he was hoping for – a large black Range Rover – and a shiver of excitement coursed through him as he spotted it. He'd picked the right day.

Moving to his left, he began threading his way between the tall wooden fence and the silent vehicles, avoiding the angle he knew was covered by the single CCTV camera. Coming to the Range Rover, he made his way around to the driver's side and squatted down by the large front wheel.

Reaching over, he carefully unscrewed the black plastic cap from the air valve and put it in his pocket. Then, taking up a small sharp stone from the ground, he used it to press in the valve. The dry rasping sound seemed terribly loud as the air escaped, hissing across his hand as the tyre gently sagged and deflated. He kept the valve pressed in until it was completely flat, then calmly got to his feet and walked on, hugging the fence as he made his way towards the station.

He approached the building from the side, drawing level with it before crossing the car park to stand against the brick wall. The ticket office and waiting room were locked up for the evening, with passenger security trusted to the ever-watchful CCTV.

*Which suited him just fine.*

Shrugging off his backpack, he unzipped it and drew out two lengths of thin metal tubing. Screwing them together, he tested them in his hands to make sure they were joined properly, then slipped around the corner of the building, keeping close to the wall. Directly above him, the long, angular body of a security camera was mounted on a single steel bracket. It was too high to reach by hand, but it was simple enough to jam the metal pole in under the lens hood and push the whole unit round until it was blindly facing the brickwork. Smiling to himself, he unscrewed the two tube sections and returned them to his backpack. Now he could move more freely. There were other cameras, but he knew exactly where they were and what they could see.

Checking his watch, he strode across to the four concrete steps that led up to the deserted platform. This was where the train from London would come in, but he had decided to stand on the opposite side, where the carriages would hide him from the disembarking passengers. The sound of his footsteps resonated in the stillness as he made his way up onto the little bridge that spanned the tracks and he paused at the top, gazing out at the trees lining the route of the railway and at the rolling fields beyond.

He certainly had a beautiful evening for it.

Descending to the other platform, he wandered calmly to the small, stainless-steel shelter and took a seat – just an ordinary person, waiting for a train.

He could sense the anticipation building inside, the growing excitement, but it wasn't time for that yet. Frowning, he looked around, checking his exits, remembering all the different ways he could get away from the station if anything should go wrong . . .

But nothing would. He had prepared too carefully.

Glancing up at the clock above him, he noted the time – 19.21 – in illuminated orange digits on the black signboard. It wouldn't be long now.

Leaning forward, he bowed his head slightly, tensing the muscles in his neck and shoulders, then relaxing them, calming his breathing to counter the terrible eagerness. Impatience was the enemy, but it had no power over him. He was ready, and there was nothing he couldn't do.

A little way along the track, the red signal winked out and was replaced by a green light. From the buildings opposite, a recorded announcement crackled into life, echoing out under the roof awning.

'Platform *one* for the *19.24* South West Trains service to *Alton*, calling at *Alton* only.' The voice had a disjointed quality – sentences and station names, assembled into an announcement by a computer. 'This train is formed of *four* coaches.'

And now he could hear it coming, the first faint ringing of the rails as the front of the train came into view – a little smudge of yellow in the distance, with two white lights glaring out, growing steadily larger as it approached.

Movement on the edge of his vision alerted him to a teenage couple who were walking up the steps onto the opposite platform, but they were engrossed in each other. In a moment, they'd be on their way – they wouldn't remember him. The resonant hum of the train's motor grew louder as the first carriages slid into the station, blocking the couple from view and swirling up a faint wave of dusty air.

Head down, he sat in the shelter, outwardly showing no interest but listening intently for the familiar chimes and hissing of the doors being released. Just a few yards away, on the other side of the train, a handful people were getting off . . . but only one of them really mattered to him. Staring at his feet, he waited until he heard the sudden rising whine of the motor, then glanced up to see the train hauling itself forward. The last of the coaches cleared the station to reveal a knot of weary passengers trudging along the platform and down the steps to the car park, among them a tall man in his fifties with wavy grey hair and a smart blue suit, moving with an imperious manner even at the end of the working day.

It was the man he'd first seen in London – a momentary flicker of eye contact between strangers as they passed each other on the Hungerford footbridge. The man he'd gone looking for, twenty-four hours later. The man he'd trailed to Waterloo Station and, eventually, to here.

The pursuit had spanned weeks – he could afford to wait a few minutes more.

As the red lights of the train disappeared into the distance, he sat there listening to the nearby sounds of car engines being started as the evening commuters manoeuvred out of their spaces and drove away. There was no hurry.

To pass the time, he reached across and unzipped the backpack that lay beside him. Feeling around inside, he drew out a thin pair of gloves and began to pull them on slowly, deliberately, working each finger in to ensure a snug fit. Once satisfied, he got to his feet and stretched, loosening up the muscles in his shoulders, then picked up the backpack in one hand to make his way along to the footbridge and up the steps. From the top, he looked out onto the car park, the long line of spaces strung out along the side of the railway – it was emptier now, and he watched as the last of the occupied cars made their way out into the lane.

But the Range Rover was still there.

The adrenalin was flowing now, and he made his way eagerly down to the platform and along the brick wall of the ticket office. Hurrying down the four steps, he turned left and walked quietly towards the big 4 x 4. His view was partly obscured by a neighbouring parked car, but that was all to the good – if he couldn't see the man, the man couldn't see him.

He slowed, stepping sideways, to better see between the vehicles . . . and there, just a few yards in front of him, was his target. Kneeling on the tarmac, the man had removed his suit jacket and rolled up his shirtsleeves before cranking the handle of a jack to raise the front of the Range Rover, oblivious to anyone approaching.

*This was what it was all about – the power of life and death, the ultimate control.*

Reaching into the backpack, he drew out a long metal spanner with quiet care, squeezing it between gloved fingers to ensure a firm grip. He was right-handed, but held the tool in his left – there was no reason to make things easy for the police. Then, with a final glance over his shoulder to make certain there was nobody else around, he took a long last breath . . .

. . . and sprang forward, moving on his toes to ensure there was no sound, curving around from the rear so that the other cars would hide his approach until the last moment, swinging the spanner down in a strong, graceful arc. He didn't flinch from the impact of steel on skull, the dull crunching sound, the feeling as the bone cracked and gave way beneath his first blow. He struck hard, snapping the man's head sideways, and the body briefly stiffened then slumped against the door panel, before toppling heavily to lie twitching on the tarmac.

*The ultimate high.*

He shuddered, staring down into the wide eyes of his feebly struggling victim, ignoring the desperate gurgling sounds, his muscles taut as he raised the spanner for a second, fatal strike. An acid taste in his mouth, his pulse thumping in his ears, he swung again, watching intently for the moment – that incredible moment – when the final choking breath sighed away and the last glimmer of life went out. The exultant moment that made him feel so utterly alive . . .

The clang of the spanner as it hit the ground seemed to ring out across the car park. He was trembling. Clenching his gloved fists, he forced himself to exhale, to get his breathing under control. There would be time to savour this achievement later – right now, he needed to get it together. Frowning, he crouched down beside the body, eyes searching for something small, something personal . . .

Not the wristwatch – somehow that just felt too obvious. His searching gaze moved on. Signet ring? He hesitated for a moment, then decided against it. Something that was personal, yes, but also something that wouldn't stand out too much. He began to roll the body over, looking for a pocket that might contain a wallet, when a glint of gold caught his eye. The dead man had loosened his shirt collar when he set about changing his wheel, and a simple gold chain was visible around his neck.

*Perfect.*

Rolling the body further onto its side to make it easier, he carefully worked the chain around, releasing it from where it was trapped in a fold of skin. Finding the catch, he unfastened it with some difficulty due to his gloves, then pulled it free and dropped it into his open palm. Simple gold links, like the souvenirs that connected his victims . . .

Standing up, he pushed the chain deep into one of his pockets, then glanced around once more.

Still nobody.

He looked down to the sprawled figure at his feet. It would be getting dark soon, but the next train was due at 19.50 and the body would quickly be discovered by passengers if it was left here in the open – he wanted to be far from the scene when that happened. Dropping to a crouch again, he braced himself against the adjacent car before half rolling, half shoving the corpse under the jacked-up Range Rover. It was difficult work – not least when the victim's shirtsleeve snagged something under the chassis – but finally the body was hidden, trailing limbs folded in under the shadowy space between the wheels.

All that remained was the jack. At first it seemed as though it wouldn't move, but he kicked it harder with his heel, again and again until it finally gave way, dropping the weight of the Range Rover to rest on its owner's body.

Satisfied, he stood up, slid the jack under the vehicle with his foot, and brushed himself down. Stooping to retrieve the spanner, he slipped it into the backpack, then made himself take a moment, checking the ground to ensure he'd left nothing behind, before turning and walking to the far end of the car park. He moved calmly, resisting the growing temptation to break into a run as he retraced his steps along the gravel track. Only now did he allow himself to take in the enormity of what he'd done, to revel in the incredible power that was his to wield. He closed his eyes for a second, drinking in the unique sensation that he felt only in these moments after a kill. It was never personal – the victims were random and their deaths irrelevant – power was the only thing that mattered.

*And yet . . .*

He paused as he came to the metal gate, his gloved hand hesitating slightly before he gripped the top bar and clambered over.

*. . . it was galling that nobody knew.*

His achievements went largely unrecognised. Yes, there had been that exhilarating period last year when the detective from Portishead had been smart enough to link some of his victims, had perhaps even come close to catching him, but in the end he'd managed to disappear again, leaving the police with nothing.

He shook his head, knowing that ought to have pleased him, knowing that anonymity was crucial . . .

It was just . . . nobody understood what he was capable of, what he had accomplished.

*And he had accomplished so much.*

Frowning he made his way along the railway embankment, the country around him silent once more, save for the soft tread of his footsteps and the sighing of the wind in the leaves. Stepping up onto the concrete sleepers, he halted for a moment to draw out the gold chain, staring at it briefly before fastening it around his neck, feeling the still-warm metal at his throat. Standing between the rails, he gazed along the track for a moment, then picked his way across to the far side of the embankment.

*The only one who appreciated his work was a detective from Portishead.*

Shaking his head, he made his way down through the bushes and disappeared into the trees.

# 6

Detective Inspector Graham Harland paused on the concrete doorstep and forced himself to smile.

'Thank you, Mrs Clarke. You've been very helpful.' He inclined his head slightly towards the earnest-looking woman who took up almost the whole width of the doorway. 'We'll be in touch.'

DS Mendel nodded his own mute goodbye and the pair of them turned, carefully stepping around the overflowing flowerpots that cluttered the narrow garden path.

Harland walked down to the open gate with the long strides of a tall man, his lean face passive until he heard the front door shut behind him.

'That was a fucking waste of time,' he muttered.

Mendel caught his eye, a wry grin creasing his heavy-set features as he gripped the iron gate with a large hand and gently drew it closed.

'You know who put us on to her, don't you?'

Harland stared at the broad man for a moment, then closed his eyes and sighed.

'If I had, I wouldn't have come.' He shook his head, pushing a weary hand through his dark cropped hair, then shrugged and turned along the street towards where they'd left the car. A fitful wind blew in from the estuary as they turned onto

Beach Road. Harland glanced down at his watch then looked at Mendel.

'It's almost lunchtime. You hungry?'

They walked on, past the car, past the bleak little bungalows with their cement gardens and the gaudy windows of the village convenience store, piled high with dusty old beach balls that would all end up in the sea. Next door was a bakery with chairs and a couple of small tables placed optimistically on the pavement outside.

A tired little bell chimed above the door as Harland pushed it open, but the woman behind the counter had a homely smile. There were pies and sausage rolls with flaky golden pastry under a heat lamp in a glass cabinet, and a tempting aroma of cooking that teased the appetite. Harland scanned the menu – a collection of handwritten options on luminous paper fixed to the wall – and paid for two bacon sandwiches.

'Cheers,' Mendel thanked him.

'That's all right,' Harland shrugged. 'I'm not in any hurry to get back. I'll only have Blake nagging on at me, and that can wait.'

'Always nice to be wanted,' the big man grinned.

Harland thanked the woman as she handed the sandwiches over the counter, passing one to his colleague as they walked outside.

'Did you want to sit?' Mendel indicated the tables doubtfully.

'No.' Fading patio furniture, abandoned on the pavement outside a parade of forgotten shops – Harland shook his head and wondered if anyone *ever* sat there. 'Come on, let's walk instead.'

They retraced their steps along the road until the line of semi-detached houses on the left petered out. Beyond, there was a boarded-up burger bar with peeling paint and weeds around it – picnic tables and vending machines, their once bright colours bleached by the elements, fenced off to wait for the summer – and in the distance, dominating the skyline, the Second Severn Crossing. The rumble of traffic came and went on the whims of the wind as they made their way up a gentle grassy slope to the promenade, a thin strip of tarmac that snaked along the tide wall towards the giant suspension bridge. A fence of stainless-steel railings ran along the top of the sea wall, and there were regularly placed benches for the elderly people this sort of place attracted.

Harland pulled his jacket closed against the cold, and trudged over to lean on the railing, staring out at the distant water, the grey beach, and the past.

'I've always hated it here,' he frowned, unwrapping his sandwich from the grease-spotted paper bag.

'It's grim today,' Mendel agreed, joining him at the rail.

Harland took a bite and stared out to the dark smudge on the horizon that was the Welsh coastline. The chill breeze made hot food taste even better, he thought. His eyes glanced along the barricade of heavy rocks banked up against the base of the sea wall below them, and settled on a figure walking a dog further out on the beach.

'Haven't been down here since they found that jogger. Vicky . . .' He paused, trying to recall the surname. 'Sutherland, wasn't it?'

'That's right.'

Harland's gaze swept the beach and he pointed to a spot where swathes of tall reeds rippled in the breeze. 'The body was over there, I think – might have been a little further along. Were you down at the scene for that one?'

'No, I was interviewing the neighbours.' Mendel inclined

his head to the left. 'She lived over that way a bit, one street back from the beach.'

Harland nodded thoughtfully, turning his face west, away from the wind. In the distance, the dark shape of the chemical works disturbed the horizon, its eerie chimneys exhaling pale breath into the sky. Further out, the three vast wind turbines at Avonmouth turned slowly in silhouette, like crosses waiting for a crucifixion.

'Miserable place to finish up,' he noted.

They ate in silence, watching the endless crawl of the waves across the estuary.

'How many other bodies did they link with our man in the end?' Mendel asked.

'At least four.' Harland finished the last of his sandwich, crumpling the paper bag in his hand. 'But I know we'd have found more if they'd let us keep the investigation open.'

He shook his head and frowned at the gathering clouds.

Mendel glanced across at him.

'He'd certainly have *killed* more, if you hadn't got so close to him.'

Harland bowed his head, a faint smile on his lips as he remembered the breathless night-time dash along the Docklands waterfront in London, the shadowed figure who'd got the drop on him.

*The killer who'd let him live.*

'Thanks, James,' he said softly. 'But he's still out there, still free.'

Mendel nodded thoughtfully.

'Yeah, well, he's a clever bastard.'

Harland turned away from the railing, straightening up, his grey eyes fixed on Mendel.

'So am I.'

He reached into his pockets and drew out a packet of

cigarettes and a lighter, but the stiff breeze made it impossible to hold a flame. Shaking his head, he glanced across towards the car.

'Come on,' he muttered. 'Let's get back to Portishead.'

Mendel smiled and took a last look out at the dark water, then walked briskly down the slope after him.

Superintendent Alasdair Blake ran a careful hand across his fine white hair as he studied the piece of paper in front of him, then looked up through his rimless glasses and gave a chilly little smile to the assembled officers.

'Thank you all for coming,' he said quietly, as though there had been any choice in the matter. 'As you may know, there have recently been one or two unfortunate instances involving the press, and I thought it prudent to get everyone together and set out our position.'

His smile, such as it was, faded and his face relaxed into its natural deep-lined expression of distaste and disapproval.

'This week saw another newspaper feature that portrayed Avon and Somerset Constabulary in a bad light.' He got up and paced slowly out from behind the table, clasping his hands behind his back. 'That's the third in less than a month.'

Sitting at the back of the room, Harland turned to Mendel and shot him a weary glance. Mendel returned a brief smile.

'It is clear to me,' Blake continued, shaking his head slightly, 'that the press are getting some of their information from *inside* the service. That we are fuelling this fire, so to speak.'

There was a murmur in the room. Blake held up a hand.

'Not from anyone here in Portishead, I'm sure. We run a tight ship.' He gave them another thin smile. 'No, I'd like to think that we in this division know better than that.'

He hesitated, as though evaluating that last statement, then turned to face the room.

'The last two pieces were written by a journalist called Peter Baraclough.' He paused, as though to underline the name. 'Suffice to say, if he approaches any of you, you speak to me, not to him.'

He glanced quickly around the room, each instance of eye contact making his words binding, before moving back to his chair.

'I strongly suggest that we're all particularly careful over the coming weeks,' he said as he sat down. 'No cock-ups, no talking out of school, *no* journalists.'

He waited for a long moment, then smiled at them once more, as though he wondered what they were all still doing here.

'That will be all, thank you.'

There was a general scraping of chairs as everyone got to their feet and started to file out. Mendel shook his head and leaned across to Harland.

'Tight ship, eh? Someone upstairs must be leaning on Blake to make him call a meeting like that.'

'Perhaps,' Harland mused. 'But you know what he's like.'

'Yeah,' Mendel said. 'This sort of thing could make him look bad, and he won't have that.'

'He won't,' Harland agreed. 'But he's smart, and if he keeps things steady while other divisions get caught talking? Well, it makes him look good by comparison.'

'Politics, Graham?' Mendel grinned at him. 'Surely not.'

They got to their feet and were moving towards the door when a voice halted them.

'Graham? And James?' The Superintendent was beckoning them to the front of the room. 'If I might just trouble you for a moment?'

Harland twisted his face into a calm expression and followed Mendel back into the room, stepping between the chairs as they approached the table.

'Take a seat,' Blake said agreeably. He looked at each of them for a moment, then leaned forward. 'I thought we might have a quick word about that business in Avonmouth . . .'

Harland sighed quietly as he sat down beside Mendel. That business in Avonmouth – a series of arson attacks on empty industrial buildings along the St Andrews Road – had looked promising at first, with several strong witness statements that narrowed the field down nicely. But in recent weeks progress had slowed and it was looking less and less certain that they'd get it over the line. He'd hoped he could avoid Blake until he had something more encouraging to report, but of course Blake wasn't in the mood to wait.

'I think I forwarded you a report a couple of days ago—' Harland began. It was tiresome, but without any new leads all he could do was restate the work they'd done so far.

'I read it,' Blake interrupted him. 'I was rather hoping to get an update on what's been happening since then.'

Harland sank slightly deeper into his chair as his progress so far was swept aside, leaving him with nothing.

'Well?' Blake sat back in his chair and stared at them over steepled fingers. 'Anything new?'

Harland looked down and shook his head.

'We know the gang that's doing it,' he said, speaking slowly, carefully. 'A group of kids, all local, small-time but nasty. The problem is nailing them with it.'

'They all swear blind they were together somewhere else.' Mendel's deep voice betrayed his frustration. 'And half of them are underage, which doesn't help.'

Blake frowned.

'What about CCTV?' he asked. 'There must be *something* usable.'

Harland shook his head. 'Nothing conclusive. Last place

they hit, the tapes went up with the building so that's no help. And coverage in the surrounding area is patchy to say the least.'

'There's too many black spots along that road to get a continuous picture of who goes where,' Mendel explained.

'I see,' Blake scowled. 'But if we know who's involved, can we not push one or two of the group to turn the others in? Some of them must have something to lose.'

'Perhaps,' Harland said doubtfully. 'There's a few slapped wrists and ASBOs among them, but nothing significant, nothing we can really use as leverage . . .'

Mendel leaned forward, his thick brows knitting together.

'They're not afraid of us,' he rumbled. 'They're afraid of grassing, of losing their mates, but they're not afraid of us.'

Blake considered this, then sat back in his chair.

'Suggestions?' he asked.

Harland spread his hands wide.

'We can run a car up and down St Andrews Road a few times each Friday and Saturday evening,' he shrugged. 'Maybe we'll get lucky – catch them at it, or at least put them off.'

Blake stared at him for a moment, then frowned.

'Very well,' he said, getting to his feet. 'Arrange for a couple of drive-bys over the next two weekends.'

He lifted his jacket from where it had lain folded over the back of a chair and draped it across his arm, then made his way round the table and walked past them, pausing as he got to the door.

'In the meantime, try and find something on one of these little bastards, anything that will help the case,' he told them. 'You've got two weeks. After that, I'm kicking it into the long grass.'

He turned and strode out of the room, pulling the door hard shut behind him.

Mendel stood up, one hand massaging the back of his neck as he straightened.

'Sometimes I bloody love being a copper,' he growled.

'It wouldn't be so bad if we didn't know who was doing it.' Harland sighed. He got up and followed the big man over to the door. 'But unless we manage to trip one of them up, there's not much we can do.'

Mendel shook his head.

'I know what I'd like to do,' he muttered darkly.

'Yeah, so do I,' Harland agreed. 'But that was in the bad old days. Everyone has rights now.'

He put his hand on the doorknob.

'Besides,' he added. 'Blake runs a tight ship.'

Mendel grinned at him.

They wandered out into the corridor and through to the main office, where two of the local constables from their team were studying something on a screen.

'Gregg. Firth.' Harland greeted them.

PC Stuart Gregg was a young officer with short blond hair and an easy grin. He'd been lounging back in his chair as he toyed with a pen, but sat up quickly when the two detectives entered the room. By contrast, Sue Firth, although the same rank, was a little older and much more mature. Her straight brown hair was tied back smartly, and she smiled at Harland as he sat down on the corner of Gregg's desk.

'Three guesses what Blake wanted to talk about?' he asked them.

'The arson attacks, sir?' Gregg replied.

'Exactly,' Harland nodded. 'So my first question is: did we get hold of the guy who owns that cul-de-sac warehouse yet?'

'Well . . .' Gregg gazed up at him doubtfully. 'I've managed to speak to him, but he seemed a bit . . . cagey, you know?'

'Cagey?' Mendel frowned.

'A bit evasive about turning over his CCTV tapes,' Gregg replied.

'For goodness' sake.' Harland shook his head. 'Did you tell him we're investigating the arson attack? The one that took place practically next door to his own building?'

'I mentioned that, yes.'

'And he wasn't falling over himself to help?'

'No, sir.'

Harland looked at Mendel for a moment, then rubbed his eyes wearily before turning back to Gregg.

'Well, get on to him and mention it again,' he said, working hard to stay calm. 'Tell him I don't care what he's got in his warehouse, or who's been in and out of the place. I just want the CCTV footage from the night of the fire.'

'You'd think he'd be keen to see these idiots locked up,' Mendel noted. 'Could easily have been his place that got torched.'

Harland shook his head.

'Depends what he's got in his warehouse,' he mused. 'Though if it *was* anything dodgy, it'll be long gone now we've spooked him.'

He sighed, then patted Gregg on the shoulder.

'Just chase him up, OK?'

'Will do, sir.'

Harland turned and looked at the screen, where a series of suspect mugshots stared out defiantly at him. Young faces, trying to look old.

'Blake wanted to know if we had anything on any of our fire-starters, anything that might persuade them to talk. I told him they were small-time . . .' He trailed off for a moment, his eyes taking in the tough-guy expressions in the photographs.

*Perhaps there was another way.*

He turned back to the others. 'Do we know if any of these kids have big brothers or other family members with current form?'

Mendel stared at him then broke into a grin.

'Lean on the older ones and let them pass it down to the kids?' He chuckled. 'What happened to your "bad old days" lecture?'

'I'm unpredictable,' Harland winked at him. 'Anyway, we're not doing anything wrong. And I'd feel a lot better about doing this than waiting around for them to light up a building that's got someone inside it.'

'No argument there,' Mendel shrugged.

'So,' Harland said brightly. 'Let's just hope we can turn up a family member who's on thin ice.'

Firth was leaning over the desk, staring at the mugshots on the screen.

'Sir?' she said. 'I might be wrong, but this kid here . . . Alex Murphy?'

She pointed to a thin, red-haired youth with watery eyes and prominent ears.

'Handsome fellow,' Mendel muttered.

'Memorable,' Harland agreed.

'That's just it, sir,' Firth said. 'I think I arrested his brother last year. Can't remember what for, but the face is really familiar. I can check up and find out.'

'Thanks, Sue.' Harland gave her an approving nod. 'Start with him, then have a look through the rest of the gang – let's get a list of relatives with something to lose, you know what sort of thing to look for.'

She smiled at him as he got to his feet, and he found himself thinking back to that evening last year when a group of them had gone down to see some film and he'd somehow wound up walking back to the pub with her, just the two of them. She'd smiled at him that night too, like someone who enjoyed his company . . .

'. . . if you want me to?' Mendel was speaking to him, waiting for a response.

'I'm sorry,' Harland shook his head. 'What were you asking?'

Mendel gave him an exasperated look, then turned and walked towards the kitchen.

'Not boring you, am I, Graham?' he asked as Harland fell in beside him.

'Just thinking about something.'

'Oh yeah?' Mendel glanced back at Firth meaningfully.

'Look, I'm sorry.' Harland held up his hands. 'Now please, what were you asking?'

'I was saying, do you want me to have a word with Bristol, and see if any of the names strike a chord with them?'

'Of course,' Harland told him. 'Please do.'

Mendel paused as they reached the doorway and turned to face him.

'You all right?' he asked.

'Yeah,' Harland shrugged. 'Just tired.'

Mendel studied him for a moment, then his smile returned.

'Well, it's Friday,' he rumbled. 'Nice relaxing weekend ahead of you.'

'Yeah.'

'Want to grab lunch on Sunday?' Mendel asked. 'I'll let you pay . . .'

'If you like,' Harland replied, then frowned. 'Actually, no I can't. Not this Sunday.'

'Don't tell me *you've* got plans?'

Harland nodded thoughtfully.

'Really? First time for everything,' Mendel grinned at him. But he didn't push it.

# 7

*Sunday, 8 June*

It was a quiet street, on a hill that overlooked the centre of Bath. Harland got out of the car and placed the bottle of wine on the corner of the glass sunroof. He turned his back on the line of smart, terraced houses, absently brushing the shoulders of his jacket as he peered up at the pale sky where the sun was trying to break through. Locking the car, he took the bottle by its neck and walked slowly back along the pavement towards number eleven. No gate, but a tidy front garden with a neat, narrow path leading up to the clean white door.

He knew it was a bad idea – had known it straight away. The last time he'd stood here, Alice had been with him. Had it really been only two years? It seemed like another lifetime.

There were white planters by the step – even their doormat looked clean and brushed. He hesitated, then sighed and rang the bell.

Why had he come? It was nice of them to invite him, of course, but why had he actually come?

He bowed his head and waited, hearing the muffled footsteps approach, the inevitable snap of the latch.

'Graham!' Christopher held the door open and beamed at him. He was a slim man with short brown hair that would become curly if allowed to grow, and pale, steady eyes. Dressed in a striped shirt and a light blue V-neck sweater, he appeared cheerful but Harland could read the tells. A little too much enthusiasm in the voice, that touch of determination holding his grin in place.

'Come in, come in.' Christopher pulled the door wide, and stepped back.

'Thanks.' Harland mumbled a greeting as he stepped across the threshold and back into the past. The door clicked shut behind him as his gaze swept the cream-carpeted hallway, the pastel walls. Familiar things seen through different eyes.

The smell of something cooking teased his nostrils as he handed the bottle to Christopher, then bent over to slip off his shoes, remembering the strict ritual that had appeared with Emily's expensive new carpets.

'Much appreciated.' Christopher hefted the bottle and glanced approvingly at the label. 'Come on through. Emily's in the kitchen.'

Harland straightened up, reflexively tensing his toes to grip the springy carpet through his socks, and suddenly felt terribly trapped. Forcing a smile, he followed Christopher along the hallway. Even though he'd never been particularly close to Alice's brother, their relationship had always been relaxed and easy-going. But now the emptiness she left behind grew suddenly unbearable again, and he was acutely aware of how much his wife had tied their family together.

'Graham.' Emily was thirty – pretty, in a formal sort of way. Lustrous dark hair worn in a bob framed a face used to smiling, and naturally long lashes gave her eyes a fascinating quality. Today's outfit was a simple white silk top and black trousers that showed off her figure – every inch the successful fashion writer. She came around the table to stand in front of him with her arms outstretched. 'It's been too long.'

His socks slid on the polished wooden floor as he stepped forward, embracing her awkwardly, aware of her breasts pushed against him, unsure what to do with his hands until he felt hers press on his back in a gesture of compassion. He gave her a gentle squeeze, feeling the warmth in her body, then pulled away.

'Good to see you, Em. Good to see you.'

Neither of them felt that, but he appreciated the effort they'd gone to.

'Drink?' Christopher opened the fridge to reveal a shelf of beer bottles.

'I could murder one,' Harland replied.

'Hey, that's a bit inappropriate coming from a copper,' Emily quipped, and they all laughed, grateful for anything that lightened the mood, however briefly.

Christopher poured him a glass and brought it over.

'Thanks,' Harland murmured as he looked out at their neat little patio and the tidy little garden beyond it. Everything in perfect order.

Emily's voice behind him broke his train of thought.

'Food will be another twenty minutes,' she said, closing a high cupboard. 'You boys go through to the living room – I'll call you when it's ready.'

Christopher smiled as she shooed them out of the kitchen, gesturing for Harland to go ahead of him.

The living room was bright and comfortable, with plain full-length net curtains diffusing the light from the wide bay windows. The carpet was thicker in here, and he felt his feet sinking into it as he walked across to one of the deep two-seater sofas, each cocooned in fitted linen covers, each with large suede cushions artfully arranged.

A broad fireplace occupied the middle of the long wall, tall bookshelves filling the space on either side of the chimney breast, but Harland's eye was drawn to the polished wooden mantelpiece, where a collection of framed photos smiled out at him from the past.

There were three pictures of Alice among them – one taken with Christopher and their parents, one with Emily, and one showing all four of them together at a wedding in Scotland. He stared at them for a long moment, then turned away and sat down, achingly aware of the empty seat beside him.

Christopher sank into the opposite sofa, looked at him for a moment, then reached forward and picked up a remote control from the small coffee table.

'It's the Grand Prix this afternoon,' he offered, one finger over the power button. 'Shall I stick it on?'

Harland was grateful for the distraction. The large, flat-screen TV bloomed into life, sweeping away the uneasy hush with a surge of engine noise and commentary, and they settled back into the comfort of their chairs, and the safety of their motor-sports small talk.

The race was still in progress when Emily looked through from the kitchen.

'Lunch is served,' she smiled. '*If* you can tear yourselves away from your racing cars.'

Christopher glanced across at him.

'Shall we?'

'Lead the way,' Harland said, getting to his feet.

Lunch itself wasn't quite the ordeal he'd feared it might be. Emily was clearly determined to give him a good meal, and she'd gone to a lot of trouble – the spotless white cloth on the kitchen table, with a full Sunday roast, served on the good china. He complimented her on her cooking, which was genuinely excellent, and she complimented him on remembering her favourite wine, which was accidental on his part, or perhaps a white lie on hers.

He ate slowly, letting Christopher talk about his job as a network engineer for an IT firm in Swindon, asking polite questions when lulls in the conversation seemed to require it.

Just before dessert, they were interrupted by a small commotion outside the back door. Harland glanced at Christopher, who just smiled.

'Don't worry, it's only Archie.'

Harland nodded, remembering the ridiculous-looking dog – some sort of enormous poodle cross-breed – that they'd bought a few years ago. Something to tide them over while they waited to see if they wanted children. He gazed thoughtfully at Emily's flat stomach as she stood up and went to see to Archie. Apparently the jury was still out on that question.

There was a wonderful lemon torte for dessert, and Harland felt almost drowsy as they stood up from the table. He wanted a cigarette, but he knew that would mean stepping out into the garden and he had no shoes on. Reluctantly, he gave up on the idea and allowed himself to be manoeuvred back into the living room for coffee and interrogation.

In the end it was Emily who asked.

'So, how are you getting on, Graham?'

*How are you doing on your own?*

He looked down, risking a weak smile as he weighed up the question. They had to ask – it was expected – but there was less expectation on him to answer, at least not truthfully.

'It's been . . . difficult, but I'm getting there.'

At least that was half true.

'You've been through such a lot.' Emily spoke sympathetically. 'I think you've been so strong.'

Harland's eyes flickered briefly to hers, before dropping back to his feet.

'I don't know about that,' he shrugged. 'Anyway, I suppose it's been difficult for all of us.'

He glanced at Christopher, who had quietly taken Emily's hand.

'For all of us,' she agreed.

'Have you thought about moving out of that house?' Christopher asked.

*Too big for you now you're on your own.*

'I've thought about it,' he replied, 'but I'm not in any rush.'

His eyes dwelled on Emily's small hand, tenderly placed on Christopher's thigh – a simple gesture of compassion that he found himself resenting.

'Anyway,' he finished lamely, 'there's nowhere else I want to be at the moment.'

*Nobody else to be with.*

They probably wondered if he was seeing anyone, but thankfully they were too polite to ask. His thoughts turned briefly to Sue, and he found himself picturing her smile, her attentive expression . . .

But this wasn't the time. And there was nothing to tell, only a confusion of guilt and desire that he couldn't understand himself, let alone explain to them. He breathed a silent sigh of relief as the conversation moved on to less painful subjects.

'So.' Christopher's voice was determinedly cheery again. 'I've thrilled you with my tales from the world of corporate IT. How's work with you?'

'Oh yes,' Emily leaned forward. 'Any juicy cases you can tell us about?'

Harland raised an eyebrow and gave her a half-smile.

'Juicy? Really, Em?'

'Sorry,' she laughed. 'You know what I mean – anything exciting?'

Part of him was still guarded about discussing work with civilians, people outside the force. They didn't appreciate the pressures, the constraints that made a difficult job almost impossible. But Alice had always encouraged him, gently steering him away from the siege mentality that was so easy to fall into after years on the job.

And so he told them about the Severn Beach case from last year. He described the strangled young woman lying face down in the mud, and explained the single, innocuous souvenir that linked her death with a series of other, apparently motiveless murders. He told them about the university lecturer, brutally beaten to death in a sleepy Hampshire village. And he recounted the chain of events that had finally led him to that ill-fated night in London's Docklands, where the killer had got the drop on him and left him lying unconscious and bleeding.

'It was a narrow stairwell, and I was completely out of breath,' he said softly. 'I'd just turned a corner onto the last flight of steps when this . . .' he paused, remembering that moment he thought would be his last '. . . this *shape* jumped down out of the darkness, caught me square in the chest and sent me flying backwards. Must have hit my head pretty hard, because the next thing I remember I was in the ambulance.'

'God!' Emily perched on the edge of the sofa, her hand over her mouth. 'Were you badly hurt?'

Harland looked down and shook his head.

'If he'd meant to kill me, I wouldn't be here now,' he said softly. 'I think he just wanted to get away.'

'I had no idea.' Christopher sat back into the sofa and steepled his fingers in front of his face. 'Didn't even know you'd been injured.'

'Well,' Harland shrugged, 'it's not something I'm particularly proud of. The bastard got away.'

'They haven't caught him?'

'Not yet.'

'What did he look like?' Emily asked, nibbling at a strand of her hair as she stared at him.

There it was, the eager thrill of proximity to danger. Harland wondered if she was becoming aroused, then frowned and put the thought out of his mind.

'I never saw his face. It was pitch-dark, and I didn't get that close to him.' He smiled ruefully. 'At least, not until he jumped me.'

Emily stared at him for a long moment, then sank back into her seat beside Christopher.

'That's absolutely amazing,' she murmured. 'You're so brave.'

'Tell it to my superintendent,' Harland grinned. 'He's not so easy to impress.'

They all laughed at that, until Emily sat upright and pressed her palm to the side of her face.

'The coffee!' She shook her head in self-admonishment, then leaned forward and patted Harland's knee as she got to her feet. 'I completely forgot about it, listening to your adventures. Sorry, shan't be a mo . . .'

He stayed for another hour, then feigned a reason to leave that they kindly didn't question. The tension eased as he got to his feet and thanked them for the meal.

'It's been really good to see you.' Christopher smiled, putting a hand on his forearm – an uncharacteristic physical contact that almost made Harland flinch.

'Don't let's leave it so long next time.' Emily gazed up at him with large, earnest eyes. 'You know you're always welcome. Always.'

'I know,' he said gratefully, but he was in no hurry to do this again. Together, the three of them merely highlighted

Alice's absence; without her there was little reason to rush back. 'Thanks.'

Secure in his shoes once more, Harland kissed Emily on the cheek and stepped out into the sunlight.

# 8

Someone had parked in his space again. No matter what time he turned the corner onto Stackpool Road, there always seemed to be a car outside his house. Not the same car – he could have done something about that – but different ones, unknown people parking here while they visited one of his neighbours. For a person who received no visitors, it seemed particularly unjust that he should so often be left without a space. He sighed and drove a short distance further up the street until he found a cramped little gap that he was able to reverse into.

Getting out of the car, he walked slowly back down the hill, still feeling bloated from his lunch with Christopher and Emily. It had been an uncomfortable visit, but at least it had occupied an afternoon; tonight he would be awkward in his own company, rather than awkward in theirs.

Opening the front door, he stepped into the quiet hallway and dropped his keys into the bowl on the hall stand. Yawning, he wandered through to the kitchen, where he lifted the kettle to check it had water in, then flicked the switch down to boil. Fumbling in his pockets, he retrieved his cigarettes and lighter, then moved over to the back door. The top bolt was stiff as always, but he drew it back with a firm pull, then turned the smooth metal key and twisted the handle.

The garden, once a comfortable little retreat when Alice had tended it, had all but disappeared. Now it was simply a narrow space between tall, red-brick walls choked with ivy. A jungle of weeds was slowly overtaking the concrete path, steadily advancing on the house. He looked out at it from the back step, then turned away.

That was a job for another day.

He hunched forward, shielding the cigarette with his hands as he lit it, then straightened his back and stared up at the early evening clouds. Not much of a scenic view – just a patch of Bristol sky, framed by high walls and the sides of buildings – but it calmed him, gave him time to think. He took a long drag, then flicked the ash, watching it flutter away like confetti across the garden.

Emily and Christopher would probably be settling down on the sofa about now – a quiet evening in front of the TV now that their entertaining was done. They were lucky to have each other.

He took another drag, exhaling and watching as the smoke drifted up and was lost in the eastern sky. Sue Firth lived over that way, somewhere on the other side of Victoria Park. She'd mentioned the street – that evening when a group of them had gone down to see a film at the Watershed – but he couldn't remember where it was. She'd looked different out of uniform, her dark hair down and her round face lit up with a bright smile as they'd walked and talked. Absently, he wondered if she was at home just now, or on duty over at Portishead . . .

From the kitchen he began to hear the kettle rattling on its base as it boiled, then the click of the switch as it turned itself off. He took a last draw, stubbed the cigarette out and dropped it into the butt-filled flowerpot by the wall before returning inside to make himself a coffee.

A main meal seemed unnecessary after the generous Sunday dinner, so he took a half-packet of biscuits from the cupboard to go with his drink, and wandered through to the front room. A quick flip through the channels confirmed that there was nothing worth watching on TV, so he put in a DVD and settled back to stretch out on the couch, his head propped up against one armrest, his feet hanging out over the other. Action films made the evenings pass more quickly, and his watch showed 9.20 p.m. when the gunfire ceased and the end credits appeared. Wearily, he pushed himself up into a sitting position, one hand moving to rub away the stiffness in his shoulder, and yawned. Then, stooping to retrieve his empty cup, he got to his feet and went through to the kitchen to clear up.

Another lonely evening, almost over.

The bathroom light flickered into life above him as he tugged the cord, then leaned over the bath to secure the plug and open the hot tap. A good soak would ease his shoulder, and help him get a good night. He knew all too well how elusive sleep could be – the thoughts that lurked in the darkness of the small hours.

Leaving the water running, he made his way along the landing and into the bedroom. It was at the front of the house, and the window looked out onto the street, but the curtains were still closed from this morning – he often forgot to open them. Yawning, Harland removed his watch and placed it on the small bedside cabinet. He undressed slowly, putting items away or pitching them into the laundry basket as he went. Then, gathering up a charcoal grey bathrobe and a large blue towel, he padded back through to the bathroom.

From habit, he pushed the door closed behind him to keep in the warmth, then paused as he glimpsed himself in the bathroom mirror. Letting the robe and towel drop to the floor, he stepped forward and leaned over the sink, wiping away the condensation to study his reflection properly.

When had he got so old?

There were lines starting to appear around his eyes, tiny crow's feet that hadn't been there before. His short dark hair was flecked with so many bright silver strands, and even his sideburns were peppered with grey. He sighed, then frowned, noting the creases in his brow, but his eyes were drawn back to tiny dark hairs that he'd spied in his ears.

*Great. Just great . . .*

Remembering the water, he bent over and switched off the tap, then returned to the mirror. Grimly, he took his razor from the cabinet and twisted it around in his hand, pressing the tiny button on the handle to activate the trimmer. Leaning towards his reflection, he angled his head to one side and eliminated the hairs, then turned and did the other ear.

He wasn't *that* bloody old.

Standing back a little, he looked at himself. From here, the grey wasn't so bad, the lines not so obvious. His body was in reasonable shape – maybe a little lean, but at least he didn't have to suck his stomach in any more – and his arms were toned.

That was probably the swimming. He'd been dismissive when his counsellor had suggested it as a way to help him get through the bereavement, but he'd tried it anyway and it had worked in a way – maybe lifting his mood a little, but certainly burning through some long, lonely hours, and tiring him so he could sleep.

He gazed at his reflection for a moment longer, pulling a hand down his jaw – he would shave in the morning, put some wax in his hair if he still had any lying around. Satisfied, he turned away from the mirror and tested the water with his toe. Far too hot. He spun the cold tap and let it run for a moment, paddling the water with his foot to cool the whole bath.

Before he got in, he retrieved the portable radio from the window sill and switched it on. Quiet voices on Radio 4, winding down the day with a muted discussion of The Arts.

He eased himself into the bath and lay back, mind and body melting away in the hot water. Steam closed his eyes and carried his thoughts once more to Sue, picturing her face, the way she looked at him – that clear smile, without any of the apprehension or pity that he saw in others when they spoke to him.

He slid deeper, so that the water gently lapped up over his chest to circle his neck.

That smile had been for him, her eyes attentive, interested. But what could he offer her? What could she possibly want from someone like him? He wasn't that much older – that wasn't the problem. It was just that she had seemed so . . . happy. Happy inside, unlike himself. He didn't want to taint that happiness, didn't want to see her face lose that spark of optimism, like his own troubled reflection.

Sighing, he turned his wrists upward, finding the hottest water just below the surface, feeling the warmth spreading through his veins. A voice from the radio mentioned that it was getting late.

He opened his eyes and reached for the soap, holding it to his nose to smell the cinnamon.

There was nothing he could do about it tonight – best to forget it for now. Sitting up and yawning, he ran the soap down his arm and began to wash the thoughts away.

# 9

She dreamed of sunlight, glittering through the trees at the end of the garden. It dappled the neatly mown grass as she twisted the pink handlebar grip back and forth, clicking up and down through the gears of her bicycle. Her small hands paused for a moment, and that was when she became aware of it – an indistinct sound, coming from the house. Resting her bike against the garage wall, she stood still, listening. At first, she thought her mother was calling her, and she skipped across the tiny square lawn to the tall patio doors. Reaching up, she tugged hard on the handle, leaning back to give all her slight weight to it with the eager abandon of a child, but as the heavy double glazing started to slide open, she suddenly heard more clearly. Raised voices in the kitchen, growing louder and louder as the door slid further, despite her trying to stop it.

'. . . I don't know why not. It's never stopped Jerry.' The shrill, mocking tone was all the more unsettling for coming from her mother.

'That's your answer to everything.' Her father's words were quieter, colder. 'I swear you won't be happy till you've turned me into a copy of that stuck-up little shit.'

He sounded so cross. Her small fingers still gripped the smooth metal handle tightly, her body swaying unhappily over the threshold as she stared across the shadowy dining room towards the kitchen door.

'At least *he* knows how to provide for his family.'

Why did her mother have to argue with him like this? Didn't she realise how angry she was making him?

There was a moment of strangled silence before her father began to shout.

'Well I'm sorry you had to settle for someone who *works* for a living.'

'Oh, give it a rest,' her mother laughed. 'It'd take a lot more than money to make a man of you, you pathetic—'The words were cut short by a stifled cry, and it sounded as though someone had fallen over something.

For a moment, a dreadful stillness blanketed the house. Biting her lip, she stepped up onto the patterned carpet and edged towards the kitchen as a quiet sobbing replaced the arguing voices, then froze as heavy footsteps moved quickly along the hall and the front door rattled and slammed.

She stood, rocking herself from side to side as she stared up at the kitchen door, waiting for everything to go quiet before she moved forward again. She didn't want to go in – she already knew what she would find – but somehow she couldn't stop herself.

The door made no noise as it swung slowly open, and she peered round it before stealing into the kitchen.

Her mother was sitting with her arms folded on the heavy wooden table, a blue cardigan draped over her shoulders, head bowed forward so that her wavy blonde hair shielded her face.

'Mummy?'

Her mother's arms seemed to tense, but she didn't lift her head or look round.

'It's all right, sweetheart.'

The words were spoken in a light, calm voice but they unsettled her more than anything that had preceded them.

With the horrible shock of certainty, she knew that her mother was lying to her. *Why?*

'What's the matter, Mummy?' She crept forward, her shoulder brushing along the edge of the table.

'I told you, it's all right.'

But it *wasn't*. She *knew* it wasn't. Reaching out, she moved closer, wanting to be held, but her mother suddenly flinched, jerking back from the touch, turning her head away.

'Will you *please* just go and play, Kim? Just . . . just go and play!'

The stooped shoulders rose and fell slowly, with a deep breath and a visible tightening of her mother's fingers. She turned her head slightly, one eye glaring out through the curtain of hair, teeth bared as though she was biting back words she mustn't speak.

Kim faltered, then took a step backwards. She'd never seen her mother so angry with her – what had she done wrong?

Retreating along the length of the table, she reached out a hand behind her to find the doorway, where she hesitated, leaning up against the uneven gloss of the wooden frame.

'That's a good girl. I love you, sweetheart.'

Her mother turned her chair away from the door slightly, tilting her head back a little. Kim managed a nervous smile, but it faded as she noticed the drops of blood, dark red beads that caught the light on the surface of the table. With a cry, she turned and tripped, stumbling though the doorway, arms tensing to save herself . . .

. . . as her eyes opened onto darkness. For a moment, she didn't understand where she was. Then she felt the soft smothering weight of the duvet, made out the dim shape of the lampshade on the ceiling above, and heard the quiet breathing beside her. Trembling, she rolled over, turning her body towards the sound, nuzzling in closer to his warmth. He stirred slightly, then reached out a strong arm, draping it around her shoulder. She wriggled closer, tucking her head in against his chest and whispering his name softly. He murmured something as his hand moved drowsily down her back and over her bottom, but she welcomed the intimacy of his touch, drawing up her knees against his and staring blindly in the dark.

'Rob?'

'Mmmm.'

'Rob?'

He groaned and moved his head slightly.

'What is it?'

She wanted to explain, to tell him what had woken her so he could banish it, but her memory of the dream was already shifting and hazy – only a confusing sense of guilt remained.

'I can't sleep,' she whispered, turning away from him, feeling foolish.

She felt him moving wearily, shuffling across into the middle of the bed, his arm gathering her and drawing her back against him.

'Come here,' he yawned, and his hand found hers, clasping it gently as he kissed her shoulder. 'It's all right. I've got you now.'

Staring into the gloom, Kim drew his arm in against her chest and held it tightly for a while, then finally allowed her eyes to close, and sleep to claim her.

# 10

Faces. Male and female, old and young, serious and smiling – just another busy Saturday in Bristol. Naysmith absently stroked a rough patch of stubble under his chin as he stared out through the café window at the shoppers drifting by, passing in and out of his line of sight as they explored the trestle tables in the food market. Little people, all of them individual, all of them insignificant.

He smiled and turned back to Kim, glancing down at the tall coffee glass on the table in front of her.

'How's your . . . ?' he gestured doubtfully at the cream-topped drink '. . . black cherry mocha?'

Kim made a face.

'Black Forest mocha,' she corrected him, then inclined her head as she raised the glass. 'I'm not sure. Maybe I should have gone for the latte. You're always safe with a latte.'

'If you don't like it, just leave it,' he shrugged. 'I can go and get you something else if you want?'

'No,' Kim shook her head, 'I do quite like it – it's just really . . . different, that's all.'

She leaned forward and used her spoon to case some of the whipped cream aside so that she could take another sip. Naysmith watched her then reached across the table to take her free hand, enjoying the way her face brightened.

'Well, you should never be afraid of trying new things,' he smiled at her.

This had been an extremely good week, all things considered. It was only natural that there would be some tension between them at first, but that had seemed to ease as Kim settled back into the safety of her normal daily routine.

Today, she was wearing skinny jeans and a tailored waistcoat that really showed off her figure – clearly she was making an effort for him. He leaned back in his chair, eyes casually flicking down to study her hands, looking for the telltale tremor, the slightest sign of nerves, but there was nothing. Steady hands. Calm. There had been the odd bad dream, but everyone had those, and she had clung to him afterwards, which was good. She really was coping well with the truth . . .

And yet he didn't want to leave it too long before drawing her even further into his confidence. It wasn't just that he was eager to do so – of course he was – but now that her perception had started to shift he knew that he needed to maintain the momentum. It was important that she didn't become too settled, start burying the knowledge too deep; that would make it harder for her to cope with the rest of what he had to tell her.

*And there was so much to tell. The man at Bentley Station. The lecturer from Winchester. The woman on Severn Beach . . .*

He glanced at his watch – it was a little after two o'clock – then looked back at Kim, admiring the smooth curve of her neck as she pushed her hair to one side to keep it clear of the whipped cream.

Patience.

There would be time enough for all that later. Just now, he wanted her to enjoy her afternoon.

'So,' he shifted in his chair and smiled, 'where next? Harvey

Nichols? Or did you want to go and have a look in that little arcade down by Broadmead?'

'Harvey Nicks,' Kim replied, dipping a finger into the whipped cream. 'I saw a gorgeous pair of boots in there last time, and I want to just try them on and see how they look on me.'

Naysmith shot her a knowing grin.

'OK.'

'I'm not going to get them,' she insisted. 'They're far too expensive at the moment. Maybe if they come down in the sales.'

Naysmith shrugged.

'Whatever you say.'

He gave her hand a little squeeze, then picked up his coffee and leaned back in his chair. Outside, a peculiar couple in their twenties caught his eye, slowing to stand just a few feet away. They looked oddly out of place among the smart shoppers – like escapees from a camping-goods catalogue. The girl was wearing a bright red fleece with grey sleeves, terribly blue jeans, and brown hiking trainers. Her partner was dressed almost identically, with the same fleece top and trainers. Even their ruddy complexions and thick blond hair seemed to match.

Naysmith smiled to himself and carefully turned his eyes back to his drink.

'Kim?'

She glanced up at him.

'Do it subtly, but take a look at the cool couple there in the window.'

Kim gazed at him with large, questioning eyes, then casually turned her head. He saw the ghost of a smile touch the corners of her mouth.

'See what I mean?' he whispered.

She turned back to the table, raising one small hand to hide her sudden grin.

'What do you think?' He affected a serious face. 'Was it buy-one-get-one-free day at their favourite boutique?'

Kim giggled and gave him a playful smack on the hand.

'Don't be such a meanie.' She tried to suppress her smile. 'They're probably just foreign students or something.'

Outside, the matching couple were now staring at something on a mobile phone that the girl was holding. Her partner was talking animatedly but they couldn't hear his voice through the glass.

Naysmith watched them thoughtfully for a moment.

'How old would you say they are?' he asked.

Leaning forward and pretending to take another sip of her drink, Kim stole a second look outside, then turned back to him.

'Not old,' she said. 'Mid-twenties?'

'Old to be students, but you may be right about the foreign part.' Naysmith nodded towards the window. 'See his backpack? It's got a Wolfskin logo on it – I'm sure that's a German brand.'

Kim gave him a triumphant little smile.

'Well, there you are then,' she said.

Naysmith inclined his head to her.

'Well done.' He leaned forward and raised an eyebrow. 'Now, for the bonus points: do you think they're a couple, or are they brother and sister?'

They both turned to look out of the window, but the couple were already moving away. As they went, the girl slipped her hand into the back pocket of her partner's jeans. Kim sniggered and turned back to the table.

'Definitely not brother and sister!' she grinned.

Naysmith shrugged. 'Depends which part of the world they're from.'

'Rob!'

He laughed and took a sip of his coffee as Kim put a hand over her mouth in feigned shock, then turned back to the window.

'People-watching can be fun,' she murmured, staring out through the shifting crowd.

*People-watching.*

Just for a moment, Naysmith froze.

Swallowing, he glanced up at her perfect profile, that delicate nose angled towards the glass, her lips slightly parted as her large eyes looked out at the drifting passers-by. His pulse quickened, the glimmer of an idea casting long shadows across his imagination.

Taking a deep breath, he leaned forward, following her gaze outside.

'OK,' he said, forcing his voice to be calm. 'Let's see how good you are – want to play a game?'

She turned to him and lifted her little chin defiantly.

'OK,' she smiled. 'What's the game?'

Naysmith suppressed a shudder of excitement and turned to look out at the shoppers browsing among the tabletop market vendors outside.

'Choose someone,' he said softly. 'Anyone you want . . .'

He swallowed again, willing his muscles to relax.

'. . . then let's see what you can tell me about them just from looking.'

A smile spread across Kim's face.

'Right,' she said, leaning across the table and sticking her tongue out at him. 'You're on.'

She turned to peer out of the window.

Naysmith leaned back, watching her concentrate. She was going to do it. She didn't understand it yet, but she was going to become a part of what he did. He felt a shiver of warmth course up through his body. It was so audacious, exceeding his wildest expectations – there was truly nothing that he couldn't do.

'How about her?' Kim was staring outside thoughtfully. 'The woman over there by the cheese table?'

Naysmith allowed himself a little shiver of delight. Previously, he'd always allowed Fate to choose for him. Now, he leaned forward to see who Kim was looking at.

'Her?' he asked.

An overweight woman in her forties, maybe five foot six, with a jolly-looking face and shoulder-length wavy hair dyed black. A deep lilac jacket was draped about her plump body, which tapered down through tight black leggings to a pair of tiny feet, giving the impression that she might topple over at any moment. Her round face creased into a broad grin as she chatted with the market trader, revealing a puffy, double chin.

He smiled as Kim nodded.

'All right,' he said slowly. 'So, what can you tell me about her?'

'Well,' Kim thought for a moment. 'She's about forty-five or so, larger figure . . . looks as though she uses a tanning salon.'

'Very good,' Naysmith mused, noting the tanned complexion. 'Is she married or single?'

Kim scrunched up her face a little as she peered outside.

'It's difficult to see,' she frowned. 'I think there's a ring on her finger though.'

It was smaller than her other jewellery, probably a wedding ring, but impossible to be sure from this distance.

'OK.' He gazed out through the glass. 'Is she well off or is money tight for her?'

Kim pondered the question for a moment.

'Well, her handbag looks expensive. And her shoes. Yes, I think she has money.'

'And yet that shopping bag doesn't look new at all.'

He indicated the woman's large canvas bag, a faded logo with the word *Chocolate* printed below it.

'Maybe . . .' Kim hesitated, then shrugged. 'Maybe it's not her bag. I don't know.'

Naysmith inclined his head towards her in acknowledgement.

'All right,' he mused. 'What would you say she does for a living?'

Kim sat back and folded her arms.

'Honestly, I haven't got a clue.' She looked at him cheekily. 'Shall I run outside and ask her?'

'No!' *That would ruin everything!* Kim looked at him curiously, but he controlled his voice and continued in a more relaxed tone. 'Just look at her and see if anything stands out.'

Kim stared for a moment then shrugged.

'I don't know . . . she's wearing a chunky necklace, big earrings. A jeweller perhaps?'

Naysmith smiled and sipped his coffee.

'Look at her hand.'

Kim leaned closer to the glass, craning to get a better view. 'What about it?'

Naysmith put his cup down on the table.

'See that blue sticking plaster on her finger?' he asked. 'That's one of those health and safety ones you need to use if you work with food.'

Kim peered out and smiled.

'Actually, she does kind of look as though she works with food.' She giggled naughtily, then put her hand over her mouth. 'Oh my, that was such a bitchy thing to say. You bring out the worst in me sometimes.'

Naysmith smiled at her.

'I'd certainly like to think so,' he murmured.

They studied the woman as she paid for her cheese and dropped her purchase into the canvas shopping bag. Naysmith frowned. Something about the way she did it, such a familiar motion . . . the bag must be hers after all. He studied the logo, trying to make out what was written around it – something *Arcade* – but the woman was turning away now. He took one last look at her, taking in each detail and fixing her appearance in his mind.

*He never forgot a face.*

Kim was looking at him when he turned back to the table.

'Well?' she asked.

'Well what?'

'I did what you wanted,' she shrugged. 'Aren't you going to play the game?'

Naysmith picked up his coffee and drained it. Placing the empty cup down carefully between them, he reached across and took her small hands in his.

'Don't worry,' he promised her, 'I'll play.'

# 11

They parked at the end of Station Road – that was the name on the sign – next to a small grey utility building. Kim glanced across at Rob as he switched off the ignition and sat for a moment, staring out through the windscreen, his face blank.

He'd been strangely quiet on the way over from Bristol. In fact, now that she thought of it, he'd been somewhat preoccupied all afternoon.

When he'd suggested going somewhere for a walk, she'd shrugged and agreed. A bit of quiet time together after the bustle of the shops might be nice, and afterwards they could maybe go to dinner somewhere.

As they'd pulled out of the car park, she'd taken a couple of minutes to study her reflection in the sun-visor mirror, fix her make-up – she wanted to make sure she looked good for him, especially if they were going to have a romantic stroll somewhere on the way home. But he hadn't driven back towards Salisbury. As she folded the visor up out of the way, she saw they were on an unfamiliar road.

'Where are we going?' she asked as she put her handbag down into the footwell.

'Wait and see,' he'd smiled, and she didn't feel she could ask again.

They passed under the Clifton suspension bridge and followed the river along the base of the gorge. Soon, the city was behind them, the high walls of the valley had fallen away and they were driving through a bleak industrial landscape.

She stole quick sidelong glances at him as he drove. Where was he taking her? Crumbling old factories and flimsy new warehouses slid by. In the distance, several huge wind turbines turned slowly, and evil-looking chimneys breathed white smoke into the sky. Mesh fences crowned with barbed wire hemmed them in on either side of the road. Not the sort of place for a romantic walk. And yet, as she looked at his profile, caught the slight spark in his expression, it was clear he knew exactly where he was going . . .

And now they were here.

Rob tore his gaze away from the windscreen and reached down to remove the keys from the ignition.

'Come on,' he smiled.

She watched him get out, then sighed, gathered up her bag and opened her door. They were at the end of a quiet, residential street, where it angled left to run along a line of small houses. There was a modern brick-built apartment block to the right, but in front of them a tall embankment cut a long, straight line across the end of the street, blocking the view. A tarmac slope led to the top, where there seemed to be a line of stainless-steel railings.

Rob was already moving towards it, walking ahead of her.

'Up here.' For a moment, she thought he was beckoning to her, holding out his hand, but then she felt foolish as she heard the car doors remote-locking behind her. 'Come on.'

Kim followed him as he went before her, striding briskly up the slope and turning to wait for her at the top. She walked up the tarmac, her own pace slowing as she climbed, and the hidden landscape ahead of her slid into view – her eyes drawn first to the Second Severn Crossing away on the right, then to the vast expanse of the estuary itself.

'Oh! Wow . . .'

'I know.' Rob smiled at her. He turned and walked over to the steel railing that ran along the length of the sea wall. Kim came over to stand beside him, gazing out at the view.

Seeing it all, so suddenly, filled her with awe. The vast sky, with towering outcrops of pale-edged cloud. Fiery cracks, where the sun cast a curtain of bright warm shafts down to heat the water into burning gold.

'This way.'

She felt very small as she followed him along the top of the sea wall, looking out through the metal railings at the beach below them. Clumps of reeds stood here and there, like dark green islands emerging from the smooth silver mud. There were no ripples on the distant water, just a void of pale grey, broken here and there by smears of dark ground. The bursts of sunlight came and went as they walked, now touching the water, now the beach, even lighting part of the bridge for a moment into pale grey and green.

A single bird wheeled around, flapping as it climbed above them, then banking to soar out over the water. Far to the west, in the haze where the coastline reached out towards its furthest point, the three great wind turbines turned slowly, silently, their long blades reaching taller than the horizon. There was a stillness now, as though the wind were gathering itself, drawing breath before sweeping down along the shoreline.

They reached the end of the railings and walked down onto the shingle and small stones above the tide's reach.

'You once asked me what it felt like . . .'

His voice startled her after the long silence, and she frowned for a second, unsure what he was referring to. And then her small steps faltered as she recalled that moment on a different beach, that single question that he'd felt able to answer.

Nervously, she turned her head to look up at him, glimpsing that same fire burning behind his eyes, that same intensity as he remembered.

*How it felt to kill.*

He was holding her hand, and for a second she felt the urge to draw away from him, but something warned her not to. She swallowed and lowered her eyes.

'I remember,' she whispered.

Naysmith turned away from the bridge, looking far off to the left where the footpath led towards the edge of the village, to the rough grass slope that led down to the beach.

'When you can see – *really see* – vast distances, it can make you feel insignificant.'

Kim glanced back to him and nodded uncertainly.

'But imagine standing here, with all of this around you, above you . . .' he gestured out at the skyline '. . . and now imagine power – limitless power – flowing through you. You're in control, in absolute control of everything.'

He paused for a moment, then added, 'Even life itself.'

Kim stared at him, unsettled but finding herself caught in his words. He slipped his arm around her waist, drawing her close to him.

'We all do bad things from time to time . . . and under certain circumstances we're all capable of *terrible* things.' His strong hand gently caressed her midriff as they stared out along the thin tarmac footpath that dwindled into the grey distance. 'But some of us are able to master the circumstances, *grasp* that power . . .'

At first she thought she was shaking, and tried to stop it, to calm herself. But then she realised that it wasn't her shaking. It was him.

'I wish I could make you understand what it's really like – it's so difficult to put into words . . .'

Kim's heart was beating rapidly, her gaze flitting between the bleak coastal path ahead of them and the eerie light in Rob's eyes. Her breathing quickened as she stood at his side, terrified but also strangely thrilled by this insight he had trusted her with.

And then, without a word, he bowed his head for a second before turning towards her. His hands rose to frame her face, his fingers gently pushing back her hair as he leaned in and kissed her.

Her eyes closed, and her thoughts spiralled away as she gave herself over to the moment. She wished it could last for ever, just the two of them together on the edge of oblivion, where all her fears and doubts gave way to this overwhelming feeling of closeness. Now, in this instant, until she opened her eyes or his lips left hers . . . he loved her, and she loved him.

When she opened her eyes, he was looking at her. The unsettling hunger was still there, but it was infused with something else now . . . a longing that made her feel so good. The idea of some stranger losing his life didn't seem real any more. It was just an abstract fragment of the past, a shadow in her confused thoughts.

Leaning in against his shoulder, she sighed and stared down at the beach. Deep down, part of her yearned to be even closer to him, to know him fully. The way he'd spoken was frightening, but also oddly compelling. She bit her lip, hesitant, unsure what to say.

He touched her chin, lifting her face towards him. For a moment, she thought he was going to kiss her again, and she parted her lips a little. But he paused, eyes glittering as he studied her face, looking right down into her soul.

'Imagine it. Imagine how it would feel to walk along this beach in the first light of dawn, rain clouds rolling in, with that sort of power flowing through you.'

Kim hesitated, her eyes flickering briefly towards the grey water. A chill ran through her as she looked at the dark shapes half submerged by the mud. She glanced back at him.

'I'm not sure I can . . .'

'Try.' His voice was soft, but commanding, kindling her desire to submit. 'Try for me now . . .'

And she did. She pushed her thoughts out along the shoreline, picturing a faceless stranger, imagining how it might feel to be so in control, not just of herself but of another; glimpsing what it would take to embrace such a terrible act and such terrible power. She felt the adrenalin tingling in her body, the fear, but also something more.

He smiled.

'Do you understand what I'm talking about?'

Kim stood there, locked in his gaze. She swallowed slightly and nodded. Her eyes broke free of his and turned to look down at the reeds, which had begun to sway in the wind.

*This was where it had happened.*

It had to be. And this was his way of telling her, she felt certain of it. Suddenly she wanted to know, wanted to be sure.

'Who was he?' She spoke quietly but her words echoed in her head as she stared out across the beach.

Naysmith inclined his head slightly to one side.

'Who was who?' He wasn't going to make it easy for her, but she couldn't stop now. She bit her lip, and forced herself to say it.

'The person who you . . .' She hesitated. 'The person who . . . was here.'

Naysmith stared at her coolly, holding her eyes for a long time without saying anything. She felt the blood draining from her as she realised he wasn't denying it, that she was right, that it *had* happened here. Then he turned away from her, to gaze out at a line of reeds on the silver mud.

'Who said it was a "he"?' he asked softly.

Kim's stomach lurched.

Without looking at her, he took her hand and led her back towards the car.

# 12

He must be asleep by now. Lying on her right side, keeping her body perfectly still, she listened carefully to his breathing, which had settled to a slow, regular rhythm. Facing towards the middle of the bed made her nervous, but if she had turned her back to him he might have fallen asleep with his arm thrown across her, his body spooning hers. This way was better.

Cautiously, she let her eyelids flicker open, just a little at first, as she fought to make sense of the shapes in the darkness. Looking across the soft curve of her pillow, she could make out the side of his head, silhouetted against the faint blue glow from the alarm clock behind him. Unblinking, her gaze bored into the shadow where she knew his eyes must be, searching for a glint, the slightest movement, anything that might indicate he was watching her.

But there was nothing.

As she grew accustomed to the gloom, she began to make out his features, so familiar to her, now so fearfully close. His eyes were definitely shut. She watched them for a moment, afraid that they might snap open, terrified that he might glimpse the doubt in her heart, but he slept on.

Good.

She listened to his breathing for a little longer, then slowly began to roll herself away from him, gradually easing over onto her back, trying not to disturb the duvet as she slid out from under it.

Reaching the point where she had to turn her head away from him, she strained to hear his breathing, measuring out the rhythm, searching for the tiniest change, but it remained steady. Her shoulder emerged from the side of the duvet, followed by one of her legs. She was balanced on the edge of the bed now, but she had to take it slowly, try and position herself without disturbing him.

One leg extended, her questing toes found the floor. She took a second to steady herself, then reached down until her fingertips brushed across the rug. Still his breathing didn't alter. Up to this point, she could probably have wriggled back under the covers without him noticing, but now she had to complete her move. Slowly inhaling, she held her breath and let her weight shift fully over, dragging her left leg out from under the duvet so that she was kneeling beside the bed.

Listening carefully, she allowed herself to exhale without making a sound. Then, walking her hands back in towards herself, she rose up on her knees and peered across the dim landscape of the bed.

He hadn't stirred.

Rolling back onto her heels, Kim rose slowly and silently to her feet, unfolding like a pale flower, naked in the dark. Drawing herself up to her full height, she glanced behind her to make sure she wouldn't stumble, then began to move backwards, balancing on her toes as she edged away from where he lay.

The door was ajar, and she half turned, carefully placing her fingers on the handle and gently drawing it just a little further open. Then, with one glance back towards the bed, she stepped gingerly through the gap and out into the still-ness of the landing.

She moved forward slowly, unsteadily, her bare feet testing the floor with each tentative step. Walking with one arm reaching out in front of her, and the other stretched out at her side, she trailed her fingertips along the smooth surface of the wall for balance. She felt the doorway more than saw it, then searched out the door itself and carefully pushed it open.

After the hallway carpet, the tiled bathroom floor chilled the soles of her feet, and she could feel a wave of goosebumps rising on her arms and thighs.

She turned and eased the door shut behind her, holding the handle down so that the latch wouldn't make any noise, her fingers seeking out the bolt and gently sliding it home. Standing there in the darkness, she let her wide eyes close for a moment, allowed herself to breathe again. Her hand reached up and outward until she felt the thin cord, took hold of it and pulled.

*Click.*

The room blazed white and she covered her eyes for a moment, giving them a chance to adjust to the glaring light. Slowly parting her fingers, she opened her eyes a little, then moved her hands to hug herself as an uncontrollable shiver ran through her. The bathroom was cold after the warmth of the bed, and her skin felt like stone. Rubbing her arms, she cast around the room, then went over to the towel rail. Mercifully, it was on, and she took the large white towel and wrapped it around her shoulders, surrendering herself to the soothing warmth. Her feet were still freezing, so she padded over and sat down on the toilet, rubbing her toes into the soft carpeted bath mat, respite from the cold floor tiles.

Only now did she dare to think about it. Up until now, she'd pushed it all away, forced herself to concentrate on getting out of the room without waking him, getting some space so she could think. But now she was here, and there was nowhere else to go, no way to avoid it. She let go just a little, and was immediately overwhelmed by a searing glare of nightmare images blazing through her mind, though she shut her eyes tight against them.

*Oh God, what had he done?*

A woman. He'd killed a woman. All the excuses she'd fabricated, all the lies she'd told herself . . . everything had been blown away in the sudden icy gale of that revelation, leaving her tattered and alone with the truth. She struggled to rationalise it, to find some justification, but there was none. It couldn't have been an accident, it simply couldn't. He'd killed a woman on purpose.

*Murder.*

It was the first time the word had come to her and somehow that made things worse. Living with a murderer. In love with a murderer. She was so stupid.

She fought them back, but the tears came anyway. Her shoulders began to tremble inside the towel, the first involuntary sobs overtaking her small body. That would have woken him, if she'd stayed in the bed, if she'd let herself think about it as she lay next to him, and how would she have explained herself then? She'd barely made it out of the room in time. How long had she thought she could keep a grip on something like this, something so . . .

Her imagination tore itself free, running on ahead of her beyond any hope of reining it back in, leading her deeper into the nightmare. Image after image, each more terrifying than the last: red blood on a woman's pale flesh, eyes rolling back, a host of different deaths. And standing over each one, that same figure, that man whom she had given herself to, his face grim and terrible.

It was too much.

Sagging forward, she wadded up a handful of the towel and pushed it into her mouth, crying into the layered material to deaden the sound, just like she used to do when she was a little girl. She couldn't help herself, but he mustn't hear her, mustn't know what she was thinking.

She wasn't sure how long she'd been there.

Sitting up stiffly, she felt exhausted and cold. Her bottom was numb from sitting on the hard wooden toilet seat – she must have been slumped over for a while.

Sniffing softly, she took some tissue from the roll and carefully dabbed her eyes dry. The crisis was past, the swell of panic had crashed over her like a breaking wave and receded. Now she just felt numb, disconnected from her circumstances, as though they were happening to someone else.

Weariness enveloped her like a fog and she yawned as she got slowly to her feet.

For now, she was all cried out. Her emotions wouldn't betray her.

*For now.*

She slipped off the towel and draped it back over the rail, shivering as her shroud of body heat evaporated. Then, lifting her chin and trying to affect a calm expression, she moved over to draw back the bolt and open the door. The light clicked off, leaving her blind in the darkness, but she knew the way. Part of her was glad, not wanting to see or be seen, ashamed of her feelings, ashamed of playing her part in a horror she couldn't understand.

Stretching her hand out in front of her, she tiptoed out onto the landing and walked quietly back to bed.

# 13

*Monday, 16 June*

Naysmith studied an email as he walked up the carpeted steps, then returned the phone to his inside pocket as he pushed the door wide and walked into the reception area.

'Morning, Amy,' he said, shifting the strap of his shoulder bag so it wouldn't crease his jacket. 'How are you today?'

Amy looked up from behind the large, curved desk and smiled at him. She was in her twenties, plain but professional, always dressed smartly, always courteous. Her straight brown hair was tied back today, which was unusual – he wondered if anyone else had noticed.

'Good morning, Rob,' she replied. 'I'm fine, thanks.'

He glanced up at the three clocks on the wall behind her.

'Are Fraser and Gina in yet?'

'Gina is. Fraser called to say he was running late but he'll be here by ten.'

'No problem,' he shrugged. 'I've got a few emails to sort through – I'll grab one of the meeting rooms for now and make a start.'

He put his hand on the internal door, then paused and glanced back over his shoulder.

'Your hair looks good like that,' he told her.

Amy beamed at him.

'Thanks, Rob.'

Fraser was a lean, likeable man in his early fifties, with thinning grey hair and a pointed chin. He put his head around the meeting-room door and gave a small nod of acknowledgement.

'There you are,' he said, as though he'd looked everywhere. 'Amy said I'd find you in here.'

'Morning, Fraser.' Naysmith smiled as he got to his feet. 'Ready to start?'

'Whenever you are.' Fraser held the door open for him as he gathered up his open laptop and bag before they walked out between the cubicles and across the main floor of the open-plan office.

'Sorry about the delay.' The older man frowned as they approached the boardroom door. 'Italian sports cars look nice but they can be rather temperamental. Had to borrow Chloe's Volvo and that lumbered me with doing the school run first.'

'That's why I drive a modest German saloon.'

'That, and because we don't pay you enough, eh?' Fraser chuckled.

Naysmith smiled.

*That, and the fact he didn't want a memorable car.*

It was important that he not stand out – imagine the risk of making all those journeys to Severn Beach in a Maserati! And it wouldn't have been nearly so easy to track down vehicles of the same make and model whose registration numbers he could duplicate on his false plates.

They entered the boardroom and Fraser shut the door behind them. Naysmith walked around the long wooden table and drew out one of the high-backed dark leather chairs.

'Good morning, Gina,' he smiled as he put his open laptop

on the polished surface and slid his bag onto the empty seat
next to him. 'If you're charged up, can I borrow your power
lead? I've left mine at home.'

Wearing a tailored pinstripe jacket and with her dark hair
styled in a smart bob, Gina glanced up from her own screen.
She was a clever woman in her late forties who, along with
Fraser, had built the business from the ground up. She
regarded Naysmith and offered him a weary look.

'You can have it for a little while, but I want it back,' she
sighed, unplugging the cable from her laptop and sliding it
across to him.

'For a little while,' he promised gravely.

There was a brief chiming sound and the large black screen
at the far end of the table flickered into life, showing two
figures sitting in a bright office by a huge glass window.

'Good morning.' The figure on the left of the screen was
a tall man in a short-sleeved shirt, with gelled black hair and
rimless glasses. He raised his hand in greeting as he settled
back into his chair. 'Good to see you all.'

'*Morgen*, Andreas,' Naysmith waved back. 'Hey there, Christof.'

'*Hallo*.' The other figure nodded towards the camera.
Christof was younger, in his thirties, with pale blond hair
and a tiny beard.

Naysmith leaned over towards the screen.

'Any chance one of you guys can get me a coffee?' He
grinned. 'The stuff they have here in Woking is pretty much
undrinkable.'

Christof laughed and held up a mug.

'I let you have some of mine,' he smiled.

On the screen, Andreas opened up his laptop, then
addressed the camera.

'Well, as you can see it is a beautiful day here in Hamburg,'
he gestured to the window behind him, the familiar office

blocks and TV tower on the skyline. 'How are things over there on the island?'

Gina smiled patiently.

'Britain is great, thanks.'

Andreas shrugged apologetically.

'Ah, it is just my little joke,' he told her.

'And a German joke is no laughing matter.' Fraser had a mischievous twinkle in his eye as he looked up from his notebook. 'So, shall we begin?'

They turned to Gina.

'OK,' she said, adopting a no-nonsense tone. 'First up, I want to know where we are with the Friedman account.'

On screen, Christof's shoulders sagged and he shook his head slightly.

'Ah, so we begin with the thing that is not the best.' Andreas gazed down at the table and nodded.

'We've discussed this several times over the last couple of months,' Fraser interjected. 'Is the situation any better?'

'No.' Christof shook his head. 'I would say it's getting a little bit worse.'

Andreas gave him a slightly pained sidelong glance, then turned back towards the camera.

'They keep requesting to change the specification,' he explained. 'What they are asking for is not so unreasonable if they are asking for it at the *start*, but we have spent already a lot of euros developing a solution which they now ask us to engineer again in a different way.'

There was an uncomfortable silence. Gina's face was unreadable but Fraser shook his head and sighed.

'This is getting expensive,' he muttered.

Naysmith leaned forward, gently turning his pen around on the polished surface of the table. A glimmer of an idea was forming.

'They're tied in for a support contract, right?' he asked, staring down at the reflections on the wood.

'*Ja*,' Christof shrugged.

'OK, how about we give them a choice?' It was coming together now – there was a way they could fix this. He turned to look at the screen. 'They can honour the original agreement and negotiate any changes at a sensible rate – which is fair enough – *or* if they keep pushing us for changes on the specification, then *we* only support what was originally specified.'

Andreas rubbed his jaw thoughtfully.

'But how would that work?' Christof asked. 'They'd have to line up additional support or the system would be vulnerable.'

'Exactly,' Naysmith replied brightly.

Christof was still frowning.

'So what's the difference to them?' he frowned. 'Won't they just keep screwing us around?'

Naysmith glanced across at Gina, noting the faint smile that touched her lips. She knew where he was going with this.

'Our support rate is approximately double the negotiated development rate,' she said coolly. 'In short, we charge them twice as much if they mess around. That's what you're thinking, Rob?'

Naysmith bowed his head to her slightly.

Andreas nodded. 'It would give us a much stronger negotiating position.'

They were all quiet for a moment, considering the implications of such a move. In the end, it was Fraser who broke the silence with a soft chuckle.

'Somebody needs to explain the perils of their situation to them.' He smiled grimly. 'Then they'll be more inclined to do a sensible deal.'

There was a pause. On the screen, Christof glanced across at Andreas, who said nothing.

Naysmith leaned back in his chair and looked at Fraser.

'I'll do it,' he said.

Fraser gave him a slow smile, then turned to the screen and raised an enquiring eyebrow.

'All right with you?' he asked.

'That would be great.' Andreas looked brighter now. 'And it would mean *our* relationship with them could still be the same. Are you sure you don't mind, Rob?'

'No problem,' Naysmith shrugged. 'Sales are my responsibility, and I'm not going to pass the buck.'

He glanced across to Gina and gave her a quick grin.

'Plus, I rather like the thought of being the bad guy.'

Gina shook her head and chuckled.

'So we have a plan.' Andreas smiled. 'Let me know about the flights, and I'll set up a meeting. Then maybe we can go for a meal with the team afterwards?'

'An evening on the Reeperbahn?' Naysmith spoke thoughtfully, then turned to smile at Andreas. 'Now how could I refuse an offer like that?'

The meeting ran on until midday, when Andreas and Christof had to leave for another appointment. As the large screen went dark, Naysmith closed his laptop, lifted his bag onto the table and started packing away.

'Hey!' Gina snapped at him.

Naysmith looked across at her, puzzled.

'Power supply.' She pointed an accusing finger at him and he realised that he'd been rolling up the cables, ready to stow them away.

'Sorry.' He smiled as he slid the power supply back across the table to her. 'Force of habit.'

'If that was a habit, you wouldn't keep forgetting to bring your own.' She glanced at her watch. 'It's almost lunchtime. Did you want to come and grab something with Fraser and me?'

'I'd like that. Give me five minutes to make a call?'

'That's fine.' She stood up and followed Fraser out of the room.

Kim answered on the third ring.

'Hello?'

'Hey, beautiful, how's it going?'

'I'm fine.' Her voice seemed subdued. Maybe he'd caught her at a bad time. 'How was your meeting?'

Naysmith leaned back in his chair, gazing up at the tiny recessed lights above the table.

'It was OK,' he shrugged. 'Listen, I'm going for lunch with Fraser and Gina in a minute, but I wanted to let you know that I'll probably need to pop over to Hamburg this week.'

'When are you going?'

'Not sure,' he replied, 'I haven't checked the flights yet – but I should only be away one night.'

'OK. Will you let me know once it's booked?'

She must be thinking about their day out together. He'd almost forgotten.

'Kim?' He softened his voice for her. I know I said we'd take the day off on Friday, but I think that might be difficult now. Any chance you can shift your day off to next week?'

'Yes, that should be all right. I'll speak to Marcus this afternoon.'

'Thanks. You don't mind, do you?'

'No, of course not.'

He thought she might have sounded more disappointed, but no matter.

'You're the best,' he told her. 'Listen, I'll call you this afternoon once I know about the flights.'

'OK, enjoy your lunch.'

He smiled and got to his feet.

'I will. Catch you later.'

It was a shame about Friday, but Kim had been very understanding, and he'd make it up to her. Leaning forward, he picked up his bag and slipped the strap over his shoulder. It was a pity about the Bristol woman too – he'd hoped to start looking for her, but now that would have to be put back as well. Frowning, he straightened his jacket and walked towards the door.

*Minor delays.*

But it wouldn't change his plans.

# 14

Kim followed Rob out of the kitchen and into the hallway, watching as he patted his pockets, checking for his passport, his wallet.

'Got everything?' she asked.

He turned to face her, his expression softening into a warm smile.

'I think so,' he said, picking up his phone and slipping it into his jacket. 'Anyway, it's just for the one night.'

He stooped to pick up his bag and retrieved his car keys from the hall stand.

'I'd better get going.'

She nodded silently, twirling a strand of hair absently across her mouth.

'Kim?'

She started, finding his eyes on her, watchful, thoughtful. 'Yes?'

He moved closer, his hands reaching up towards her throat, but she managed not to flinch. They moved higher, gently cupping her face and lifting it to his. She exhaled, hoping it sounded like longing rather than relief.

'I want to kiss you goodbye.' His eyes were smiling again. She let her lips part, relaxing into his embrace. Her eyes

closed but the troubling images remained, despite the remembered desire she felt in her own kiss.

He released her and turned away, not noticing the trembling
she felt in her body, not seeing the cracks she could feel in
her own expression.

'Right, now I really do have to go,' he said, opening the
front door and stepping out into the grey morning light.

'Take care,' she called from the shadow of the doorway.

'I always do,' he grinned, walking across to the car and
unlocking it. 'See you tomorrow.'

Kim watched as he pulled away, the red brake lights glowing
brightly, until the car turned onto the road and disappeared
round the corner. She stood there for a moment longer, then
closed the front door and was immediately hit by the silence
of the house. It was an almost tangible blow, like a wall of
water that crashed over her and washed down the hallway,
blanketing everything in a terrible stillness. Turning, she made
her way through to the kitchen, walking softly to try and
make her footsteps seem less noisy. In the middle of the
room, she paused beside the table, her eyes flitting around
the walls.

*A quiet prison.*

She frowned and bit her lip. This was home. Their home.
Her home. But there was something troubling about the place
now.

She found that she was holding her breath, and forced
herself to exhale. What was the matter? Walking over to the
counter, she reached for the kettle, but her hand felt clammy
as it touched the handle, as did the other when she placed
her palm on the worktop.

Was she sick?

Her breathing was still irregular, trying to balance itself
back into a normal rhythm, but she couldn't quite master it.

She turned and walked back into the hallway, hesitating, unsure where she should go.

Part of her wanted to scream, to drive out the creeping quiet with a howl of anguish. Tears pricked in the corner of her eyes, but the rising storm of thoughts stole her ability to cry. She trembled, rooted to the spot, until finally she sagged to her knees. Down was the only way she could move, fingers clawing at the carpet as she crumpled and curled up as though in pain.

That cold knot in her stomach, now a block of ice that burned, weighed her down. Her cheek touched the carpet, and a tear slid across her temple. Her mouth opened as though to cry out, but no sound would come.

How long would she have to lie here, waiting for something to happen?

She blinked away another tear and stared out across the floor. The hallway seemed long and tall from down here, the familiar made foreign and unsettling. Her nails gouged into the carpet once more as she managed to force out a strangled sob, tensing all her muscles as hard as she could before releasing them, gulping down a breath to make up for the ones she'd forgotten to take.

What was she going to do?

Everything was wrong. She raised her eyes to the front door, a tall and distant barrier looking strange from this angle.

*The front door.*

She closed her eyes, fearful of even the thought. Trapped behind a door that she was afraid to open. Afraid to step through. Because of the terrible uncertainty that lay on the other side.

Her body stiffened again, knuckles whitening, knees pressing together, teeth clenched and eyes screwing more tightly shut – desperately trying to drown out the noise that roared in her head.

And then, rising above it, there was a strange, despairing sound, like an animal crying in pain, rising in pitch and volume until it filled her ears and her mind. She felt her lungs empty, pushing out every last ounce, her throat twisting the air into a scream that shook the house.

When she came to herself, she was on her back, staring up at the pale ceiling. Her breathing was shallow now and her throat hurt. She felt weak, but sensed that she could move again.

At first, she just turned her head, gently rolling it to one side to look at the skirting board. Her fingers tensed and relaxed, the heel of her hand brushing the carpet. Drawing in a deep breath, she pushed herself up to a sitting position, swaying as her head came upright, a little faint.

She felt very small, a forlorn figure sitting at the foot of the stairs, walls on either side of her. But her eyes turned again to the door. Another breath – this one felt easier than the last, her body was levelling out. Good.

With one hand, she rubbed her eyes, surprised at the wetness on her lashes, the dried tears on her face. Had she managed to cry?

She got to her feet, steadying herself with a palm against the wall. The plaster felt cold, but her hand was no longer sweating, and she lowered her arms to her sides as she stared down the hallway.

*She had to get out.*

And now she was moving quickly, running up the stairs with an adrenalin-fuelled urgency, as though he might have somehow felt her thoughts and returned home to burst in through that terrifying door. She raced along the landing and into the bedroom, reaching for her handbag and checking for her purse. Her phone was beside the bag and she swept it up.

*Sarah!*

She would call her sister, tell her everything . . . Her finger hovered over the speed dial as she tried to imagine how she would say it.

No. Not now, not over the phone. She slipped the handset into her bag and went back out onto the landing. She needed to think. She needed to get out.

At the top of the stairs, she hesitated for a moment. What if he came back? What if he'd forgotten something and was driving back to the house? If he found her like this, sobbing and shaking . . .

*Stop it!*

She closed her eyes and rubbed her temples with clenched fists. Then, taking a gulp of air, she half stumbled down the first few steps, her eyes peering down to the hallway, her ears straining to hear the door.

But he didn't come. She found herself at the foot of the stairs, with the silence drawing in around her, as though the entire house was waiting for something. Picking up her keys and grabbing her jacket, she took the final steps towards the front door and stood beside it, listening intently. Then, with a violent lunge, she snatched the handle and jerked the door wide open.

There was nobody there. She was on her own.

# 15

Kim slammed the car door shut, and fumbled her key into the ignition. It wasn't cold, but she could feel herself shivering and turned the heater up. Gripping the steering wheel, she took a deep breath and looked out at the sleepy village, and their house.

*What was she going to do?*

She bit her lip, then frowned and dragged her gaze to the road.

*Sarah. She would go and see Sarah.*

She eased the car to the junction, then turned left and drove slowly away. At the main road, she turned left again, accelerating up the hill until the houses and trees slipped away behind her, and she emerged into the open countryside.

Her heart was still racing as she followed the road along the side of a broad green valley, and she had to brake suddenly for a speed camera that loomed up ahead of her. Nothing seemed real.

She wondered what she would say to her sister. How should she tell her – gradually, or just blurt everything out in one go before she lost her nerve? And what would Sarah say? Support her? Or shout at her for being so stupid?

She still remembered that night, all those years ago. She remembered the bare bulb, hanging by its twisted brown flex, the harsh glare, and the long shadows it cast along the upstairs hallway. Everything had seemed unnaturally still as she walked towards the bathroom – even the TV down in the lounge was silent, as though the whole house was holding its breath. And then a momentary hiss of anger from below, the frustration of someone trying to be quiet, reached her ears and drew her to the landing at the top of the stairs. Reaching out with small hands, she gripped the white-gloss banister struts and leaned forward to rest her head between them, listening.

Her mother's voice, indistinct snatches of conversation, with the odd loud word punctuating a rapid tirade of low fury. Her father's voice, harder to discern, as they tried to talk over each other, then descended into angry whispers again.

Kim turned her head so that her ear was between the struts, straining to hear, but she couldn't make out what they were saying. After a moment, she straightened up and started to edge her way down the stairs, one hand sliding fitfully along the banister rail.

Stepping down onto the carpet, she peered around the corner to look along the dark hallway. Her parents never closed the kitchen door properly, but they had this evening – tiny cracks of light bled out from under it. Why had they decided to shut her out?

Fearful but desperate to understand, she crept forward.

The voices were clearer now, harsh words from just a few feet away.

'That's crap, John.' There was disgust in her mother's tone. 'The reason you didn't take the job is because you were afraid you couldn't hack it. You've always been scared of things like that. No courage.'

'What the bloody hell do you know about it?' Her father sounded bitter. 'You know *nothing* about the situation and *nothing* about—'

'I know one thing,' her mother cut in. 'I know I married a bloody coward.'

It was as though the temperature suddenly dropped; the rhythm of their argument faltered.

'What?'

'You heard me.'

'Coward, am I?' he snarled, his voice rising, but she either didn't notice or didn't care, her voice shrill, goading.

'What are you going to do, hit me again?'

Kim flinched, waiting for the explosion, but it didn't come. There was a long, uneasy silence before her father spoke again.

'No.'

Her mother started laughing, but it was a humourless, mocking sound. 'You can't even—'

'No! I've had it. With you, with everything.' He sounded horribly calm. 'It's over.'

'What do you mean?' Her mother wasn't laughing now.

There was the sound of a chair being scraped back, and shadows shifted in the crack of light under the door.

'Congratulations.' The way he spoke was different, unsettling. 'You've won. I'm leaving you.'

Kim stared up at the door, trembling, her small hand pressed flat against the wall. Her father didn't sound angry any more. He didn't even sound like her father now – it was as though some part of him had broken inside, and this cold quiet voice was all that was left.

She strained, waiting for something more, something to pull the argument back from the edge, but, when it came again, her mother's voice was cruel.

'Good. You can go tonight.'

Kim choked. She began to back away from the door, hand dragging along the wall to steady herself as the tears overtook her. Turning, she stifled a sob and ran up the stairs, almost stumbling as she reached the top, and raced along the landing to burst into her sister's room.

Sarah was sitting propped up on the bed, her Walkman on and a magazine spread open on her lap. She looked up, startled, as the door flew open.

'What's wrong with you?' she frowned, pulling her headphones off. 'I've *told* you to bloody knock.'

'It's Mum and Dad.' Kim gulped down a breath, struggling to get the words out. 'They've had a really bad fight—'

'I *know*,' Sarah scowled, holding up her headphones. 'What do you think these are for, stupid?'

'No, listen!' Kim fought down the tears – she needed to tell her sister, needed somebody to tell *her* that it would be all right. 'It's different this time. Something's happened and . . .'

Her voice broke, and she began to cry again, sobbing the words out.

'I was downstairs listening and I heard them arguing and Mum said some things and then Dad said . . .' She took a breath, rubbing her eyes. 'He said it was over and he said he was leaving, and Mum said it was good, and he's going tonight.'

Sarah was staring at the floor, her face ashen.

'What are we going to do?' Kim pleaded, stumbling forward, arms outstretched.

Sarah's head snapped up, her eyes dark and tearful.

'Get away from me,' she hissed. 'Get out!'

Springing off the bed, she pushed Kim's open arms aside, and bundled her little sister out of her room.

'Out!'

Forcing her into the hallway with a final shove, she stepped back and jerked her door shut.

The sound of her mother's voice drifted up from below,

yelling out a stream of abuse. Kim rushed forward, turning the handle, pushing on the door, but Sarah was holding it closed from the inside.

Downstairs, the pleading and the cursing grew louder, moving into the hallway, echoing up the stairs. Her mother, bitter and defiant, shrieking out one final insult . . .

And then the front door slammed, her mother's voice faltered, and a terrible silence fell over the house.

But that was years ago. Kim blinked away her tears and sniffed. Things were different now. Sarah would understand.

The road curved on ahead of her, the repetitive flash of the white lines oddly soothing. She found that she had no recollection of driving the previous few miles. There was a roundabout ahead, and she slowed as she approached it.

What if she were wrong? What if she were making a huge mistake, one that could cost her everyone she cared about, everyone who cared about her? She didn't want to be pushed away – not again.

Ahead of her, she could see the exit for Taunton and, further round, one signposted to Bristol.

She needed time to think, and Sarah would be at work anyway.

An impatient horn sounded from a car that had come up behind her, jarring her back to the present. Cursing the driver in her rear-view mirror, Kim pulled forward onto the roundabout. Gripping the wheel fiercely, she drove past the Taunton exit and continued along the main road, putting her foot down as the long straight tarmac opened out in front of her.

Now, an hour away from home, the anguish of that morning seemed hazy, overtaken by the terrible fear of doing the wrong thing. She couldn't afford to screw this up – she had to be sure.

A sign slid by: *Bristol 32 miles.*

Bristol – where he'd brought her the previous week, where he'd suggested they drive out of town and go for a walk on that bleak stretch of shoreline.

And suddenly, she knew where she was going.

At first she wasn't certain of the route they'd taken, but she remembered passing under the Clifton Bridge and that was somewhere to start. As she drove beneath it and along the deep cut of the gorge, she wondered why he'd not told her before that it was a woman, why he'd waited to fill in such a crucial detail.

Hadn't he realised how important it was? No, he was smarter than her. He must have guessed how that would hit her, and tried to cushion the blow by not telling her everything at once. He understood her, and was trying to protect her . . .

*Stop it!*

She shook her head and choked down a sob. What was wrong with her?

The road swept her along below a concrete motorway overpass, and she peered out, trying to remember the way they'd come before, trying to distract herself just a little longer.

The houses all looked the same now and she wasn't sure if she'd taken a wrong turning. Playing fields and garages slid by, but she carried on, reasoning that she would come to the coast at some point.

And then, ahead of her, she saw the windmills – their pale arms rising above the scatter of low buildings, turning against the distant grey clouds. The road brought her to a large roundabout in the shadow of a tall, derelict building that stood stark in her memory. She swept around to the right and drove along the long straight road, fenced in on either side and disturbingly familiar.

Not far now.

There were the factory chimneys, reaching up before her, sighing out their swirling fumes into the overcast sky. The road climbed as it passed over the railway line, revealing the dark swathe of the Severn estuary on her left and the jagged piers of the bridge, rising bone white above the water.

She indicated left at a sign for Severn Beach and drove slowly into the village, trying to recall which street Rob had turned down. A line of trees slid by, small houses and parked cars. The sound of children drew her eye to a school playground that she didn't remember, though it had been Saturday last time she was here . . .

And then she saw it – the sign for the railway station. Turning left, she followed the narrow road round. This was the place – she remembered it from the previous visit, the neat little houses with their tiny gardens. There was the entrance to the station, a red sign on a tall pole, the little café and the entrance to the caravan park.

She coasted forward until she came to the end of the road and parked at the foot of the tarmac slope. After a moment, she switched off the engine and sat, staring out through the windscreen.

*What was she doing here?*

But deep down, she knew.

Opening the door, she got out and locked the car. It felt cold after such a long drive with the heater on full blast, but she hugged herself and walked up towards the promenade, following in her own footsteps, recalling Rob's words to her. As she crested the rise, the dark water slid into view once again and she stood there, gazing down at the broad beach, just as she had less than a week ago.

What had he done here?

*'You once asked me what it felt like . . .'*

That was what he'd said to her.

*'Imagine it. Imagine how it would feel . . .'*

She stumbled as the images surged into her mind, flashes of red, wide eyes and muffled screams. Her trembling hand gripped the metal railing and she gulped down a deep breath. 'No!'

It was all too much.

She steadied herself and moved back from the edge of the sea wall, the steep drop and the unsettling expanse of the beach yawning below her. Turning away, she gazed back along the promenade.

An elderly couple were coming towards her, their pace slow, eyes turned out to the water. Kim straightened and walked over to them.

'Excuse me,' she asked, forcing her voice to remain calm. 'Where's the nearest police station?'

Portishead was only a fifteen-minute drive back down the Severn, but it took her a while to locate the police station. It was a small, ugly building, set back from the road at one end of the main street – the sort of place you didn't notice unless you were really looking for it.

The officer at the front desk looked at her dubiously when she walked into the reception area, but after listening to her for a moment, and noting down her address, he picked up a phone and spoke in hushed tones – to someone senior, judging by the number of times he said 'sir'. His eyes never left her the whole time he was on the phone, and when he was done he ushered her into a narrow corridor and showed her to a tiny bare room with a table and four flimsy-looking chairs.

'Someone will be along to see you in a moment,' he told her, before closing the door.

There were two letter-box windows set high in one wall, too small for anyone to squeeze through. She sat on her own, staring at the battered old table, its corners worn smooth, wondering what sort of people had sat there before her. Cold fluorescent light glared back up at her from the scratched Formica surface, and she began to shift uncomfortably on her chair, but stopped as the door handle clicked and a broad man in a jacket entered the room, followed by a uniformed officer.

'Kim Nichols?'

'Yes.' She stood up, flinching at the sound as her chair scraped on the floor.

'Good afternoon,' the broad man said, extending a large hand. 'I'm Detective Sergeant Mendel and this is PC Jamieson. I understand you have some information for us?'

He sat down and indicated she should do the same.

'I'm not really sure where to begin . . .' Kim said, dropping back into her seat.

'You told the duty officer that you might have information about a death?'

Kim met his gaze for a moment, then looked down at the table.

'Yes,' she said, steeling herself. 'I don't have many details, but I think my partner may have . . .'

This was it – she had to say it, however difficult it felt. The silence swelled, dragging the words from her.

'. . . may have killed someone,' she managed, taking a breath. 'Here. Or near here.'

She glanced up and found Mendel gazing at her. His expression hadn't changed.

'Can you tell me your partner's name?' he asked.

'It's Rob.' Kim swallowed, her throat suddenly dry. 'Robert Naysmith.'

'And he lives at the same address as you?'

Kim trembled.

'Yes,' she replied. 'I live with him.'

Mendel leaned back in his chair and considered her for a moment.

'OK,' he said slowly. 'And what do you think your partner may have done?'

Kim took a deep breath. She couldn't stop now.

'He told me he'd killed someone,' she said, then added, 'and I think it was deliberate.'

'Did he say who he'd killed?' Mendel asked.

Kim looked away.

'I'm not sure,' she replied. 'A woman . . . He never told me who it was, just that he had . . . you know.'

Mendel scratched his chin thoughtfully.

'Can you remember his exact words?' he asked.

Kim thought back to their recent walk on the beach, and further back to that moment at the cottage.

'It was a while ago. I knew he was keeping something from me and I ended up asking him what it was.' She frowned, trying to recall everything he'd said to her. 'He told me . . .'

She hesitated, caught in the big detective's unyielding stare.

*He had never actually said it!*

'Yes?' Mendel prompted her.

Kim looked at him helplessly.

'He didn't put it into words, but I asked him if he was in trouble, if he'd done something bad . . . when I asked about killing someone, he sort of . . . nodded.'

The two policemen stared at her.

'Look, I realise how that sounds, but it was absolutely clear to me.' Her voice was becoming shrill and she found she was gripping the edge of the table.

*They didn't believe her.*

Mendel shifted in his chair.

'It's OK,' he said quietly, 'just tell us what was said. Whatever you can remember.'

Kim glared at him for a moment, then lowered her eyes again.

'A while later, he took me to Severn Beach. While we were there, we started talking about it again, and I got the impression that this was where it had happened . . .'

'What did he say?'

'It's not so much what he said.' Kim sagged in her chair. 'It was just like he was . . . reliving something. You know, like retracing his steps or something?'

Mendel watched her, his face unreadable.

'Did he say anything about who he'd killed? Or when it was supposed to have happened?'

Kim leaned forward.

'Look,' she snapped. 'I've told you who he is, and what he said. Aren't you going to do anything about it? Arrest him? Question him?'

Her voice sounded loud, urgent.

Mendel gave her a long, level gaze, then scraped back his chair and got to his feet.

'Excuse me for a moment,' he said calmly. 'I just want to go and check on something.'

Turning away from her, he moved towards the door. The uniformed officer nodded to him but remained in the seat opposite, watching her. The door closed with a loud click.

Kim slumped back against her chair in frustration.

They didn't believe her. They were sitting here, listening to her, but they weren't going to do anything. She scowled at the uniformed officer. He looked disinterested, as though he were going through the motions.

And then her frustration melted away as a terrible dread crept over her.

What if they *did* question Rob, then let him go?

He'd know it was her, know that she'd betrayed him. What was she thinking of, coming here?

'Are you all right?'

The uniformed officer was looking at her, his face now showing concern.

Her eyes filled with tears and she shrank back from him, hiding her face with her hand as she started to sob uncontrollably.

*Shit. Shit! What the hell had she done?*

# 16

Harland stirred his coffee and dropped the teaspoon into the sink. Lifting his mug, he turned and walked out of the kitchen, back towards his office. Mendel passed him in the corridor, wearing a thoughtful expression.

'Kettle's just boiled.' Harland gestured back towards the kitchen.

'I'm in the middle of something just now,' Mendel frowned. 'Some woman just walked in off the street saying she thought her boyfriend might have killed someone, but she's not sure who it was or when it was.'

Harland looked at him.

'That's it?'

'Pretty much.'

'Not exactly conclusive.' Harland grinned.

Mendel rubbed the back of his broad neck with a large hand.

'It is a bit thin,' he agreed. 'The only reason I was interested was because she said it had something to do with Severn Beach.'

Harland looked at him intently.

'The jogger who was strangled? Vicky Sutherland?'

Mendel nodded. 'Trouble is, the more I asked her, the more vague she's become. Not sure if her boyfriend was just trying to creep her out, or if she's paranoid . . .'

Harland considered this for a moment. A lot of people had read about that case – Peter Baraclough had mentioned it in a recent piece highlighting Avon and Somerset's failures – and press coverage often brought the crazies out.

'Did you run their names through the computer?' he asked.

'I did a preliminary search – nothing came up on either of them.'

Harland took a sip of coffee.

'What's she like?' he asked.

Mendel shrugged.

'Nervous, angry. Sit in and see for yourself if you want.'

Harland looked at him.

'She's still here?'

The big man smiled.

'Got her in the interview room now,' he said.

Harland tapped his colleague on the shoulder as they approached the door.

'What was her name again?' he asked in a low voice.

'Kim Nichols.'

'OK.'

Mendel opened the door and beckoned Jamieson out of the room, then went inside. Harland followed him, gently pushing the door shut behind him.

'This is Detective Inspector Harland,' Mendel said, pulling out a chair and sitting down.

Harland stepped forward and extended his hand towards Kim. She was very pretty, with an almost delicate quality, and he saw the hesitation before she leaned forward and shook his hand. Her large eyes looked bright and wet – Mendel hadn't mentioned that she'd been crying. Had the tears come after he'd left the room, and if so what had upset her?

'Hello,' he said, taking a seat. 'You were telling my colleague about your partner . . . ?'

He glanced at Mendel.

'Robert Naysmith,' the big man prompted.

'. . . Robert Naysmith.' Harland gazed across the table at Kim. 'Can you tell me a bit about him? What he does for a living?'

She stared back, tired but still wary. He knew that look – had seen it many times right here in this room – and he knew that everything depended on getting her talking. The more she said, the easier it would get.

Kim shifted on her chair, then looked down at the table. Her voice, when she finally spoke, sounded soft and sad.

'He's a sales director,' she said quietly. 'He works for Winterhill – a software company in Woking.'

'What about yourself?'

'I work for an accountancy firm in Salisbury.'

'OK,' Harland nodded. 'How long have you known Robert?'

'Almost three years now.'

*Hardly any pause before answering. Good.*

'Do either of you have any connection with this area? Through your work? Or family? Friends?'

Kim was shaking her head. 'No, nothing.'

'All right.' Harland looked at her for a moment. 'So I understand you have some concerns about something that Robert may have done?'

He left the question open, deliberately vague, to see how she would respond.

'He told me—' She broke off, taking a breath, then spoke more slowly. 'I think he may have killed someone. A woman.'

'Go on . . .' Harland encouraged her.

'He never gave me specifics,' she shot a brief, cold look at Mendel, 'but I think it happened just up the coast from here.'

'Do you know when this was?' Harland asked her.

'No.'

'Any idea who the woman was?'

'No, I'm sorry.'

Harland sat back in his chair. If she *was* one of the crazies, wouldn't she be better informed? She didn't seem to know very much about the case, not even the stuff that had made it into the media. He frowned and glanced across at Mendel.

'You aren't going to arrest him,' Kim said, half to herself.

Mendel turned towards her.

'We'll make some enquiries and—'

'No!' She leaned forward, gripping the edge of the table. 'If you speak to him, he'll know I came to you. He'll *know*!'

'We need to look into the things you've told us,' Mendel pressed on, adopting a reasonable tone. 'Make some enquiries, then decide what course of action to follow.'

'Forget it!' She was shaking her head now, eyes wide but her gaze avoiding their faces.

'I understand you're concerned,' Mendel sighed, 'but we have to—'

'I said forget it!' she snapped at him. 'Look, I made a mistake, OK? It was probably just a stupid joke and I'm wasting your time.'

Mendel held up his large hands in a calming gesture.

'Let's just slow down a moment and—'

'No! It's just a joke, OK? OK?'

Harland watched her, noting the panic in her movements, the urgency in her eyes, the tension in her neck. She really was very attractive. And very scared.

'Please—' Mendel began, but she cut him off, scraping her chair back noisily across the floor and rising to her feet.

'I want to go,' she said firmly.

Mendel kept his seat and looked up at her.

'If you'll just sit down for a minute—'

'Am I free to go?'

Her voice was louder now – pitched higher – and her eyes moved quickly, looking at them, looking at the door.

'Am I free to go?'

Mendel started to say something, but Harland raised his hand and gave a slight shake of his head.

'Kim?'

She looked at him as he stood up and moved past Mendel to rest his hand on the door handle.

'You're free to go,' he told her quietly.

The change in her was immediate. Her shoulders dropped in relief and she quickly gathered her bag close to her chest as she walked towards him, casting one nervous sidelong glance at Mendel as he stood and allowed her to pass.

Harland reached into his pocket, drew out a small card and offered it to her as he opened the door.

'My number's on here,' he said. 'Keep it, and call me if you need to. OK?'

Kim looked hesitantly at the card.

'OK?' he asked again.

Kim looked up at him, her large eyes anxious.

'Don't speak to him,' she said in a small voice. 'Please. Not without warning me.'

Harland stared down at her.

'Don't worry,' he said.

They stood for a moment, then Kim looked down and took the card from him.

'Thanks,' she mumbled, and hurried out into the corridor.

Harland walked slowly into his office, yawning as he moved around his desk. Mendel closed the door and leaned back against it, his broad brow furrowed.

'What do you reckon?' he asked. 'Wasting police time?'

Harland glanced back at him and shrugged.

'Your guess is as good as mine.' He sank down into his chair and rubbed his eyes wearily. 'No real information, and she wouldn't be much good as a witness if she keeps changing her mind so quickly.'

He paused, then looked up.

'She was definitely scared of something though.'

Mendel nodded slowly.

'So what do you want to do?' he asked. 'The Vicky Sutherland case is tied up in the Met's investigation. Want to pass it over to them?'

Harland leaned back and thought for a moment.

'Blake was pretty bloody specific,' Mendel reminded him. 'We're not touching that one again.'

Harland tilted his head to one side.

'Who says this is anything to do with Vicky Sutherland?' He gave Mendel a half-smile. 'Just some woman off the street, with a vague – genuinely vague – concern about her boyfriend.'

Mendel regarded him doubtfully.

'What did you have in mind?'

'Honestly?' Harland spread his hands apart and sighed. 'Not much we *can* do. Let's just check her and the boyfriend out. Discreetly. See if either of them has any links with the victim list – you know the drill. I doubt it'll turn into anything though.'

Mendel gave him a long look.

'Well, I suppose we have had more than one body turn up along that stretch of coastline,' he admitted. 'But first sign of anything linking it to Vicky Sutherland, and I'm dropping it right in the Met's lap, just like Blake told us.'

'Of course,' Harland agreed.

Mendel made his way over to the door, then turned back, his face serious.

'For your sake, Graham,' he frowned, 'just be sure you do the same.'

# 17

Stepping out of the warm restaurant, Naysmith shivered in the cool evening air and gazed out along the Reeperbahn – a steady flow of people, dark figures silhouetted against the bright windows and neon signs, drifting from one pleasure to another. Laughter and indistinct conversations, stray words in German and other languages, woven through a backdrop of dance music. He smiled and turned to Andreas.

'That was the best steak I've eaten in months,' he sighed, pulling his jacket closer around him. 'Do you know what I miss most about English cooking when I'm away?'

The tall German thought for a moment, then shook his head.

'Nothing at all,' Naysmith laughed. 'Come on, let's go and get a beer.'

They made their way along the busy pavement, weaving between the slow pedestrians, then crossed the road and turned down a cobbled side street.

'It was good to see the team again.' Naysmith raised his voice as a car passed, techno booming out from its lowered windows. 'And I'm glad I finally got to meet Jurgen.'

'You did not meet him in January?'

'He was away last time I came over. Seems to know what he's doing though.'

'*Ja*, he is doing some good work,' Andreas agreed. He paused, then smiled. 'Come, I know a great bar for us and I have a little bit of Hamburg to show you on the way.'

They turned aside and walked into a broad alley between the solid, three-storey buildings. Tall barriers overlapped to block their view of the street ahead, and a sign on one read *Zutritt für Jugendliche unter 18 und Frauen verboten* – 'No entrance for juveniles under 18 years of age and women'.

'Ah,' Naysmith grinned. 'I think this is the place you keep promising to show me.'

'You know this place?' Andreas enquired. 'It is where you can come for the . . . sightseeing.'

They passed between the barriers and walked through to the cobbled stretch of Herbertstraße. There were fewer people here, but everyone moved more slowly, their eyes drawn from the illumination of one full-length window to the next. Behind the glass on either side of them, women in their underwear sat on tall chairs or perched on bar stools, their state of undress surreal to those in the chill evening outside. Plastic canopies above the windows advertised different names, but the story was the same all down the street.

'So?' Andreas chuckled as they wandered down the alley. 'What do you think?'

'It's like being in Amsterdam,' Naysmith replied thoughtfully with a smile. 'But without the canals.'

His eye caught a movement across the street, where a slender young woman was drawing open the heavy red curtain that had covered her window. He paused for a moment, watching as she stretched up to pull it all the way back, enjoying the tension in her limbs. Her long dark hair tumbled over her bare shoulders and her skin shone pale against the lacy black bra and thong. Stockings and stilettos completed the look as she turned away to reveal a striking rear profile before easing herself up onto a chrome bar stool.

'Someone just made some money, I think.' Andreas inclined his head towards the window.

'What?' Naysmith looked back at him for a moment. 'Oh, yes, I see what you mean.'

*The woman must have had the curtains closed while she was with a customer.*

He glanced back at the window, taking in the elegant curve of her neck, the calm expression on her face, and felt the eagerness grow in him. She looked a lot like Kim.

'Rob?' Andreas was looking at him. 'You want that I go for a walk? Maybe meet you in the bar a little later?'

Naysmith laughed.

'No, no, she just reminded me of someone,' he explained. 'Anyway, I generally manage without paying for it.'

The tall German held up his hands.

'My friend, we all pay for it,' he said solemnly. 'One way or another.'

'Andreas! When did you get so cynical?' Naysmith exclaimed. 'Come on, where's this bar you were telling me about? I think you need a beer more than I do.'

He woke up alone, which was unusual for a trip to Hamburg. Blinking, he leaned over for his phone and checked the time. Then, with a lengthy yawn, he propped himself up against the headboard and looked thoughtfully at the empty half of the bed beside him.

He'd certainly had motive, and the bar that Andreas led him to had presented plenty of opportunities, but last night Naysmith had been distracted. As they'd stood there, studying the local talent, watching the glittering eyes of the St Pauli girls, his mind had been elsewhere, thinking about someone else. Andreas had looked somewhat crestfallen when they finally stumbled out into the cold night air without a conquest – not even an anecdote about the one that got away – but Naysmith had been strangely content as he slumped into the taxi.

Now he reached across for his phone, his thumb tapping the speed dial for Kim. He stifled another yawn, then held the handset to his ear for a moment, but the number was beeping. Unobtainable, or a network error – he lost track of which tone meant what in some countries – but it didn't matter. He would call her later. Placing the phone on the bedside table, he threw off the duvet and padded through to the bathroom.

It was his favourite hotel in Hamburg. Maybe not the most exclusive, and certainly not the most expensive, but the Gastwerk had real character – a grand old industrial building hollowed out and filled with efficient interior luxury, all housed within a brutal iron framework. Metal gangways soared above beautifully appointed spaces, while light rippled across the surface of the water in large, open culverts. The rooms varied considerably in both size and style, but they always pleased him. Today, as he pulled his jacket on, he considered the exposed-brick walls, the high, recessed windows and the dark comfort of everything around him – only in Germany.

Smiling, he swept up his key card and went downstairs.

Andreas would be punctual for their breakfast meeting, but he still had a few minutes before the hour and redialled Kim's number as he made his way across the foyer to the dining room. A brief moment of silence before the 'unobtainable' beep again. He sighed – should have called her last night. His eyes scanned the room, but there was no sign of Andreas yet, so he eased himself into a comfortable seat at a table with a good view of the door. He had just finished sending a text message to Kim when he spotted the familiar figure of his colleague approaching and held up a hand to beckon him over.

'*Morgen!*' The tall man grinned at him, dropping heavily into a chair. 'I hope you slept well?'

'Very well, thanks.' Naysmith smiled. 'I'm feeling good this morning.'

'Well, it is a very nice hotel.' Andreas looked around, then leaned forward and lowered his voice. 'Much better than the other place, the one that the Americans use.'

'The one over by the station?'

Andreas nodded.

'They like to be close to the Alster – the lake – but it's not a good area at night.' He held up a hand to bring the waiter across. 'They call it the needle forest.'

'Needle forest?'

'*Ja.*' The German mimed injecting himself with a syringe. 'Because of the junkies, you know, needle forest?'

They ordered coffee from the waiter, then went over to the breakfast buffet. Spotless chromed lids hinged up to reveal hot bacon, sausages and eggs steaming in their broad trays. Cold meats and different breads were accompanied by fresh fruit and pastries. Naysmith ignored the cereal selection and returned to the table with a fully laden plate.

'Hungry, yes?' Andreas grinned his approval.

'Hangover prevention,' Naysmith replied. He picked up his knife and balanced it thoughtfully across two fingers. 'I appreciate you coming over this morning. I've not got long before my flight, but I wanted to have a quiet word about the other accounts that the Hamburg team are running.'

'Of course.' Andreas nodded earnestly. 'What about them?'

'I don't want any more situations like the Friedman one. We'll take a look over all the key accounts and make sure nobody is taking advantage of you.'

'OK.' Andreas leaned over and pulled his laptop from its bag. 'And if we find something we don't like?'

'Same as Friedman.' He hefted the knife so it was pointing at Andreas, and gave him a cold smile. 'We teach them not to do it again.'

He was back in London by lunchtime, breezing through the arrivals hall and outside to the courtesy buses. As he walked to the car, a plane roared down the runway, filling the air with the distinctive aroma of aviation fuel. He took out his phone and considered calling Kim again, then decided against it – she'd mentioned something about working from home today – and he wanted to surprise her. Reaching the car, he opened the passenger door to slide his bag down into the footwell, then placed the bouquet of flowers carefully on the seat before hanging his jacket in the back.

He smiled to himself as he got in and started the engine. It was going to be an excellent afternoon.

As he turned off the main road into the village, he was tapping his fingers on the steering wheel, in time with the music on the stereo. Past the bowling green and over the bridge, following the tarmac as it swept around under the trees; he slowed as he came to the pub, turning off a moment later to park outside the house.

He got out and stretched, loosening his muscles after a morning of travel, then retrieved his jacket and pulled it on. He slung his bag over his shoulder, then gently lifted the flowers and walked to the front door. Keys in hand, he reached up to the deadlock, then paused and smiled to himself. He moved his hand across to the door knocker and rapped it smartly three times.

And waited.

# 18

The noise made her jump. Pulling the lid of her laptop closed, Kim stood up from the table and moved across the kitchen to peer out into the hallway.

*She knew that knock – it was him.*

She wavered for a moment, then walked silently to the front door.

Her hand reached out, fingers brushing over the temptation of the safety chain before grasping the deadlock and turning the knob. Forcing her face to relax into a neutral expression, she pulled the door open to let him back in.

He was smiling at her – that same easy smile that always used to make her feel so needed, so wanted.

'Hey.' Rob drew a large bouquet of flowers from behind his back. 'Busy? I got the earlier flight so I thought you might like to go into town and get a coffee.'

She stared at him – the man she'd fallen for, the man who protected her . . .

*. . . the man she'd tried to turn in.*

The confusion of feelings that had driven her to Severn Beach were gone now, and she wondered what she'd hoped to achieve by her foolish actions. Whatever he'd done was in the past – the fact that it might have been a woman didn't really change anything – did it?

'Kim?'

'They're beautiful,' she managed, taking the flowers from him. 'Thank you.'

Talking to the police might have changed things, though. What had she been thinking? Blurting out a stupid accusation without really knowing anything. She had no evidence, no real understanding, just a reckless desire to tell someone. Even if it was true, if he *had* done something terrible in the past, there was nothing the police could do about it.

And they probably hadn't believed her anyway. The big man, Mendel, certainly didn't take her seriously – just sat there asking her a lot of questions she couldn't answer. Harland had seemed different – genuine even – and his voice had been kind when he told her not to worry . . .

. . . but she did worry. She knew her actions could have had serious consequences for Rob – for both of them. Why had she been so stupid?

As he stepped into the hallway, laying his bag down and softly kissing the top of her head, she suddenly hated herself for trying to betray him. Whatever else he was, he still cared about her.

It was better this way, she decided. They'd work through it together, and everything would settle down and be just like it was before.

'So, was it lonely without me?' Rob leaned in close to gaze into her eyes.

She stared up at him for a second, then put her arms around his neck and buried her head in his shoulder.

She wouldn't drive him away. Everything would be all right. Everything would be like it was before.

'I'm glad you're back,' she said.

# part 2
# SORROW

# 19

*Sunday, 6 July*

It was a clear, bright morning. Rob had already opened the curtains and sunlight streamed into the room, hurting her eyes as she stretched and wriggled up into a sitting position. The clock on his side of the bed said 8.23 – he was up early for a Sunday. She flexed her toes under the duvet and yawned, wondering whether or not to snuggle back down for a while, but she knew that she needed the bathroom. Reluctantly, she moved to the edge of the bed and drew the duvet around her as she stood up and shuffled across the bedroom to get her bathrobe.

The reassuring smell of toast reached her as she padded out into the hallway, and she found herself smiling as she placed a small hand on the cool gloss of the banister.

'Rob? Are you making breakfast?' she called down.

'It's almost ready.' His voice drifted up to her, indistinct from the kitchen. 'Down you come, sleepyhead. The weather's too good to stay in – I want us to go out and make the most of it.'

They were on the road by ten, heading west out of the village and cruising down quiet roads that swept them along beneath a clear blue sky.

'Do you think it'll stay like this?' Kim asked, reaching up to slide back the shade on the sunroof.

'Forecast is good all day,' Rob told her. He was wearing a pale linen shirt, with a faded pair of shorts that she liked him in. 'It's going to be hot this afternoon.'

Kim closed her eyes and let her head tilt back, welcoming the sun's touch on her face, the warm glow through her eyelids.

'How far did you want to go?' she murmured.

'I don't mind. Maybe that place by the aqueduct; maybe further. See how we feel.'

'You're the boss,' she said softly.

The car park was already filling up when they reached Bradford on Avon. Rob got a ticket from the machine while Kim slipped on her scruffy trainers, then he took her hand as they made their way down the slope towards the long expanse of still, green water. They'd walked the Kennet and Avon Canal quite often – sometimes just a couple of miles along the embankment, sometimes further. Once, they'd wandered all the way up to Bath, though she hoped that Rob wasn't feeling quite so energetic today.

A red-faced woman with powerful arms was cheerfully calling instructions down to a barge in the depths between the lock gates, and laughing with a wiry old man on the other side of the water. After a moment, they took their positions at the end of the long wooden balance beams and began slowly to push the gates closed, leaning in hard and bracing their feet against the arcs of white brickwork set into the ground.

Kim slowed a little so that she could watch as the first spurts of water began to stream in at the other end of the lock, glistening in the sunlight and releasing a rainbow spray that rose up between the wet green walls.

'Fascinating, isn't it?' Rob was standing beside her, gazing down at the swirling water that had begun to lift the barge.

She nodded, her eyes tracing the red and gold paintwork on the barge, noticing the open packet of biscuits sitting on the deck. Such a lovely way to see the countryside.

'I'd like to try it sometime,' she said thoughtfully. 'You know, just sitting there, relaxing, letting the water take you wherever it wanted to.'

They stood for a moment longer, watching as the cabin roof rose up into the sunlight.

'There's a lot of power in that water,' Rob murmured.

Kim turned and looked at him, suddenly reminded of another conversation. Was there an ulterior motive to their walk? Had he brought her out to tell her something?

*Please no, not today.*

She watched him gazing at the water as it gushed in below them, but there was no light in his eyes, none of that terrible eagerness she'd seen previously. He seemed calm, and she allowed herself to relax, reproaching herself a little for thinking badly of him. She was lucky to have someone like Rob.

They crossed the road where it passed over the water, and made their way down to rejoin the canal by a busy local pub, where the rattle of crockery drifted out from the kitchens and families jostled for tables underneath the plastic awnings. Soon, the noise diminished and they began to hear the crunch of their own footsteps as the towpath narrowed and the town slipped away behind them. They overtook one or two slower walkers, and were overtaken themselves by a couple of cyclists, but as they followed the canal out into the open countryside, there were periods when they seemed to have the whole waterway to themselves.

'Glad you came?' Rob asked her.

Kim nodded. 'It's beautiful.'

'Better than staying at home,' he said, and smiled.

They wandered on through stands of trees, keeping the

stillness of the water on their left as it meandered along the side of the valley. To the right, the ground fell away into a tangle of bushes and brambles, with the River Avon some way beyond.

They came across several groups of barges, moored together in twos and threes. Some of them clearly hadn't moved for a long time – weathered garden chairs, old gas cylinders and children's toys spread out along the grass beside the path, evidence of their inhabitants gradually putting down roots into the bank.

Rob paused by one beautifully decorated barge and smiled at a small tabby cat that got up from sunning itself on the deck, stretched and ambled over to them.

'Guarding the boat while the owners are away,' he said with a grin.

The cat went to Rob and brushed itself against his ankles.

'Not much of a guard,' Kim said, smiling.

Rob dropped to a crouch and stroked the little cat, tickling behind its ears as it rubbed itself against him. He smiled as it raised its head so he could rub under its chin, a quiet delight in his expression.

Kim watched him thoughtfully, wondering why he didn't have a cat himself. Perhaps it was too much of a commitment – after all, he wasn't someone who would let himself be tied down. She turned to gaze out across the fields, pushing her hair back and tightening the elastic that held it away from her face. And yet, he did seem to have committed himself to her.

Rob stood up with a contented look on his face and they continued along the towpath. The cat followed them for a few yards, then sat down in a spot where the sunlight came through a gap in the trees and watched them go.

The sun grew warmer as the day drew on, and they saw

more people as they walked. The calm water was disturbed by occasional tourists and trippers sailing their rented narrowboats from one pub to the next – overweight men with spotless rugby shirts and determinedly cheery wives in expensive casual clothing, or outdoor enthusiasts with a lot less style but more genuine faces. And yet, they were all of them – the trippers, the cyclists, the walkers – just passing through. This place really belonged to the barge families.

She'd seen them before – crusty old souls with tanned, leathery faces who sat like organic extensions of their boats, staring down at the water, oblivious to passers-by. Then there were the younger ones – travellers with beautifully grungy clothing, who sat on the grassy bank with their guitars or bent over crafting things from wood and old metal. A little boy with dreadlocks watched her from an open gangway and smiled at her as she caught his eye. There was an elusive sense of contentment about them that awoke a longing in her, but their life was a million miles from hers, even though she passed within a few feet of them.

'Must be strange growing up on a boat,' Rob murmured as she returned the boy's smile.

'I suppose,' she agreed, though the idea of waking up and looking out onto the water seemed very appealing.

'No satellite TV, no Internet,' he mused. 'It must be like growing up in the seventies.'

Kim cast a glance back over her shoulder at the barges moored along the towpath behind them.

'They look happy though.'

She found herself wondering about her own happiness. It was a beautiful day, and she had everything she could ever want.

*Everything she could ever want, and something she never wanted.*

*Fergus McNeill*

She wished she didn't know about it. She wished he had never told her, but it was her own fault for pushing him so hard.

She glanced up at him as he walked beside her, his eyes turned away to look out across the valley.

No wonder he hadn't wanted to tell her – he'd been trying to protect her. Suddenly it was all so obvious. He'd been shielding her, but she'd forced the issue. It must have been so difficult for him, but that just proved how much he cared for her.

*And she'd nearly ruined everything by going to the police.*

Without knowing what he'd done, without understanding the reasons, she'd taken his trust and betrayed him. She bit her lip as she walked, and slipped her hand into his.

It wasn't something she could forget, but it was in the past – she had to try and move on.

'Mind your back.' Rob put his arm around her and drew her in towards the side of the towpath as a cyclist came past from behind them, followed by two more, peddling at speed – muscular bodies swaying from side to side in their Lycra, a welcome distraction from more troubled thoughts.

'Do you think it's some sort of race event?' she asked, rejoining the path with a wary look in both directions. It would be a bother if they had to dodge speeding cyclists all day.

'Doubt it,' Rob replied. 'I expect it's just random people out for a bike ride.'

'They seemed to be taking it pretty seriously.'

'How do you mean?'

'Well,' she shrugged, 'they all looked so similar, all dressed up in the same Lycra shorts, the same headgear.'

Rob looked at her thoughtfully, then nodded.

'Maybe they think it makes them go faster.'

Kim shook her head and grinned.

'Maybe they'd go faster if they went on the road, instead of dodging in and out of walkers on a footpath.'

She squeezed Rob's hand and they walked on, dappled in the sunlight that filtered down through the trees.

There were a few wild flowers here and there along the grassy bank, but an explosion of colour greeted them as they came to a small house, walls of warm brown stone surrounded by blue delphiniums, where the canal angled sharply to the right. Around the corner, the narrow towpath broadened into hard ground, with a long metal rail guarding the edge of the deep still water, and they got their first glimpse of the aqueduct.

Thrusting out across the green valley, it carried the canal high above the trees and fields and the snaking river below, a mighty fortress of stonework with paved footpaths on either side of the continuous calm water. A collection of sturdy old buildings huddled about the near side, with a couple of small shops and a country pub set back into the slope of the hillside.

They wandered along the footpath, moving slowly out onto the aqueduct as a brightly painted barge came gliding along the canal beside them, its engine puttering quietly, leaving long, lazy ripples in its wake. Kim turned away from it, moving over to the thick parapet to stand beside Rob. The old stone felt cool beneath her hand as she looked down through the trees at the River Avon spilling across a broad weir and drifting under the arches below them.

Rob stared out along the valley, then glanced down at his watch.

'Are you feeling hungry yet?' he asked.

She looked at him, then followed his gaze towards the nearby pub. It had a stepped garden, set into the side of the valley, with tables and chairs overlooking the broad water below the weir. Walking in the fresh air had reawakened her appetite.

'That might be nice,' she nodded. 'Shall we go and see what it's like?'

They retraced their steps along the footpath and turned aside at the end of the bridge, following a tarmac slope that led down beside a line of whitewashed stone buildings and a New Age shop that sold crystals. The pub itself was a long, uneven building nestled in against the hillside. Beneath the high gables, a white wall bore the name 'The Cross Guns' in large black letters.

A low doorway led into the bar, and Rob stood aside to let her go first. However, as she stepped across the threshold, a stocky man with a ruddy complexion and a faded T-shirt appeared from within, jostling into her as he emerged into the sunlight. Beer slopped over the side of the glasses he was carrying and trickled down over his large hands.

'Aw, for fuck's sake—' he bellowed, straightening up to glare down at her as she backed away, feeling clumsy, foolish.

And then Rob was there.

'Hey.' His voice was quiet but firm. The big man glanced at him, then back to her again.

'HEY!'

The snap of command stopped the advancing man dead. He glared, but hesitated as Rob stepped forward, placing himself slightly in front of her.

'You should apologise to my girlfriend,' he said, speaking quietly again, but in a tone that was gravely serious. The man scowled for a moment, then seemed to sag a little.

'Sorry,' he mumbled, his angry eyes downcast. 'Didn't see you there.'

Kim found that she had been holding her breath.

'It's OK,' she stammered. 'Really, no harm done.'

Rob stood aside once more and held out his hand, gesturing for her to go first. The big man wordlessly moved out of her way to let her pass inside.

She stepped over the threshold into the cosy little bar area, turning to make sure that Rob was following. Something about the encounter frightened her – the way the man had reacted, as though he'd seen something in her partner that she had missed. And yet, she knew more, knew how far he could really go. Had the man sensed who was speaking to him? And if he hadn't, if he'd stood his ground, how far might Rob have gone?

Her breathing had become swift and shallow, but then Rob came through the doorway, his smile calm, assured, and the idea suddenly seemed stupid.

'You OK, Kim?'

She was being silly. He was just protecting her, like he always did.

'I'm fine.' She managed a small smile.

He drew her close to him and planted a kiss on the top of her head, then took her hand and led her over to the bar where a middle-aged woman acknowledged them through a gap beneath a shelf of suspended glasses.

'What shall we have?' he asked.

They ate outside, at a small wooden table some way down the garden, close to the riverbank. The rushing noise of the weir came to them faintly from further upstream, beyond the weeping willow trees that trailed their long fingers in the swirling water.

Kim watched Rob cutting into a rare sirloin, then contemplated the steak and ale pie on her own plate. It was delicious, but her thoughts were still elsewhere.

'Rob?'

He looked up at her.

'That man up there,' she glanced up towards the pub on the slope above them. 'I can't believe how you got him to apologise to me.'

Rob shrugged.

'Did you mind?' he asked her.

'No, I didn't mind . . .'

In the distance, a two-tone horn blared out a warning, and Kim caught flashes of colour through the trees as a train rattled along the opposite side of the valley.

'What if he'd got out of hand?' she asked.

Rob held up a finger to indicate that his mouth was full.

'Not him,' he replied after swallowing. 'His type is all mouth. And I didn't like him getting mouthy with you.'

*Always protecting her.*

'Thanks.' She smiled. 'But it wasn't necessary for him to apologise.'

'I think it was,' he said seriously.

Kim lowered her eyes and took a mouthful of her pie.

'All that is required for idiots to prevail is for smart people to do nothing.'

Kim looked up at him, questioningly. 'What?'

Rob smiled and shook his head.

'I'm paraphrasing,' he chuckled. 'There's an old saying: "All that is required for evil to prevail is for good people to do nothing."'

She stared at him for a moment as he cut another piece of steak, considering his words, then turned her eyes away to look out across the river.

# 20

*Saturday, 12 July*

Sometimes it was hard to switch off. Walking through the drifting Saturday-night crowds in the city centre, Harland found himself tensing at every raised voice, every drunken shout. It wasn't his job – he wasn't on duty – but the instinct clawed at him.

They'd arranged to meet at a bar on King Street, and the old town was packed. Harland stepped between the groups of smokers outside and walked past the doorman, who was busy impressing a couple of girls. Inside, the place was noisy – a wall of indistinct voices, bass and the clatter of glasses. He glimpsed Mendel, Gregg and some of the others at the far end of the bar and started to make his way over, squeezing through the crush of warm bodies, muttering a futile succession of 'Excuse me's.

'Graham!' Mendel had spotted him now. 'Over here.'

Harland waved in acknowledgement and forged his way to the bar.

'Evening,' he nodded when he reached them.

'All right, sir.' Gregg smiled then returned to a conversation with his girlfriend.

Harland eased in beside Mendel and looked around.

'Been here long?' he asked.

Mendel raised his glass, which was almost empty.

'Not that long,' he surmised. 'What are you drinking?'
'I'll get them,' Harland replied. 'Same again?'
'Thanks.'

Harland manoeuvred himself so that he was half facing the bar, money in hand.

'So how old are you, anyway?' he asked.

'Same as I always was,' Mendel shrugged. 'My birthday's not until tomorrow, and by then I'll be too hung-over to care.'

The bar staff looked so young – harried waifs in black T-shirts, scurrying back and forth through the noise – but Harland finally managed to get served. He pocketed his change, then turned to pass one of the pint glasses across.

'Cheers.'

But Mendel was looking over his shoulder, his face breaking into a grin.

'I don't believe it.' He lifted his voice and called out, 'Ray, you long-lost hooligan.'

DCI Raymond Pearce was an East End diamond in his late forties, with dark grey hair and an ancient scar that ran down his left cheek. He moved lightly, but there was an imposing solidity to him, like a retired rugby player who hasn't let himself go. Harland watched him calmly shouldering his way between two groups of people, then halting to raise an eyebrow theatrically as a skinny youth almost backed into him. He emerged from the crowd beaming at Mendel.

'Evening, James,' he chuckled. 'How's the birthday boy then?'

'Mustn't grumble,' Mendel smiled. 'Didn't expect to see you tonight.'

'Well, if that's how you feel . . .' Pearce turned, pretending to leave, and noticed Harland for the first time. 'Blimey, didn't see you there, Graham.'

He extended a firm hand and clasped Harland's warmly.

'Not still working with this old gorilla, are you?' he asked with a wink at Mendel. 'I thought they'd have found you someone decent by now.'

'Ah, it could be worse.' Harland grinned at him. 'Much worse. But DS Pope joined your lot, didn't he?'

'Please!' Pearce's face showed disgust. 'Tell me that bastard's not coming tonight, or I really *will* do a runner.'

'You're all right,' Mendel replied. 'I made a point of forgetting to invite him.'

Pearce brightened.

'Thank fuck for that,' he said, then clapped his hands together and glanced towards the bar. 'Right then, gents, what are you drinking?'

Before long, there was a group of them and they'd managed to occupy a corner at one end of the bar.

'Still stuck in Portishead then?' Pearce smiled over his drink.

'That's right,' Harland nodded. 'Very pleasant in the summer, out there on the coast.'

'Picturesque,' Mendel agreed.

'But plenty of action?' Pearce teased them. 'Lots of big cases to get your teeth into?'

'Stolen bikes, missing cats, even the odd bit of graffiti.' Mendel shook his head gravely. 'Honestly, I don't know how we cope sometimes.'

Pearce laughed.

'Blake still running things over there?'

'Oh yes.' Harland gave him a bleak smile. 'Blake's still there. He runs a very "tight ship".'

'Sounds cosy.'

'Those two haven't been best pals recently,' Mendel interjected. 'Blake's as far up his own backside as ever, and Graham's been doing his best to get fired.'

'Seriously?' Pearce looked at them, surprised.

'It was just a bit of a misunderstanding,' Harland shrugged it off, 'over that Severn Beach murder.'

'Graham didn't understand what "leave it alone" meant,' Mendel explained.

'Thanks for that.' Harland raised his glass sarcastically. 'Anyway, speaking of our favourite people, how's life with Pope?'

'Never see him, thank goodness,' Pearce frowned. 'He's busy sucking up to Command at the moment, and as long as he's doing that he isn't bothering me.'

Mendel shook his head, then turned to look over his shoulder.

'Happy birthday, *sir*,' said a voice.

It was Firth. She eased her way out of the crowd with a mischievous smile.

'Don't you start,' Mendel joked. 'Anyway, all this birthday talk is making me feel old.'

'Never mind,' she laughed, leaning forward and giving him a hug. 'We'll have a whip-round and get you a nice walking frame.'

Mendel chuckled, then looked at his watch.

'Thought you weren't coming,' he rumbled. 'Or is this what you call fashionably late?'

'Don't blame me,' she protested, turning and pulling a tall man into the circle. 'Someone else took their time getting ready. Everyone, this is Richard.'

Harland's heart sank. She was seeing someone. When had that happened?

'Hi,' the man smiled. 'And don't listen to her – she's the slowcoach. Ouch!'

He nursed his arm where Firth had punched him.

'Police brutality,' Pearce chuckled.

Firth turned back with a grin, but it faltered for just a second as she spotted Harland.

'Oh hi,' she said, then looked away quickly.

And that made it worse. He hadn't been sure until now, but that one awkward flicker of regret in her eyes finally confirmed what his instincts had been saying all along.

Now he'd missed his chance.

'Come on,' she said, clasping Richard's hand and steering him towards the bar, 'you can buy me a drink.'

He watched them move apart, feeling an irrational surge of anger towards Richard, a man he'd never met before. Not particularly good-looking, but he had an easy, uncomplicated manner about him. No angst. No hesitation. Bastard.

Harland rubbed his eyes wearily and downed the rest of his pint.

As he put the glass on the bar, he caught Pearce looking at him, then glancing across at Firth.

'Don't ask,' Mendel said firmly.

It was cold when they emerged onto the pavement, but Harland didn't notice it. He gazed up beyond the lights to the darkness of the night sky and felt the street sway around him.

'Cheers guys.' Mendel's voice was behind him, cutting through the laughter and conversation that bled out from the doorway. 'See you next week.'

The noise from the bar muted as the doors swung shut, and the big man came over to stand beside him.

'I don't know about you, but I need a taxi,' he yawned.

They walked slowly along the cobbled streets, weaving between groups of people who were making their way home and others who were getting ready for the clubs.

'Nice to see old Pearce again,' Mendel said as they came

to the end of King Street. 'We did a year together when I'd just made sergeant.'

'He's always seemed like a decent bloke,' Harland said. Ahead of them, he could just make out a couple, intertwined in the shadows between two buildings. The girl had her hands on her partner's face as they kissed, eyes closed in the gloom.

He sighed, then noticed Mendel looking at him.

'What?'

The big man looked away and frowned.

'It's none of my business, but . . .' He paused.

'Spit it out,' Harland sighed.

'I think it's great that you're . . . looking around again.' Mendel spoke slowly, carefully. 'I'm not sure that work colleagues are a good idea though.'

He gave a sympathetic smile and started walking again.

'What?' Harland went after his friend, coming alongside him and looking at him questioningly.

'Just saying.' Mendel shrugged. 'Maybe it's for the best, you know?'

Harland stopped and stared at him.

'I don't know what you're talking about,' he scowled.

Mendel looked over at him and smiled.

'Yeah you do, but never mind.' He pointed towards the line of taxis across the street. 'Come on, we'll share a cab and I'll drop you off.'

# 21

Naysmith stood on the pavement and stared at the list in his hand – a series of brief names and addresses on a folded piece of paper, easily discarded. Not the sort of list he'd want to keep on his phone. Most of the names were crossed out – locations quickly checked and quickly dismissed – but this place was proving difficult to find. Looking up, he turned around, eyes sweeping back along the length of the street. It had to be around here somewhere.

A dark uniform caught his attention, the unhurried movement of a policeman on patrol. Naysmith hesitated for a moment, then smiled.

*Why shouldn't he?*

Tucking the list into his pocket, he wove his way through the milling shoppers and students and approached the officer.

'Excuse me,' he asked brightly. 'Do you know where the Clifton Arcade is?'

A young constable with a friendly face, alert and eager to help.

'Yeah, it's easy to miss.' He turned and pointed back up the hill towards a triangle of grass and trees. 'If you go back up that way, then turn right just at the newsagent. It's tucked away behind that line of shops.'

'Much obliged.' Naysmith smiled at him.
*If only he knew.*

Turning off Clifton Down Road where the policeman had
said, he found himself on a narrow street, unevenly paved,
that ended in a cul-de-sac. Away from the main road, the
shop names became unfamiliar and interesting – boutiques,
custom jewellers, delis and cafés.

At the end of the street, beyond the crowd of tables that
seemed to have spilled out from a small bistro, a narrow
stone arch led through to a leafy green square. As he
approached, Naysmith noted the dark blue awning on the
left, golden letters spelling out the words 'Clifton Arcade'.

He didn't walk in right away. This street was new to him
– somehow he'd missed it on previous visits – and he skirted
calmly around the tables, his curiosity leading him on
through the arch to gaze at the quiet square on the other
side. Grand old sandstone buildings set about a central
square of grass and trees, oddly reminiscent of the architecture in Bath. Looking around, he noted a blue plaque
on the nearest corner, declaring that a famous cricketer had
once lived here. Such a lovely oasis of calm in the bustle
of the city . . .

But he had work to do. Turning, he made his way back
through the arch.

Two women were sitting at one of the pavement tables,
comfortable in their affluent forties. One of them glanced up
at him, holding his gaze as he moved slowly around the tables.
Her friend was busily talking, but she gave him a slight smile,
then demurely looked away as he returned it.

At another time that might have led to something interesting.
But not now. Not today. He'd spent a lot of time scouring the
city and he needed to stay focused until he found what he

was looking for. Leaving the bistro behind, he stepped up under the entrance awning and passed inside.

The arcade felt tall and cramped, like an old chapel, with a carpeted aisle in the middle and a congregation of eclectic storefronts huddled on either side. At the far end, steps ascended to an unseen upper level below an ornate rose window. Naysmith paused, turning his face up to the sunlight that filtered down from the glass ceiling, and smiled to himself. Kim would love this place.

He made his way through the mingled aromas of bath soaps and incense, politely standing to one side so that an elderly couple had room to pass, then turned his attention to the task. Each business displayed its name on a small hanging sign, and his eyes scanned the aisle until he located the one he was looking for.

*Edible Arts.*

There it was, a few yards ahead on the right, halfway along the aisle. He didn't rush, but began to move slowly towards it, pretending to browse in a couple of windows as he went. Antique jewellery in one, Mexican crafts in another. The shop he was interested in was just next door . . .

. . . and suddenly he could see her. The woman he had been searching for was standing there, just a few feet away from him. She was wearing a dark brown apron with the shop's name embroidered on it, her black hair swept back under a headband as she leaned over a marble work counter, pressing delicate petals of icing into the side of a wedding cake. Through the plate-glass reflections, Naysmith watched her, surrounded by an army of miniature piping bags and little tubs of coloured icing, her plump face creased with concentration as she worked.

Her life was his.

He turned away as a violent shiver of anticipation ran

through him – the heavy sense of inevitability – but he forced himself to walk on slowly, studying another couple of shops. Two doors further on, he found himself peering into a confectionery store called Biba Chocolate and suddenly recognised the logo he'd seen on the woman's shopping bag.

He smiled.

There were still a number of shops ahead of him and he made himself walk the entire length of the arcade before turning and drifting calmly back along the aisle.

As he passed Edible Arts again, he allowed himself the luxury of one final glance, to fix her image more firmly in his mind, her tanned skin and her small eyes, her heavy arms and double chin. She was surveying her work, a can of Diet Coke in her hand.

*Poor thing – now he'd found her, there was really no point worrying about diet drinks.*

Smiling at that, he was about to move away when his eye settled on a small, handwritten sign taped inside the window by the door.

*Hours: 10 a.m. to 4 p.m. – Closed Mondays.*

He checked his watch and thought for a moment. Kim might get a bit silly about him coming home late, but he was eager to move things forward now that he'd found his target, and he'd made so many trips to Bristol already.

It was only a few hours to kill and he wanted to learn more about this woman. Satisfied, he walked on down the aisle and out into the bright daylight.

# 22

He knew that she shut her shop at four. The handwritten sign in the window had been very helpful and it allowed him to spend a relaxing afternoon exploring the narrow side streets on the hill near the suspension bridge. He found a perfect little café that specialised in artisan chocolates and spent a glorious hour in there, sampling handmade truffles from the beautiful selection on display and sipping a dark spiced cocoa drink while he read the paper.

A little treat before it was time to get serious.

At half past three, he stood up and went over to the counter to pick out a small selection of chocolates for Kim. Previously, he'd felt uneasy about letting her into his thoughts when he was hunting, but now those dividing lines were shifting, blurring. She was beginning to understand, beginning to appreciate what he did. Naturally he still had to be careful not to overwhelm her with too much knowledge too quickly, but it wouldn't be long before he could tell her more about the game he played. And this one had an extra edge to it, as she had chosen the target herself.

He smiled and thanked the Mediterranean-looking woman behind the counter as she handed over the tiny ribbon-wrapped box, then made his way outside. Standing on the pavement, he slipped the box into his jacket pocket, then set off down the hill.

There was a friendly feel to these streets – a welcoming

neighbourhood built around a succession of relaxed cafés and independent shops. As he walked, he drew out his phone and powered it off – he didn't want any interruptions, and there was no sense leaving a cellular trail to the victim's home.

The arcade was quiet when he arrived. A number of the shops in here seemed to close at four, and there weren't many customers around for him to blend in with. He frowned as he studied the layout, noting the second exit that he'd need to cover and checking the sight lines to determine where he should wait. In the end, he settled on an antique-furniture store that had a tall mirror with a beautifully carved wooden frame in the window, finding the best place to stand so that he could see the Edible Arts storefront in its reflection.

Just before the hour, he saw her. Switching off the lights inside her shop, she emerged wearing a well-made turquoise jacket over her simple black top and dark floral-print skirt – loose-fitting clothing to hide her figure.

She exchanged pleasantries with another shopkeeper further down as she locked up, before rattling the flimsy door to check it was secure. Then, gathering up her bags, she turned and walked towards him. Naysmith gently stepped closer to the mirror as she approached, concentrating on her brisk footsteps and the swish of her skirt as she passed just behind him. He pretended to check his watch, giving her a moment to get ahead, then casually turned to follow her.

He was glad he'd noticed that second exit – she was approaching it now, pushing through a pair of windowed wooden doors and into a covered walkway that cut through one side of the building. He lost sight of her for a moment, then approached the doors himself. There she was, a plump silhouette, walking down the passage towards the daylight at the far end. She disappeared off to the right.

When Naysmith emerged into the open, she was about

twenty yards ahead of him, hurrying down the narrow side street that led out to the main road. She wasn't difficult to follow. That turquoise jacket made her easy to spot, and her short stride didn't cover a lot of ground, even though she appeared to walk quickly.

He watched to see which way she would turn when she reached the street, but she slowed and stopped, waiting to cross over to the other side. Fortunately, she had her back to him, so he was able to catch up to her without being noticed and he walked a little way down the hill before turning round.

She had crossed over and was walking uphill, but soon reached a bus stop. On the opposite side of the street, Naysmith paused and scowled.

*Buses.*

They were an unwelcome complication – in such a confined space it was much tougher to follow someone without leaving some sort of impression, some subconscious memory that would give them déjà vu if they saw you later near their home. Still, it couldn't be helped. He'd just have to play it by ear and see how far he could go.

Not wanting to get any closer until the last possible moment, he busied himself looking in the shop windows, frequently glancing down the hill to check if the bus was coming. Staring at the glass, he could just make her out in the overlapping reflections as she stood by the shelter, waiting.

And then she was gathering up her bags, her body language changing. Naysmith glanced down the hill – yes, there was the bus, moving slowly towards them. He waited until it had passed him, slowing and pulling in, before he crossed over to the other pavement, carefully pacing his approach to the shelter and calmly joining the short queue of people getting on.

She was facing the driver now – Naysmith strained to hear where she was going, but she held up some sort of travel pass and was waved aboard.

*Damn – no indication how far they were going.*

He didn't turn his head, but his eyes followed her as she moved inside the bus, taking a seat about halfway down the aisle. There were quite a few passengers and there might not be much room, but he knew he had to try to find a seat nearer the back. He certainly couldn't risk her seeing him, even subconsciously, for the whole journey or she'd be too aware of him when they got off and he wouldn't be able to follow her.

It was his turn to step up into the bus.

'Is there an all-day ticket?' he asked quietly.

'Four quid,' the driver replied.

'Thanks.'

He took the ticket and made a point of yawning so that he could cover the lower half of his face with his hand as he approached his target and moved past her. Luckily, there were two empty seats in the rear section and he chose the one furthest back from her and slumped down as low as possible against the dark purple fabric. Leaning back, he noted the small glass CCTV eye above him, but that was an unavoidable part of public transport – one more thing to factor into his planning.

As the bus pulled away, Naysmith settled down, gazing out of the window, logging the landmarks, memorising the route. They crossed the park that led down to the suspension bridge and followed the road as it swept down a tree-lined hill. A green matrix sign above the gangway displayed the names of principal stops – CLIFTON ZOO, REDLAND, CITY CENTRE – and he wondered which one was the target's destination. Every time the bus slowed, he'd glance forward, watching to see if she made any move to get up, then relaxing when he saw that she didn't.

He could see the angular cathedral spire in the distance, jagged shards against the sky, and then it was lost behind a succession of imposing buildings that rose up above tall hedges to look out over the downs.

Passengers got on and others got off, but the target gave no indication that her stop was close. Perhaps she was going all the way to the city centre? The bus had turned off and was now rattling down a gentle slope through a residential area lined with large stone houses and ironwork balconies, before turning back onto a broader road and climbing again.

There was something oddly familiar about the view as he stared out through the glass, and a moment later he recognised the entrance to Clifton Down railway station.

He closed his eyes for a moment, recalling the young blonde woman he'd tracked here last year before following her back to Severn Beach where she'd lived.

*And died.*

He could feel the hairs standing up on the back of his neck as he recalled her final, desperate moments . . .

But this wasn't the time for reminiscing. Snapping out of his daydream, he cast a hurried glance forward, but it was all right – the target was still there.

At the top of Whiteladies Road, they turned right and were soon coasting downhill again into Redland. And now, finally, the woman began to move, gathering her bags together, reaching out with one puffy hand to press the 'Stop' button.

Naysmith was ready but remained in his seat, watching as she got up and walked forward, her broad figure swaying from one handrail to the next while the bus slowed. Just in front of him, an elderly man with fine white hair and a military moustache was struggling to his feet and Naysmith stood up to help him.

'Take your time,' he smiled, holding a hand out to steady the old man as he shuffled to the front of the bus and stepped stiffly down to the pavement.

'Thank you,' the pensioner crackled as the doors hissed shut behind them.

'My pleasure,' Naysmith nodded to him. He prided himself on always being courteous, but the delay had also allowed the target to move away and open up a respectable gap, exactly as he'd hoped. It would have been awkward if he'd been too close.

The woman had crossed the road and was now on the opposite pavement, walking back the way the bus had come. Naysmith didn't cross over yet. On this side there were no houses, just a long strip of green park, and the footpath led down beneath a line of trees. At the bottom of the slope a gently arched footbridge with white iron railings led across the railway cutting towards the small brick buildings of Redland Station.

He kept slightly behind her, glancing across every now and again to match her pace, only losing sight of her when he reached the footbridge and she disappeared behind the stone parapet of the road bridge on his left. He quickened his stride for a moment, then slowed down again as he reached the other side, just in time to see her turn off into a quiet lane on the opposite side of the road.

He had to wait for a couple of cars to pass before he could cross, then he stepped smartly over the tarmac and joined the narrow pavement some thirty yards behind her. There was no traffic here. A sign, almost obscured beneath an overhanging bush, announced this as Kensington Road, a sleepy little side turning that ran along the top of the railway cutting. A long line of mossy old garages stood apart on his left, and behind them he heard the rattle of a train passing along the line below, before the quiet descended once more.

She didn't take the first turning but walked on, following the old stone wall as it snaked unevenly along, disappearing behind it when the pavement bent round to the right. He walked a little faster now, stepping out into the street, trying to keep her in sight, but as he passed the bend there was no sign of her.

*Shit.*

He hurried forward. There was only one turn-off, just ahead on the right, and he noted the name – Alexandra Park – as he drew level with it. There she was! He smiled as he caught sight of her once more. She was on the nearside pavement, so he drifted across to follow on the other side, but as he started to cross she turned abruptly and disappeared between a pair of stone gateposts.

*This was the place.*

It was a narrow street, with big, stone-fronted houses on either side, and hers halfway along. He wandered slowly past, memorising the number on the gatepost. Her place was a large semi-detached, with pale stonework and tall bay windows; the front door was at the side of the property, accessed by a straight concrete path and walled-off from the adjacent house. He slowed just a little, checking for security lighting, signs of a dog or any other problems, but there was nothing obvious.

*Keep moving.*

It wasn't the sort of street he could stake out – too many twitching net curtains. If he spent any time here, someone would notice, and remember him when the police came to ask about their poor dead neighbour.

He glanced back over his shoulder as he walked on.

There was nothing remarkable about the house, except that it was sizeable and clearly expensive. There was no driveway, so it was impossible to tell which of the parked cars belonged to her, if any. And no sign of children, which was encouraging.

But he still needed to know if she lived alone or not.

It was such an important part of his planning. Who else might be in the house if he decided to take her at home? When would the body be discovered? Or how long before she was reported missing? Information was crucial, and he needed more of it.

As he approached the top of the road, he slowed, frowning as he considered what to do next. One more look, then he'd go – he turned and crossed the road to walk back down.

The front gardens were all quite small, with low stone walls, small trees and neat little groups of different coloured bins arranged at every gate. He shook his head at the conformity, the willingness to fill such small gardens with so many of them, and the mess where one of the bins had tipped over and strewn old newspapers and junk mail across a meagre flowerbed.

And then he smiled.

He continued on down the road, casually stealing one last sideways glance at the house. She had the same collection of recycling bins at her gate too.

*Good.*

He made his way down to the end of the road and turned back towards the railway station. It would be dark in a few hours. He would come back.


Dusk drew in to shroud the city and the short street lamps cast isolated pools of dim light onto Alexandra Park. As Redland settled itself into the routine of late evening, a lone figure walked unsteadily along the road, a can of strong lager held loosely in one hand. On he came, stumbling against the garden walls, head bowed as he passed beneath the lamp posts, so the long shadows hid his eyes.

*Just another drunk weaving his way home.*

Naysmith moved slowly, forcing himself to slouch, to walk with an uneven gait. His glance flickered up now and again, checking the house numbers, counting ahead. As he approached the address, he paused, pretending to steady himself against a parked car, turning his head so that his eyes could sweep the street. Would he have to wait? No, there was nobody around.

He pushed himself away from the car and lurched the few remaining steps to the open gate. As he drew level with it, he appeared to trip over something, falling awkwardly to his knees, one hand going to the concrete gatepost for support. He remained there, stooped over, catching his breath for a moment – but at the same time, quietly and carefully, he opened the top of the small plastic recycling bin with his sleeve. Reaching inside, he brushed aside the empty cans and cartons, searching with the backs of his fingers until he felt what he wanted.

*Paper.*

Turning his hand, he grasped the wad of newspapers, flyers, and envelopes, and carefully drew it out. Angling his prize so that it caught the cold glow of the street light, he peered down at it for a moment, then allowed himself a small smile of satisfaction.

*OK. Time to get back in character.*

He grasped the top of the gatepost and struggled to his feet, tucking the papers inside his jacket before staggering on. From his brief glance at the printed junk mail he now knew the woman's name was Lesley Vaughn – there were several envelopes addressed to her, plus a number for a Mr Phillip Vaughn, presumably her husband, though it could conceivably be her father.

At the bottom of the street he turned left, allowing himself to straighten his back as he turned the corner. Walking smoothly now, he followed the pavement round a slight bend and on towards the main road. He stopped just once, to drop the still-full can of lager into a rubbish bin and leaf through the rest of the papers he'd collected.

Among the post, there were several catalogues addressed to Mr & Mrs Vaughn – which seemed to confirm that they were indeed a married couple – and, intriguingly, two dental-trade magazines. Naysmith shuddered as he looked at the glossy photo of a dentist's chair on the covers, noting that they were addressed to the husband. He hated dentists. There was nothing more of interest so he tipped the pile into the bin, but it had been a worthwhile exercise. Knowing more about them would certainly help with his planning.

And it was pleasing to have a name for his target.

He shot his cuffs and straightened his jacket. So far, his day had gone well, but there was still the tricky matter of Kim. She'd be suspicious, wondering where he'd been this evening, but he couldn't tell her what he'd been doing. Not yet anyway.

He checked his watch – with luck, he'd still be in time to catch the train back from Temple Meads. Satisfied, he strode away into the darkness.

# 23

The car in front of her slowed suddenly and Kim had to stamp on the brakes, feeling herself thrown forward against her seatbelt. She blinked and swore as the other vehicle turned off onto a narrow driveway, her heart rate quickened by the near miss. Gripping the steering wheel, she frowned and concentrated on the road, checking her mirror and reminding herself of the speed limit.

A musical beep sounded from her handbag on the passenger seat – text message – but she frowned and ignored it. She'd be home soon, it could wait until then. Moments like this – near misses and narrow escapes – were warnings to be heeded. If she reached for her phone now, she knew she'd probably run into a bus.

She reached the junction and even remembered to indicate left – she never indicated normally – before turning onto the tree-lined road that led into the village. A few minutes later, she pulled up at the side of the house and switched off the engine.

Her pulse was still thumping in her ears, but, she told herself, she was lucky.

*It was a near miss. She was OK.*

Lost in thought, she gathered up her bag from the seat beside her and got out of the car. Remembering the shopping, she went and opened the hatchback, working her small fingers through the handles of the plastic carrier bags. Then, slamming the boot shut, she turned and made her way round to the front step. Rob's car wasn't there – he must not be back from Bristol yet – so she had to balance the bags against the door as she searched for her keys.

The house felt quiet as she made her way down the hallway, the carrier bags rustling noisily in her hand, her heels clicking on the hard kitchen floor as she walked over to dump everything on the table.

She would put it away in a minute. Right now, she wanted a drink.

Turning to the counter, she checked there was still water in the kettle, then pressed the switch in. She took a mug from the cupboard and looked for the coffee.

*Of course. That was what she'd stopped off to get.*

She rifled through one of the carrier bags and took out a new jar, piercing the gold foil and inhaling the rich aroma. Opening the drawer, she was taking out a teaspoon when another musical beep came from her handbag on the table.

Another text.

She stopped what she was doing and rummaged through the bag until she found her phone, unlocking it and staring at the screen. There were two messages, both from Rob.

*Hi. Taking client for meal. Back late. R.*

*Don't wait up. R.*

Kim frowned and put the phone down on the table. She stood for a moment, biting her lip, then pushed her hair back and away from her eyes. Behind her, the kettle started to bubble and boil.

It didn't mean anything, she told herself. He was often late.

She went to the fridge, then remembered the milk was still in the carrier bag on the table. She busied herself for a moment, unpacking everything, adding milk to her coffee before putting the shopping neatly away. There was a large foil tray with some spiced chicken fillets, but that would have to wait – she would be cooking for one tonight.

It didn't matter. She sat down at the table with her drink, feeling the silence of the house swell around her. Her phone lay there in front of her, and she found herself staring at it.

He'd had quite a few clients up in Bristol recently.

She picked up the phone and turned it absently in her hand.

*Don't wait up.*

She tried to picture him, imagining where he was right now, who he was with. Sitting in a wine bar with some dreary fat businessman bore? Or was his client female?

In her hand, Kim swivelled the phone around, hit 'Reply' and began tapping out a series of responses.

*Don't lie to me.*

*Who is she?*

*I know what you're doing.*

Each time, her thumb hovered over 'Send', but each time she relented and deleted the message, her angry words left unsaid. Too many doubts, not enough certainty.

She stared at the kitchen wall as she drank her coffee.

In her mind, the client was tall and voluptuous, a confident woman who smiled at Rob as they laughed together. Was he flirting with her to get the deal? No, he wouldn't do that. Was he flirting with her to get her into bed?

*Stop it!*

She screwed her eyes shut for a moment, and took a deep breath. Then, frowning, she got up and went to the drawer to find some paracetamol – she could feel a headache coming on. Her hands were shaking as she prised the white tablets out of their foil strip.

Why tonight? Why did he have to worry her tonight?

She turned to the cupboard and started to plan a meal. Pasta would be quick, and there was a small tub of sauce that could go in the microwave. And a glass of wine. She found the bottle and poured herself one.

*Where was he right now?*

She put the bottle down and leaned back against the kitchen counter.

He was so strong, so confident. If he made up his mind that he wanted someone, he would succeed. And there had been a lot of travelling lately, a lot of late nights.

Kim sighed. She turned and put the pasta back in the cupboard and returned the sauce to the fridge. Maybe she would feel more like it later.

She picked up her phone, in case he tried to call, then took her wine and walked slowly through to the living room.

Sinking down into the corner of the sofa, she picked up the remote and switched on the TV. She spent a few minutes clicking through the channels, flitting from one show to another without really watching anything.

He had to be seeing someone else. *Had* to be.

She pulled her feet up onto the sofa, hugging her knees as she wondered where they'd met, and whether it was serious.

What was she like? Blonde? Brunette?

She reached for her phone and started typing out another message:

*Who is she, Rob?*

But once again, the doubts gripped her. What if she was wrong? What if he wasn't cheating on her, and her accusations pushed him away? She shook her head bitterly. To drive away someone who cared about her – she was turning into her mother.

Restless, she got to her feet and went upstairs.

There was a heavy stillness in the bedroom and she found herself moving quietly, almost as though she was afraid to disturb something. But she was alone.

She was about to sit down on the edge of the bed, then turned to face his wardrobe, gently opening the doors wide to reveal the neat array of clothes. She moved closer, reaching out to run one finger along the line of jackets, her eyes searching for a telltale blonde hair on his shoulder. If only she knew for certain. Leaning forwards, she brought her nose close to the dark material of a favourite suit, sniffing in case she could detect a trace of unfamiliar perfume. Her small hands snaked into the inside pockets, searching for something, anything . . .

And then she stopped.

*What was she doing? What was the matter with her?*

She withdrew her hands slowly, blushing with embarrassment even though nobody was there to see her.

*Paranoid, that's what she was.*

Maybe he had been a bit naughty in the past, but that was before. Before they got serious. He was honest with her now – too honest, in fact. He had told her he wasn't cheating at the same moment he'd revealed his terrible secret. Why would he lie about one and not the other?

She had to believe him.

Ashamed of herself, she leaned forward, burying her face in his clothes, taking comfort in the familiar scent of his aftershave. Why was she always so suspicious? Whatever he was doing, he wasn't cheating on her.

She allowed herself a moment of respite.

He probably *was* out with a client. Again.

A frown crossed her face.

*Back late . . . Don't wait up.*

She shook her head. He wasn't cheating on her, and if he wasn't cheating on her, what else *could* he be doing?

In the distance, a church bell chimed.

*What else could he be doing?*

She lifted her face and stepped slowly back from the wardrobe. Suddenly, she found herself believing his assurance that he wasn't sleeping with anyone else. But now there was no comfort in it, as a different possibility began to uncoil itself in her mind.

*No.*

She went back downstairs, numb.

In the living room, she picked up her phone and read the messages again. Then, very carefully, she put the phone face down on the coffee table before sinking back into the corner of the sofa.

*No!*

She was being stupid, imagining things. He'd be home in a few hours and everything would be all right. She just had to be patient. Frowning, she reached for the remote control and switched on the TV again, then settled down to stare at the screen.

Everything would be all right.

# 24

There was a single tree at the end of Badenham Grove. Someone had draped an old bed sheet between the lower branches with a birthday message daubed in pink paint, but it had obviously been left hanging there for some time as the letters had bled downwards in the rain. Harland slowed, then turned right, pulling his car in and bumping it up so that two wheels were on the pavement, like the other vehicles that lined the street. Most of the residents hadn't left for work yet.

It wasn't really a bad area. Two-storey semi-detached houses, and most of them were nice enough – well kept behind their neat little hedges – but there were a few with cracked-concrete gardens, weeds struggling up between the uneven grey cement. The place he was looking at now had no hedge or garden wall – just a car parked sideways under the front-room window, covered by a faded tarpaulin that sported a layer of moss. Somebody had once cared for the car, but it hadn't been touched for months. Harland wondered if Leroy's dad was in prison.

It had been a stroke of luck, he couldn't deny that. Josh Gilmour was the one who'd mentioned it at the end of yesterday's shift as they'd sat together in the main office area at

Portishead. A group of kids – four of them by all accounts – had been dropping house bricks onto the M49 from the Kings Weston Lane bridge. Fortunately, nobody had been killed, but one brick had punched a two-foot dent in the bonnet of a passing car and the driver had got straight onto his mobile and shakily called it in.

There was a CCTV camera on a motorway-sign gantry right next to the bridge. The control room had immediately informed Traffic, and someone – he wasn't sure who, but they deserved a medal – had turned the camera round and caught the kids in the act.

'But that's not the best bit,' Josh had told him, beckoning him over to his monitor. 'Check this out.'

Harland had gone over to peer at the images moving on the screen.

'See what I mean?' Josh chuckled as he paused the footage. 'Right there – that kid on the right is actually pointing up at the camera like a complete halfwit.'

'Should have covered his face first,' Harland smiled. He leaned closer, peering at the grainy image for a moment, his expression growing thoughtful.

'Sir?'

'Do me a favour, Josh.' Harland sat down on the desk. 'Remember that gang that was torching industrial units along the St Andrews Road? Pull up their mugshots for a moment.'

He watched as Josh accessed the file, then leaned in close, studying the faces.

'There!' He jabbed a finger at the photograph of a skinny-looking youth with a long face and short blond hair. 'That's him, isn't it? The idiot who looks up at the camera?'

'Leroy Marshall.' Josh read the name below the photo, then brought up the CCTV image again. 'Yeah, I think you're right – it does look like him.'

Harland sat back and pulled a hand across his jaw.

'Where does he live?' he asked after a moment.

'Hang on . . .' Josh clicked the mouse. 'I've got an address in Badenham Grove.'

'Sorry. Remind me . . . ?'

'It's just off Long Cross. Next to the primary school.'

Harland stood up with a grim smile.

'And about five minutes' walk from that motorway bridge.'

A rap on the glass jarred him from his thoughts and he turned to see a police uniform stooping close beside his car. He wound down the window.

'Ready, sir?' the officer asked him.

'Sorry, yes.' Harland shook his head and took a deep breath. 'Let's go.'

He got out of the car and locked it. Nobody was going to steal anything, not with the other police cars pulled up at the house, but it was a habit – if he always did it, he'd never forget to.

Stretching for a moment, he massaged his shoulder to loosen the stiff muscles, then followed the four dark uniforms across the road. Josh was there, but he didn't know the others. Two of them went up the side of the house to cover the back, while Josh and another officer went to the front door and began knocking loudly.

Harland stood on the pavement, stifling a yawn as he gazed up at the bedroom windows.

*That's right. Wakey wakey.*

He saw a woman's face, pale and drawn, appear briefly at the curtains, and he waved to Josh that someone was coming. A moment later, the door opened and the same face, weary but suspicious, stared out at them.

'What time do you call this?' she rasped unhappily. 'All that banging, waking everyone up.'

'Mrs Marshall?' Josh began, but she ignored the question.

'Jason's not here,' she told him. 'And I don't know where he is, so it's no use you asking.'

'Mrs Marshall?'

'Yes. What?'

'We're not here for Jason,' Josh told her. 'We're here for Leroy.'

Her face fell, just for a moment, and then she turned away, stepping back into the house and shouting angrily up the stairs. As Josh and the other officer followed her inside, Harland could hear raised voices coming from within. It sounded as though Leroy had more than just the police to worry about.

*Good.*

Harland patted his jacket pockets. Were his cigarettes in the car? No, they were here. He found the packet, drew one out and lit it while he waited for the noise in the house to die down.

Mrs Marshall was still shouting as Leroy was led from the house, his face pained, as much from his mother's anger as his actual arrest.

'I ain't done nothin',' he whined as Josh steered him firmly down the step, past the tarpaulin-draped car and out onto the pavement.

There were faces appearing at other windows now, as neighbours opened their curtains to see what was going on. Mrs Marshall glared up at them balefully, then swore and went back inside.

Harland threw away his cigarette and walked over to where Leroy was standing, a wretched figure in the grey morning light, bleary-eyed and thin, with his short blond hair sticking up. He was wearing a red T-shirt and black tracksuit – maybe the same clothes as the night before if they were lucky.

'Has he been cautioned?' Harland asked.

'Yes, sir,' Josh nodded.

'Good.' He turned to Leroy. 'Bored with starting fires, are we?'

'Eh?' The youth eyed him with contempt.

'You heard me.' Harland gave him a bleak smile, then leaned in closer. 'And *don't* fuck me around.'

He straightened up and shook his head wearily. Josh kept his poker face, but Harland could tell he was enjoying this.

'You're going down anyway, Leroy – chucking bricks off a motorway bridge will get you some prison time, guaranteed. But unless you want the full six years for attempted murder, you'd better start giving us some names. Starting with whoever torched those places on St Andrews Road.'

Leroy's eyes darted from face to face, and though he puffed his chest out in defiance, he suddenly looked very small, and very scared.

*Got him.*

'When I get back to the station, you're going to tell me everything I want to hear, understand?' He turned to Josh. 'Put him in the car.'

'Yes, sir.'

Harland watched as they led Leroy away.

They'd got lucky on this one – he knew that. But with results so hard to come by, he wasn't complaining. And if this let them clean up the St Andrews Road case too, it might get Blake off his back.

Better late than never.

# 25

The road climbed as it wound its way out of the village, and Naysmith had to work hard to propel the bike up the long slope. Soon, the houses gave way to hedgerows and old stone walls, colours and textures that normally blurred past in a car made suddenly sharp. Cresting the rise, he changed gear, the pedals easier now as he rode out into the countryside. The rattle of an approaching train drew his eyes to the right – the railway line had drawn in beside him and he smiled, thinking that he would soon be returning past this point, looking down on the road from a carriage.

Ahead, his view opened out across rolling hills and newly harvested fields. Bales of hay were stacked on the horizon, golden monoliths like standing stones against the skyline. He lifted his head, relishing the breeze that rushed by his ears as he coasted down the hill, leaning in to follow the curve of the tarmac as it swept down below the level of the railway embankment.

A mile or so later, he left the main road, bearing right at a small village, pedalling along a street without pavements, and on through stands of old trees and open green fields. There was a freedom to cycling out here, an enjoyment in escaping the confines of the car, and every so often, as he thought about the day ahead, a surge of adrenalin coursed through his body to strengthen his legs. Away from the main road there was little traffic – few people to remember him, and he'd made sure there was nothing memorable about his appearance. Thatched stone cottages and small, sleepy hamlets slid by as he made his way quietly and swiftly west.

It took about half an hour – slightly longer than he'd planned, but he was in no hurry. The first houses of Tisbury peeped out at him through the trees at the foot of the hill. It wasn't a big place – a small market town, a name on a signpost some way off the beaten track – but that was just the point. It was quiet, it was out of the way, and it had a station.

He'd spent some time considering how to make his journey. How to reach the centre of a busy city, and get out again, without leaving any trail. In the end, it was Kim who had given him the idea.

'Rob, I think my car's due for a service.' She was reading a letter from the local garage, one of their annual reminders to drum up more business. 'They can collect it, but I'd need you to give me a lift into Salisbury . . .'

'No problem.' He looked up at her, standing at the kitchen counter, and the thought came to him even as he was speaking. 'You can use my car if you like, as long as it's a day when I'm working from home.'

It would be great if he could arrange it. However much he wanted to trust her, he felt uneasy about burdening her with too much knowledge too soon. And this way, she wouldn't need to know until long after it was all over.

'You don't mind?' Kim asked.

'Let me check my plans,' he told her with a smile.

And he had checked. He'd chosen a Monday when he knew she'd be working late, and they'd dropped her car off the night before. This morning, wrapped in a bathrobe, he'd

kissed her goodbye at the front door and watched her from
the window as she pulled away in his car, indicated left and
turned onto the road. Knowing that his mobile phone,
switched to silent mode, was safely tucked into the pocket
of his jacket in the boot.

*No interruptions today, and nothing to track where he was
going.*

And then the clock was ticking. With everything prepared
and Kim on her way to work, Naysmith went upstairs and
into his study. From under his desk he drew out the backpack
and checked its contents one more time.

Everything was in place.

He nodded to himself and went through to the bedroom,
quickly dressing in new, nondescript clothing he'd bought
from a supermarket. Jeans and a plain T-shirt, a baggy grey
hooded top and cheap trainers – standard lines, sold in every
town, unremarkable and untraceable. No jewellery other than
the gold chain around his neck, no wallet, just a handful of
banknotes jammed down in his pocket.

*He was ready.*

Scooping up the backpack, he went downstairs and gently
nudged the telephone handset so that it was off the hook.
Then, turning away from the front door, he went out the
back way. Stepping quietly into the small courtyard garden,
he locked the back door and slipped the key under a plant
pot. Moving to the tiny garden shed, he brought out his bike,
checking the tyres again, just as he had done the night before.
Then, wheeling the bike over to the high wooden gate that
opened onto the lane, he paused to listen.

*Nothing.*

Calmly, he unlatched the gate and pushed the bike
outside, gently shutting the gate behind him. Glancing over
his shoulder to ensure that nobody was around, he swung

his leg up and coasted quietly down the lane that ran behind the houses, the tick-tick sound of the chain seeming oddly loud in the accusatory village silence.

And now, just half an hour later, he rode down the hill to Tisbury Station. The old red-brick railway buildings stood closed, a backdrop to the self-service ticket machine that had replaced them – ideal for someone keen to preserve his anonymity.

He paid for his ticket in cash, then wheeled the bike onto the single station platform, raising his hood and inclining his head away from the CCTV cameras, whose placement he'd noted on a previous visit.

There were only two other people waiting – an elderly woman with a distant expression and a middle-aged bearded man wearing a battered suit. They both politely ignored him until the train arrived and, when it did, chose other doors to board.

Lifting his bike easily, Naysmith stepped up into the carriage and slotted the bike into the rack. Then, casually rubbing his nose to obscure his face from the train's interior cameras, he sank into one of the narrow rows of seats and slouched down out of view.

It was only ten minutes or so until he had to change, and he passed the time gazing out of the fingerprint-marked window. Kim would be at work now. How would she react if she knew? Closing his eyes, Naysmith pictured her face, trying to visualise her expression flickering between fear and awe as she saw him for what he really was. He felt the hairs rise on the back of his neck and smiled to himself.

At Salisbury, he changed trains, boarding the 9.41 to Cardiff Central. He could feel the excitement rising, but it wasn't time for that yet. Pushing it down, he forced himself to breathe, willed himself to be calm. For now, he had to focus on the task before him – leaving no trail.

He was going to Bristol, but he got off at the earlier station of Bradford on Avon. Even with his other precautions, he couldn't risk taking the train straight through. Lifting his bike down onto the platform, he made his way beneath the cream-painted ironwork of the shelter, hurried over the footbridge and out into the station car park.

*So far, so good.*

He mounted his bike and pedalled away, past the old stone buildings, beautiful, sturdy architecture from another time – rural England the way the Americans pictured it. Riding over the railway bridge, he followed the road until he came to the old tavern, where he turned aside onto the canal towpath.

It was flat here and he picked up his pace, ever conscious of the aggressive timetable he was following. Soon, the last of the town's brown stonework was behind him and he was coasting quickly along, ducking now and again to avoid overhanging branches. At this time, on a weekday morning, there were very few people around. He'd passed one or two elderly dog-walkers near the outskirts of the town but now he was alone – just him and the calm dark water, curving along the side of the valley.

The trees gave way and he emerged into the sunlight for a brief spell, passing a couple of decaying old riverboats encrusted in sickly green moss and abandoned to their over-grown moorings, but there was nobody around – the occupied barges were still some way further on.

And now the trees closed in again. There were no boats here, and little light. Approaching a bend, he took a quick glance back over his shoulder to make sure that nobody was following, then squinted as he checked everything was clear ahead.

*Perfect.*

Skidding to a halt, he dismounted quickly and wheeled the bike down off the embankment into a dark stand of trees on the slope below the canal. Propping the bike loosely behind a bush, he moved deeper into the tangle of undergrowth until he could no longer see the towpath. There, screened by the foliage, he quickly shrugged off his backpack and took out a pile of folded clothes.

He paused once more, holding his breath as he listened for any warning sound, then began to undress. His T-shirt rode up as he pulled the big hooded top over his head, and he dragged them both off together before undoing the laces on his trainers. He slid his jeans down carefully, making sure that nothing fell from his pockets, then turned and picked up the cycle shorts and stepped into them. The Lycra top felt cold against his skin as he pulled it on before donning the lightweight riding helmet and tinted sunglasses. He laced up his trainers and transferred the money and train tickets from his jeans before finally pulling on the thin black cycling gloves. Then, checking the ground as he went, he gathered up his discarded clothes and folded them neatly into the backpack, which he tucked under a bush where it wouldn't be found.

Cautiously, he picked his way back up the slope to where his bike was waiting and wheeled it out onto the towpath, glancing quickly each way as he emerged.

Still nobody around. He had chosen the right spot.

And now he set off at speed, eager legs powering him along the narrow track as it followed the gently curving line of the grassy canal bank.

He passed several groups of barges as he approached Avoncliff, some with wisps of pale smoke curling from their stovepipe chimneys, others with their doors flung wide as their occupants bustled around with the tasks of the day. Nobody looked up as he sped by, just another cyclist hurrying along.

He could hear the roar of the weir now, white water foaming noisily away to his right. Passing the lonely stone house on the corner, he swept round by the Cross Guns pub and out onto the huge aqueduct, high above the valley floor. A quick glance at his watch confirmed that he had made good time – he had several minutes to spare – so he allowed himself to slow a little, gazing out over the parapet at the huge weeping willows and the meandering river below. Such a beautiful view – once he'd briefly considered buying a house round here, but decided against it because of the influx of weekend tourists in the summer months. On a day like today, though, it was perfect.

He reached the far side of the aqueduct and dismounted before bumping his bike down a long flight of steps to a tiny station – two narrow platforms hugging the tracks. Leaning his bike against the small wooden shelter, he checked his watch again, then smiled. Everything was going to plan.

The solitary cyclist that boarded the train at Avoncliff was unrecognisable from the man who'd disembarked at Bradford on Avon. Naysmith kept his sunglasses on and his head down as he settled into his seat for the rest of the journey. The carriage was half full, but it grew busier when they stopped at Bath, where a lot of passengers got on; he wedged himself back into a corner, feigning sleep to discourage anyone from sitting next to him or, heaven forbid, trying to engage him in conversation.

Arriving at Bristol Temple Meads, he allowed the other passengers to go first, not getting to his feet until the doors were open and people were spilling out. Retrieving his bike from the rack, he guided it down onto the platform and let the crowd go ahead of him, funnelling down the steps. The under-pass was brightly lit, and the smell of baking hung heavy in the warm air as he wheeled his bike between the pasty shop and the coffee kiosk. A passenger lift at the far end allowed him to avoid the CCTV camera above the stairs and a moment later he emerged onto the main platform, where the diesel throb of an InterCity train echoed down from the vast canopy roof.

Pausing at the barriers, he showed his ticket to a red-faced woman, thanking her politely as he passed through. Emerging from the ticket hall into the open air, he looked out at the line of blue taxis waiting on the cobbled station approach, and at the waiting city beyond.

It was time to pay a visit to Mrs Vaughn.

Some of the hills were hard work, but the bike allowed him to cut quickly across the city centre, slipping down the quieter side streets, breaking his trail and avoiding the obvious CCTV traps. Now, as he descended from the heights of Cotham, freewheeling down the hill towards Redland Station, he could feel the adrenalin rising. Nothing was certain – there remained the tantalising possibility that she might live. The street could be busy and, with time still a factor, he would have to abort. Or, more likely, she could have gone out for the day . . .

*But if she was home, then he was less than a mile away from her, and drawing closer every moment.*

He coasted across the railway bridge and turned left off the main road, drawing up just in front of the garages at a point where trees blocked any view from the overlooking houses. Glancing up to make sure nobody was around, he reached forward and released the long steel wrench arm that was taped to the underside of the bike frame, resting its weight across the handlebars and gripping it with his gloved fingers as he set off again.

Alexandra Park was on a hill and he'd decided to ride past the foot of it for a preliminary look, before circling round and approaching from the top end. The street appeared quiet as he drifted past, so he powered on, taking the next turning and working up the incline between the looming terraced buildings. Reaching the junction at the far end, he turned right, following the road round until her house came into view again.

*Still nobody around. Green light.*

He swerved up onto the empty pavement, gently free-wheeling down the slope, obscured from view between the hedges and the parked cars, until he reached her gate. He didn't stop, just steered smoothly in and coasted quickly down between the houses, like an expected guest would do. Dismounting quietly, he lifted the bike around so it was facing outwards and propped it carefully against the wall. Then, turning to face the side of the house, he stood on the door-step and rang the bell. This was the moment – was she here?

He tightened his grip on the wrench arm, allowing it to hang casually at his side, two feet of solid steel, turning his body so that it wouldn't be visible.

*Movement.*

He could hear someone approaching, muffled footsteps coming towards the door, the sound of the latch turning. The door opened inward, and suddenly there she was, dressed in a loose floral-print top and dark blue jeans, peering out at him in polite puzzlement.

'Hi, Lesley!' He spoke quickly, beaming like an old friend to keep her off balance. 'Is Phillip home?'

'Er, no . . .' She answered without thinking, opening the door just a little wider as she struggled to work out who this was.

Naysmith smiled.

'That's OK,' he shrugged, and swung the wrench.

It was a perfect blow, catching her under the chin and knocking her head backwards before she could react. He was already moving, calmly stepping across the threshold before launching himself forward with a snarl, knocking the stumbling woman to the floor, letting his full weight crash down onto her soft stomach to silence her, control her. But whether from the steel hitting her jaw, or the impact of her head against the floor, she was unconscious as he crawled up her body, the wrench raised over his head, ready to administer the fatal strike.

She was still breathing.

Straddling her torso, he held himself still for a moment, listening. But there was no sound, no approaching footsteps, no voice calling from another room.

She was still breathing. And he had her all to himself.

Getting to his feet, he quietly shut the front door and, leaving the prone figure sprawled on the carpet, made his way along the hall into the kitchen. Working quickly, he opened a couple of drawers beside the sink before his eyes came to rest on the knife block, tucked away in one corner of the worktop. Selecting a long, broad blade, he hefted it in his hand for a moment, then turned back towards the hallway.

She hadn't moved. Still lying there, eyes mercifully closed, a crumpled heap at the foot of the stairs. He was struck by how thick her ankles were, how much extra weight she was carrying – it was so much more apparent when her body was relaxed. For a moment, he wondered if he should steal something – to suggest a robbery motive – but the anticipation was killing him and he knew the clock was ticking. Better not to spend longer in the house than he had to.

Knives could be messy, but it was a change from his usual preferences. The blood was a risk – he wouldn't have favoured a stabbing if he hadn't had the time and privacy – but here was an opportunity to do something different, and it always paid to break from routine, make things a little harder for the police. Also, it might suggest a more personal, vindictive attack, rather than a random execution.

*Better make it look convincing.*

Kneeling down beside the woman, Naysmith placed one gloved hand carefully across her mouth, then raised the knife in his other, and turned his face away. He was naturally right-handed but would strike with his left. This was it – the moment when her life was finally and completely his – and he allowed himself to savour it for a few, rapturous seconds . . .

And then, it was time.

Her body stiffened with the first blow, but he held her firmly, stabbing again and again until she shuddered and relaxed beneath him. Without loosening his grip on her, he cautiously turned back to look.

Dark stains were blooming out across the fabric of her top but there was surprisingly little blood spatter. He had learned from experience to push the blade in quickly but draw it out slowly, and holding the body down had prevented her from spreading things around too much. He released his grip on the knife, leaving the blade in her chest. His gloved hand dripped red, and there was a little trickling along the under-side of his forearm, but nothing too serious. He could feel the wave of nauseous excitement bubbling up in his stomach, but he forced it down for a moment.

*First things first.*

He got to his feet and walked unsteadily through to the kitchen, turning on the cold tap with his dry hand and rinsing the blood off his arm. Satisfied, he thought about turning the water off but decided to leave it running – less chance of any traces remaining in the sink trap. Turning, he went back into the hallway and knelt beside the body, bowing his head for a moment as though in prayer, calming himself.

There was still something he had to do.

Gazing down at her, his eyes settled on the heart-shaped silver pendant at her throat – a delicate piece of jewellery, the sort of gift that lovers exchanged. Nodding to himself, he leaned forward and pushed the dead woman's hair aside, finding the clasp and undoing it. Cradling the back of her head in one gloved hand, he lifted it so that he could slide the pendant free before jamming it down into his pocket, making sure it was deep enough not to slip out.

Reaching up to his own neck, he located the fastener on the gold chain he wore and loosened it. Looping the chain around her throat was difficult, but after a couple of moments it was in place and he briefly lifted her head once more, ensuring her hair wasn't caught anywhere, that there were no inexplicable tangles.

He stood and surveyed his handiwork. The gold chain didn't look out of place on her. Smiling, he stooped to retrieve the steel wrench handle, then forced himself to check the floor for anything he might have dropped, anything amiss. Finally, he inspected his clothing for any telltale signs before moving carefully around the body and reaching for the door latch. Outside, everything was quiet – just another sleepy lunchtime in the suburbs. He drew the door closed behind him and went to his bike.

Balancing the wrench across the handlebars again, he mounted and coasted quietly out into the street, turning down the hill. Only now, as he turned into another road, did he allow the euphoria to claim him, feeling it surge up like an explosion of energy. The pedals were light beneath his feet as he powered back up the side roads that would take him away from the scene, and the awesome sensation of power made him want to shout. He controlled life itself! There was nothing he couldn't do.

And one day, quite soon, Kim would know what he was capable of – she would see him as he truly was – and she would worship him. Grinning to himself, he crested the hilltop and began freewheeling back down into Bristol.

He had timed it perfectly. Slipping into Temple Meads Station via the side entrance, he merged into a group of other passengers. Holding his ticket aloft, he was waved through the barriers without question, and wheeled his bike along the main platform, scanning the overhead monitors for departures from behind his tinted glasses.

His train was on time.

Descending to the underpass, he made his way across to platform 12, where he found a quiet spot away from the scrutiny of the cameras, and waited for his train to arrive. This was where it became an art form. Anyone could lash out, even extinguish a life if they were brutal enough, but the skill lay in going undetected. He could drift in and vanish away again without leaving a trail. And if his timings went to plan, even Kim wouldn't be able to guess how he'd managed it.

The journey to Avoncliff took half an hour. One other passenger got off there – a rustic old man with unruly white hair and hearing aids in his prominent ears – but Naysmith hung back on the platform, allowing him to labour up the steps to the aqueduct before climbing them himself. Fortunately, his timetable was a little more forgiving on the return journey. He waited long enough for the old man to cross the river and turn down towards the pub before getting onto his bike and riding back along the towpath.

The backpack was exactly where he'd left it. Unzipping

the main compartment, Naysmith drew out his clothing, then gratefully peeled off the Lycra top and shorts, enjoying the shiver of cool air on his bare skin as he located the stolen pendant and held it up to admire.

Once dressed, he double-bagged the cycle gear in a pair of black plastic bin liners and stowed them in the backpack, ready to go to the charity bins at a not-so-local supermarket. Transformation complete, he climbed back up to the towpath and set off for Bradford on Avon.

The train got into Salisbury a little late, but he still made his connection. It wouldn't have been a disaster if he'd had to cycle back from there, but just in case anyone ever managed to trace his route, he wanted the trail to end somewhere hopelessly rural, rather than the busy city so close to where he lived. As it was, he enjoyed a pleasant ride home, following quiet country lanes through the rolling Wiltshire landscape. Nobody saw him slip in through the back gate, and he had the kettle boiling when he heard Kim's key in the front door.

He smiled as she walked into the kitchen. 'Coffee's on.'

'Thanks,' she said, putting her bag down on the counter. 'Did you hear anything from the garage?'

'Not yet,' he shrugged. 'I'll take you round there in the morning. By the way, remind me to check the boot of my car – I think I left my jacket in there, and my mobile's in the pocket.'

'A whole day without your phone . . .' She sat down at the table and stifled a yawn. 'Did you manage to get anything done?'

Naysmith poured the hot water. And smiled.

# 26

It rained all the next day. Midway through the afternoon, there were a few brief rumbles of thunder and the office lights dimmed momentarily.

'Uh-oh.' Marcus appeared at the door with a concerned expression. 'Everyone make sure to save your work, just in case there's a power cut.'

In her cubicle, Kim moved her mouse and clicked 'Save', then leaned back, allowing her chair to turn gently away from her desk. She gazed out through the droplets of water trickling down the window and looked across the neighbouring roof-tops. Salisbury could be lovely in the summer but it was a depressing place in the wet – an unwelcoming huddle of old bricks and concrete, like a bleak Northern town transplanted to the South, complete with its weather.

She turned back to her screen and sighed.

*Only six more sets of figures to prepare.*

Her hand strayed to the heart-shaped silver pendant Rob had bought her as she glanced up at the clock. Ten past three. She really didn't want to stay late again tonight. He had phoned and surprised her with cinema tickets. The film didn't start until eight, but she wanted to go home and change before they went out.

She leaned forward and began working through the next set of numbers.

'Kim?'

She glanced up to see Jane, who had got to her feet and was peering over the cubicle wall that divided them.

'Yes?' Kim frowned, annoyed at the interruption. She would need to start again from the top of the page. 'What is it?'

'I can't find the files for the third quarter.' The new girl was young and quiet, with short blonde hair. She was supposed to be a replacement for Dennis but, without his experience or work ethic, her principal contribution to the firm seemed to be that she was cheap. She certainly wasn't carrying Dennis' share of the workload.

'Why do you need the quarter-three files?' Kim asked. 'I thought you were supposed to be going through quarter-two?'

'I was,' she shrugged, 'but Marcus asked me to update all the linked sheets, and I need to reference the third-quarter files for that, don't I?'

'You do, but . . .' Kim pushed her chair back from her desk and took a deep breath, 'the quarter-three files aren't actually complete yet. Marcus . . .'

She tailed off.

*Marcus should have checked with her first before wasting Jane's time.*

'So what should I do?' Jane asked her.

Kim sighed and started to get to her feet.

'We need to go through and check for any files that haven't been updated since . . .' She hesitated, then shook her head and sat down again. 'Actually, no. You need to go back to Marcus and ask him to help you update the files. I have to get on and finish these figures.'

She couldn't allow herself to be taken for a ride again.

'Sorry,' she added, concentrating determinedly on her screen.

'No problem,' Jane shrugged, turning and moving away. She had that special sort of calm that you only found in people who simply didn't care.

Kim frowned and began working through the numbers again. She'd had just about enough of people taking her for granted.

Outside, the skies stayed dark. Kim worked hard and was just finishing the last set of numbers as the clock hit five thirty. Saving the last of her work to the server, she raised a hand, sliding it under her hair to massage the back of her neck, smiling as her fingertips touched the delicate silver chain. It had been a long afternoon, but the figures were done. She switched off her computer and gazed out at the rain for a moment before getting to her feet. Then, gathering up her bag and jacket, she walked out of her cubicle.

Marcus had pulled up a chair by Jane's desk and the pair of them were working through a large set of spreadsheets.

*Served him right.*

She waved to them as she walked towards the door. 'See you tomorrow.'

'Er, Kim?' Marcus was looking at her wretchedly.

*Trying to summon the courage to ask her to stay behind and help.*

'Don't worry, Marcus,' she smiled brightly. 'I got all the figures done for you.'

Wrong-footed, he blinked at her for a moment, then nodded.

'Yes, of course.' A resigned smile. 'Thanks for doing that.'

'No problem,' she replied, moving towards the exit. 'Bye.'

Marcus looked crestfallen as she turned away, but there had been no uncomfortable confrontation and she knew she'd done the right thing.

Hurrying down the stairs, she paused to dig out her umbrella before pushing the door open to look out at the rain. It was still quite heavy. Bracing herself, she stepped outside and raised the umbrella, hurrying to the car and watching her feet to avoid the puddles.

Rob's car wasn't there when she got back to the house. She scampered round to the front door, keys in hand, and shook the rain from her jacket as soon as she got inside. Gathering up the post from the mat, she pushed a hand through her hair and walked into the front room, where she picked up the remote control and switched on the TV. She was going to sit down, but the rain had left her feeling cold, so she turned and went back through to the kitchen and filled the kettle. A hot drink would warm her up.

As she waited for the water to boil, she sifted through the envelopes but there was nothing with her name on it – everything was for him.

She left the post on the kitchen table, made her coffee and went into the hallway to go upstairs and change.

'. . . have launched a murder investigation following the discovery of a woman's body in Bristol yesterday.'

The voice came from the TV. Kim paused and glanced through into the front room, where the picture changed from the newsreader to a view of a solid-looking man in a grey suit, his serious face lit by the flicker of photographers' flash-guns. He cleared his throat and spoke with a strong London accent.

'Officers were called to an address in Redland at half past six yesterday evening by the husband of a woman who was discovered at their house in Alexandra Park. Officers attended with an ambulance but unfortunately the woman – Lesley Vaughn, aged forty-six – was pronounced dead at the scene.'

A caption at the bottom of the screen read: *DCI Raymond Pearce, Avon and Somerset Police.*

'Upon attending the scene, a murder enquiry was immediately launched. It was obvious that the woman had been assaulted and most likely died of her injuries. However, a forensic post-mortem is taking place at the moment, and the results of that will confirm the actual cause of death.'

The man paused and glanced up from his notes. He had a no-nonsense look about him, with dark grey hair worn short, and a faint scar down his left cheek.

'We currently have a number of detectives working on this case, and we're drafting in additional resources from other parts of the Avon and Somerset area. The team are working round the clock to catch whoever is responsible for this appalling crime and bring them to justice.'

Another pause, another barrage of camera flashes.

'We're appealing for witnesses or anybody with any information. We believe that Lesley spent much of yesterday at home, where her body was discovered at approximately six thirty p.m. We're appealing for anyone who may have seen anything suspicious in the Redland area of Bristol to come forward with any information they might have . . .'

Kim leaned against the door frame. She was annoyed at herself for even considering the idea, but she couldn't help it.

*He couldn't have done something like this, could he?*

No, thank goodness – Rob had been here all day yesterday. She'd taken his car and left him to work from home. Her body unknotted itself a little. It couldn't have been him.

Behind her, the metallic rasp of a key in the lock made her jump.

*Rob!*

She gasped and turned towards the front door, then hesitated. Stepping quickly into the front room, she snatched up the remote control and changed the channel. It was stupid, but somehow the thought of him coming in to find her watching a police press conference made her deeply uncomfortable. She dropped the remote on the sofa and hurried back into the hallway.

'It's really coming down out there.' Rob was standing there by the front door, dark hair dripping, shaking the water from his jacket.

'You're soaked. Let me get you a towel.' Kim turned away from him quickly, walking into the kitchen, not trusting herself to make eye contact. Behind her, she heard him chuckling appreciatively.

'Always thinking of me, aren't you?'

She stopped in the middle of the kitchen floor and bit her lip.

*Yes*, she told herself. *And that was the problem.*

# 27

The afternoon sunlight was streaming in through the windows, throwing long shadows across the upstairs office. Mendel leaned back in his chair and rubbed his chin thoughtfully.

'Alexandra Park,' he muttered. 'Just round the corner from Redland Station, isn't it?'

'Yes, a couple of streets away.' Harland stood with his back to the wall, staring down into his coffee cup. 'Nice area – last place you'd expect something like this to happen.'

Mendel shook his head.

'Not good,' he mused.

'I know.' Harland looked up from his coffee. 'Apparently she was stabbed six times.'

'Bloody hell.' Mendel looked at him. 'And they don't fancy the husband for it?'

Harland shrugged. 'Early days, I suppose.'

He pushed himself away from the wall and walked across the room to gaze out of the window. Things were too quiet just now, and he was suddenly restless.

'Did they find the weapon?' Mendel asked.

Harland frowned, trying to recall what Jamieson had told him.

'I think it was at the scene,' he replied, turning back to face into the room. 'They've found a knife, anyway.'

There were footsteps in the corridor outside, and Josh leaned around the open door.

'Ah, there you are,' he called to Harland. 'The Superintendent wants you, sir.'

Blake's door was closed and Harland stood outside for a moment, taking a calming breath before knocking.

'Enter.'

Grasping the handle, he assumed a neutral expression and opened the door.

'Graham.' Blake looked up from his desk and his face brightened. 'Come in and sit down.'

'Sir.'

Harland stepped into the scrupulously tidy room and pulled the door closed behind him. Blake seemed happy enough, but he knew to his cost just how deceptive the old man could be. Lowering himself into one of the chairs that faced the Superintendent's desk, he tried to work out what he'd been summoned for.

'I was hoping to have a chat with you, Graham.' Blake spoke as though things had just occurred to him, as though he hadn't prepared every word in advance. That was why it was so important not to let your guard down. 'How are things with you?'

'Er . . . fine thanks.' Harland wasn't sure what he was being asked.

'I'm glad to hear that.' Blake settled back into his chair and folded his arms. 'I've always believed that maintaining good officer morale is terribly important.'

*Ha!* Harland suppressed an ironic smile.

The Superintendent studied him for a moment, then continued.

'I've been keeping an eye on you, Graham. Ever since last year, with that poor woman they found on the beach.'

*Where was this going? What had he done wrong?*

'I appreciate how frustrating it must have been for you to relinquish that case to the Met – for your whole team, in fact – but as more senior officers it's our job to lead by example, and deal with the workload we're given in a professional manner.'

Harland stared at him, waiting for the rebuke that must surely follow. But Blake was still smiling.

'I've been impressed with your efforts on some of the recent cases, Graham.' He sat forward to lean his elbows on the desk. 'And most importantly, you've managed to get some really good results. The arson attacks along St Andrews Road, for example – things like that can make such a difference.'

'Thank you, sir,' Harland said warily. Had he really been called in for a pat on the head?

'Yes, a few arrests like that really take some of the heat off the Portishead division,' Blake mused. 'Of course, everyone's preoccupied with the stabbing in Redland at the moment . . .'

He paused, and glanced at Harland.

'What have you got on your plate just now, Graham?' he asked.

'A break-in over at Sea Mills, and an aggravated assault here in town,' Harland replied. 'Not much else.'

Blake stared at him thoughtfully.

'We've been asked if we can spare any manpower to support the Redland investigation,' he explained. 'You live in Bristol, know the area . . . I wondered if you might like to join the Bristol team for a week or two, and help them out?'

'Certainly, sir.' Harland leaned forward. He was eager for a change of scene, and the prospect of a serious case to work on was a welcome surprise.

'I take it by the look on your face that you find the idea agreeable,' Blake said pleasantly. 'That's settled then.'

'Thanks,' Harland told him. 'I appreciate this.'

The Superintendent shook his head to indicate that it was nothing.

'Do you know DCI Pearce?' he asked.

'Yes,' Harland nodded. 'He helped us out on the Clevedon murder a couple of years back.'

'Excellent. Our chance to repay the favour then,' Blake concluded. 'Give the break-in and the aggravated assault to Mendel, and then you can report to Bristol . . . tomorrow morning?'

'Yes, sir.'

'Well, I'll let you get on then.'

Harland got to his feet and moved towards the door.

'Graham?'

'Yes, sir?' He turned back to see what the Superintendent wanted.

Blake gave him a long look.

'It's good to see you smiling again,' he said.

Harland walked back into the office and sat down on the corner of Mendel's desk.

'You look cheerful.' The big man frowned at him. 'What's up? Has Blake decided to take early retirement?'

'If only,' Harland replied. 'He's sending me over to Bristol to help out on the Redland case.'

'Nice,' Mendel nodded appreciatively. 'You can give my regards to Pearce when you see him. When are you off?'

'Tomorrow.'

'Good. I hate long goodbyes.'

'Very funny. Listen, you know the Sea Mills break-in, and that stupid assault case? I'm going to have to dump them on you. Sorry.'

'No worries,' Mendel chuckled. 'I'll wrap them up soon enough.'

'Thanks.'

'And you do realise I'm going to steal your office while you're away, don't you?'

It was Harland's turn to laugh.

'Fair enough,' he grinned, 'but there's an unopened packet of biscuits in the filing cabinet, and it better still be there when I get back.'

'You'll be lucky,' Mendel rumbled. 'Anyway, if you're swanning off to Bristol, you know what that means?'

'What?'

'Last trip to the White Lion for a while . . . if you're not too busy this evening?'

Harland smiled.

'I wouldn't miss it,' he promised.


The following morning dawned grey, with an ugly overcast sky, but Harland was in a good mood. He didn't have nearly so far to travel, but he left the house at his usual time, turning the car radio up and reminding himself to turn right at the end of the street rather than left.

He found that he had an appetite, so he stopped at the supermarket on Coronation Road to grab some breakfast. The pastries at the bakery counter were still warm, and he picked up a small bottle of orange juice before walking back to the car.

Traffic was starting to build up as he made his way around Redcliffe, but once he got past Temple Meads it thinned out again, and he was soon following the line of the river as it led away from the city centre. Nobody lived out here – it was just car dealerships, tool-hire places and anonymous business units behind high steel fences. Shortly before the flyover, he turned right onto a narrow side street and followed it round to the large car park.

Switching off the engine, he unfastened his seatbelt and sat there for ten minutes, quietly eating his pastries and staring up at the pale grey building in front of him. It was seventies-ugly – a large, blocky construction, with a tall transmitter mast jutting up high above the roof – but Harland looked at it with enthusiasm. He'd been here before, of course, but only for brief visits. After all the frustrations of the last year, a proper stint with Bristol CID seemed very appealing.

Identifying himself at the front desk, he was directed to the stairwell and made his way up to the second floor. Pushing through a set of double doors, he entered the main corridor and smiled as he recognised DCI Pearce walking towards him.

'All right, Graham,' he beamed. 'What are you doing here?'

'Blake's renting me out to you for a week or two,' Harland replied. 'You know, to help with the Redland murder.'

'I had no idea, but that's great – we need some good people on this one . . .' He paused, then consulted his watch with a grin. 'Blimey, you're keen, aren't you? I wasn't expecting the cavalry till nine.'

'I live just off Coronation Road,' Harland explained. 'It only takes me five minutes to get here.'

'I retract the compliment then,' Pearce winked at him. 'We're supposed to be getting some extra bodies in from Taunton and Bath too, so we're going to be mob-handed on this one . . .'

He paused and reached into his jacket pocket to draw out a mobile phone, which was vibrating quietly. After reading the name on the screen, he frowned and answered the call.

'Andy, can you just hang on a moment? Cheers . . .' He covered the mouthpiece and spoke quickly. 'Sorry, Graham, need to take this one. There's a briefing at nine fifteen in the conference room – grab yourself a drink and I'll see you there, OK?'

He clapped Harland warmly on the shoulder, then turned away, already speaking into the phone he held pressed to his ear.

There was a canteen on the ground floor – a broad room with polished lino flooring and Formica tables that caught the light from the windows. Harland wandered across to the long stainless-steel counter, standing far enough back to avoid being questioned by the solemn-looking woman who watched him over the heated trays. The smell of frying bacon tempted him to order a full breakfast, but he bravely resisted – the pastries would keep him going until lunchtime. Turning aside from the hot food, he got a surprisingly good Americano from the large coffee machine at the end of the counter. The cramped little kitchen back at Portishead suddenly seemed very poor by comparison.

He glanced at his watch – not even nine yet. He briefly thought about going outside for a cigarette, but he wasn't sure where people went to smoke here. He could wait. There was bound to be someone else at the briefing who smoked, and it would be a good chance to get to know them.

Walking to the nearest table, he eased himself down into a plastic chair and took out his phone. A few rounds of solitaire would calm him down and exercise his mind. He was just starting his second game when a familiar voice spoke from beside him.

'I didn't expect to see you here.'

He looked up to see DS Russell Pope – sub-six-foot, with that same puffy face, those same piggy little eyes staring out from behind his glasses – and groaned inwardly. They'd not spoken in the months since Pope got his transfer away from

Portishead, indeed they'd hardly spoken since Harland had slammed him up against a wall in the station corridor the previous year, and that had suited both of them just fine. Now, though, he was on Pope's turf, and whether it was the passage of time or territorial advantage, something had emboldened the wretched little man.

'Morning, Russell. How's it going?' He should at least *try* and be civil.

'I'm doing very well, thanks,' Pope replied. He stood awkwardly for a moment before his artless curiosity got the better of him. 'So, what brings you to our little breakfast bar?'

*Our* breakfast bar. He'd only been transferred out of Portishead two months ago and already he spoke as though he owned Bristol CID. Harland could feel the muscles in his shoulders tensing up, but forced himself to speak nicely.

'The Redland murder,' he replied. 'Blake asked me to come and help out for a couple of weeks.'

'I'm surprised. But I suppose if he feels he can manage without you . . .'

'Cheers.' Harland gave him a withering smile and turned back to his phone.

'Still,' Pope added, 'it means we'll be working together again.'

Harland looked up.

'Really?' he said, without enthusiasm.

'Oh yes. DCI Pearce has had me on the case for a day or two. I've been reading the file on it – some rather interesting little facts in there that should lead to a good quick result—' He sounded as though he was about to launch into a long droning speech, but Harland cut him off.

'Sorry, Russell.' He indicated his wristwatch, and smiled apologetically. 'I just wanted to have a quick cigarette before the briefing starts – where do people go to smoke around here?'

He didn't want to create any more tension between himself

and Pope, but the little idiot was beginning to get to him and he needed to put some space between them. Before, he'd just been annoying – now he was a reminder of Harland's own weakness. In the event, Pope seemed pleased to show off his superior knowledge.

'I don't smoke myself,' he said loftily, as though they hadn't known each other for the last two years, 'but I know that some people go along to the end of that corridor – there's a covered outdoor area set aside—'

Harland was already getting to his feet.

'Thanks, Russell,' he said, then seeing that Pope looked as though he might follow him, he added, 'I'll see you upstairs in a minute.'

'Conference room,' Pope told him. 'Second floor.'

*Patronising little git.*

Harland waved his thanks and stalked down the corridor, shoving his way through a glass door that opened onto a tiny paved area hidden behind a panel fence. The cigarette was already in his mouth and he clicked the lighter as soon as he was outside, drawing in the smoke and breathing out the resentment he felt.

Gazing up at the grey sky, he was dimly aware that Pope was just trying to be helpful, in his own annoying way – the little man didn't know that he'd been upstairs and met with Pearce already, so it was just a common courtesy to explain where the briefing would be. He sighed and pushed the thought from his mind.

He didn't like Pope – nothing could change that – but more importantly, he hated the person he became when Pope was around.

By nine, the conference room was more than half full. A lot of the officers were obviously from Bristol – Harland nodded to a few whom he knew by sight – but a couple of groups came in late and sat together chatting, presumably the reinforcements from other divisions. At the far end of the room, beyond the rows of chairs and the single table, the broad front wall was dominated by a projector screen, currently displaying an Avon and Somerset screen saver.

He took out his phone and switched it to silent mode. The clock on the screen read 9.14 a.m.

There were quite a few people talking and Harland didn't hear the door, but when he glanced up again DCI Pearce was striding across the front of the room, pausing beside the table to pick up a small remote control.

'All right, boys and girls, let's settle down. Thanks.' He waited until the buzz of conversation died, then looked around the faces in front of him. 'Right, first of all, good morning, and I want to welcome those of you who are joining us from other divisions – good to have you all on the team, sorry it has to be under these circumstances.'

He pushed some papers aside and perched on the corner of the table.

'Anyway, let's get down to it.'

He studied the remote for a moment, then glanced back at the screen as he pressed a button. The projection changed to show a single slide with two words on it: *Operation Kingsfell.*

'Now then,' Pearce began. 'As you all know, there's a lot of media interest in this case.'

He looked at them meaningfully.

'Needless to say, we *don't* talk about it – we don't even *speculate* about it – with anyone who isn't in this room. Agreed?'

There were murmurs of assent from the assembled officers. Pearce held their gaze for a moment longer.

'Good,' he said quietly. 'Now, brace yourselves while I show you why this is so important.'

He pressed a button on the remote. Behind him, the screen showed a jarring photo of a dead woman. She was sprawled on her back, chest gashed, her clothes and the carpet beneath her stained dark with blood. There was nothing peaceful about the body – from the flailed limbs to the awful staring expression on her bruised face, everything spoke of a frantic, brutal death.

There were one or two sharp intakes of breath in the room. Pearce looked at them and nodded gravely.

'Yeah. This is Lesley Vaughn, forty-six years old, reportedly found by her husband when he got home from work on Monday evening. She's been frontally stabbed six times, and her jaw's fractured – you can see the discoloration below her mouth.' He broke off, then leaned forward. 'It's not pretty, but I need you all to really know what you're dealing with, because *you lot* are going to catch this sick fuck and get him put away.'

Harland stared at the bruising around the woman's chin. Someone had struck her very hard – a powerful blow to incapacitate the victim maybe? He frowned, trying to remember something, but Pearce was speaking again.

'Post-mortem didn't find any evidence of sexual assault. Indications are that she'd been lying for a few hours when we got to her, so time of death looks like late morning or early afternoon – last phone call from her mobile was at ten fifty-five, so, assuming that's genuine, she was still alive then.'

He paused, turning to look up at the image on the screen, then shook his head. 'No sign of forced entry to the property, and the position of the body so close to the front door suggests that she may have let the killer into the house herself . . .'

Over the next hour, Pearce laid out the background of the case. Lesley had a small cake shop in the Clifton Arcade – nothing special but it seemed to be doing all right. She and her husband Phillip were reasonably well off – he had his own dental practice in Chippenham – and there was no suggestion that they were anything other than happily married. Two grown-up children, Jack and Louisa, both away at university, and nothing but good words from the neighbours.

No enemies, no money problems, no motive. And yet, Lesley was dead.

'I *am* aware of the rumours about a sexual-assault allegation made against the husband by a former patient a couple of years ago, but I think we can safely disregard that now,' Pearce told them. 'I heard back from the investigating officer on the case – just this morning – and it turns out the patient was actually an ex-employee with an axe to grind. There was even some talk about charging the woman with wasting police time, but she had a history of mental-health problems and ended up getting some sort of medical referral. She's living in Scotland now and Strathclyde Police are checking up on her. Either way, though, it doesn't seem the husband has anything to hide on that score.'

He gestured with the remote control again. On the wall, a wide-angle photo of the downstairs hallway was replaced by a huge close-up of a bloody kitchen knife.

'Ah yes.' He turned back to face them again. 'It looks as if the murder weapon belonged to the victim. There was a matching set of these in her kitchen, and it has her prints on it, as well as a few telltale smudges. Chances are, our killer wore gloves – the SOCOs are still processing the house, but they haven't turned up anything definite yet.'

He got to his feet and paced slowly around the table.

'So.' He clapped his hands together and faced the room. 'Now we've got some grafting to do. Some of the team have already been taking statements and pulling in CCTV, identifying people who would have been in the area, running down car registrations, and so on. I need you to get to work on that list – get out and speak to potential witnesses and start building up a detailed picture of what happened on Monday, particularly between eleven and three o'clock.'

Turning to gaze at the screen, Pearce paused for a moment, then hit the remote and shut the projector off.

'I want to know anything relevant. Passers-by, strange cars, delivery vans, the lot.' He came back round to stand in front of the table. 'And stay alert, people. You never know when you might be speaking to the killer.'

# 28

The train pulled slowly out of Woking and Naysmith leaned back in his seat, stretching his arms over his head before settling down to relax. All his paperwork was finally wrapped up, the sales meeting had finished early, and he was effectively done for the day. Next week he'd begin preparing for his trip to Montreal to discuss terms with a potential new software reseller, but for now he was simply looking forward to a lazy weekend.

Gazing out of the window, he watched the low hills rising and falling, the trees and fields slipping sedately by. This train was quieter than the later one he usually caught, and he'd even managed to get a table seat in the one coach he knew had power outlets. Unzipping his bag, he drew out his laptop and plugged it in to charge while he read through the preliminary figures that the Canadian company had sent over.

Sitting opposite him, a nervous-looking man in his forties with rimless spectacles and a faint beard was reading the paper, shaking out the creases unnecessarily every time he turned a page. Naysmith frowned at him but the man didn't notice.

Diagonally across from him on the other side of the aisle, a blonde woman in her thirties was engrossed in a book. Naysmith settled back to study her. She wore a modestly unadorned black dress that hinted at an attractive figure, black stockings and elegant shoes. Her straight hair was feather-cut, just brushing her shoulders, and a simple gold necklace hung around her neck. Behind a delicate pair of glasses, her long lashes all but hid her eyes, and a natural shade of lipstick gave her an innocent quality. But it was her expression that fascinated him – so wonderfully vulnerable, with tiny flickers of emotion playing out on her face as she read.

Absently, he wondered how difficult it would be to seduce her. There was no wedding ring visible as her hand came up to turn a page – not that that had ever stopped him before.

No, the only thing really stopping him was Kim.

It wasn't as if she'd find out. He'd enjoyed so many women without her ever actually catching him. And yet somehow she seemed to sense when he was deceiving her, and he could see how much it pained her. He certainly didn't want to hurt her . . .

. . . but it didn't hurt to look.

He glanced back wearily as the man opposite made another noisy page turn, and his eye was suddenly drawn to an article with the headline 'REDLAND KILLING' on the folded back side of the paper. Leaning forward, he tried to read the smaller print below it, but the man turned another page and the story was gone.

Scowling, Naysmith leaned back in his seat and turned his head so he could study the blonde woman again, taking in the gentle rise and fall of her chest as she sat there, oblivious to all around her . . .

But his mind was elsewhere now.

They had just left Basingstoke when the man finally put his paper down on the table, yawned and sat back to look out of the window.

Naysmith leaned forward.

'Pardon me,' he spoke lightly, as though it were of no matter to him. 'Would you mind if I took a look at that?'

'I'm finished with it,' the man replied, pushing it across the table towards him. 'Be my guest.'

'Thanks.'

Naysmith took up the newspaper and began browsing through the pages, spending a moment or two on each one until he found the article he wanted.

### REDLAND KILLING: MURDER WIDOWER'S DARK PAST

*Police investigating the brutal stabbing of Bristol cake-maker Lesley Vaughn, 46, are remaining tight-lipped about serious sexual-assault allegations levelled at her wealthy husband. Phillip Vaughn, 49, who owns a successful dental practice in an affluent town near Bristol, was accused by a female patient who claims he took advantage of her in the dentist's chair. Friends of the former public schoolboy are said to be 'stunned' by the news. Meanwhile, police continue to appeal for any information relating to the crime, which has shocked the local community.*

There was more, but he had read enough. Smiling to himself, he folded the paper quietly and slid it back into the middle of the table, then leaned his head against the seat and rested his eyes for a moment.

He'd always imagined that it might be problematic if the press took an interest – *really* took an interest – in one of his victims. A huge media appeal championing the police investigation, galvanising witnesses to come forward . . . that would be a worry. But thinly veiled accusations levelled at the dead woman's husband, and snide comments about the boys in blue?

*It was so easy.*

Relaxing his shoulders back into the upholstery, he almost felt sorry for the police.

*Almost.*

Opening his eyes, he blinked at the brightness coming from the window, recognising the familiar scenery as the train began to slow for the stop at Andover. He turned back to gaze at the blonde woman. She was putting her book away now, closing her handbag and lifting her chin to look around the carriage. Their eyes met for a second and the corners of her mouth twitched in a faint smile as she got to her feet. Her figure was better than he'd thought, and his eyes followed her as she turned and made her way, swaying from seat to seat, down to the end of the carriage.

*Damn.*

He sighed and drummed his fingers on the table as the station slid into view and the train came to a standstill. He'd been so very restrained recently. Outside, he watched the blonde woman walking along the platform, turning her head slightly to catch his eye as she passed the window. He smiled at her before she was swallowed up among the other passengers, then sat back against his seat and stared up at the ceiling.

And thought of Kim.

# 29

It had rained overnight, but the dark patches of damp were retreating into the pavement cracks now, drying like last night's tears. Redland felt different today, shocked and sobered by the brutal killing in its midst.

Police Appeal posters stared out from plate-glass windows as he passed – 'MURDER' picked out in block capitals along the top, above the woman's face, frozen in that same smile he'd seen in all the local papers and TV news reports. He wondered where she had been when it was taken. A party perhaps? Or a night out with friends, laughing and enjoying herself, oblivious to how famous her image would become, or why. All the neighbourhood businesses seemed to have it – restaurants and coffee shops displaying it in their polished windows, shops with it taped up inside glass doors. A community's cry for help.

Harland slowed, staring through his own reflection at another of the pale sheets. This one had a second flyer beside it, older and faded by sunlight, appealing for information about a missing tabby cat. He considered the two posters for a moment, little A4 rectangles of tragedy, side by side, then shook his head and walked on.

Ahead of him, two middle-aged men were sitting at a pavement table – the smokers' section – outside a small café.

Steam rose from their mugs of tea as they scraped their chairs in and one coughed as he drew the ashtray towards him.

'Yeah, that's what the paper said. Stabbed to death in her own home.'

'Well, it'll be the husband that did it.' The second man took out a pouch of tobacco and carefully unfolded a cigarette paper. 'This used to be a nice neighbourhood, but now we've got murderers and all sorts living here.'

Harland stepped down into the road as he passed their table. It was the subject of almost every conversation he'd overheard this week. A whole city suburb, young and old, working class and affluent, all stunned by the thought that something so terrible could happen here.

He frowned to himself at that.

It really shouldn't matter where these things happened. That it had occurred in a quiet street, in a desirable area. That the victim had been a respectable middle-aged woman. That she had been killed in her own home.

People turned up dead all too often in the city without ever catching the public's attention or the media's interest – but they were usually in (or from) the poorer parts of town, where it was assumed that nobody could be entirely innocent. It would be gang-related, or drug-fuelled, and it would get a single headline and a day's coverage before the reporters dropped it and moved on. If a woman was sexually assaulted, there might be a more vocal campaign, but even that would soon degenerate into a bandwagon for the professional cause junkies that such crimes always seemed to excite. And if it happened too far outside the city, it would largely slip under the radar, like that poor girl they'd found on Severn Beach – somewhere else's problem. There had been pressure enough on that case. He thanked his lucky stars he wasn't leading this one.

The Redland murder was becoming a nightmare. It ticked all the boxes and the press were settling in for a long campaign, positioning themselves as the champions of the public, stirring the pot with that constant, irritating question: *What are the police doing?*

Harland clenched his fists as he walked. Did they really expect the force to show their hand, to broadcast their progress so the murderer would know when the net was drawing in around him? Did they really think that because the police were saying nothing they were also *doing* nothing?

No, they just wanted to sell papers. The questions they asked – the self-appointed, self-righteous indignation – this was what they turned to when the real world didn't suit their own personal schedules and publishing deadlines.

*What are the police doing?*

Harland shook his head in irritation. The police were doing what they *had* to do – legwork, building up a true picture of events, searching for those tiny pieces of information that might lead to an arrest *and* support a conviction.

And the media certainly weren't helping.

He paused and took a deep breath. It wasn't good for him to get angry – he had a job to do. Glancing up at the line of shopfronts, he checked the street numbers. The café he wanted was just a few doors further along. Reaching into his jacket pocket, he drew out a small notebook and reminded himself of the name he'd been given, then walked forward.

It was a small place, squeezed in between a letting agent and a picture framer, halfway along a parade of shops that crowded the narrow pavement. Harland pushed open the door and stepped inside. There were no customers, and he walked slowly up to the long counter where a woman with frizzy red hair was unwrapping the clingfilm covering from a tray of muffins.

'Won't be a moment.' She glanced up at him with a slightly harassed expression. 'I can assure you we are open, just running a little behind this morning.'

'Gill Evans?' Harland asked her.

She stared at him, then put the tray down and regarded him cautiously.

'Yes?'

'Detective Inspector Harland.' He drew out his warrant card and held it up for her to see, noting how she relaxed once she knew he was a police officer. Normally, people tensed up when he identified himself, but since the murder more had remembered that the police were there to help them. He wondered how long it would last. 'I understand you were working here last Monday?'

'Oh yeah,' she said, understanding dawning. She had a soft Welsh accent and she wiped her hands on a cloth as she faced him across the counter. 'Pam called and said the police had been round and how you might want to speak to me, 'cause she was off that day.'

'Pam?'

'Pamela Bellar – she's the owner.'

'So you were working here last Monday?'

'That's right,' Gill told him. 'I do four mornings a week, Monday to Thursday. I was in from about eight o'clock till lunchtime – can't remember what time I finished exactly, it depends on how busy we get.'

Harland took out his notebook and scribbled down the times.

'Can you remember anything that happened that day?' he asked her. 'Anything out of the ordinary?'

Gill shook her head.

'Nothing ever happens in here,' she sighed. 'It's always the same customers – people who live or work nearby.'

'Any strange cars or vans parked outside?'

'None that I remember, sorry.'

Harland gazed at her for a moment.

'That's all right,' he said. 'Can you tell me where you live, and how you get to and from work?'

'I live over in Montpelier,' Gill explained. 'I usually just walk – it's only about twenty minutes.'

Harland closed his eyes for a moment, picturing the layout of the streets.

'You come up by Redland Station?' he asked. 'And then up Alexandra Park to here?'

'I used to,' she replied, then her expression darkened. 'Don't like going past that house now – it gives you the creeps, knowing that he might be in there.'

'Knowing who might be in where?' Harland quizzed her.

'That pervy dentist,' Gill said earnestly. 'You lot still haven't arrested him, so I go down Fernbank Road instead.'

Harland sighed and massaged his temples. Everywhere it was the same story – since the piece in the paper, nobody could see past the husband, despite the fact that he'd been virtually ruled out as a suspect.

'I'd like you to think back to last Monday,' he told her patiently. 'As you were coming to work, or as you were going home, did you pass anyone or see anyone unfamiliar?'

Gill nodded seriously.

'Pam and I were discussing this the day after it happened,' she told him. 'You know, wondering if we might have actually passed the murderer in the street.'

She gave a little shudder.

'And?' Harland pressed her.

'Well, it was mostly the usual people – local people who you pass, that get familiar after a while. But I don't know their names or anything.'

'You said "mostly",' Harland mused. 'Any strangers on your walk?'

'Well, Bristol's a big place, so there's always strangers,' she replied. 'There was a woman jogging with her dog near the station . . . oh, and a delivery van outside the deli place on Gloucester Road, but it's mostly parents and kids going to school at that time in the morning.'

'How old was the woman?' Harland asked.

'In her thirties, blonde . . .' Gill shrugged. 'One of those athletic, hard-body types . . . I hate them.'

A smile touched the corners of Harland's mouth.

'Can you remember anything about the van? What colour it was?'

'It was quite big – like a transit van – and I think it was white, or a light colour anyway. I'm not really sure, sorry.'

'No, you're doing fine,' Harland told her as he finished writing down what she had told him. He looked up from the notebook. 'And what about on your way home?'

Gill sighed and frowned.

'Nothing really,' she said, picking up a bottle of water and unscrewing the top. 'Mostly familiar faces. A couple of old biddies that I hadn't seen before, and some bloke on a bike who passed me down by Redland Grove. But I didn't see the husband, if that's what you're asking.'

Harland ignored that.

'Where were the old ladies?' he asked.

'Up near the top end of Zetland Road, but they were both really old.'

'And the cyclist, what did he look like?'

Gill thought for a moment.

'Couldn't tell you,' she frowned. 'He was wearing cycling stuff – you know, Lycra shorts and one of those cycle helmets . . . He wasn't fat, if that helps?'

'Thanks . . .' Harland noted everything down, then stood thinking, tapping his pen against his chin.

Gill watched him for a moment, then leaned forward over the counter.

'So?' she asked conspiratorially. 'When are you going to arrest the dentist?'

# 30

The skies were clouding over again as Harland locked the car and turned towards the grey CID building. He yawned and walked slowly, his mind sifting through the conversations of the last few days, trying to discern anything important, anything that would help.

Pearce had a lot of people on the ground, but the team still needed that first decent opening – something to steer them in the right direction, something to indicate a suspect other than the husband . . .

. . . because it was only a matter of time before the press would be demanding they arrest him.

He frowned to himself, frustration overtaking the weariness. If only the media hadn't got involved.

Walking between the parked vehicles, he heard a car door slam and looked around. His heart sank as he saw Pope's squat figure striding towards him, but they were both making for the entrance – there was no way to avoid him.

'Morning, Russell,' he said, waiting for the shorter man to catch up.

Pope raised a hand in acknowledgement.

'Hello,' he replied. 'You look gloomy – everything OK?'

Harland gave him a bleak look, then sighed. Pope was only speaking the truth.

'Just thinking about the Redland case,' he admitted. 'And wondering when we'll get a break.'

'Still interviewing witnesses?'

'Trying to.' Harland shook his head. 'I ask them what they remember, and *they* ask me when we're going to arrest the dentist.'

Pope looked down.

'It's a pity about that,' he said quietly. 'At first, the husband looked like a dead cert for it, but . . .'

Harland nodded, a wry smile touching his face.

'It's never quite that simple, though,' he said. 'Except in the papers of course.'

Pope glanced up, then lowered his eyes once more.

'Yeah, that was unfortunate,' he agreed.

They walked round to the front of the building.

Harland reached into his pocket to find his cigarettes, then thought better of it.

'I don't know which is worse,' he said. 'Having no suspects, or having one we know didn't do it.'

Pope gazed at him thoughtfully.

'Very true,' he murmured.

He held the door open for Harland and they went inside.

The investigation had made good progress at first – one fragment of information leading to another, then another – and the palpable sense of momentum had urged them all forward. Now, however, Harland could feel the incident room becoming tense as the need for progress became more urgent.

He watched DCI Pearce speaking in hushed tones to a pair of dark-suited officers he'd not seen before, then turning to face the room. He felt guiltily glad that it wasn't him up there.

'All right, thanks, everyone.' Pearce looked around, waiting for the murmured conversations to cease, then got up and walked around to the whiteboard. 'Right then. I know you've all been out and about, running down bits and pieces, but we've got to a point where I thought it was best just to get you all in here and bring you up to speed on where we are.'

He spoke calmly – same old Pearce – but Harland thought he could sense a fresh resolve in the way he moved. Was there something new?

'So,' Pearce rubbed his hands together and nodded to a colleague at the back of the room, 'let's recap. Steve, can we get the projector on? Cheers.'

Projected onto the whiteboard beside him, a map of the north-west quarter of Bristol appeared, annotated with a number of yellow markers, and one red one.

'OK, here we are . . .' He pointed to the single red marker. 'Alexandra Park in Redland. Mrs Lesley Vaughn is at home on her day off. Sometime between eleven and three or four in the afternoon, there's a knock on her front door and she opens up to find her killer standing there. He incapacitates her with some sort of heavy metallic object, then stabs her six times in the chest with one of her own kitchen knives.'

Pearce paused, then resumed at a slower pace.

'Naturally, nobody saw anything, as many of you who've been helping with witness statements will know.' He turned back to the map. 'But with the railway running along the end of the road, there's only a few ways out of there – which brings us to the CCTV.'

He looked across to the side of the room and beckoned over a woman in her thirties with short blonde hair.

'Most of you know DS Michaela Thompson – her team have been ploughing through all the hours of footage we pulled in. Michaela, do you want to go over the perimeter sightings?'

DS Thompson walked over to the whiteboard.

'Thank you, sir.' She squinted as she stood in the projector beam, turning to the map and tracing a large semicircle around the area north of the railway line. 'We were pretty fortunate with the CCTV footage we retrieved, because we had enough to cover pretty much every way in and out – a perimeter fence if you like. We knew roughly when the crime occurred, and it's a pretty quiet neighbourhood, so we started looking at who came into the area, who went out of the area, and how long they spent there.'

'We figure the killer was with Lesley for at least ten minutes or so,' Pearce interjected. 'May have been longer, but there's no sign of robbery or any sexual assault. Sorry, Michaela, carry on.'

'That's all right, sir.' Michaela moved so that her face was out of the projector beam. 'The bottom line is, we've been able to discount the vehicles and pedestrians who were just passing through – who weren't inside the perimeter long enough – and focus on tracking down people who entered and left at the right sort of time.'

'Which is where this guy comes in.' Pearce signalled for the next slide. The image on the whiteboard changed, the map giving way to a grainy CCTV snapshot of a crossroads, with a freeze-frame blur of a figure on a bicycle, turning right to join the main road. 'Our solitary cyclist.'

Harland leaned forward, remembering his conversation with Gill Evans. She had mentioned a cyclist.

Another slide illuminated the wall, showing the same figure riding up a hill beside a line of parked cars.

'Thanks to your efforts, we've been able to identify most of the folk who were in the area at the time of the murder.' Pearce glanced over his shoulder at the blurred image behind him 'But not this bloke, right, Michaela?'

'Right, sir,' she agreed. 'He shows up at least nine times on different cameras across the city.'

A new map appeared, showing a series of green and blue markers dotted between Redland and the city centre.

'The green shows sightings we believe occurred before the murder, the blue afterwards,' she explained. 'Once we put this together, we did a second lift of CCTV from the city centre, and we got a bit of luck. Steve?'

Another slide – a sharper image this time, looking down on a pedestrian crossing. The cyclist was circled, just to the left of the frame, head turned away from the camera.

'This is about the best shot we have of him,' she said. 'And it may be nothing, but I'd just like to mention that whoever he is, this man *never* looks up near the cameras. Not once, which is fairly unusual.'

'Thanks, Michaela.' Pearce moved over to stand beside the whiteboard. 'So there he is. About six foot one, six foot two, athletic build, a clean-shaven male with dark hair, from what little we can see under that cycle helmet. Everyone got that?'

Harland stared at the image, trying to see the man beneath the cycle gear, but the cameras hadn't captured much.

'Now, this may be connected, or it may not, but we've also turned up a name that needs looking into.' Pearce waved to the back of the room, and a photograph of a well-groomed man in his fifties flashed up behind him. 'This is Reuben Cort. Used to run a catering business with Lesley, and officers were called to a disturbance involving the two of them at the beginning of last year. There's clearly some history there, and maybe a motive if we're lucky – I've got some people on him and I'll update you soon as poss.'

Harland studied the pink face, the shiny bald pate and the clipped white hair; noted the expensive designer spectacles.

'Right then, boys and girls.' Pearce clapped his large hands together, and inclined his head towards the door. 'Don't let me keep you.'

# 31

Harland walked out into the car park at dusk and stopped for a moment, yawning and rubbing the back of his neck. The urgency and the hours of a major case were tiring, but in a good way – plenty to occupy him and keep his thoughts from straying, turning inward. He gazed up at the nearby concrete flyover, listening to the constant rumble of traffic passing by as he reached into his pocket for the cigarette packet. There hadn't been much time to smoke today, or to eat – lunch had been a chocolate bar from one of the vending machines – and he realised that he was extremely hungry. There was probably something in the freezer at home, but the thought of cooking seemed like too much trouble tonight. Promising himself something better, he left the cigarettes in his pocket and began walking to his car.

It was a little out of his way, but he seemed to hit mostly green lights as he drove through the centre and he was in an unusually good mood when he parked on Princess Victoria Street. Getting out of the car, he stretched, then walked back along the pavement. The plate-glass windows of the fish and chip shop were large and spotless, with a welcoming light streaming out from the bright interior, and the tempting aroma of hot food to draw him in.

It was busy, but there was always a queue in here. Taking his place at the back of the line, he gazed up at the menu boards and smiled, remembering his first visit. Mendel had brought him in on the way home from Portishead one evening and had quietly pointed out the number of Scottish accents among the clientele. 'Always a good sign, that is,' the big man had whispered. 'Those Jocks can always sniff out the best chip shops.'

There were three people serving behind the polished-tile counter, all wearing smart matching aprons. When Harland reached the front of the queue, a short woman with curly blonde hair flashed him a hurried smile.

'Hi, what can I get you?'

'Large cod and chips, please,' he said, glancing at the menu, then looking towards the glass-fronted fridge. 'Oh, and a bottle of 7Up.'

She turned quickly and got his drink, setting it down on the counter.

'There you are. It'll just be a couple of minutes for the fish, OK?'

'Thanks.'

Harland paid her, then took his bottle and went to perch on one of the few unoccupied stools at the window. Staring out through the gold letters painted on the glass, he watched people hurrying along on the opposite side of the road – well-dressed, respectable types – while his mind slid gently back to the case. This was only a couple of streets away from where Lesley Vaughn had worked. It was a nice enough area – you'd think you were safe round here. Then again, hadn't Vicky Sutherland worked somewhere nearby too? Of course, both women had been killed in other places – Lesley at home in Redland, and Vicky over at Severn Beach . . .

He paused, frowning slightly.

*They both worked close by. Maybe a mile and a half, two miles apart?*

He closed his eyes, trying to picture the layout of the streets, quickly travelling the route in his head, looking for . . . what? Two murders in the same city didn't mean anything. There was nothing to connect the victims, and the killings were very different. And yet . . .

'Excuse me?'

He opened his eyes. Several people were staring at him as his glance swept along the queue to the woman leaning impatiently across the counter.

'Large cod and chips, yes?' she repeated, giving him a stern look.

'Sorry.' Harland jumped to his feet.

'Salt and vinegar?' the woman asked.

'Please.' He moved to the front of the queue and offered her an apologetic smile as she handed his food to him, neatly packed in a warm cardboard box, but she was already turning to smile at a more attentive customer.

It felt chilly, stepping outside, after the cosy interior of the takeaway, but his thoughts were firmly back at work now.

*Two victims, both working in the same neighbourhood, with no obvious reason for either killing.*

For a moment, he thought of taking his phone out and calling Pearce – but what would he say?

No, better to think it through a bit first, not tip his hand too quickly like he'd done with Blake the year before. He'd sound Pearce out gently. There might be no connection between the two murders. But if there was, then that changed everything. And he would have a lot to contribute to the investigation. Lost in thought, he carried his fish and chips back to the car.

# 32

*Tuesday, 5 August*

An extra briefing had been scheduled for eleven o'clock and the room was already full when Harland arrived, picking his way to the back to find a seat. Pearce walked in just before the hour, shirtsleeves rolled up, carrying a bottle of water. Spotting someone sitting at the front, his face broke into a broad smile and he changed course to greet him.

'All right, Nick, didn't expect to see you this morning,' he nodded. 'You not over in Bath?'

'Paula's doing it instead.' Nick was a broad man, with spiky brown hair and a dark jacket.

'Blimey, they won't know what's hit 'em. Anyway, glad you're with us.'

Pearce clapped him on the shoulder then continued his walk to the table at the front of the room, where he put the bottle down and turned to face his team.

'All right then,' he said, raising his voice a little. 'Let's settle down, everyone, thank you.'

He sat on the edge of the table as the murmured conversations died away.

'OK. First off, I just want to say that I'm pleased with the work you lot have been putting in on this. Things have been moving quickly, and there's not been a lot of time to chat, but credit where it's due and all that.'

He glanced across the assembled faces and flashed a quick grin.

'Anyway, that's enough of the sentimental stuff. Down to business.'

He reached across for the bottle of water and started to unscrew the cap.

'It looks like we've got a development on the Reuben Cort angle. Most of you know DC Peter Leighton – Pete, why don't you come up here and fill us in.'

Leighton got to his feet and moved to the front of the room. He was a thin man in his forties, with short dark hair swept back and a pale complexion. Wearing a tan jacket and black trousers, he approached the table stiffly and cleared his throat.

'Thank you, sir.' He turned to address the room. 'Most of you were here when we discussed Reuben Cort before – single chap in his fifties, Lesley Vaughn's former business partner.'

There was a murmur of agreement from the room.

'Now he's not got any form *as such*, but there was an incident in March last year when uniformed officers were called out to a disturbance at the company's former premises over in Bishopston. There's nothing in the reports to indicate that it was anything more than a shouting match, but in light of recent events we looked into it a bit further. The responding officer was Jackie Hughes – some of you may know her – and she remembered it quite well.'

He cleared his throat again, then continued.

'At first, Reuben and Lesley had been running it as more of a general catering firm, doing weddings, corporate functions, that sort of thing – apparently he had some aspirations of being a chef – but the business was essentially failing. At some point, Lesley bought him out and decided to try specialising in *her* area of expertise, the cake-making.'

Leighton had warmed up a little now, and was pacing back and forth in front of the table.

'Business picked up and she started making money – Reuben wasn't too pleased. He said she'd taken *his* clients, felt she owed him, but she wasn't having any of it. That's when things came to a head – Reuben decided he was entitled to some of his old company property. Basically, he showed up one day, tried to walk out with a load of equipment, and Lesley called the police. When Jackie got there, they were screaming at each other. She doesn't remember any specific threats, and she managed to calm things down, but there was no love lost between them.'

Pearce took a swig of water, then leaned forward.

'I asked Pete to go and have a word with Reuben, sound him out a bit.'

'Yes, we spoke to him yesterday,' Leighton continued. 'He lives in a semi-detached place over in Ashley Down, seemed really edgy when we showed up. Understandable, I suppose – Lesley's been all over the news and things weren't good between them – but even so . . .'

He frowned and shook his head.

'First thing he said when he opened the door to me was that he didn't have anything to do with it, and he just got more and more defensive from there on.'

'You reckon his alibi's a bit thin, yes?' Pearce interrupted.

'That's right,' Leighton agreed. 'He was vague about his movements for that Monday. Says he spent the afternoon in the city centre – did some shopping, went for a coffee, that sort of thing – but there was nobody with him. So to my mind, he's still very much in the frame.'

Pearce got slowly to his feet.

'Cheers, Pete.' He paused, then addressed the room. 'Now, this Reuben bloke may well have nothing to do with the murder, but until we can rule him out, he's going to be a person of interest, and that's a bloody short list at the moment. We're already running down a credit-card receipt he's given us, and DS Thompson's team . . .' he cast around the room until he spotted her '. . . are working through CCTV from the shops around Broadmead and Cabot Circus. It shouldn't be hard to figure out whether his story's accurate or not, right, Michaela?'

'Right, sir,' DS Thompson replied.

'Good. In the meantime, I think we want some of you to nose around discreetly, see what we can learn about this bloke. General background's OK, but we're particularly interested in his movements and behaviour around that Monday, immediately before and after the main event.'

Pearce nodded to Leighton, who returned to his seat.

In the front row, Nick raised his hand.

'What about the cyclist?'

'We're still after him,' Pearce replied. 'I want to know who he is, even if it's just to rule him out. More CCTV for Michaela's lot to go through.'

Harland hung back a little as the room emptied, then followed Pearce out into the corridor.

'Got a moment, sir?' he asked.

'Sure.' Pearce turned to face him. 'What's your mind?'

Harland took a deep breath. *How best to put it?*

'Well,' he began. 'I was just thinking about Lesley's personal effects, and the Redland crime scene . . .'

'Yes?'

'I was wondering if there was anything missing . . .' He hesitated. 'Or added.'

'Added?' Pearce frowned. 'What do you mean?'

Harland shrugged noncommittally.

'Objects that just . . . don't belong,' he explained.

Pearce looked at him thoughtfully.

'You reckon this isn't an isolated killing?' he asked quietly.

'I think it's something to consider,' Harland replied.

Pearce studied him for a moment, then turned and motioned for him to follow. They walked along the corridor to a small, windowless interview room. Pearce closed the door behind them.

'All right,' he said. 'What sort of objects are we talking about?'

'Small, innocuous things,' Harland explained. 'A door key that doesn't fit, someone else's supermarket loyalty card, that sort of thing.'

Pearce nodded to himself.

'I'll check again, but there was nothing out of place as far as I know.' He shot Harland a meaningful look. 'In the meantime, I really need you to be a hundred per cent focused on Reuben Cort.'

'OK.'

'Because if Blake hears you're still banging on about the Severn Beach thing . . . well, that doesn't do anyone any good, yeah?'

Had he been that obvious? Harland closed his eyes briefly then sighed in agreement. 'Yes, sir.'

Pearce looked at him carefully, then smiled.

'Good man, Graham.'

Downstairs, the smoking area at the back of the building was deserted. Harland pulled the door shut behind him and gazed up at the grey sky.

Was he losing his perspective? Obsessing about old cases?

He took out a cigarette and turned towards the wall, shielding the flame as he lit up, then sighed out the smoke. There was something about the Redland murder, about the way it was done and the complete lack of evidence, that troubled him. He'd had that same feeling on the Severn Beach case.

*And hadn't that one involved an initial incapacitating blow too?*

There had been nothing on that case for months . . . apart from the woman who'd stopped in at Portishead. He frowned, wondering if he could get away with requesting a ping for her boyfriend's phone, just to see where he'd been that day – it was galling to have a suspicion and not be able to check it. But a mobile check would cost money, and that would doubtless bring it to Pearce's attention. He couldn't risk that, not now, but there might be another way.

Jamming the cigarette into the corner of his mouth, he reached into his pocket and drew out his phone. Thumbing down the list of numbers, he considered calling Mendel, then decided against it – partly because he felt foolish after Pearce had seen through him, partly because he knew what Mendel would say. He dialled the number for Portishead instead, and asked to be put through to the main office.

'All right, sir.' Josh sounded surprised to hear from him.

'Hi.' Harland did his best to sound cheerful. 'Can you do me a quick favour?'

'Sure.'

'I need a mobile number for Kim Nichols? I think she lives in Salisbury or somewhere near there, but she came into Portishead a while back, so she'll be on the file.'

'Kim Nichols . . .' Josh's voice repeated it slowly, with the faint clatter of the keyboard as he typed in the name. 'Is this for the Redland case?'

'No, no.' Harland assumed a disinterested tone. 'Just something that's been niggling me, something I want to clear up.'

'How's Redland going?'

'Early days, Josh. How's everyone back there?'

'OK, thanks, usual stuff . . .' He paused. 'Ah, Kim Nichols. Here you go.'

He read out the number. Harland held the phone up with his shoulder as he scribbled the digits in his notebook, then thanked Josh and hung up. Straightening, he took the cigarette from his mouth and stubbed it out.

It was probably nothing. Kim hadn't even been sure if her boyfriend had done anything at Severn Beach, and there was nothing to link that case with Redland. But it wouldn't do any harm to check.

He weighed the phone in his hand for a moment, then dialled and lifted it to his ear.

One ring . . . two . . . three . . . click.

'Hello?'

'Hi,' Harland greeted her. 'Is that Kim Nichols?'

'Yes.' Her tone was slightly guarded. 'Who's this?'

'It's DI Graham Harland from Avon and Somerset Police. We spoke when you came to Portishead?'

There was a long pause before she answered. 'Yes?'

'Are you able to talk for a moment?' he asked her.

'Um . . .' She was hesitant. 'Can you hold on?'

'Of course.'

Harland listened to a succession of muffled sounds. Was she covering the mouthpiece? Moving to somewhere with more privacy before she spoke to him? He wondered where she was . . .

'What is it?' Her voice came back suddenly, but she was speaking in an urgent whisper now. 'Why are you calling me?'

'I'm sorry to trouble you.' He suddenly felt bad for spooking her. 'I just wanted to ask you something—'

'I told you before,' she hissed. 'That was all a mistake. Please, I really don't want Rob to know that I spoke to you.'

'Kim, it's all right.' He tried to sound calm. 'I'm not contacting him, I'm contacting you.'

'But why?'

'I just have a question, something I wanted to check, OK?' There was another long pause.

'I don't see what good it will do.' She still sounded suspicious, but the initial shock of his call was wearing off. 'What's the question?'

'I appreciate your help,' he told her. 'I was just wondering if you knew where Rob was on the twenty-first of July? That was a Monday, the week before last.'

'Monday before last?' She seemed almost relieved, as though she had feared a more troubling question. 'I think he was working from home . . . yes, he was at home all day that Monday.'

There was no hesitation in her voice now.

'You're sure?' Harland pressed her.

'Yes, I remember because it was the day I had my car serviced.'

Not defensive, just matter-of-fact. Harland rubbed his eyes and sighed in frustration. It had only been a feeling, and yet . . .

'Why?' Kim was becoming wary again now. 'What's this about?'

'It's nothing,' he told her. 'Just something I wanted to check, but you've cleared it up for me.'

'You're not going to tell Rob about me, are you?' She sounded anxious, like she had done on that afternoon back in Portishead.

'Don't worry,' he reassured her. 'That's all I wanted to ask. I'm sorry to have bothered you.'

'That's it?'

'That's it. Thanks for your help.'

'Oh.' There was relief in her voice. 'OK. Well, goodbye then.'

'Bye.'

Harland ended the call and stared at his phone for a moment before putting it back into his pocket. It looked as though Pearce had been right.

# 33

Kim stood motionless, a lonely figure on the rickety metal fire escape that jutted out from the top floor of the old white building. Behind her, the gabled Salisbury rooftops huddled together like gloomy slate peaks, obscuring the narrow streets and the bustle of the city centre below.

She stared down at the phone in her hand, the back of it still warm from Harland's jarring call. Perhaps this was good. Perhaps this meant it was finally over. Ever since her stupid visit to Portishead she'd been on edge, worried that the police would make some clumsy move and betray her to Rob. But Harland had sounded as though he was satisfied. Maybe she could forget all about it, try to move on.

A breeze gusted up through the gap between the buildings, stirring old cigarette butts on a section of flat roof just below her. She'd come outside with just her thin blouse, but she folded her arms against the cold air, not ready to go back inside just yet, needing a moment more to compose herself. Part of her yearned to call Rob, to hear his voice and make-believe that everything was all right, but she couldn't tell him what had upset her. She couldn't tell anyone.

Sighing, she began picking absently at the flaky black paint on the fire-escape handrail, watching the pieces twirl down into a mossy gutter below.

*Rob . . .*

Her thoughts went to him, and she turned her face to gaze

up at the sky. He was working from home again today, like he had been that Monday. She wondered why Harland had asked her about that, but quickly decided to put it out of her mind. Whatever it was, Rob wasn't involved. He'd been at home all day, thank goodness. There was nothing to worry about.

She turned, her heels clicking noisily on the metal fire escape, then stooped to move the brick she'd used to wedge open the door before stepping back inside. Pulling the door shut behind her, she started down the corridor, her mind still on that Monday.

She'd taken his car to work because hers was at the garage. They hadn't spoken during the day as far as she could remember – but of course, he'd left his phone in the boot of the car.

Walking slowly back into the office, she went across to her desk and sat down. Placing her hand on the mouse, she moved it to wake the computer, but her gaze drifted down to stare at the tiny snapshot of Rob she kept in a little heart-shaped frame beside her computer.

*What had happened on the twenty-first?*

She looked up at the screen, tempted by the Internet icon and the thought of searching for things that had happened on that day . . .

*No.*

Everything was fine. He was at home all day, she knew that. He must have been.


'Are you all right?'

Rob was studying her, genuine concern on his face.

'I'm fine.' Kim gave him a brief smile and let her eyes drop back to the mug of hot chocolate she was holding. 'Just thinking about something that happened at work today.'

'Want to talk about it?' he asked, reaching forward to touch her hair.

She shook her head.

'Fair enough.' He leaned back into the sofa and yawned.

She had felt uncomfortable around him all evening, withdrawing from him, avoiding conversation. It was like that first day at the cottage, after he'd told her. But there were no tears this time, no release, just that gnawing sense of dread.

He yawned again, and got slowly to his feet, stretching.

'I've got an early start – Nottingham tomorrow,' he told her. 'You coming up?'

Kim glanced at the paperback on the coffee table, then gazed up at him.

'I think I'll sit and read down here for a while,' she said softly. 'I'll try not to wake you when I come to bed.'

'OK.' He leaned over her, kissing the top of her head, then wrapping his arms around her. 'Goodnight.'

She closed her eyes, feeling the warmth of his embrace. But there was no comfort in it any more.

'Night.'

She sat alone, huddled into the corner of the sofa, knees drawn up to her chest, pressing her toes into the cushions. Above her, she heard the vague rush of the bathroom cistern filling, and the muffled footsteps as he came through to the bedroom. Her eyes watched the ceiling, following his movements, listening for the faint creaking as he got into bed and settled for the night.

Now, the house was silent. Her book lay untouched on the table. All the other distractions were gone and she was alone with her fears.

She unfolded herself slowly, sitting forward and lowering her feet to the floor. Getting up, she moved quietly, padding through to the kitchen to retrieve her work bag, then hurrying back to the relative warmth of the living room. Glancing up at the ceiling again, she paused to listen for any sounds, then unzipped the bag and drew out her laptop.

*It was silly. She already knew where he'd been that Monday. What good would this do?*

But the doubts and the curiosity were overwhelming. Harland had called her for a reason, and she had to know.

Opening her laptop, she stared at the screen for a moment, then opened a browser window. Setting the search for 'News', she hesitated, then entered 21 July and pressed the 'Enter' key.

Part of her had already guessed what the top story might be, but she hadn't been sure of it until the words came up on the screen in front of her. The Redland murder had been on the news all that week – *and it had happened on the Monday.* Her stomach knotted and she lurched forward, one hand across her mouth, the other gripping her side as she hugged herself.

*No!*

He wouldn't have done something like that. He *couldn't* have. And there was no way he could have made it to Bristol and back – not from the village, not without a car.

She clicked frantically to close the browser window, then pulled the screen forward until her laptop snapped shut. Taking a breath, she got uncertainly to her feet, trying to reign in her imagination.

*Stop it! He was here all day.*

She hesitated, then walked slowly out into the hallway, pausing at the foot of the stairs.

*He couldn't have done it.*

Her hand reached out to touch the banister rail as she stared up into the darkness.

*Could he?*

# part 3
# SWITCH

# 34

Dessert, when it arrived, was faultless. Naysmith had decided to try one of the specials – a beautiful tarte au citron, delicately seasoned with ginger and lime, while Kim had asked for her usual dark chocolate brownie with mint. Both were presented exquisitely, like everything else they'd enjoyed, and the waiter set the gleaming white plates before them with a deferential nod.

'I'd like an espresso please,' Naysmith told him, then turned to Kim. 'Do you want anything?'

She was wearing a simple blue-grey dress, with her dark hair down and tumbling across her pale shoulders, waking an impatient arousal in him.

'Just a cappuccino, please,' she said quietly.

'Of course.' The waiter turned and walked away.

Naysmith gazed at her for a moment longer, then took up his fork and sliced off a thin piece of the tart, tasting it thoughtfully.

'Oh, you should have ordered this,' he sighed as his face melted into a grin. 'I've tried some serious desserts here, but . . . wow!'

She looked at him and, for a brief instant, there was a flicker of something troubled in her expression, but she seemed to brighten a little, reaching over to his plate with her own fork.

'Hey!' he protested. 'Just a taste.'

'You can have some of mine.' She deftly cut a corner off the tart.

'You know I don't care for mint.'

'Sorry,' she shrugged, popping the stolen piece into her mouth. 'Oh, you're right. That's good.'

'I told you,' he gently scolded her. 'You should listen to me.'

Another strange look flickered across her face, but then it was gone again.

'I do listen to you,' she said softly.


Naysmith held the door open for Kim and followed her out into the quiet stillness of the village evening. The sounds of the restaurant faded behind them as they walked under the darkening sky.

'I wish I wasn't going tomorrow,' he sighed, gazing up at the shadowy clouds that had crept in from the horizon. 'A couple of days off, a relaxing meal with you, and suddenly the idea of Montreal isn't appealing at all.'

Kim was staring across the road to the tree-lined village green.

'Look,' she whispered.

Three wild ponies were grazing quietly on the cricket pitch opposite them, dim brown shapes against the dusky gloom of the woods. Naysmith smiled. They were inside the bounds of the New Forest here, where the roads had no fences and animals were able to roam at will.

'They look so beautiful,' she murmured. 'So free.'

'Beautiful,' Naysmith agreed, running his hand down the back of her dress and caressing her bottom. 'Come on, let's get you home.'

He turned and walked across the gravel to the broad grassy

verge where they'd parked. Kim stared at the ponies for a moment, then followed him to the car.

It was dark when they got home. Naysmith was feeling eager now, and he toyed with the idea of taking her straight upstairs to bed, but Kim disappeared into the kitchen and emerged with a tall glass of Bombay Sapphire and tonic.

*What the hell. It would give their food time to go down.*

They settled down in the living room to watch an episode from the French crime series box set he'd bought.

'A good chance for you to brush up on your *français* before you go,' she told him.

'*Je veux te baiser*,' he said innocently.

'What's that?' she asked.

'It means, "Where is the post office?"' he lied. She was wedged into the far corner of the sofa, and he reached across, pulling her close and putting his arm around her. 'Come here. I won't be able to do this tomorrow night.'

'No,' she agreed, leaning her head against his shoulder. 'You won't.'

He enjoyed the show, settling back and stroking Kim's hair as the warmth of the gin soothed him, but towards the end of the programme, Kim groaned and sat up.

'What's wrong?' he asked her.

'I don't know,' she replied, shifting position as though trying to get comfortable. 'I'm not feeling that great.'

'What did you have tonight?'

'The scallops . . . but they tasted fine.'

Naysmith frowned, patting her gently on the back. A few moments later, Kim shook her head.

'I'm sorry, Rob, I'm feeling rotten,' she said quietly.

He reached over, touching her forehead.

'You don't have a temperature,' he said. 'Is it your stomach? Do you feel as if you're going to throw up?'

'I'm not sure,' she replied. 'I just feel awful and my head is starting to hurt. I think I should go and lie down.'

'Do you want me to come upstairs with you?' he asked, rising to steady her as she got to her feet.

'No, no.' She smiled at him weakly and pushed him back onto the sofa. 'You finish your drink and watch another episode. I just want to lie quietly and let this pass.'

She moved unsteadily from the room. Naysmith watched her go, then turned to scowl at the TV. After a moment, he reached for the remote control and rewound the DVD a couple of scenes, then slumped back in his seat and stared at the screen.

Upstairs, he heard the rush of water as the toilet flushed. A moment later, his eyes turned to the ceiling, tracing the muffled footsteps above him. She was getting into bed.

When the episode ended, he got to his feet and wandered through to the kitchen. The blue bottle of gin was on the table and he poured himself another, topping it up with tonic and a handful of ice from the freezer. At the foot of the stairs, he hesitated.

There was no point in disturbing her too soon. Maybe let her rest a while and hope she felt better.

He turned around and trudged back to the living room. Sinking down onto the sofa, he took a long sip of his drink, then pressed 'Play' on the remote and settled in for a lonely evening.

It was late when he finally switched off the lights and went upstairs. The house was silent apart from the soft creak of his feet on the steps and he made his way along the landing to the bathroom. Tired now, he leaned against the wall as he used the toilet, then flushed and went over to the sink. The face that stared back at him from the mirror looked dejected. This wasn't the evening he'd had in mind.

The bedroom was in darkness, and he used the light from his phone to find his way across the carpet before switching on his reading lamp. Kim was lying motionless, long hair tumbling over her bare shoulders, her face turned away from him. He undressed quietly, dropping his clothes in the laundry basket as he went, then pulled back the duvet to get into bed.

Easing himself down, he reached out a hand to stroke her back. Oddly, she was still wearing her bra and, as his hand worked lower, her underwear too. She really must have been feeling poorly.

He caressed her for a moment, running his hands over her smooth skin, down the length of her back to reveal the beautiful curve of her bottom, but she showed no sign of stirring. Finally, he gave it up, and gently pulled the duvet back to cover her again.

*Definitely* not the evening he'd had in mind.

With a sigh he let his head fall back into the pillows, stared up at the ceiling, and waited for sleep to come.

# 35

She got up early, sliding silently out of bed so as not to wake him. Listening to his steady breathing, she crept around the bed and clicked the switch on the clock radio, turning the alarm off. He looked so different when he was sleeping – still strong and attractive, but without the edge of menace she felt when he looked at her. She stood there for a minute, gazing down on him thoughtfully before the memory of the previous evening came back to her.

Just a couple more hours to get through.

Yawning, she went down to the kitchen and made herself a coffee. Sitting at the table, she sipped her drink cautiously, inhaling the steam as she closed her eyes and listened for any sound from upstairs. But there was nothing.

How would he be this morning?

She glanced up at the clock – it was almost nine and he'd have to be on the road by eleven. Quietly, she got to her feet and opened the fridge to find the bacon and eggs, then slowly started preparing a large breakfast. The less time he had this morning the better.

When she did go upstairs, she found him still fast asleep. Sitting down on the edge of the bed, she reached out a hand and gently stroked his hair.

'Hey, sleepy.'

He stirred, his face creasing into a frown, then rolled over onto his back, one arm flung across his eyes to shield them.

'What time is it?' he asked her groggily.

'It's nine thirty,' she told him calmly. 'Breakfast is ready.'

'What?' He struggled up into a sitting position and rubbed his eyes. 'Shit, why didn't you wake me?'

'You looked like you needed the rest.' She ran her hand down the duvet, following the outline of his leg. 'Come downstairs and eat before it gets cold.'

By the time they'd finished eating, it was after ten. Kim stood up and took the plates over to the counter. Rob yawned and stretched in his chair.

'Feeling better this morning?' he asked her.

'A bit better,' she said, remembering that she was supposed to have been ill last night. 'I think I just needed to sleep it off, whatever it was.'

She heard him sliding his chair back, the quiet footsteps behind her before his arms encircled her waist, drawing her backwards against him. Her heart sank as she felt his hardness rubbing against her.

'Somebody's excited,' she said lightly.

He bowed his head, nuzzling her neck as he pressed his body close to her.

'You smell so good,' he whispered.

She found a suitable smile and wriggled around so that she was facing him.

'Hey,' she said, looking up at him. 'Don't get yourself too excited. You have a plane to catch, remember?'

'We've got a little time . . .' he murmured, his hands snaking downwards.

'Please, Rob.' Her hand gently took his and moved it back

up. 'Let's not rush it this morning. You're only away till Tuesday.'

She stood up on tiptoes and kissed him lightly on the lips, then untangled herself from his arms.

'You'd better go and get ready,' she said, nodding towards the clock on the wall.

He stood there, his face suddenly unreadable, like a stranger's. For a moment, she felt a flutter of fear, wondering if he could sense her thoughts, see what was concealed behind her eyes. Her pulse quickened, but she found it impossible to look away. Shit, maybe she'd have to distract him, offer to relieve him before he left for the airport . . .

But then he groaned, and smiled – suddenly familiar again.

'I'm going to be uncontrollable by the time I get back,' he warned her.

'Sounds exciting,' she said softly.

He stepped forward quickly, surprising her, and kissed her deeply. She closed her eyes as his arms pulled her tight against him, letting him kiss her until he had to break off. Releasing her, he shook his head longingly and grinned.

'Damn,' he said. Then, before she could say anything, he turned and hurried upstairs to get ready.

'Have you got everything?' she asked him.

Rob stood in the hallway, pulling his laptop bag over his shoulder and extending the handle on his travel case.

'I think so.' He patted his pockets, then checked inside his jacket. 'Passport, mobile, laptop, wallet – that's all that matters. If I've forgotten anything else I can always buy it when I get there.'

He moved close to her and kissed her tenderly on the forehead, then raised his hand to gently lift her chin so he could gaze down into her eyes. She smiled shyly for as long as she could, then looked down as the panic began to grip her.

'Go on,' she told him. 'You'd better get moving. I don't want you driving too fast and taking risks.'

Rob smiled. Grabbing his case, he opened the front door and stepped outside, where he glanced over his shoulder.

'My beautiful girl . . . you really do care about me, don't you?'

He turned and walked over towards the car. Kim stood on the doorstep and watched him leave.

He was right, of course, and that was what made it so difficult. Part of her really *did* care about him. But that wasn't enough any more.

'Goodbye,' she whispered.

She pushed the door, feeling it shut with a heavy click, then stood alone in the hallway, listening to the silence. She had got this far, but the hardest part was still to come. Turning, she took a couple of steps forward, wondering which room to go into first, but as she hesitated the enormity of what lay ahead threatened to overwhelm her.

She had the whole weekend. Another hour wouldn't make any difference.

Biting her lip, she started slowly upstairs, breaking into a run as she reached the landing and rushing to throw herself down onto the bed. Eyes screwed shut, she sobbed quietly into the duvet, letting the frustration spill out. Why did it have to be this way?

She found herself curled up, hugging his pillow, as though it might comfort her.

As though anything could comfort her now.

Sitting up, she rubbed her eyes and dried her tears. She had four days, but she knew that if she didn't make a start now, she might lose her courage completely. Getting to her feet, Kim looked around the bedroom.

It was time.

She spent the next few hours wandering through the house as though in a waking dream, picking things up, trying to decide whether they mattered or whether they could be discarded. Everything she touched tore at her, stabbing her with guilt – she was a thief, stealing her own possessions.

The wardrobes didn't upset her as much as she thought they might. She knew she couldn't take all of her clothes, but perhaps that wasn't such a bad thing. Over the course of the afternoon, she picked out her favourite winter things and stowed them carefully at the bottom of her large suitcase – she wouldn't need them for a while – and managed to perform a heartbreaking initial triage on her shoes.

She forced herself to keep going, but it was all just too upsetting. And she hadn't even thought about the more personal things – jewellery, photographs, letters. She bowed her head.

Why did it have to be so hard? Why did things go wrong with everyone she ever cared about?

*Stop it!*

She couldn't afford those kinds of thoughts, not now. Taking a deep breath, she got slowly to her feet and went downstairs to make herself a coffee.

Sitting there at the kitchen table, she leaned forward, propping up her forehead with one hand, allowing her mind to wander. Another relationship, another disaster. Why couldn't things work out for her?

She began to think about putting it off, about giving him time, a chance to change . . .

But as her fingernail traced out invisible heart shapes on

the rough wood of the table, she reminded herself that he couldn't change the past.

He had killed a woman.

Nothing would alter that. Nothing would bring her back. And nothing could erase that knowledge, or prevent her seeing a murderer when she looked at him.

Opening her eyes, Kim drained her coffee and slowly got to her feet. She knew she had to do this.

She unplugged the phones at the wall and switched off her mobile. Upstairs, she went into Rob's wardrobe and found the pile of emergency cash that he kept in the house. Folding the wad of notes, she added it to the bulging brown envelope that she had hidden in her bag. She had been quietly with-drawing money for the last few days – on Monday morning, she would go to the bank and empty their joint account. She wondered if he'd understand. It wasn't about revenge – far from it. She just wanted out – *needed* out – and she knew she wouldn't be able to escape him without money.

As she closed her bag, she briefly wondered about leaving him a note to explain, to beg him to let her go . . . but what words could she possibly write to him now?

She sighed and sank down onto the bed. Suddenly, she felt so very tired. Surrendering to it, she gratefully lay back on the duvet and wondered what she was going to do. Whatever happened, this time there would be no coming back.

# 36

Harland stood back from the urinal and zipped up his trousers. There was a splutter and a hiss as water flushed down into the white porcelain, filling the bathroom with the caustic smell of citrus and bleach. Behind him, the door opened.

'All right, Graham.' Pearce strode across to the urinals and took his place, staring grimly at the tiled wall.

'Morning, sir.' Harland leaned over the sink and worked the soap dispenser.

'You heard? About Reuben *bloody* Cort?'

Pearce sounded angry. Harland glanced across at him.

'No,' he said, turning on the tap. 'What is it?'

Pearce closed his eyes, as though composing himself.

'Remember there was a gap in his afternoon? A couple of hours when we couldn't find him?'

'Yeah.' Harland nodded.

'Well, we found him,' Pearce scowled. 'Turns out he was busy shagging some young guy in a hotel on Temple Way.'

'Oh!' Harland paused, then continued washing his hands. 'Explains why he was being evasive, I suppose.'

Pearce snorted.

'I don't give a toss if he's a shirtlifter or not. But apparently "some money may have changed hands", which was why he didn't feel inclined to tell us.'

Harland shook his head. 'Charming.'

'Yeah,' Pearce grinned. 'And not really the sort of chat to be having when you've got your knob out.'

Harland chuckled, turning away and placing his hands under the dryer.

'So we've got all his time accounted for now?' he asked.

'Yes.' Pearce moved across to the sinks, raising his voice to be heard over the noise of the dryer. 'Hotel receptionist remembers him and his little friend, and we're getting CCTV to confirm. But the stupid bastard's put us back days chasing his shadow.'

Harland moved aside so that Pearce could dry his hands.

'So if he's out of the picture, where does that leave us?'

'We're back to the cyclist,' Pearce shrugged. 'Michaela reckons she may have a sighting at Temple Meads. It's not confirmed yet, but she seems pretty sure.'

Harland held the door open as they walked out into the corridor.

'Well, I suppose that's something,' he shrugged. 'Do we know what train he got on?'

'Yeah, Michaela figured it out.' Pearce smiled grimly. 'Unfortunately, this is where things get harder. She went back to First Great Western about getting CCTV footage from the train, but by the time she got to them it had been deleted . . .'

He paused, looking out of the window at the Bristol skyline.

'We're checking stations along the route, but there are different operating companies and not many keep their footage this long. If our cyclist got off at one of the bigger towns, we might find something, otherwise . . .'

He sighed, turning back to Harland

'Anyway, I just wanted to say it's been good having you with us.'

Harland looked at him questioningly.

'Am I going back to Portishead?' he asked.

'Yeah,' Pearce nodded. 'Wrap up whatever you're doing by the end of the day. The boys from MCU are getting involved now. They'll be following up on the cyclist, so we'll be standing down our own reinforcements. Sorry I couldn't keep you longer.'

'I appreciate that,' Harland shrugged. 'It's been good.'

Pearce clapped him on the shoulder, then started down the corridor. A moment later, he turned and called out.

'Oh, and do us a favour, Graham?'

'Sir?'

'Take that genius Pope with you?'

Harland smiled as Pearce raised a hand in farewell and strode away.

# 37

Naysmith couldn't sleep. Peering uncertainly through the darkness, he squinted to make out the red digits on the bedside alarm clock: 04.53. He turned over for a moment, trying to get comfortable, trying to shut out the steady hum of the hotel air conditioning, but his mind was awake. Sighing, he reached out a searching hand for the lamp switch, shutting his eyes against the sudden glare of the light.

The sheets were tangled around his feet and he threw the covers to one side as he sat up, pushing himself back to lean against the headboard. Yawning, he rubbed his eyes, then stretched. Waking this early was irritating.

He looked at the clock again. What time was it in the UK? Five hours ahead, so it must be almost ten. He picked up his phone from the bedside table and dialled Kim's mobile number. There was a short delay, then the familiar ring tone, though it sounded quieter, distant. He listened as it rang several times, then clicked and went to voicemail.

Naysmith stared at the handset. Had she just busied him? He scowled and put the phone down, leaning his head right back to gaze up at the ceiling. Maybe she couldn't talk just now – she'd call him back in a few minutes.

He rubbed his eyes, then leaned across for the remote control, frowning as he studied it, looking for the 'On'

button. At the foot of the bed, a TV in a large wooden
cabinet fizzed into life and he began slowly clicking through
the numbers: the hotel's own channel; a succession of
French-language programmes; endless shopping networks
. . . When he finally came across an English-language
channel with the morning news, he dropped the remote and
watched for a few minutes.

The top story seemed to be the unfolding drama of a
library that had flooded – no shootings, no murders, not even
a robbery. He thought back to the evening before, when he'd
been out for a meal with Pascal, the CTO from Systemiq.
Pascal had told him what a wonderfully safe place Montreal
was, how it wasn't like America, how you didn't have to worry
about the person next to you being a killer.

Naysmith had smiled.

His mouth was dry. Yawning, he swung his legs over the
edge of the bed and got to his feet. Interlocking his fingers,
he stretched his arms up over his head, glimpsing his naked
reflection in the tall mirror, lit by the bedside lamp, seeing
the muscles tighten and relax. He felt good. Padding across
to the writing desk, he picked up the bottle of water,
unscrewed the cap and took a long drink. The carpet was
springy under his toes as he moved to the window, pulling
back the heavy curtain to look out on the domed cathedral.
The early-morning light threw long shadows across the ornate
stonework, drawing beautiful lines against a backdrop of
monotonous skyscrapers. Steam rose up from vents on the
buildings below, and one or two small figures hurried along
the pavements, early starters on their way to work.

He let the curtain fall closed, and padded through to the
bathroom, where the cold marble tiles chilled his bare feet . . .

*Just like the kitchen floor at home.*

He turned and went back to the main room, retrieving his

phone from the bedside table. No text messages, no missed calls. He locked the phone and brought it through to the bathroom, placing it on a glass shelf beside the sink.

In the shaving mirror, his own face gazed out at him, sharply magnified. He hesitated, staring at himself in extreme close-up, noticing the faint lines, the glint in his eyes, the doubt.

He scowled, pushed the mirror back towards the wall and went to get dressed. He needed some air.

Emerging from the lift, Naysmith turned right and walked out into the lobby, a broad space of white columns and marble flooring, dark wood and patterned wallpaper – dated but pleasing. Passing between the groups of easy chairs, he made his way to the narrow escalator that led down below street level and then along a thickly carpeted corridor that swallowed his footsteps.

Shining brightly through the glass wall on his left, the harsh lights of the hotel gym left nothing to the imagination – like some hideous porn show where the sweating participants were red-faced businessmen panting together on their cross-trainers. How old were they? Late forties? Fifties? Competing against themselves in a contest they could never win, while real excitement – real challenge – passed them by. He shook his head and walked on, past the hotel boutiques, where the expensive women would come while their husbands recovered from the gym, frowning out through their age-revitalising make-up, bored beyond belief. Easy targets, if he'd been interested.

He pushed through a set of heavy glass doors that led out into the network of underground walkways and shopping malls that ran for miles below Montreal's streets, insulating people from the weather. It was still early for

the malls but another escalator took him down towards the
railway station, where the food courts would already be open
for the morning commuters. He felt hungry – unsettled and
frosty from his disturbed sleep – and allowed the aroma of
baking to draw him onwards. Low ceilings and warm
lighting gave the place a snug feel, while signs in French
described the golden loaves and glistening pastries piled
high behind the glass.

He chose a counter that had a long queue of commuters
– locals always knew the best places – and waited his turn.
When he made it to the till, a pretty black girl smiled at him
– '*Bonjour*' – switching seamlessly to English when she heard
him speak.

He ordered a Danish and coffee – he needed something
to wake him up – and handed over a ten-dollar bill, which
was enough to cover the price plus the various unspecified
taxes. As he took his change and moved along the counter
to wait for his drink, he turned to look back down the
passageway. More of the shops were opening now – their
owners sliding back the concertina shutters, arranging tables
or display stands. And all around him, the steady stream of
people emerging from the railway station, phones pressed to
their ears.

Naysmith frowned to himself and reached into his jacket
to check his phone. Kim still hadn't called.

It was a thirty-minute journey back to the airport. The taxi
driver had dark skin and spoke with an Arab-sounding accent
but there were rosary beads hanging from the rear-view
mirror. Naysmith watched them swinging as the cab wallowed
around the downtown corners – that same soggy ride you
felt in American cars – and wondered if the man was Catholic
or if he was driving someone else's taxi.

They emerged from streets of sturdy old stone terraces that huddled about the feet of the skyscrapers and soon hit the dull concrete and asphalt of the highway, the muffled rhythmic bumps marking time on the uneven surface. The back seats were clean and the whole interior smelled of that sickly air-freshener that valet companies used. Naysmith kept his mouth closed and breathed through his nose as he stared out of the window at the railway tracks running alongside, lined with battered cargo wagons and tall boxcars bearing the Union Pacific logo. Vast trucks with polished chrome and elaborate paintwork kept pace on the inside lane until the taxi slowed and cut across to the off-ramp. They were near the airport now, with the telltale scatter of wretched business hotels, grey blocks of misery beneath neon names. Overnight incarceration for those not worthy of a place in the city – for the reps with their samples and their brochures, and their stink of desperation.

It was a flat fare from downtown – thirty-eight dollars – and he handed his last two twenties to the driver before getting out. Extending the handle of his case, he made his way inside the airport and went to check in.

There was a long queue for security, but he used the time to assess the passengers in front of him, identifying which of them would be slow and making sure he wasn't behind them at the X-ray machines.

The departure area felt like a European airport – long and quiet and bland. There were rows of black faux-leather seats for people with no lounge access, and a few duty-free shops, but everything seemed more expensive than it should. He found a bottle of perfume for Kim, then checked his wallet and frowned. Not something he could charge to the company credit card, so he turned and made his way to the nearest cash machine.

Inserting his card, he tapped in his PIN and gazed down at the small screen. There was a pause before it cleared and displayed a message he hadn't seen before: *Insufficient Funds*.

Insufficient funds? He'd only asked for a hundred dollars. Straightening up, he hit the 'Cancel' button and took his card, staring at it. There had been four or five grand in that account; he hadn't made any withdrawals on this trip, nobody could have stolen his details . . .

Turning away from the machine, he took out his phone. Kim had a card on the account, but she never withdrew more than twenty or thirty pounds at a time . . .

He hit the speed dial for her name and lifted the phone to his ear, but the call went straight to voicemail. Again.

*A whole weekend without a call or even a text message.*

Naysmith stared at his phone for a long moment, then slowly returned it to his pocket. Sudden suspicions rose in his mind, like the first wisps of smoke, but he stamped them down before they engulfed him – there was nothing he could do until he got home. Unclenching his fists, he forced his shoulders to relax, then turned and made his way towards the departure gate to wait for his flight.

He slept fitfully. The plane was half empty, so there was no chance of an upgrade, but one of the flight attendants had taken a shine to him and moved him to the emergency-exit row, where he could stretch out in relative comfort. She woke him as they began their descent into London, fastening herself into the jump seat opposite him a few moments later. He watched her as she clicked her seatbelt into place – early thirties, bottle-blonde hair, with nice eyes and the mandatory excess of make-up.

'Good trip?' she asked him.

'Not bad.' Naysmith smiled reflexively. Flirting became an

automatic response after a while. 'More business than pleasure, unfortunately.'

She grinned at that.

'What is it that you do?'

He smiled to himself.

'I work with people,' he mused. 'Keep track of them, get to know how they function, who they are. Helps me to deal with them better.'

'Like a corporate headhunter? Or more of a troubleshooter?'

'It's kind of a unique role, but I suppose headhunter is close enough.' He sat back for a moment, openly admiring the curves of her figure accentuated by the smart airline uniform, then leaned forward with a grin. 'Now, let me see what I can guess about *you* . . .'

By the time he got home, his mood was black. An endless succession of calls to Kim, starting as soon as he stepped off the plane, and every one had gone straight to voicemail. He'd wondered if she'd lost her phone, but there was no reply from the landline number either.

Nothing since he'd left for Canada.

He wanted to be concerned about her. Angry, even. Mentally, he was ready to shout at her when he got in, to tell her off for worrying him with her silence.

But she wasn't there and, as he put his bags down in the hallway and walked to the foot of the stairs, it dawned on him that he'd known she wouldn't be. Something was wrong, and it had been wrong before he left.

There was a folded piece of paper – a conspicuous white square – propped up on the hall table. She had left him a note. Closing his eyes for a moment, he steadied his breathing, calming himself before he opened it.

*Rob,*
*I'm so sorry. Please don't be angry, but I just can't do this. If you*
*care about me, please don't try to contact me. Just forget about*
*us, and forgive me if you can.*
*Goodbye.*

*K*

He stood absolutely still for some time, staring down at the paper. There was a terrible, cold knot in his stomach, and he became aware that his hands were sweating.

*Breathe, damn it!*

He took a moment, centring himself, then read the letter again, committing it to memory. All the pieces were fitting together now – all the little warning signs that in his folly he'd ignored – and he suddenly understood.

His hand crumpled the note, screwing it up into a tight little ball of paper.

He needed to think, think clearly. And then, when he was *fucking* calm, he would find Kim and bring her back. It might take a while, but time meant nothing to him. He wasn't going to lose her – not now, not ever. Dimly, he was aware that his fingernails were gouging into his palm and he unclenched his hand.

It would be a game like no other.

# 38

Taunton was just as she'd left it. The same small town, with the same small shops – an unglamorous, in-between sort of place that she'd been so desperate to escape ever since her childhood had run aground. And now she was back.

The sunlight was harsh and she squinted as she walked slowly down towards the river and leaned on the black railings. Below her, the water slid lazily by, drifting beneath the bridges as it wound its way through the town. On the opposite bank, weathered old men were dotted along a low pontoon jetty like statues, their fishing rods motionless while orange floats gleamed bright against the murky brown.

A group of young girls made their way along the path towards her, turning aside to descend on one of the benches in the small strip of grassy park, laughing, gossiping. She'd sat there herself so many times, with a teenager's impatience to escape, certain that the grass would be greener elsewhere, but that seemed like a long time ago now. Taunton might not have changed, but she had.

She turned to stare at the white ironwork of the North Street bridge, and the reflection gently rippling on the smooth surface of the water below it. Why couldn't things have worked out just a little bit more simply for her?

Pushing herself up off the railing, she wandered slowly along the concrete riverbank. To her right there was a large paved area where boys were pulling tricks on their skateboards, rumbling down the slight slope then clattering up against the low walls and down again. Practising their moves to impress the girls.

She remembered coming here with boys, catching the flicker of interest in their wandering eyes, learning how to keep their attention, especially as she came to realise how much she desired it. She was never quite sure what it was that they saw in her, but the way they watched made her feel like she was worth something – a temporary escape from the shadow of her popular sister. At first she'd tried to keep control, to set limits, but the ones who *would* take no for an answer always seemed to condemn her for it afterwards. *Frigid, tease, bitch* – she'd grown to hate those names. Maybe that's why she was drawn to the edgier guys. Somehow they were always the most exciting, the most honest. There was an inevitability about being with them and she accepted it. Friends whispered behind her back, but she knew it was just jealousy – she dared to go where they wouldn't. It took courage to surrender, and there was freedom in letting go.

And so she had come to value those relationships, working hard to hold on to them. She had finally realised how little men wanted from her.

*And how much.*

The tarmac path sloped up to join the road bridge and she turned right, gazing idly in the shop windows as she wandered towards the town centre. There were a lot of coffee shops here now – that was new – but the rest of the shopping area looked disappointingly familiar. She bought herself a frappuccino, then started to make her way slowly back down towards the river.

Sarah wouldn't finish work until after five thirty. She checked her watch – 3.35 p.m. Still much too early . . .

... but the bed and breakfast place would be open for check-in now. She sipped the last of her drink, then dropped the empty container into a litter bin with a sigh.

Might as well get it over with.

She'd found the B & B on the Internet. It wasn't far from her old school – an imposing Victorian house set back from the road, the harsh brick frontage softened by tall trees. Along the front of the property ran a long wall topped by white stonework – matching the brick and stone of the building itself.

It was only a couple of minutes' drive from where she'd left the car and there was no difficulty finding it – a large wooden sign with gold lettering painted on a maroon background boasted of en-suite bedrooms, colour TVs and four-poster beds.

She turned left, bumping across the pavement and passing between the two grand, sculpted gateposts. Beyond the perimeter trees, the gardens had been levelled and tarmacked over – a smooth grey sea of car park, with the house jutting up in the centre like an island.

There was only one other vehicle – a small blue minivan, its nose tucked neatly against the fence that lined the side of the property. Kim pulled in beside it and switched off the ignition. As she got out, she glanced up at the house – three storeys and very tall, looming against the bright sky, dark windows glaring down on her.

Lifting open the hatchback, she hefted the two smaller bags out onto the tarmac, then stood for a moment, staring at them. So little to show for her life away from Taunton, she thought. The big case would have to stay in the car – it couldn't come with her just now.

Trundling the bags across the car park, she followed signs

directing her around to the far side of the building, where a stone portico housed a flight of three steps leading up to the windowed front door. A small card taped inside the glass announced 'Vacancies'.

Inside, there was a terrible hush that made her think of visiting elderly relatives when she was a child. Every sound seemed magnified – the creak of the door closing behind her, the clatter of her shoes on the polished wooden floorboards – and the weight of the house's disapproval pressed down on her, as though her very presence disturbed the peace. She decided to carry her bags rather than pull them.

Ahead of her was a wall with a small serving hatch closed off by a pane of frosted glass, and below it a semicircular table with an old brass desk bell.

She glanced around, then tapped the top of the bell, listening as its loud ring slowly died under her hand. On the other side of the wall there was movement, the unhurried approach of purposeful footsteps, and the frosted glass slid open to reveal a severe woman in her fifties with immaculate short grey hair.

'Good afternoon?' It was more question than greeting, and she peered over the top of her spectacles as though the arrival of guests was a terrible trial for her.

'Hi, I'm Kim Nichols. I've booked a room?'

The woman, wearing a navy-blue buttoned cardigan, studied her for a moment longer, then consulted a large, leather-bound book.

'Ah yes, here we are.' She glanced up. 'For a week?'

'That's right. Maybe longer, I'm not sure . . .'

The landlady looked at her doubtfully.

'It depends on my work,' Kim explained. *And on escaping Rob.* 'Can I let you know in a couple of days if I'll need the room longer?'

'Well, we do get so very busy,' the woman told her gravely. 'The earlier I know the better . . .'

She hesitated for a moment, before her desire for money overtook her disapproval, then leaned closer to the hatch as though bestowing a great kindness. 'But I can probably let you have it a little longer as things stand at the moment.'

'Thank you.' Kim smiled.

The woman nodded to herself.

'Now, if you'd care to fill out one of these . . .' she handed a registration form through the hatch '. . . and we require an imprint of your credit card, or a deposit of two nights' stay in advance.'

Kim handed over her credit card and filled in the form.

The landlady seemed to brighten once she'd authorised the payment. She received the completed form graciously and passed Kim's card back to her along with a room key on a heavy plastic fob.

'I've put you in our number eleven,' she explained. 'It's very cosy, up on the second floor, I would have offered you something on the first, but a young lady like you won't be troubled by the stairs, as some of my older guests would be.'

'I'm sure it'll be fine.'

'Breakfast is served between seven and nine and is taken in the room at the end of the hall there . . .' She indicated it with a slight tilt of her head. 'And the stairs are behind you.'

'Thank you.'

And then the woman was closing the hatch.

'Do let us know if there's anything else you require. Good afternoon.'

The hatch slid shut, and the footsteps moved away.

Jamming the massive plastic tag into the pocket of her jeans with some difficulty, Kim picked up her bags and approached the old wooden staircase. An ornate, carved

banister gleamed with polish, though the narrow strip of
elderly carpet that ran down the centre of the steps was held
in place by scuffed brass rods.

She climbed noisily to the first floor, where the stairs ended
and a broad hallway traversed the length of the house.
Engraved brass plaques indicated 'Rooms 6–8' to the left and
'Rooms 7–10' to the right.

*Which way was number eleven?*

And then she noticed one door that was different to the
solid dark wood of the others – a magnolia-painted fire door,
with a small brass plate that read '11 & 12'. Passing through,
she found a steep flight of grey-carpeted steps squeezed in
between two walls, so narrow that she almost had to take her
bags up one at a time. At the top, the steps turned sharply
onto a tiny landing with a skylight window and two doors.

Kim fished out the key, opened the door to number eleven,
and peered into her room.

*At least it was clean.*

She was right up inside the roof of the old house – she
could tell from the odd shape of the walls and the sharply
sloping ceiling. It was very small and the only light came
from a tiny dormer window, showing the minimal furnishings
that between them managed to fill the cramped little room.

An old portable TV occupied one end of the dressing table,
with a single wooden chair beside it, and there was a built-in
wardrobe with three anti-theft clothes hangers. One corner
of the room had been partitioned off to make the en suite,
but it was only big enough for a toilet and a washbasin.

Kim sighed.

There were no four-poster beds up here – no room for
them. She pictured herself a young damsel from a nineteenth-
century novel, imprisoned at the top of the house until she
surrendered herself to an arranged marriage. Smiling sadly

at the thought, she sat down on the bed, feeling the dip in the middle where it had seen one too many nights of passion.

*'It's very cosy, up on the second floor . . . I can probably let you have it a little longer . . .'*

Kim let herself sink back onto the bed, resting her tired eyes for a moment.

*No wonder the landlady thought it might remain available.*

But it was clean and, more importantly, it was cheap. And right now, she didn't know how long she'd have to make her money last, how long it would be before she was free of Rob. She prayed it wouldn't be *too* long.

It was a little after seven when she turned onto Gordon Road. She knew there was just enough room to turn around at the end of the narrow cul-de-sac, but she managed to find a space and pulled up almost outside the terraced house she'd shared with Sarah for so many years.

She switched off the ignition and sat for a while, listening to the ticking of the engine as it cooled, trying to think what she would say. She'd sent her sister a text message to tell her she was coming, but that was all – no reason for her visit, no hint of what had happened. It wasn't the sort of thing you did over the phone, but now that she was here, the prospect of doing it face-to-face seemed impossible too.

The street was so familiar – an unbroken line of two-storey houses on either side, pressed in tight to the narrow pavements. This was where she'd felt her first taste of freedom, her first step away from her old life, even if it had meant staying in the same town.

This was where she'd lived before she met Rob.

But she knew she couldn't stay here now – it simply wasn't safe. He'd been here too often, picking her up and dropping her off in their early days together, spending the night sometimes – he'd brought her back here for Sarah's birthday, and at Christmas.

No, she couldn't stay. She would get in and get out as quickly as she could. That would be safest, and the less inter-rogation she had to face the better.

She opened the door and got out, smoothing down her clothes. Should she take the case out of the car now? No, not yet. Sarah would wonder what was going on if she turned up on the doorstep with a suitcase, and she didn't want a barrage of questions before she even got inside. She would drop it off as she was leaving.

Locking the car, she made her way towards the house. Sarah had painted the little iron gate in a dark shade of green, and there were new curtains hanging in the front-room window that she wasn't sure about . . .

. . . *but this wasn't her home any more.*

She took a deep breath and rang the bell.

After a moment, she heard quick footsteps and the door opened.

'Hi, sis!' Sarah was everything she wasn't – confident, curvaceous and blonde, taking her looks from their mother. Kim's colouring was more like her father's – perhaps that's why she'd been his favourite, and why her mother had grown so distant after he left.

'Hiya,' Kim smiled.

'Come in,' Sarah beamed, looking past her into the street. 'Is Rob not with you?'

'No, it's just me.'

'Well, come on through. I was just going to open a bottle of wine.'

They walked down the narrow hallway and into the kitchen. Kim dumped her handbag on the counter, just as she used to, and looked around. It was as if she'd never been away.

*If only.*

She sank into her old chair with a sigh and looked across at her sister, who was taking a couple of glasses from the dishwasher. How was she going to tell her?

Sarah straightened up and came over, setting the glasses and a bottle down on the table.

'So,' she smiled as she sat down and started opening the wine. 'What brings you back here? Everything all right?'

Kim stared at her.

*Just say it!*

'It's Rob,' she began. Her hands felt clammy and she looked down at the table. 'I've . . . left him.'

'Oh, babe! I'm sorry.' Sarah was immediately on her feet, sweeping round the side of the table to put her arms around her. 'You poor thing.'

They hugged for a moment, and Kim felt her eyes filling with tears. She should have done this a long time ago.

Sarah gave her a last little squeeze, then moved back to her chair again.

'Oh Kim,' she said, reaching a hand across the table to console her sister. 'Is it serious?'

*Is it serious?*

Kim wasn't sure whether to laugh or cry.

'Yes,' she managed, her voice trembling. 'It's really bad.'

It was so difficult. She wanted to open the floodgates, blurt out everything, but suddenly she was afraid – afraid of involving Sarah, and afraid of what Sarah might think of her if she did.

She gave her sister a brave little smile before the tears rose once more.

Sarah waited for a moment, then gently pressed her hand. 'Was he cheating?' she asked.

Kim raised her head to nod, wiping her eyes on her sleeve.

That was true as well: he *had* cheated on her, at least in the beginning. But that was only half the story.

'Cheating, lying . . . everything's a lie,' she sniffed.

'Poor babe.' Sarah looked at her for a moment, then poured two glasses of wine and slid one over. 'You think you know someone . . .' She tailed off and shook her head sadly.

They sat there quietly together until Kim dried her eyes and lifted her drink, summoning the courage to tell her sister the rest of it. She just needed a moment to compose herself.

'Now I don't want you to worry,' Sarah said suddenly. 'You can stay here as long as you want. The back bedroom's got some of Simon's stuff in it, but I'll make him clear some space for you and we can get you settled—'

'No.' Kim shook her head and managed a faint smile. 'I'll be all right, really.'

It was the shock on Sarah's face that caught her attention, as though she'd been completely wrong-footed.

*Not used to her little sister saying no.*

'I've booked myself into a B & B,' she explained.

'A B & B?' Sarah stared at her, her expression somewhere between confused and offended. 'What d'you want to do that for? What's wrong with staying here?'

Kim picked up her wine glass. It looked like one from the set she'd bought when they first moved in.

'I just think I need to be on my own for a while,' she said softly. 'Take some time to get my head together. You understand, don't you?'

'Of course.' As always, Sarah recovered quickly and she was smiling as she reached for the wine bottle. 'But you know you're always welcome here.'

'I do know,' Kim said with a grateful smile. The house was still in her name, but Sarah meant well. 'And I appreciate it.'

'Well, any time you change your mind.'

'Actually, I've got a case in the back of the car.' Kim hesitated and looked enquiringly at her sister. 'Would you mind if I left it here for a little while?'

'That's fine. I'll get Simon to stick it upstairs when he gets home.'

'Thanks.' Kim sat back in her chair, relieved to have got this far. But there was so much more she needed to say.

Sarah had drained her glass and was pouring another.

'Anyway,' she said in that tone of voice she used when she'd made up her mind about something, 'you might not think so now, but it's probably for the best.' She thought to herself, then added, 'Don't get me wrong, Rob was charming, but I was always a little bit wary of him.'

Kim looked up.

'Why's that?' she asked.

Sarah met her eyes for a moment, then looked away.

'Oh, just little things,' she replied. 'There were a couple of times I'm sure I caught him looking at me . . .'

One of her hands had strayed up to absently toy with a button at the front of her blouse.

Kim stared at her coldly. Was Sarah just a little bit pleased about that?

Suddenly she felt a lot less sure of things between them. Perhaps Sarah wasn't the person she should be talking to.

# 39

Harland leaned back in his chair and rubbed his eyes. It had been a long day. He yawned, then stretched out a hand and switched off the monitor, grateful as the harsh glare died. Pushing his seat backwards, he eased himself wearily to his feet and picked up his jacket. Then, walking around the desk, he stepped out into the corridor and pulled the door shut behind him.

Mendel and Josh were standing outside the kitchen and he stifled another yawn as he walked over to them.

'We boring you?' Mendel asked gravely.

'Not yet,' Harland grinned. 'I was going to pop into the White Lion. You can bore me over a pint if you like.'

'Sounds good,' Josh smiled.

Mendel nodded. 'Always got time for a pint.'

They walked downstairs, said goodnight to Francis, who was stuck with desk duty, and made their way outside into the cool evening air. Harland fumbled in his pockets, drawing out his cigarettes and lighter.

'How did you find working with Bristol CID, sir?' Josh asked as they came to the pavement.

Harland shot him a wry smile, leaning forward and cupping his hands around the flame as he lit up.

'Just like working here,' he replied. 'Same dog, different bit of string.'

'Hey,' Mendel warned him. 'Ask if you want to borrow my catchphrases.'

'Sorry,' Harland smiled. He followed the others out onto the pavement and turned down the hill towards the main road.

Behind them, a car door slammed shut.

Harland turned to see a woman with long dark hair who hesitated as he looked at her, then ran down the slope towards him.

'Detective Harland?'

'Yes?' The face was familiar but it took him a moment to place her. 'Kim?'

Dressed in jeans and a short tailored jacket, she stopped a few feet away from him. Mendel and Josh had turned around to see what was going on.

'We spoke on the phone, about my boyfriend . . .' She broke off, struggling, steeling herself. 'You said before that I could call you,' she finished helplessly.

Harland took a long drag on his cigarette and studied her – nervous posture, eyes beginning to glisten with tears, tremble in her voice.

*Genuine.*

'That's right,' he said softly. 'What can I do for you?'

She stared at him for a moment, as though about to speak, but her face fell as she looked past him to the others. She turned back to him in mute desperation.

Harland glanced at Mendel.

'On you go.' He tilted his head down the road. 'I'll catch you up.'

Mendel frowned at Kim for a moment, then shot a meaningful look at Harland.

'See you down there,' he muttered. 'Come on, Josh.'

The two of them turned away and walked on down the hill. Harland returned his attention to Kim.

'Now,' he said, in as kindly a tone as he could muster.
'What is it?'

'It's Rob.'

'Robert Naysmith?' Harland asked. 'The man you live
with?'

'Lived with,' she corrected.

'OK . . .'

'I'm sure he's killed someone,' she stammered. 'I don't have
any proper proof, but I'm sure of it and I really need you to
. . . do something.'

Harland looked at her, then glanced back towards the
station house.

'Do you want to come inside and talk about it?'

She followed his look, then nodded nervously.

'I'm sorry, it's just that I can't cope with this any more.'
She put the back of her hand to her mouth, composing herself
for a moment. 'I didn't know who else to go to.'

'It's all right.' Harland turned and walked slowly back
towards the building, Kim following him nervously. 'I'll take
you in and we'll get you a cup of tea. Then someone can
take your statement—'

'Can't *you* take the statement?' Kim stopped and looked
at him with a pleading expression. 'The other officers didn't
believe me last time. Please, I'd rather tell you.'

Harland stole a quick glance at his watch and sighed to
himself. The pub would have to wait. Mendel might grumble,
but it wouldn't be fair of him to simply dump this woman
on the next shift. Besides, there was something about her . . .

'All right.' He took a last drag on his cigarette and threw the
butt aside.' We'll have a talk and see where we go from there.
Fair enough?'

She gave a brief little nod and followed him to the door.

                    *    *    *

Even in the cramped confines of the interview room, she looked small – a forlorn figure who sat across the table from him, her large eyes hunting round anxiously.

'So.' He opened his notebook, then leaned forward slightly so that she would focus on him rather than on what he was writing. 'Let's continue. You'd been living with Rob for a while, and you felt he had some sort of secret . . . ?'

He tailed off gently, leading her into what he hoped would be a safe starting point.

Kim stared down at the table for a long time, then began to speak in a soft voice.

'I asked him once . . . asked him if he was keeping something from me. At first I thought it was another woman, but he told me it wasn't and this time I really knew he was telling the truth.'

It was almost as though she was talking to herself, reliving a moment, once more searching her partner's face in her mind for any trace of deception, and finding none.

'But I was sure there was something else, something that he was holding back.' She swallowed, her eyes darting up nervously as she once again became aware of where she was. 'So I kept on at him.'

'And what did he say?' Harland asked quietly.

'He said there *was* something, but when I asked him if he would tell me . . . he just said not yet.' She frowned, as though upset with herself for allowing that admission to pass unchallenged.

Harland sat back and gazed at her thoughtfully. She had a delicate, vulnerable beauty that he found oddly compelling.

'What did you think it was?' A slightly off-centre question, to see how she reacted, to make sure it wasn't all rehearsed.

'Money, I suppose.' She answered without thinking, her eyes gazing into the distance before focusing on Harland, as though noticing him again. 'At the time I thought maybe he had done something dodgy at work.'

'What do you mean? Like fraud?'

'I don't know. Maybe.' She shrugged. 'Kickbacks or something illegal . . . Back then I never imagined it would be anything so serious.'

Harland paused for a moment, watching her twirling a strand of hair around a slender finger.

'But later he told you it was something other than kickbacks . . . ?' he prompted her.

Kim nodded slowly.

'We were away for a few days,' she murmured. 'And he seemed sort of different. Preoccupied.'

'Yes?'

'It was as though he needed me to know something, so in the end I asked what the matter was. But he just stood there, watching me . . .' She bit her lip, eyes downcast behind long, dark lashes. 'So I started asking him different questions. Had he done something bad? Had he hurt someone?'

Harland leaned forward, nodding at her to continue, but she didn't seem to notice.

'He was staring at me in a really odd way, and I started to get frightened.' She faltered and looked up, her eyes suddenly bright with tears. 'So I asked him if he had . . . killed someone, because I really needed him to tell me that he hadn't.'

'But he didn't deny it.'

'No, he didn't.' She sniffed, as though determined to push through to the end of her recollection. 'He's never denied it.'

'And what did you do?'

Kim bowed her head.

'I cried. I shouted at him. And he just stood there and took it all.'

'Why didn't you call the police? Or just walk out?'

Her head came up quickly and she gave him an agonised stare. But there were no words – she could only shake her head.

'It's OK.' Harland could sense that cracks were beginning to appear in her resolve, and knew he had to keep her talking before she froze up on him.

'When did you first hear about Severn Beach?' he asked.

She seemed relieved to move on from the previous question, leaning forward a little, reaching up to place her small hands on the table.

'He took me there,' she said after a moment. 'We'd been in Bristol, and he suggested going for a walk. Then he drove us out to Severn Beach.'

'And what happened?'

'We walked along that path – you know the one that runs along the top of the sea wall?'

'I know it,' Harland nodded.

'Well, we were there when he started to talk about how it felt.' She frowned. 'I'd asked him, you see – back when he first told me – asked him what it was like. And now he was explaining it, about the sense of power, about being totally in control . . .'

Harland could see her concentrating, working to replay the scene in her mind. Whether her partner was involved or not, *she* was certainly telling the truth.

'Go on . . .'

She closed her eyes for a moment, reciting softly.

'"Imagine how it would feel, walking along this beach in the first light of dawn, rain clouds rolling in, with that sort of power flowing through you . . ." It was something like that.'

Harland frowned.

*First light of dawn? Rain clouds?* He thought back to the

weekend when they'd found the body on the beach. *How did Naysmith know what Vicky Sutherland's last morning had been like?*

'Did he say anything about the victim?' he asked.

Kim looked at him, then nodded.

'I did sort of push him about who it was, but I said "Who was *he*?"' She lowered her eyes again, reliving it all once more. 'Rob just smiled and asked me why I thought it was a "he".'

They sat in the interview room for almost an hour. Apart from the conversations with Kim, there was little to link this Robert Naysmith to the murders from the previous year. He seemed to have no particular connection to Severn Beach or Oxford, or to any of the locations they'd flagged before the investigation was taken away from them. There was no motive. Nothing.

It was true that his work took him all over the country, and allowed him to keep his own hours. But as Harland sat there gently coaxing the words from this frightened woman to build up a picture of Naysmith, he began to see a clever man, a controlling man, a careful man. Someone who wouldn't make mistakes.

*Someone like their killer.*

It was a pity about Kim. She really was very attractive, even in the midst of her tears, and it had taken some courage for her to come back to him. He wished he could help her more, but Blake's instructions had been absolutely clear: the case was now with the Met, and there was to be no further action without the Superintendent's express permission. Right now, the best thing he could do for her was to let her go home.

'Are you OK?' he asked her, closing his notebook.

She nodded mutely, one small hand nervously touching her lips as her eyes glistened with tears once more.

It was so unfair. But he'd have to give it to the Met – they would interview Naysmith and check him out.

Tired now, he pushed back his chair and got to his feet.

'We'll look into this,' he assured her. 'It's tied in with an investigation that another division are running, but you've got my number, so you can call me if you think of anything else, or if you want to know how things are going.'

He wanted to come across as confident but in his own ears the words sounded lame.

She moved towards the door, then turned to him.

'You believe me, don't you?'

He thought of all the polite things he usually said, the carefully non-committal phrases, but her large eyes begged for the truth.

'Yes,' he told her simply. 'I believe you.'

She trembled slightly – was she about to cry again? – then startled him by quickly moving close and throwing her arms around him. For the few seconds that her head was on his shoulder, the scent of her hair took him back, to Sunday mornings in bed, long ago when he wasn't alone. He stood awkwardly, unsure what to do, then gently let one arm enfold her in what he hoped was a reassuring gesture. She felt warm and soft against his body.

'Thank you,' she whispered as she pulled away from him. There were new tears in her eyes but also, he thought, a glint of hope. She turned and hurried out of the room.

Harland stepped out and watched her small figure as it disappeared down the corridor.

# 40

It was an insistent knock. Not hers. And not the way a neighbour would knock, unless there was some emergency. Frowning, Naysmith stood up from his desk and hurried down the stairs. He opened the front door and stared out at the two men, his pulse quickening as he saw that one of them was a uniformed police officer.

Which made the other one . . . a detective? He tensed slightly, but fought down the instinct to run. If they had any idea who he was they'd have brought a lot more people. And they wouldn't have knocked.

Anyway, he'd been careful. He was ready.

Forcing himself to breathe, he regarded the two men and asked, 'Can I help you?'

'Robert Naysmith?'

The detective was shorter than him – a dumpy man in his forties, brown hair thinning on top but worn longer and thicker on the sides, presumably to compensate. His suit was the shiny kind of thing you bought from a supermarket, and the shirt looked worn from too many washes.

'Yes?' He allowed himself to adopt an expression of concern. Normal people looked concerned when the police came to the door.

'I'm DI Cadnam and this is PC Barden. Can we have a word?'

'Of course.' He stood back and opened the door wider. 'Come in, please.'

He ushered them into the hallway and closed the door behind them.

'Can I get either of you a drink? Tea? Coffee?'

'We're fine, thanks.'

The uniformed one – Barden – was tall and powerfully built, seeming to fill the hallway. Absently, Naysmith wondered if he would be difficult to take down, or if it was just bulk.

'Go through to the living room.' He indicated the door on the left and followed them.

The house seemed very quiet as they walked in, their eyes sweeping the room, cataloguing and searching. As if he would be stupid enough to leave any clues lying around in here. As if he would be stupid enough to leave any clues anywhere.

He gestured towards the sofa and remained on his feet until they sat down, forcing them both to look up at him, just for a moment. Then, conscious of the seriousness of the situation, he dropped into his own armchair and gazed levelly at each of them.

'So.' He adopted a business-like tone, as though he was eager to know what brought them here. 'What can I do for you?'

'We're making enquiries about a crime that took place last year in the Bristol area – the murder of a woman.'

They were both watching him carefully, studying him for any reaction that might give something away – he would have to play it just right. DI Cadnam had left a momentary pause to see if he would volunteer something, but if he was innocent he wouldn't know what they were talking about yet. So he leaned forward and nodded earnestly, waiting to see what they told him next.

Cadnam frowned.

'In the course of our enquiries, we've identified a number of people who may have information that could aid our investigation.' He paused for impact, then added, 'Including yourself.'

Naysmith let his face register shock.

'What are you talking about?' he protested – a little anger, a little concern, smoothly raising the pitch and volume of his voice. 'What information? What's this about?'

'Please.' Cadnam was holding up his hands in a calming gesture. 'We have to speak to any potential witnesses – you never know what will prove important.'

He was doing his best to sound reasonable, and his use of the term *witness* was a deliberate attempt to defuse the situation – or perhaps throw him off guard? Still, Naysmith reasoned, an innocent person would find the word reassuring. Certainly preferable to *suspect*. He leaned back in his armchair and gazed at them warily for a moment, then shook his head.

'Sorry,' he frowned. 'I know you're only doing your job. What was it you wanted to know?'

Cadnam took out a small notebook and opened it.

'Can you tell me anything about your movements on Friday the twenty-fifth and Saturday the twenty-sixth of May last year?' he asked.

Naysmith stared at him blankly.

'Last year? No idea.'

He waited until the detective was about to speak, then added, 'I can check my diary if you like?'

Cadnam looked at him.

'If you wouldn't mind,' he nodded.

Naysmith got to his feet.

'I'll be right back,' he told them.

His face displayed concern until he was out of the room, fading to mild annoyance once he was beyond their sight. Walking through to the kitchen, he picked up his laptop from the table, then turned and went back through to the living room, remembering to look anxious as he did so.

Cadnam was eyeing the laptop as he sank down into the armchair again.

'You keep your diary on there?' he asked.

'I have to,' Naysmith replied. 'My schedule's pretty hectic and it varies from week to week.'

He opened the laptop and hit the power button to wake it.

'I try and keep track of everything on here.'

Cadnam settled back a little into the sofa.

'What is it that you do exactly?' he asked.

'I'm the sales director for Winterhill – a software company in Woking,' he replied. 'Not very exciting, I'm afraid, but it pays the bills . . .'

*The nervous banter of a mediocre man.*

The laptop chimed its start-up theme and displayed the desktop. Naysmith clicked on his diary icon and looked up.

'What were those dates again?' he asked.

'Friday the twenty-fifth and Saturday the twenty-sixth.'

'Sorry, which month?'

Cadnam wasn't going to catch him out like that.

'May.' The detective looked mildly irritated now. 'Last year.'

Naysmith moved his finger across the trackpad and paged back to May.

'OK, here it is.' He turned the screen so they could see. 'Thursday was a sales meeting in Woking, but Friday I was working from home.'

Cadnam leaned forward to peer at the screen, then glanced up.

'Do you often work from home?' he asked.

'Yes. A lot of what I do is calls and emails, so I can do that from here – saves the commute.'

'And you were alone all day on that Friday?'

Naysmith knew he ought to look worried by that.

'Well, until Kim came home – my girlfriend . . . ex-girlfriend now.' He let them see a flicker of regret that wasn't entirely feigned. 'She would have been home around six.'

She hadn't been of course. That Friday she'd gone to stay with her sister – he'd dropped her at the station before getting ready to travel to Severn Beach – but an innocent man wouldn't remember one Friday more than a year before, and chances are neither would she.

'And how about the Saturday?'

*The morning he'd killed Vicky Sutherland.*

Naysmith spread his hands wide, allowing his demeanour to become a little more agitated. They still hadn't told him what was going on, and that would be worrying for an ordinary person.

'I don't remember. We usually went shopping in Salisbury, or Southampton.'

He shrugged, looking at them for more information.

Cadnam regarded him for a moment, then consulted the notebook.

'Would you mind checking another date for me, please?'

'Of course.' Naysmith frowned. 'When do you want to know about?'

'Wednesday the twenty-fifth of July. Last year.'

Naysmith turned back to the laptop and paged forward to July, his mind recalling that terrible stormy night, the university lecturer, the sickening sound as metal had shattered bone and another game had ended.

He showed them the screen.

'There you are. Networking drinks evening in London,' he explained. 'I usually have one of those every month or so.'

Cadnam stared at the screen for a moment, his eyes taking in all the other entries on the page.

'Would you like a printout of my calendar for last year?' Naysmith asked him. A calendar that he'd carefully maintained, covering his tracks, against just such a situation as this.

Cadnam shook his head. Barden sat quietly, watchful and slightly unnerving.

'In that case . . .' Naysmith leaned forward '. . . I'd appreciate it if you'd tell me what this is about.'

Cadnam relaxed back into his seat and looked at him for a moment, considering his next move.

'Tell me, have you ever been to Severn Beach?' he asked.

It was poorly played – a clumsy attempt that gave away too much.

Naysmith made a point of frowning, then rubbed his eyes wearily as he slumped back into the armchair.

'Yes,' he nodded. 'Once.'

He sighed, as though disappointed by something.

'Well?' Cadnam leaned forward.

Naysmith looked at him, his face expressing the regret of a person wronged.

'I went there once, with Kim.' He glanced at Barden, then back to Cadnam. 'That's what this is all about, isn't it?'

The detective looked at him thoughtfully, pen hovering over his notebook.

'Go on,' he said, carefully noncommittal.

'Kim, my ex—' He broke off, as though understanding something for the first time. 'I took her out to Severn Beach after we'd been in Bristol one weekend. It must have spooked her more than I thought.'

'Spooked her?'

'We talked about that woman,' Naysmith explained. 'The one who got washed up on the beach.'

She hadn't been washed up – he hoped the detective noticed his mistake.

Cadnam frowned.

'Can I ask how you knew about the woman?'

'There was a reconstruction on TV. And it was in the papers for a while.' Naysmith shrugged. 'That's what gave me the idea.'

Cadnam shot him a wary look.

'Strange thing to do, take your girlfriend to visit the scene of a murder . . . ?'

Naysmith looked down, awkward now, as though some embarrassing prejudice or grubby sexual secret had been found out.

'I know, it's a bit weird, but if you knew Kim . . .' He paused as though torn, as though reluctant to speak ill of her. 'She responded to some unusual things.'

Cadnam narrowed his eyes.

'I'm not sure I follow you,' he said.

Naysmith hesitated.

'Danger turned her on. I just played on that a little, you know? A bit of theatre – get her thinking about what happened there, get her excited . . .' He looked at each of them in turn, then stared down at the carpet again. 'It's not something I'm particularly proud of, but the whole relationship was pretty screwed-up.'

He waited, feeling their eyes boring into the top of his head, waiting for one of them to speak. After a moment, Cadnam broke the silence.

'You said you knew what this was all about?'

*A change of tack – good. But not good enough.*

Naysmith raised his head slowly.

'Kim and I didn't part on the best of terms,' he admitted. 'I assume she's said something, and that's where you got my name from.'

He looked at them questioningly, but Cadnam turned it back on him.

'Can you elaborate?'

'OK,' Naysmith sighed. 'She was always fairly . . . suspicious. Always accusing me of seeing other women, even when I wasn't.'

He dropped that in – another deliberate piece of carelessness for them, reassurance that they really were so much smarter than him.

Cadnam took the bait.

'And when you *were* seeing other women?'

Naysmith looked at him for a moment, as though considering whether or not to deny it, then let his shoulders drop.

They had 'outsmarted' him.

'She got very angry. I mean, *really* angry.' He allowed his voice a wistful edge, choosing his words carefully so that the decisive blow would sound casual. 'And she was really clever about it too. In the end, she waited until I was out of the country on business, then cleaned out one of my bank accounts and disappeared.'

'Really?' Cadnam glanced at Barden and scribbled something in his notebook.

Naysmith nodded ruefully.

'I can show you the statement if you don't believe me,' he sighed.

'How much did she take?'

'A little over six grand.'

The detective tapped the end of his pen against the notepad for a moment.

'Did you report this?' he asked.

Naysmith shook his head.

'There didn't seem much point. The account was in both our names, and I actually thought I'd got off lightly. She could have trashed the house or taken a pair of scissors to my suits . . .' He smiled at them sadly, then looked down again. 'And I suppose I did sort of deserve it. I know I didn't treat her too well.'

He could feel Cadnam staring at him. Good. Let that idea do its work for a moment, establish itself in their thoughts, erode Kim's credibility.

He lifted his head sharply.

'But I never thought she'd do anything like this! I know she's always been a little unstable, but if she's trying to set me up with the police . . .'

He let it hang there, filling the room with doubt.

Barden shifted slightly in his seat.

'I'm right, aren't I?' Naysmith pressed. 'This is all because she figured out I was cheating on her?'

Cadnam exchanged a brief glance with Barden, then softly closed his notebook.

'I appreciate your time,' he said, getting to his feet. 'If there's anything further, we'll be in touch.'

It only sank in as they left. Naysmith's heart was racing when he closed the front door and bowed his head against it. Standing there in the silence of the hallway, he took a deep breath and shuddered.

She'd done her best – credit to her for having the courage to try – but it hadn't worked. And now he was even more eager to find her again. It would be a uniquely personal challenge.

# 41

*Tuesday, 26 August*

Kim pushed through the glass door and stepped out onto the broad swathe of paving stones that fronted the office. She halted for a moment, smoothing down her skirt, which was riding up a little, and doing up the top button of her blouse. Maybe she should have worn her light grey suit with these shoes, but that was in the case she'd left at Sarah's.

It didn't matter – she was just glad that another job interview was over. She always found them a little unsettling, but as she walked away from the building she still couldn't decide if the office manager was dreary or creepy.

*Or which was worse.*

She made her way between the lines of cars to where she'd parked. Slipping off her jacket, she folded it carefully and put it on the passenger seat with her handbag.

Working in Exeter would be a long commute unless she moved, but the money was good.

She started the car and found her way out of the car park, trusting the satnav on her phone to guide her through the town and onto the motorway. It would be good to get clear of Exeter before the rush hour – assuming they had a rush hour down here.

Being in the wrong lane meant she had to go round the roundabout twice, but eventually she spotted the right exit

and drove up the ramp to join the M5 for the journey back
to Taunton. Merging with the rest of the traffic, she wondered
if the long commute might make it impractical to stay there.

*Oh well, every cloud had a silver lining.*

She smiled at that, then her face grew serious again.

Until the police dealt with Rob, it really didn't matter where
she was. Just as long as she was far away from him.

There had been an accident earlier in the afternoon and the
queue of slow-moving traffic meant it took her well over an
hour to get back. Leaving the motorway, she considered going
back to the B & B to change clothes, but the thought of that
cramped little room was just too depressing. She'd promised
to drop in on Sarah this evening anyway, so she pulled over
at the side of the road, rummaged through her handbag and
drew out her phone.

'Hello?'

'It's me. Just wanted to check you were home before I
popped round?'

'I've been back for a while. See you when you get here.'

'Give me fifteen minutes.'

Kim put the phone back in her bag and waited for a gap
in the traffic.

After stopping at the off-licence on East Reach, she threaded
her way down the narrow streets and turned onto Gordon
Road. There was a space on the opposite side to the house,
a few doors down. Getting out, she pulled on her jacket, then
grabbed the bottle and her handbag from the passenger seat.

*She wouldn't stay late.*

Sarah opened the door with a grin, turning away and
hurrying back down the hallway. Kim followed her, and the
aroma of cooking hit her as soon as she stepped inside.

'Something smells good,' she smiled, walking into the kitchen.

'I'm glad you think so.' Sarah looked over her shoulder. 'I'm making it for you.'

'Oh, you didn't have to.'

'It's no bother.' Sarah peered into a large saucepan. 'So how did the interview go?' She looked at the bottle in Kim's hand. 'Are we celebrating or commiserating?'

Kim sank down into a chair.

'I'm not sure,' she laughed. 'Both, I think.'

'Both?'

'I think there's a good chance they'll offer me the job,' she explained. 'And the money's good . . .'

She tailed off.

'So?' Sarah turned to look at her. 'What's the problem?'

'The guy who interviewed me . . .' Kim placed the bottle on the table and frowned. 'He was really creepy.'

'So?'

'He was sort of quiet, wouldn't make eye contact. Oh, and . . .' she spoke in an adenoidal monotone '. . . he had a really interesting voice.'

Sarah sniggered.

'He's probably just a harmless little nerd who collects comics or builds model aeroplanes. You know the sort – talking to women always makes them nervous. I think they can be kind of sweet.' She flashed an evil smile. 'And you can have *so* much fun with them.'

Kim looked at her doubtfully.

'Anyway,' Sarah continued, 'so long as he's not a sex pest or a mass murderer, what does it matter?'

*Murderer.*

Kim swallowed. How messed up was her sense of perspective? How could she be bothered by this guy after Rob?

'Sis?' Sarah was staring at her, concern on her face. 'Do you want a glass of water? You look really pale.'

The risotto was delicious, especially after several days of sandwiches and takeaways. As they cleared the plates from the table, Sarah frowned and turned to the freezer. She took out a packet of melting-middle chocolate puddings and read the instructions on the side of the box.

'Bollocks,' she muttered. 'I forgot these need to defrost for an hour.'

'It's OK.' Kim put a hand on her stomach. 'I'm stuffed.'

'Trust me,' Sarah tapped the box. 'These are just *gorgeous*. Honestly, they're better than sex.'

'Don't let Simon hear you say that!'

'A little bit of criticism does him good. Don't want him getting too sure of himself.' She gave a dirty laugh.

'Where is he tonight?' Kim asked. 'I don't think I've seen him since New Year.'

'He's working in Cambridge today,' Sarah replied. 'But he said he'd be home by nine.'

She opened the box and put the desserts on the counter.

'There. We'll stick a DVD on while these thaw, and you can see Simon before you go.'

Kim's eyes flickered to her watch, and Sarah sighed.

'Come on, sis. What have you got to rush back for?'

It was a fair point. What *did* she have? Another miserable evening trapped in her little attic room at the B & B, staring at the walls?

'All right,' she nodded. 'Anything you like, just so long as it's not got Leonardo DiCaprio in it.'

The film was almost over when they heard Simon's key in the lock.

'We're in here,' Sarah called from the sofa.

'Who's "we"?' Simon replied, coming into the front room and breaking into a broad smile when he saw Kim. 'All right, stranger, how are you?'

He was broad but tall, with a round, cheerful face. He wore a nondescript suit, a dark blue shirt with the top button undone, and his brown hair was gelled into its usual messy style. Kim stood up and he gave her a suffocating hug before stepping back and gazing at her.

'Looking very smart,' he noted approvingly.

'Thank you.'

'You didn't have to dress up on my account, though,' he added with a wink, before turning to Sarah. 'Any food left? I'm starving, me . . .'

'Yeah babe,' Sarah replied, still half watching the TV, then jumped up and chased into the kitchen after him. 'But leave those chocolate puddings alone! They're not for you . . .'

It was getting late when Kim left. She waved goodbye to Sarah, who was standing on the doorstep, then walked across the road to her car. There was a chill in the air and the seats were cold against her legs – sometimes she really hated wearing a skirt. Starting the engine, she turned the heater on full, praying it would warm up quickly, then eased out of the narrow space and along to the end of the cul-de-sac.

*It had been a lovely evening – exactly what she needed.*

With familiar ease, she turned the car in the cramped dead end, but Sarah had already gone inside and closed the door when she passed the house again.

*Oh well.*

At the end of Gordon Road, she turned left, passing a line of parked cars on Queen Street before turning right again. Holding a hand in front of the air vents, she felt only cool air and started to shiver as she drove slowly through the town centre and down towards the illuminated white ironwork of the bridge, the lights glittering on the water below . . .

*Maybe Taunton wasn't so bad for now. And she had left before, so she could do it again.*

She turned off at the junction and followed the road until she saw the wooden sign, indicating for the benefit of the car behind her as she slowed down and turned in at the gate. There was a space close to the front wall and she edged into it before switching off the engine and getting out into the cool night air.

The tall gables of the B & B loomed over her, those tiny upper windows dark, unfriendly. She suddenly felt so terribly isolated – unable to stay in the welcoming familiarity of her old house; a small unhappy figure, shivering in the shadows of a guest-house car park.

But she'd done what she had to do. She'd finally got away from him, and she'd gone to the police. Now she just had to lie low here . . . and wait.

# 42

Naysmith hesitated as his fingertips were about to touch the brass handle, withdrawing his hand and easing the door open with his forearm before passing inside. He strode calmly across the floor, making no attempt to be quiet, his polished leather shoes clicking confidently on the aged floorboards. There was something rather lovely about big old houses like this, with their high ceilings and long corridors, but it was rather a pity to see them reduced to guest houses or, worse yet, converted into flats. Approaching the glass hatch, he noted the half-moon table set below it, and the waiting desk bell with a 'Please ring for attention' sign. He smiled and rapped the top of the bell smartly with the side of his hand, listening to the sound bursting through the stillness to resonate around the building.

And waited . . .

Kim had been careless. It had taken him less than three weeks to find her and, for a moment, the hope flared in him that perhaps she wanted to be found. Perhaps she was playing her own, mixed-up little game with him, to test if he really wanted her, to see if he'd come running after her. But deep down, he knew that couldn't be true. She didn't yet know his methods, how *capable* he was of hunting people. She probably thought she was being clever. She probably thought she'd given him the slip.

In any event, she should have parked somewhere else. That was her biggest mistake. That was what made it all so disappointingly *fucking* easy. She knew the area – there were plenty of other obscure little streets round there – but he'd spotted her car practically outside the house on Gordon Road. His third trip to Taunton, and he'd found her already.

*No challenge at all.*

Once he'd seen the car, it was simple. He found a place to park on Queen Street, nicely tucked in between two other vehicles, where he could watch the end of Gordon Road – and just about make out the front of the house – without being too visible.

She'd stayed quite late. At first he'd wondered if she might be spending the night there, if she'd been foolish enough to move back in with her sister. He'd looked at the dashboard clock and thought about calling it a night, heading for home.

Simple Simon rolled up around ten. Naysmith watched him fiddling with his keys on the doorstep before letting himself in. As the front door slammed shut, he'd rubbed his eyes and stifled that first, wearying yawn.

*But something told him to wait.*

And then, just before eleven, he'd sat up in his seat, eager eyes staring out through the darkness. Light spilled from the doorway, illuminating the gateposts, and two figures appeared, silhouetted against the yellow glow from the inside.

There she was – his beautiful Kim. He smiled despite himself, watching as she hugged her sister and walked across to her car. His hand reached for his own ignition, but he didn't start the engine yet – in a quiet neighbourhood, the noise might make them look in his direction. Anyway, he had time – she was parked the wrong way and would need to turn around.

As her rear lights came on and she pulled out, he saw Sarah step back into the house and shut the door.

*Good.*

He started the car but left the lights off as the engine idled.

*Not until she was past.*

A moment later, he slid down low in his seat as the beam of her headlights illuminated the vehicles ahead of him and her car turned left. He switched on his own lights and pulled out behind her as she turned right onto South Street and drove down to the junction at the end.

She went left through the sleeping town centre, with him trailing behind her, trying to keep his distance – there wasn't a lot of other traffic, just those two points of red light that led him on past the darkened windows of the shops. They crossed the river and went on towards the station, but she turned off onto a side road.

*Odd. Where was she going?*

He followed her down the road, noting the large old houses, the walled gardens and spreading trees.

And then he saw the amber flash of her indicators; she was turning in somewhere. He didn't brake, just lifted his foot from the throttle to let the car slow a little as he cruised past the tall gateposts that marked the entrance to the car park, and finally lost sight of her.

She was staying at a bed and breakfast, rather than taking the risk of staying with her sister. He smiled to himself.

*Nice try, Kim.*

A hundred yards down the street, he pulled over to the side and stared at the road behind in the rear-view mirror. The fact that she'd at least tried to cover her tracks pleased him for some reason. Perhaps because it meant his brave little girl was still thinking about him.

After a moment, when there was no traffic, he did a U-turn

and crept slowly back along the road. He read the sign and
noted the name 'Geddes Guest House' as he drew level with
the gate. There was her car, parked up by the fence, and he
stared up at the house for a moment, lost in thought.

Then, as he'd peered up through the trees, a yellow light
had blinked on in one of the tiny top-floor windows. He'd
gazed up at it for a moment and smiled to himself before
setting off for home.

And now, in front of him, the pane of frosted glass slid aside
with a rasping scrape and the stern face of a middle-aged
woman appeared at the hatch.

'Can I help you?' Aloof, grey hair, affected accent. But
better that than the overfriendly small hoteliers who wanted
to get to know their clients.

'Good afternoon. I'm Robert Hanage,' Naysmith lied
politely. 'I telephoned this morning. I believe you have a room
for me?'

She studied him over the top of her spectacles, assessing
his manner, his clothing . . . then smiled warmly.

'Mr Hanage, yes of course.' She nodded approvingly, then
made some show of consulting a large, leather-bound book.

Naysmith leaned forward, but couldn't see enough to read
the details of the other guests.

*No matter.*

'Here we are.' The woman was passing a registration form
and a pen through to him. 'I've put you in number nine – it's
our most comfortable room.'

'How thoughtful of you,' Naysmith smiled at her. 'I've a
feeling I'm going to enjoy my stay.'

That evening he had an excellent meal at an old country-
house hotel a few miles outside of town and got back a little

after ten. He parked down a quiet side street – Kim would be bound to notice his car otherwise, and he didn't want her to run again. Taunton was deserted tonight. The pubs would be closing soon, but he passed no one as he made his way round the block to the guest house.

There were several lights on in the imposing old building, but the little window at the top was in darkness and there was no sign of her car.

Where was she? Visiting Sarah again perhaps?

Reaching into his pocket, he drew out the key with its large plastic fob and approached the entrance to let himself in. His room commanded an excellent view of the car-park entrance. She would doubtless be back in the next hour or so, and when she did, he would be ready.

# 43

Harland drained his first coffee of Wednesday morning and yawned. Leaning back in his chair, he worked the muscles in his shoulders, trying to loosen them, then returned his attention to the stack of witness reports on his desk.

When his mobile rang, it was a welcome relief. He peered at the screen for a moment – London number – then hit the answer key.

'Hello?'

'DI Harland?' A voice he couldn't quite place.

'Speaking.'

'Good morning. This is DI Cadnam – we talked before?'

Harland paused for a moment, then leaned forward.

'About the Severn Beach witness, yes.'

'That's right.' Cadnam's voice was flat, unreadable. 'I just wanted to let you know, we've now followed up on the information you gave us, but it was a dead end.'

Harland frowned.

'The statement from Kim . . .' He broke off, trying to remember her surname.

'Nichols.'

'You checked into it all? Took a look at the boyfriend?'

'We did. Seems he'd been cheating on her and she found out about it. Draw your own conclusions, but he has no connection to any of the known victims and she's . . .' Cadnam paused, measuring how much to tell. 'Well, let's say she probably felt like getting her own back.'

'That wasn't how she came across.' Harland shook his head. He thought back to that small figure sitting in the interview room, the very real sense of fear he'd got from her. 'Did you actually speak to her yourself?'

The faintest note of annoyance crept into Cadnam's voice.

'I did better than that,' he replied. 'I spoke to this Naysmith guy. Honestly, I know you want a result – we all do – but this one isn't going anywhere.'

'She was scared of something,' Harland persisted. He wasn't wrong about this one.

'I'm not arguing with that,' Cadnam said. 'But you know how it works, and there's just not enough to justify reopening the case at the moment. I'm sorry.'

Harland sighed.

'I know how it works,' he said wearily.

'If you turn up anything else, let me know and I'll do what I can. OK?'

Harland gave a wry smile.

*Yeah, because that worked out so well for everyone this time.*

'Sure,' he said. 'Thanks for calling.'

'Bye.'


Harland put the phone down on his desk and spun it slowly around for a moment with his finger. Relinquishing an investigation was never good, but he'd really hoped that something might come from rattling this Robert Naysmith's cage.

Rubbing his eyes, he yawned again, then reached for his mug and found it empty. Barely half past nine and already the day was going downhill. Sighing, he got to his feet and made his way through to the kitchen.

Mendel was by the sink filling the kettle when he walked in. The big man glanced up at him, then moved across to set the kettle on its base.

'What's the matter?' he asked as he switched it on.

Harland shook his head and stepped forward to rinse out his cup.

'Remember that woman who came in?' he said after a moment. 'The one who thought her boyfriend was the Severn Beach killer?'

'Yeah, I remember her,' Mendel nodded. 'What are the Met doing?'

'Nothing.' Harland opened the cupboard and took out the coffee. 'They think she's making the whole thing up.'

'Maybe she is.'

Harland put his mug on the counter and leaned back against the wall.

'I don't think so – she was scared. Genuinely scared.'

Mendel looked at him for a moment.

'So we're no further on than we were before,' he shrugged. 'That's life.'

'I suppose so.'

The kettle boiled and Mendel poured water into both their mugs. 'There you go.'

'Thanks.'

He picked up a teaspoon, then looked at Harland.

'So what's the problem?' he asked. 'It's been off our radar for months.'

Harland bowed his head.

'The problem is what do I say to her?'

'Why say anything? Let the Met deal with it.'

Harland looked at him.

*Because she had come to him. Because he had persuaded her to talk.*

'I suppose you're right,' he said. Stirring his coffee, he rinsed the spoon under the tap and left it on the side to dry.

'Course I'm right,' Mendel told him. 'Anyway, you should be happy. We've got Leroy Marshall in court soon, and he's given us his whole gang. That's a decent result.'

'I know, it's just . . .' Harland sighed and shook his head. 'Never mind.'

He stalked back to his office and closed the door. Slumping down into his chair, he took a sip of coffee and closed his eyes. Kim wasn't making it up – something *was* scaring her – but without any evidence, what could Cadnam's team do? He stared down at the pile of papers on his desk for a moment, then frowned and started looking for her number.

Picking up the phone, he made it as far as the last digit, then hesitated and hung up. Mendel was right. The Met would call her.


The clock at the bottom of the screen showed 7 p.m. Harland massaged his temples, then leaned across to switch off the computer. The after-image remained for a moment, a pale rectangle imprinted on his retina, and he rubbed his eyes until it faded. Another day done.

He stood up and stretched for a moment, then took his jacket from the back of his chair and slipped it on. The corridor was quiet as he pulled his office door shut, but he could hear voices near the kitchen.

Mendel was there, rinsing out his cup, while Stuart Gregg was propped up against the far wall, leafing through a handful of papers and shaking his head slowly.

'How's it going?' Harland asked.

Mendel gave him a wry smile.

'Slowly,' he said. 'You done for the night?'

'Yeah,' Harland sighed. 'Fancy a quick drink in the White Lion?'

Gregg glanced up hopefully, but Mendel looked at his watch.

'We've just got one more thing to wrap up here – maybe see you there in half an hour?'

'See you there,' Harland nodded.

He made his way downstairs, raising a hand to acknowledge Firth's wave from through the glass-partitioned front office, then walked outside into the cool evening air. As the door swung shut behind him, he paused to reach into his pocket, fumbling for his cigarettes. Jamming one into his mouth, he clicked the lighter and took a long first drag, then walked out towards the street.

'Hey!'

Harland turned quickly, his eyes settling on a slender figure walking tentatively down the pavement towards him.

'I trusted you.'

*Oh no.*

His shoulders sagged as he recognised Kim, one small hand pointing at him in accusation, the other steadying herself on a parked car for a moment then tightening to a tiny fist as she came closer.

'Kim?' He moved towards her as she came to a halt and stared at him with eyes red from crying.

'I trusted you,' she hissed again. 'I made a statement, just like you said, so you could get Rob.'

'Kim, it's not—' he began, but she interrupted him.

'Today someone phones me up and says he's spoken to Rob, but there's insufficient . . . I don't know what.'

'Look, I know it's not what—'

'Just tell me if they're going to arrest him. Just *tell* me!'

Harland looked down and shook his head.

'I don't think so.'

Kim stared at him. Her hands, hanging at her sides, began to tremble.

'But now he knows. He *knows* I went to the police about him.'

Harland looked at her wretchedly. He could smell the alcohol on her breath now.

'I can't go home,' she wailed. 'Had to quit my job. What the fuck am I going to do?'

'I'm sorry.'

'Sorry? Is that all you've got?' She jabbed an accusing finger. 'You told me it would be all right. Why did you put me through this if you didn't believe me?'

Harland moved closer to her, putting his hand on her arm.

'I do believe you, Kim.'

She stared at him in despair.

'And the rest of them don't?'

He wanted to say something positive, something that would encourage her, but there was no way to dress this up.

'Something like that.' She trembled and sagged against a car. He moved to try and steady her, but she flailed at his arm, pushing him away.

'Leave me alone.'

She pushed herself upright and began to walk off, rummaging in her handbag for something. Harland heard the jingle then saw the glint as she drew out her keys.

*Car keys.*

'Kim?' He started after her. 'How much have you had to drink?'

'I said, leave me alone!'

'I can't let you drive if you're drunk.'

She spun round to face him.

'What are you going to do?' she sobbed. 'You want to arrest *me* now?'

'I just want to help you.'

'Help me?' She gave a bleak little laugh. 'You can't help me. You couldn't help anyone.'

And that was the worst of it – the hated truth – that he laboured in vain, that all his efforts came to nothing. When it came down to it, when it really mattered, what difference did he make?

'Where are you staying?' he asked.

'Taunton,' she murmured, moving towards her car.

'Kim, that's almost an hour away. Isn't there anyone who can come and pick you up?'

Her shoulders tensed and she whirled round to face him.

'Like my sister?' she snapped, then shook her head bitterly. 'Don't you get it? I've put my family in danger already thanks to you.'

She turned back towards her car. Harland walked after her, pushing a hand through his hair in exasperation.

'Look, I can't let you drive . . .'

He stepped in front of her, placing his body between her and the car. He'd done nothing wrong but responsibility weighed heavily on him.

'Why don't you find a hotel, come back for your car in the morning? *Please.*'

She shook her head.

'What does it matter?' she said wearily. 'Just go.'

'No.' Mendel and Gregg would have to wait. He couldn't abandon her now. 'Look, I'll drive you, OK?'

'Where? I don't know anywhere.'

'We'll find you somewhere.'

She glared at him for a moment, then shook her head and shrugged in defeat.

Gently he led her back down the slope, around the station building to where his car was parked. She seemed quieter now, as though he'd broken her will and the last of her fight had drained away.

*Even doing the right thing made him feel bad.*

He unlocked his car and held the door open for her, watching her as she got in. She didn't look at him, just sat staring straight ahead as he shut her door and went round to the driver's side. Sliding into his seat, he looked across at her.

'Are you OK?'

She said nothing, just turned to look at him. He put the key in the ignition, then paused. Where should he take her?

'There's not much round here, but I know a few places in Bristol. It's on my way, and you can easily get a bus back in the morning to collect your car.'

She nodded slightly, just once, then turned away from him, touching her mouth with the back of her hand as she stared out of the passenger window.

Harland sighed.

'All right . . .' He started the engine and gripped the wheel. 'Bristol it is.'

It was only a twenty-minute journey at this time of the evening but her silence made it seem longer. As they drove out of Portishead he tried to engage her with a couple of questions about herself but she ignored him, winding down the passenger window and turning her face towards the rush of cold air that swirled into the car. By the time they crossed the M5 he'd given up on any conversation, but as they descended into the outskirts of the city, she finally spoke.

'Why are you doing this?'

He glanced across at her, startled to hear her voice, thrown by the nature of her question.

'It wouldn't have been safe for you to drive,' he replied,

waiting for her to say something else. But the silence returned, awkward seconds dragging out until he felt compelled to fill them. 'I didn't want anything to happen to you.'

She kept staring straight ahead for a moment, and then, on the periphery of his vision, he sensed her turn towards him.

'What do you care?' she asked.

*What sort of a question was that?*

Ahead of them, traffic lights changed from green to amber, but he put his foot down and accelerated over the crossroads.

'Look, I care, all right?' He could hear the frustration building in his voice and strained to master it. 'I care. It's just . . . I can't always make things work out the way I want.'

He didn't look at her, just watched the road, but he could feel her eyes boring into the side of his head. He sighed and indicated left. In the distance, the Clifton bridge twinkled on the skyline, but it was quickly lost from view as they swept down under the dual carriageway and emerged onto the built-up streets of the suburbs.

'So what will happen to him?' she asked quietly.

'Sorry?'

'If they won't arrest Rob, what will happen?' There was nothing sluggish about her speech now.

He stared out across the steering wheel for a long moment as they approached the river.

'It's not up to me—' he began, then broke off.

*No. None of that official-vocabulary bullshit.*

He wasn't going to mislead her again. Better to be straight with her.

'I think that unless something changes – like if they get some new information . . .' He tailed off.

*Was she crying?*

He heard the first timid sobs and glanced across to see her bent forward, head in her hands. Her small body shook as she wept.

'Kim . . .'

He tried to do the right thing – maintain his professional detachment, concentrate on the road – but it was no use. Her distress touched something deep inside, cutting through months of loneliness and reminding him of the person he'd been before Alice died.

He could sense the crisis coming – for him as well as her. Checking the rear-view mirror, he took a deep breath and pulled over beside the trees that followed the line of the river along Coronation Road.

She was sobbing now, indistinct words and anguished sounds muffled behind the hands that cupped her face.

'Kim?'

'Everything's wrong.' She gulped a sudden breath. 'Everything!'

He placed an awkward hand on her back, uncertain how he should console her.

'It's OK,' he said softly. 'It'll be OK.'

'No.' She straightened a little, head still downcast, staring at the floor. 'He's going to find me, and there's nothing I can do to stop him. And nobody will even believe me until it happens.'

Harland put a cautious arm around her, gently drawing her closer until she allowed her head to rest on his shoulder.

'I believe you,' he said.

She turned her head to look up at him, her face suddenly very close. Her large eyes stared into his, long lashes dark with tears that ran down her cheeks. He felt he ought to pull away, but instead he hesitated as she moved closer, her lips parting slightly.

And then instinct took over and he met her kiss with his mouth, closing his eyes to shut out all the doubts and all the confusion for one brief, soft moment.

Her hand was on his shoulder as she broke off, and he opened his eyes to see her draw back just a little, gazing up at him with an anxious expression.

'Sorry . . . You're not married or anything?'

Harland shook his head.

'No,' he said simply.

She looked up at him, her face glistening, then pulled him down and kissed him again. He felt more tears falling, trickling on his hand as she pressed her mouth to his, but she gradually became more insistent, giving herself to the kiss. This one lasted a long time, and Harland's pulse was racing when she finally drew away and he could breathe once more.

'Where can we go?' she asked him.

*Was she saying what he thought she was saying?*

He stared at her. A clamour of thoughts rose in his mind but he dismissed them all.

'I live just a few streets from here . . .' He left it open.

'OK.' She leaned her head against his shoulder again and put her hand on his thigh – her touch rippling out through his body, leaving him in no doubt. He gunned the engine and pulled away.

They didn't speak, but she held his hand as they walked down the pavement and up to the front door. Neither of them wanted to break the spell now – lots of contact, lots of touching, but no words. He turned the key in the lock, and let her inside.

As the door closed behind them, she kissed him again. There was no time to think, no time to question anything as they climbed the stairs and entered the bedroom. Another kiss, and then they were undressing each other, her small hands working quickly, her breath warm on his chest as she undid the buttons of his shirt.

Their lips met and they stumbled over to the bed – Harland guiding her down onto the duvet, breathing quickly, finding freedom in the inevitability of it all. She was so fragile, so vulnerable, so beautiful. Kim arched her back so he could slip her underwear down and then pulled him on top of her.

As he pushed himself up the bed and she wrapped her legs around him, he stared down at a face that momentarily seemed to mirror his own sadness, his own sense of loss. And then he moved, and her eyes closed as she gasped and bit her lip – the vision was gone and his thoughts dissolved into sensation.

# 44

She woke gradually, drifting gently up to the surface of consciousness, comfortable and calm. Her mind slowly began to register things – the pillow against her cheek was different, the duvet felt wrong. She opened her eyes, struggling to make out the unfamiliar blur of the room around her.

And the unfamiliar heat of the body next to her.

She slumped back down into the pillow for a moment as flashes of the previous evening coalesced in her mind, but the movement brought a dull aching in her head. Her mouth was dry and she could feel the edges of a hangover.

She was glad he hadn't let her drive.

After a couple of minutes, she sat up gently, quietly. Sprawled beside her, face down, Graham murmured something and shifted slightly. She gazed down at his shoulders, exposed above the line of the duvet, the short hair tapering down at the nape of his neck, watching as his lean body rose and fell steadily, peacefully.

This wasn't like her. It was such a long time since she'd woken up in a stranger's bed, and yet somehow it didn't feel like that. There was no regret, no doubts, just a quiet calm after the release of so much tension – clearing skies after a long-awaited storm.

She needed the bathroom.

Easing her legs out from under the warmth of the duvet, she lowered her feet to the soft carpet and carefully rolled herself into a sitting position at the edge of the bed.

Graham didn't stir.

Rising to her feet, she tiptoed over to where her clothes lay scattered on the floor – evidence of last night's abandonment – and wriggled into her pants, then picked up her blouse. The house wasn't cold, but she felt more comfortable, less exposed. Slipping her arm into the sleeve, her eyes began taking in details of the room – a glass bowl filled with smooth stones in the empty fireplace, a selection of coloured candles on the hearth, the slender white vase on the shelf beside the window, a pale ribbon wound around the frame of the dressing-table mirror. So many delicate touches.

She frowned.

At one side of the dressing table there was an ornate jewellery box – pale polished wood with inlaid Japanese carvings. Propped neatly beside it, a tan leather make-up bag, with a little gold dolphin charm hanging from the zip.

Her eyes swept the rest of the room and settled on a small handmade picture frame on the shelf. She moved closer, peering at the photograph inside – Graham and a blonde woman, obviously a couple, comfortable and happy in each other's presence.

Kim felt a brief flutter of panic.

*Had he lied to her? Was he married?*

She turned to glance back at the bed, wondering if she should just gather her things and go, then looked again at the items on the dressing table.

*Something wasn't right.*

Jewellery box, make-up bag . . . but where was the rest? As she looked around the room, she could see his things everywhere – pressed shirts hanging on the outside of the wardrobe door, deodorant and aftershave on the dressing table, an untidy pile of books by his side of the bed – but little belonging to her. Just those few things, the photograph . . . mementos.

She bit her lip and padded quietly out into the hallway. The bathroom was at the far end of the landing and she closed the door behind her. A quick glance in the cabinet above the sink saw the pattern continue. Razor, shaving foam and a single toothbrush. Everything was his. As she closed the cabinet door, her own reflection gazed back at her thoughtfully. He definitely lived alone, but who was the woman in the picture?

Downstairs, she found a tidy kitchen with a window that looked out on an unkempt garden, and made her way over to the sink. She took a tall glass from the draining board and filled it from the tap, swallowing the cold water quickly to counter the dehydration and lessen her headache. Then, returning the glass to its place, she filled the kettle and switched it on. The cupboards were largely bare of food, but there was half a jar of coffee and an unopened box of tea bags in one of them. She guessed coffee and made two cups before returning upstairs.

He was still asleep when she entered the bedroom – a profoundly tranquil expression on his face – but stirred as she set the cup down on his bedside table.

'Morning,' she said awkwardly.

He sat up quickly, blinking at her in surprise for a moment before his features relaxed in recognition and he sank back against the headboard and rubbed his eyes.

'Good morning,' he said, gazing up at her for a long moment. Then, remembering the cup, he reached out a bare arm to take it and shot her an uneasy smile. 'Thanks for this.'

He leaned forward, inhaling the steam.

'I wasn't sure how you took it so I left it black,' she said.
'Black is fine,' he nodded.

The silence grew louder as she stood there, suddenly self-conscious, holding the front of her blouse shut, aware of his nakedness under the duvet. She turned away for a moment, then moved slowly towards the small picture frame, looking at it once again, waiting.

'That was my wife. Alice.'

*Was?*

Behind her, his voice suddenly seemed far away.

'She died two years ago.'

Kim turned towards him, but he wasn't looking at her. His eyes were downcast, his face transformed into a stoic mask of sorrow.

'Car crash,' he said simply, then shrugged to himself.

'Oh.' She wasn't sure what to say. Part of her was relieved, pleased he hadn't lied; part of her was disappointed in herself for thinking that way. After a moment, she moved back towards the bed. Her hand stopped clasping the front of her blouse as she reached out to steady herself against the wall and kiss him on top of his bowed head.

'I'm sorry,' she said softly.

He glanced up, suddenly back in the present. Looking at her, he smiled, then sighed.

'No. *I'm* sorry,' he said after a moment. 'About last night, I mean . . .'

He tailed off and looked away from her.

'Don't be,' she told him. 'I'm not.'

*So strong, yet so vulnerable.*

He smiled sadly, eyes downcast as he waited for the words to come.

'I never meant . . .' he dragged his gaze back to hers '. . . never meant for *this* to happen.'

'I know.'

Perhaps that was why it felt different. Because he hadn't tried to seduce her, hadn't tried to do anything other than protect her.

'I was worried for you. I just wanted to help.'

'I know,' she told him. 'And you did.'

Easing herself down onto the duvet, she leaned across and extended her arms, drawing him close before settling down to rest her head on his chest, his heartbeat reassuring and steady in the quiet of the room.

'What will you do?' he asked after a while.

Kim closed her eyes for a moment, then shook her head slowly.

'Honestly? I don't know.' She felt strangely calm, but things would be difficult now – the money she'd taken wouldn't last for ever. 'Keep looking for a new job, I suppose. I can't ever go back home now.'

Lying quietly, she gazed at the photograph of Graham and Alice, wondering what she'd been like, if they'd been happy together.

'You could stay here for a while,' he said after a moment.

Kim drew back and stared at him.

'I'm not your problem.' She wasn't helpless. She could take care of herself.

'I didn't mean it like that.' His expression was pained, as though he'd forgotten how to speak to a woman. Perhaps he had. 'I just meant for a day or two, if it helps. Where are you staying just now?'

She regarded him carefully for a moment, then relented.

'At a B & B in Taunton.'

He nodded, choosing his words carefully.

'I'm just saying, you can stay here until you get yourself sorted. If you want.'

He really seemed to mean it.

'Oh, and I didn't—' He broke off, eyes flickering to hers then quickly away again. 'There's a spare room. If you want.'

He trailed off into an awkward silence. *So honest, nothing hidden.*

Slowly, she relaxed back down to lay her head on his shoulder, smiling to herself.

'We'll see,' she said.

# part 4
# SACRIFICE

# 45

Saturday-morning sunlight glimmered in the gap between the curtains as Harland blinked and opened his eyes. He yawned and went to roll over, pausing as he felt Kim's arm draped across him. Turning his head, he gazed at the tangle of brunette hair on the pillow next to him, listened to the soft rhythm of her breathing.

Had he made a mistake? Inviting a stranger into his house, into his life? A confusion of different emotions rose in his mind and he closed his eyes against them for a moment, sinking back down into the mattress.

Beside him, she stirred a little, then settled again, the warmth of her body oddly soothing.

They'd made love again last night – the first time since the first time. He hadn't wanted to push things with her, and though she'd shared his bed each night, he'd known it was because she didn't want to be alone. But last night, as he lay there looking up at the ceiling, she'd climbed on top of him and silenced his questions with a kiss.

Now, he sat up slowly, gently lifting her arm and moving out from beneath it. Visible above the edge of the duvet, her white camisole top rose and fell steadily as she slept on. Getting out of bed, he stood up and stretched, then moved towards the door, walking carefully to avoid waking her. It would take a while to get used to having someone else here again, and suddenly the house felt strange, but not in a bad way.

In the bathroom, he caught sight of himself in the mirror and turned to lean over the sink, studying his reflection and catching the ghost of a smile. The aching loss was still there in his eyes, but for the first time it seemed diminished, pushed aside by . . . what?

Lust? No. She was lovely, and he wanted her, but it was more than that.

He made his way downstairs and into the kitchen. Pausing to yawn again, he checked there was water in the kettle and switched it on.

His instinct was to protect, to worry – instincts he normally had to suppress. So many women seemed to respond to indifference, to easy-going confidence – things that didn't come naturally to him any more. But with her, there had been no time to pretend. He had been himself and it had been enough.

As he went to get the milk, his eyes settled on the old photo of Alice and himself, stuck on the fridge door.

*He had been himself.*

Perhaps that was why he felt no guilt.

They had a meagre breakfast at the small kitchen table – usual for him, but he found himself wondering if she normally ate more. There was still so much he didn't know about her. He'd thought about going to the supermarket on his way home last night, but somehow the idea of buying lots of different food seemed dangerous, like tempting fate. If he started acting as though they were living together, it would break the spell and she would go. Day by day was fine for now.

She looked sleepy but she had dressed before coming down – still very much a house guest. When they had finished their coffee, he picked up the cups and took them over to the sink, wondering if she had plans for the day, hoping that she didn't.

'Doing anything later?' He tried to sound casual about it. Kim yawned.

'Not really thought about it,' she said.

Harland felt himself smiling as he rinsed out the cups, then turned around to face her.

'Look, I know that wasn't much of a breakfast . . .' He shrugged as she lifted her head to gaze over at him. 'Did you want to maybe go out and find somewhere to eat?'

*And some neutral territory so she could relax with him.*

'OK,' Kim said slowly. 'I don't really know Bristol that well.'

'We could take a walk, if you want. There are lots of good places.'

'I'd like that,' she nodded, stifling a yawn. 'I'm not really hungry just now, but a walk sounds good.'

It was bright and warm as they waited for a break in the traffic before crossing Coronation Road. Walking beneath the trees, Harland turned left and led them out across the old footbridge. They gazed down, through the rusty iron lattice-work with its peeling red and white paint, to the silted brown river that crawled below.

On the far side, they went right, following the road as it hugged the north bank of the river, sweeping round in a gentle, tree-lined arc. They spoke little at first, sensing how fragile things might be between them, aware of how little they knew each other.

Ahead of them stood an old corner pub at the end of a three-storey terrace. A covered Georgian balcony, supported by slender ironwork legs, wrapped around the curved face of the first floor, hinting at the beauty of its heyday.

'I love those old verandas.' Kim smiled as she gazed up at it. 'There's something very romantic about them.'

'You see a few of them around the older parts of the city,' Harland noted. 'Come on, let's cross over here.'

They left the main road and walked down a brick-paved lane that ran along the edge of one of the smaller harbour basins. Stepping in and out of the shade, beneath the trees that lined the quayside, they gazed out at the moored yachts and narrowboats, their reflections shimmering gently on the water.

'This really is beautiful,' Kim murmured. She looked serene in the sunlight. 'You're lucky to live next door to all this.'

Harland smiled to himself. He'd not thought of himself as 'lucky' for a long time. And yet . . .

'So much prettier than Salisbury,' she added.

'Is that where you're from?' he asked. 'Originally, I mean?'

It was a bad policeman's habit, always questioning. He scolded himself silently, but she didn't seem to mind.

'Salisbury? No, I'm from Taunton.' She shook her head slightly. 'I don't know which of them I like least.'

'I've been to Taunton a couple of times.' Harland shrugged. 'It wasn't that bad.'

'You didn't have to grow up there.'

'Not a fun place, then?'

'It's not that . . .' Kim hesitated, then sighed. 'I was just glad to leave.'

She looked troubled now. Had he said the wrong thing? Touched a nerve?

They walked on in silence until they came to the end of the quay where the footpath turned to follow a narrow inlet channel. A footbridge led across to a sea of wooden tables outside the Ostrich pub – a few already occupied even though it was early – but they stayed on the cobblestones that led back to the main waterway.

'Sorry,' Kim said after a moment. 'I didn't mean to— I just have some bad associations with Taunton.'

'OK.' He wasn't sure what to say to that. Should he ask? Or just shut up for a moment and let her tell him if she needed to?

She seemed to sense his uncertainty, glancing up at him, then turning away to look out across the water.

'My father finally walked out on us when I was ten,' she said softly. 'After that I never really liked the place very much.'

'Sorry to hear that.'

She managed a brief smile as they turned and walked back towards the centre of town.

'What about you?' she asked, her voice brightening a little as she changed the subject.

Harland looked down at the ground and smiled.

'My father was in the police,' he shrugged. 'We lived in a few different places when I was growing up. A bit of time in London, a bit of time here.'

'Any brothers or sisters?'

'Only child,' Harland told her. 'But don't worry, I'm remarkably well adjusted, considering.'

Kim nodded to herself.

'There were times, growing up, when I wished I was an only child,' she reflected.

They walked on towards the towering grey dock cranes that stood dark against the clear blue sky.

'You've just got the one sister.' Harland frowned. 'Sarah, right?'

'That's right,' Kim smiled up at him. 'Nice to see you've been listening.'

Harland inclined his head to her modestly.

'And she still lives in Taunton?'

'Yes,' Kim replied. 'Technically, it's my house. We lived together for a few years. It's not a very big place, but when I moved out, she and her partner were able to spread out a bit.'

'Where did you live after that?' The moment he said it, he knew it was the wrong thing to ask.

Kim slowed, looking down at her feet before glancing up at him from behind her hair.

'I moved in with Rob,' she said, a strange tone creeping into her voice. Fear? Or something else?

They stood there for an uneasy moment, until he reached forward and took her hands in his.

'It'll be all right,' he promised her. 'We'll get him. I'll speak to the Met again, maybe start looking into it myself – quietly – until I find something that we can use, some way to take him down.'

She stared up at him, managing a brave little smile. So troubled, but so beautiful.

'Can we talk about something else?' she said softly.

Harland gazed into her eyes a little longer, then nodded.

'I just want you to know that you're safe now, OK?'

She didn't speak – just looked up at him and squeezed his hand.

He wouldn't let anything happen to her. Somehow that thought lifted him, and he found that he was smiling.

'Come on,' he said. 'Let me show you around.'


They walked across the swing bridge near the Arnolfini building, pausing to look along the old dockside with its cranes and warehouse buildings to a distant terrace of multi-coloured houses on the hill overlooking the river.

'I often come down here,' Harland told her. 'There are some beautiful spots around the old harbour.'

He pointed out towards the curved facade of a building across the water.

'If you go along that way, there's a path that takes you right along the riverside . . .'

He stopped and turned to look at her ruefully.

'Sorry,' he said. 'I'm doing all the talking. And don't feel you have to be dragged along – tell me if you want to stop somewhere.'

'No, it's OK.' The uneasiness had passed, and she seemed happy again. 'We can keep going.'

They followed the cobblestone quayside around the side of the Arnolfini and walked out onto the gentle arch of Pero's Bridge. Halfway across, a pair of buskers were playing a beautiful rendition of 'Ave Maria' – one on violin, the other on cello – and Kim held back a little to hear them finish.

'You too?' Harland said softly, as she brought a hand up to touch her chest.

She nodded. 'I've always loved that piece of music.'

On the far side of the bridge, they wove their way through the sounds and smells of the Watershed market, stopping to sample olives from a quayside vendor before they emerged from the covered walkway and turned left onto Park Street. As they came to the foot of the hill, Kim pointed at a large mural painted on the plain end wall of a building.

'Is that a Banksy?' she asked.

'That's right,' Harland replied. He gazed up at the stencilled image: a life-sized open window, revealing an angry-looking man in a suit and a woman in her underwear standing behind him while her naked lover hung by one hand from the window ledge.

'Always makes me smile,' he murmured. There was an odd

excitement about seeing something so familiar with her beside him – like seeing it for the first time. He turned to face her. 'Do you feel like a coffee? I know the perfect place . . .'

They made their way up the hill, slowing now and again to nose in the little shop windows. Near the top, Harland stopped outside a cheerful-looking café.

'What would you like?' he asked her.

'Um . . .' Kim studied the menu in the window. 'Just a cappuccino, please.'

'OK. I won't be a moment.'

'There are seats inside,' Kim frowned. 'Aren't we going in?'

Pausing in the doorway, Harland looked over his shoulder at her.

'This isn't the place I meant,' he said.

Coffees in hand, they turned off Park Street and made their way up a steep side road. The pavement climbed suddenly, a flight of worn stone steps leading up to a raised section of aged flagstones. Below, garages and storerooms opened out onto the street, while on their right-hand side a stepped terrace of beautiful old townhouses marched down the hill. There were more of the covered balconies here, their ornate ironwork painted white and cascades of trailing plants hanging down above their heads. Kim gazed up at them as she walked, a faint smile on her lips.

At the top of the incline the narrow street abruptly angled left and sloped down into the city again, but a set of steps led on into a park. They made their way up, passing under the shadow of some old-established trees to emerge on a sloping pathway that wound steadily higher as it curved round the side of an open, grassy hill.

To their right, trees and bushes circled the summit, where a sturdy stone tower stood proud and tall against the sky, but Harland followed the path on until it broadened out into a flat area on a lower crest. Here, high above the city, a line of benches sat at the top of a long slope, gazing out across the tiny streets and houses and on towards the far green hills and the horizon.

'Oh!' Kim walked over to the edge. 'What a view!'

'*This* is the place I was talking about,' he smiled.

She stood there for a moment, sipping her coffee and gazing out into the distance. Behind her, Harland reached into his pocket and drew out his cigarette packet, then frowned and put them away again.

*Not now.* If they were going to kiss, he didn't want the taste of smoke to put her off. He moved forward to stand at her side. Sunlight glittered on the leaves of the trees below the glorious blue sky.

'So, what do you think?' he asked. 'Better than the café, isn't it?'

She smiled and slipped her small hand into his.

# 46

He was being so sweet. Standing here, on this grassy hill with the whole of the city spread out below them, she felt oddly free. Squeezing his hand, she saw his face break instantly into a smile.

So honest. So unguarded. So opposite to everything she'd known before.

She turned back to stare out across the city – the sloping streets, the sturdy old buildings, the colourful houses. It felt welcoming, inviting.

*But it wasn't home.*

With Rob still out there, it was hard to think of anywhere as home.

She took a couple of steps and sat down on one of the benches. Graham stood a moment longer, and she glanced across at him – a lean silhouette against the bright sky. He was a good person – she felt sure of that now. At first, she'd been wary of his offer to stay, waiting for him to make a pass or try and take advantage of her, especially after the way she'd behaved that first, drunken evening. But the pass had never come. She knew he wanted her, but he'd seemed content simply to hold her when he found her in his bed the following night. He made her feel safe.

She bowed her head and sighed. It wasn't right. She should really find her own place before things went too far. Before she screwed things up. Before he got hurt.

'You should see the sunsets from up here.' He was speaking again and she raised her head to look at him as he stared out at some distant memory. 'It's like sitting on the edge of the world.'

'Graham?'

Something in her tone of voice must have warned him. He turned and looked at her, doubt clouding his face.

'You've been really good to me,' she began. The fact that he really had made her feel even worse.

'That's all right.' He was guarded now, wary of what was coming next.

She bit her lip, then sighed.

'It's not all right though,' she said, avoiding his gaze. 'I feel as if I'm taking advantage of you.'

That was true as well.

'You're not.' He said it flatly, as though it were a simple, obvious fact. 'I'm happy for you to stay with me.'

'But—'

'I *want* you to stay.' There was no pleading, no desperation, but she knew he meant it.

'I'm not sure I can do what you want . . .' She hesitated as it dawned on her what she had meant to say, then added, 'I'm not sure I can *be* who you want.'

His eyes left hers, and for a long moment he stared out towards the skyline. Finally, he bowed his head.

'What do you mean?' he asked, but it was obvious from the hollow tone in his voice that he understood; he just needed to hear her speak the words.

'You lost your wife.' She hated herself for saying it, but it couldn't be helped. 'You lost your wife, and I found out I was living with a murderer.' She shook her head. 'We're both . . . running away from really bad things.'

She expected him to walk away – to get to his feet, snarl

some cold rebuke and stride off down the hill – but he didn't. She could see the upset in his face, but he mastered it and turned back to her, holding her gaze steadily.

'So?' Just the one word, spoken softly, as though inviting her to hit him again.

It was impossible. Couldn't he see she was trying to spare him?

'You've been so sweet – you've been so kind . . .' She reached out a hand and gently touched the side of his face. 'I just don't want you getting hurt.'

'What makes you think I'm going to get hurt?'

'Because I'm bad luck to be around,' she snapped. 'Sooner or later, I *always* screw things up. *OK*?'

'I don't believe that.' He didn't flinch, just carried on looking at her.

'It's true,' she insisted. 'I always drive people away. I always have.'

Her father. Her mother. Even Rob. Everyone who ever cared for her, and she had pushed them all away.

'Do you want to drive *me* away?'

She looked up sharply. 'What?'

'I said, do you want to drive *me* away, Kim?'

'No, of course not, but—'

'Then don't.' Again, the matter-of-fact tone, as though it were as simple as making a decision. 'I *want* to be with you, that's the choice I've made. Stop worrying about me and let's just see where things go.'

She lowered her eyes, but he leaned forward and held her gaze.

'Please, Kim . . .'

She stared at him, not knowing what to say. What more *could* she say?

'Kim?'

Slowly, she moved her head close to his, gave him a sad little smile and kissed him. As her eyes closed, she felt his arms enfold her and she rested her head against his shoulder. She had warned him.

# 47

It had been a frustrating couple of weeks.

When Kim hadn't returned to the guest house in Taunton, Naysmith had been mildly annoyed, but not particularly concerned. Standing at the window of his room in the small hours of the morning, gazing down at the half-empty car park, he assumed that she had spent the night with Sarah. In the morning, he'd risen early and driven across town to check the streets around her sister's house.

No sign of her car. No sign of her.

Two days later, he'd passed through Taunton late at night, checking both locations, and again on his way back from an appointment in Exeter the following week. Still nothing.

Kim had disappeared.

Part of him was annoyed that she'd given him the slip, but on another level he knew it would help to prolong the chase, and that was a positive.

Back at home, he found himself restless, rattling around a house that suddenly seemed a little too big, a little too quiet. Annoyed at his own foolishness, he stretched himself out lengthways across the sofa, staring up at the ceiling, watching as the dark wooden beams reflected the flickering glow of the TV set.

He needed to pick himself up, test himself so that he felt alive again. It was a pity that she'd gone when she had. He'd loved the thought of her selecting his targets. Whom might she have picked out for him next?

He leaned across, taking a glass of gin from the table beside him and sipping reflectively before returning it to its coaster and letting his head ease back onto the armrest. If only she hadn't chosen to go to the police . . .

He paused as the glimmer of an idea came to him.

But she *had* chosen. She had chosen the police!

He stared up at the ceiling, a cold smile spreading across his face.

*Yes.* A most fitting target, and there was an elegant symmetry to the whole thing.

He dropped his feet to the floor and rolled upright into a sitting position.

Who better to represent the police than the man who had almost caught him before? The man whom he could so easily have killed . . .

Naysmith nodded to himself. He and Detective Harland had unfinished business to resolve. They'd actually met twice, though Harland didn't know it. Once, when they'd raced along the Docklands waterfront in the small hours of the morning, two silhouettes running through the darkness, until he'd got the drop on the detective and left him unconscious. And before that, they'd passed within inches of each other when Naysmith had, rather recklessly, followed him into a pub in Portishead . . .

*Portishead. That was the place to start.*

But he couldn't afford to be reckless this time. Harland must surely have seen his photograph by now, so he would need to be extremely careful if he was to track down the detective without being spotted. And of course, the nature of his job meant it would be almost impossible for Naysmith to take him when he was at work.

But what an accomplishment it would be. What a challenge!

He would need to get to know Harland, understand his routine and learn where he went. It would be fascinating to study his adversary, and that would surely make the conclusion of the chase so very satisfying.

And then, once he'd dealt with Harland, he would devote his attention to Kim.

He was busy for the next few days, and it was Monday before he was able to slip a false appointment into his work diary. He woke early, but lay in bed for some time, knowing that there was no point rushing. He already knew where his target worked.

After a leisurely breakfast, he finally set off just before eleven, locking the door on the empty house behind him. There was no need for elaborate cover stories or careful excuses now – it was just him and the target today. Like it used to be, in the days before Kim.

He sighed and walked across to the car. Sliding in behind the wheel, he started the engine, then sat for a moment, flicking through the radio channels, looking for something that would distract him.

He was intrigued by Harland and found himself eager to know more about him. What lay beneath that grim exterior? What sort of man was he?

And he wondered how he would feel about his adversary when the time came to finish things.

Frowning, he put the car into gear, and set off out of the village.

He followed the valleys, coasting along quiet roads through rolling green countryside as far as Bath. There he turned aside, hopping on the motorway to skirt around the north side of Bristol, then sweeping down the M5 as it crept out towards the coast. The sun was hot now, and there was a deep blue sky behind the towering red cranes and pale wind turbines that broke the horizon. Anticipation stirred in him as he saw the sign for his exit and moved across to the left-hand lane, but he mastered his impatience, reminding himself that this was only the beginning of what ought to be an intriguing game.

He stopped at some motorway services for a dreadful lunch and several cups of coffee, finally driving into Portishead late in the afternoon. Getting there too early would have been dangerous – a lone man spending the whole day sitting in his car would surely attract attention, and he couldn't afford that.

Turning onto South Avenue, his eyes swept along the line of parked cars, looking for a space. There! He would go up to the end of the road and turn around so that he was facing down the hill, better able to see who came and went from the police station.

He didn't know what time Harland's shift finished – he wasn't sure if the detective was even at work today – but that was all right. He was prepared to take his time on this one.

Finding a place to turn the car, he crept back down the slope and pulled into the space, close to the pavement. Switching off the engine, he undid his seatbelt, feeling the warmth of the sun through his shirt as he wriggled about in his seat, trying to get comfortable. Then, leaning back against the headrest, he settled in for a long wait.

Last time he'd come here it had been on a whim. Idle curiosity about the man who was investigating him, and a few spare hours in Bristol, had brought him to this quiet street. This time he had a purpose, and the thought of what lay ahead invigorated him, an eager thrill that coursed through his body.

What was Harland really like? Did he live here in Portishead or somewhere further away? Was he married or living with anyone? There were so many questions to answer. Clearly he was an intelligent man, which was a relief, as an idiot would have been poor sport and this was one game he wanted to savour.

Gazing down the road, he studied the squat police building – two storeys of functional bricks and windows, mercifully screened by trees – and the entrance porch, with its notice-board and anti-crime posters.

Was Harland inside? And if he was, what time would he finish work?

He'd seen one or two people go in and out – uniformed police officers for the most part, plus one overweight woman with a small dog in tow. He wondered what she had been there for – to report lost property probably. She certainly didn't look like a criminal.

He smiled to himself.

Wasn't that one of the reasons why he'd never been stopped? People's prejudices blinded them to so much. They were instantly wary of the wrong accent, the wrong clothing, the wrong neighbourhood. But they couldn't see past his manners, his grooming, his success.

By the time they realised who he was, it was always much too late.

He stretched then rubbed his eyes for a moment, shaking off the drowsiness that the sun and the warmth of the car encouraged. It was important to stay alert – he mustn't doze off. Sitting up, he switched on the radio and forced himself to concentrate on the presenter's chatter as his eyes glanced back to the police-station entrance.

★ ★ ★

It was just after six when the glass door opened and the familiar lean figure emerged. There, just a few dozen yards away from him! Naysmith gripped the steering wheel and sank lower in his seat as Harland stepped down onto the concrete paving and paused to light a cigarette. The man looked tired as he exhaled a pale breath of smoke, then continued his weary walk round the building. Was he going towards the car park? Excellent!

Wide awake now, Naysmith watched as Harland disappeared from view. Eyes never leaving the side of the building, he reached forward and started the engine in readiness. Sure enough, moments later, a metallic-grey Ford emerged from behind the police station.

Pulse thumping in his ears, Naysmith pulled out and stole down the road after it.

They turned left at the old whitewashed pub where Harland had once brushed past him, and accelerated out of the town. It was the same route he had followed on his way down here – were they heading for the motorway?

Approaching the circular junction above the M5, Naysmith had to brake gently so as not to get too close. Up until now there would be nothing odd about having one car in your rear-view mirror – this seemed to be the main route in and out of Portishead – but from here on he'd need to start being less visible. As Harland pulled onto the roundabout, Naysmith delayed a little, allowing another car to slip in between them. They passed over the motorway, as though they were going round to join the southbound carriageway, but the grey Ford drifted across to the left-hand lane and exited onto a road signposted for Clifton.

*Clifton . . .*

Naysmith smiled to himself.

The road climbed steadily now, sweeping through a couple

of tiny hamlets as it pushed on towards high, open ground. Cresting one particular rise, Naysmith thought he could glimpse the Severn Bridge, looking oddly small in the distance, far away to his left . . .

. . . but this was no time to become distracted – he had to keep his eyes on the target.

There were two cars between them now, but Harland was still only a short distance ahead. Naysmith had promised himself he wasn't going to rush things, wasn't going to take risks. He'd let Harland get away from him if he had to – he could always lie in wait for him, now that he knew the car – but so far he'd been lucky.

As they came down the hill into Bristol, the car in front of him turned off, leaving just one vehicle between him and his target. They reached the outskirts, crossing a roundabout and negotiating a bewildering couple of junctions – for a moment, Harland was directly in front of him until another car merged in between them as they drove out from an underpass.

The city started abruptly – suddenly there were Victorian terraces lining the right-hand side of the street, while sturdy old industrial buildings loomed up on the left. Naysmith leaned forward to gaze up at one particularly impressive red-brick warehouse, then dragged his attention back to the road again and scowled.

The car in front of him was going very slowly – Harland was opening up too much of a gap, getting too far ahead of him.

*Come on, for God's sake!*

There were trees on the left now, and larger houses on the right. No chance to overtake here – too much traffic coming the other way. Ahead of him, Harland's grey Ford disappeared from view around a bend in the road.

*Come on!*

Naysmith's fingers gripped the steering wheel in frustration as they cruised onwards, following the tarmac as it curved round to the right. There! A little way ahead, he could see the grey Ford waiting, indicating right before disappearing down a side street.

*Yes!*

He slowed and waited for a break in the oncoming traffic before turning into the quiet little residential street. It didn't look as though it was on the way to anywhere – he must be getting close. The houses were pressed in tightly here and the curve of the road obscured his view. Was that Harland's car further along, turning right again? It was difficult to see, but he couldn't rush – he had to be careful.

There was no sign of the detective when he got to the turning, but he decided to follow his instincts and take the right-hand way – a sign on one of the houses read *Stackpool Road*.

This was a very narrow street, climbing steadily as it curved. Naysmith drove slowly, leaning forward to peer out over the steering wheel.

*Grey Ford, grey Ford . . .*

There were cars parked on either side of the street. He edged forward, eyes narrowing.

Was that it up ahead? Yes!

Sighing with satisfaction, he leaned back into his seat, driving on slowly. There was Harland now, that same lonely figure walking back down the pavement – he must live in one of the semi-detached houses that Naysmith had passed on the left-hand side.

No matter – he would find the right one soon enough.

Naysmith smiled to himself . . .

. . . and then jammed on the brakes.

There. Parked a few doors further up the street from the grey Ford.

*It was Kim's car.*

And suddenly, in one terrible moment, he understood. A crushing wave of nausea swept over him and the cold knot of jealousy tightened in his stomach.

His hand shook as he clawed at the gear stick, ramming it into first as he accelerated away up the hill, his breathing shallow as he tried to get his head round the flood of images that rose unbidden in his mind. *Harland taking her hand, leading her inside, closing the door behind them.* The engine shrieked as he over-revved it, moving faster still, swerving up the narrow street, parked cars whipping by in a blur. *Kim resting her head on Harland's shoulder, placing her small hand on his chest, looking up into his eyes . . .*

And then he was thrown forward, stamping the brake pedal into the floor as his subconscious registered a red Mini turning out of a side road, both cars skidding to a shuddering halt.

It was impossible to control the rage, but his seatbelt held him back, restrained him for a vital few seconds while his eyes stared wildly at the other driver – a man in his thirties who was stupidly getting out to confront him.

Jabbing at the release button, Naysmith flung off the seat-belt, ignoring the metal fastener as it cracked against the window. Throwing his door open, he sprang out to stand on the tarmac, furious and eager.

He saw the bluster and bravado drain from the other driver's face, noted the hesitation, the involuntary step back.

'Get out of my *fucking* way!' he snarled, fists clenching in readiness.

'Hey, what the hell—!' the man began, but Naysmith silenced him.

'Move!' he roared, advancing towards him, using all the

self-control he had to turn his anger on the car rather than on the driver. 'MOVE!'

He struck out with his leg, smashing his heel into the front grille, then again, and again, shattering the nearside headlight.

The man was already scrambling back inside, jerking his door shut as he threw the car into reverse. The Mini lurched backwards, weaving an erratic retreat down the side street, to leave Naysmith alone, taut and shaking in the middle of the crossroads.

He turned and gazed back down the hill. Towards the house. Towards her.

Harland had crossed the line. Now, it was personal.

# 48

There was a reassuring air of chaos in the little café. The two women behind the counter appeared to be mother and daughter – one in her thirties, the other her fifties – and they fussed and argued with a lifetime's familiarity. An exasperated sigh greeted each new customer, and there were grave warnings about how long it might be if people wanted anything hot – 'We're unusually busy today!' – despite the place being half empty. And yet the food always arrived, and everything tasted good.

Harland put the last bit of scrambled egg into his mouth and laid down his knife and fork. Opposite him, crammed into the tiny space between the table and the wall, Mendel used a piece of toast to mop up the last of the sauce from his beans.

'Better now?'

'Worth the wait,' the big man nodded.

Harland watched as the younger woman ran the gauntlet of sizzling hotplates behind the counter, bearing a tray for one of the tables. She began setting the food down in front of a gnomish old man, then seemed to hesitate and started to gather the plates up again.

'Eggs, bacon, sausage, beans, tomato, granary toast and tea?' she asked suddenly.

'Er . . . yes,' the man replied.

'Thank God,' the woman sighed, setting the food down again. 'Enjoy your meal.'

Harland grinned as she raced back to her station and got caught up in a confusion of 'After you's with her mother, who was bringing out someone's omelette and blocking the narrow gap behind the counter.

'Dinner *and* a show,' he murmured.

Mendel chuckled, then glanced down at his watch.

'So, are you heading back to Portishead now?' he asked.

'No,' Harland replied. 'Pearce asked me to nip over this afternoon. Said he wanted to chat about the Redland case.'

'They're still running with it?'

'As far as I know.'

Mendel drained the last of his tea and set down his mug.

'At least the media seem to be easing up a bit,' he rumbled.

'Well, there was nowhere for them to go with the story after they tried to set up that dentist.'

'And he was definitely innocent?'

'Oh yes, completely.' Harland knew one of the detectives who had interviewed him, and had heard from the liaison team who were trying to pick up the pieces after the newspapers waded in. 'First he loses his wife, and now his dental practice will go bust because he's the "perv dentist".'

'Poor bastard.' Mendel shook his head sadly.

'Poor bastard,' Harland agreed. *And if the poor bastard topped himself as a result of those stories, the papers would probably report that a well-loved family man had been let down by the police.* He sighed. 'Pearce wasn't happy, but I suppose his hands are tied unless he can deliver the real killer.'

Mendel scowled for a moment.

'Are they making any progress?' he asked.

'I'll see what he says when I go down there, but I don't

think so.' His thoughts drifted briefly to Kim as he picked up the salt and pepper shakers and placed them next to each other in the centre of the table. 'Last I heard they'd tracked down enough witnesses to know that the cyclist wasn't on the train by the time it got to Westbury, so they've been checking the stations between Temple Meads and there.'

'Which means it's down to CCTV now,' Mendel said with distaste.

'Pretty much.' Harland gazed through the steamy windows at the street outside, where a couple were holding hands as they tried to read the prices on the menu.

He turned back to the table to find Mendel staring at him thoughtfully.

'You don't seem that bothered,' the big man noted.

And it was true. Normally, this sort of situation would get to him, but for some reason, the fires of his temper were burning low just now.

'Well, you're always telling me there's no point in worrying about things you can't change,' he said, picking up his mug.

'Yeah,' Mendel nodded, 'but you never listen to me.'

Harland drank the last of his coffee and put the mug down with a smile.

'There is that,' he agreed.

They got up, and Mendel waved his thanks to the women behind the counter. Harland followed him towards the door, then turned back and picked up a pack of chewing gum from a rack of sweets beside the cash register.

'Eighty pence,' prompted the younger woman, who seemed relieved to sell something that didn't require cooking.

Harland paid and received his change.

'Thanks.'

When he turned around, Mendel was standing in the doorway, a faint grin creasing his heavy features.

'So who is she?' he asked.

'What?' For a moment he genuinely didn't know what his friend was talking about.

Mendel folded his arms and gave him an appraising look. 'I've been sitting there for the past half-hour, trying to figure out what's up with you.' He glanced down at the chewing gum, then back up at Harland again. 'You're seeing someone, aren't you?'

*Shit.*

'What makes you think—'

But Mendel was smiling broadly now.

'I knew it!' he grinned. 'She's a non-smoker, right? And you're not exactly carbon neutral.'

Harland looked down at the incriminating gum packet, then slowly shook his head. There was no point trying to deny it.

'You should be a detective,' he said with a wry smile.

'Thanks.' Mendel inclined his head in a mock bow. 'So you finally started seeing someone?'

Harland nodded reluctantly.

'That's great.' The big man's face darkened for a moment. 'It's not Firth, is it?'

'What? No.' He'd moved too slowly with Firth.

'Good.' Mendel looked relieved. 'It's not that I've anything against Firth – she's great – but seeing someone from your own nick . . . ?' A sympathetic smile. 'Well, you deserve a break, and the last thing you need right now is a complicated relationship.'

*A complicated relationship.* But was there any other kind?

'Thank you, Doctor Mendel.'

'You're welcome.'

They went outside and stood on the pavement while Harland took out a cigarette and hunched over to light it.

'So,' Mendel prompted him, 'when do I get to meet her?'

Harland straightened up, blowing a cloud of smoke into the air. Mendel and Kim hadn't exactly hit it off when she came to the station. He decided to ignore the question.

Mendel's eyes narrowed.

'Do I know her?' he asked.

Harland glanced across at him, just a little too quickly.

'Give me a break, James,' he said. 'It's early days yet.'

A non-committal answer, but Mendel had already noted his reaction.

'Be mysterious then.' He smiled thoughtfully. 'Catch you later, Graham.'

Harland walked across the car park, gazing up at the drab grey building with its huge transmitter tower jutting up against the overcast sky, and wondered why he had been summoned. Had there been some new developments in the investigation? Did they need to speak to him about one of the witnesses he had interviewed? He thought back to the people he had questioned, the faces he had studied, but nothing stood out. Still, he would find out soon enough.

Pearce was waiting for him at the top of the stairs, a bright smile and an enthusiastic handshake at the ready.

'Graham, good to see you.' He clapped Harland on the shoulder, then held the door open and gestured for him to go ahead along the corridor. 'How's it going?'

'Good, thanks. You?'

A weary expression passed over Pearce's face.

'Could be better,' he said pointedly. 'Come on through to my office and we'll have a chat.'

They followed the corridor to the far end of the building, where Pearce opened a door and ushered Harland into a small, glass-partitioned room. There were two framed photos of police football teams on top of the filing cabinet, surrounded by a collection of small plastic trophies, and a signed England shirt hung on the wall, mounted in a large box frame.

'Grab a seat, Graham,' he nodded, walking around to his side of the desk. 'Sorry, did you want a drink or anything?'

'I'm fine, thanks,' Harland said as he sat down.

'Smart move.' Pearce made a face. 'Between you and me, the coffee isn't all it's cracked up to be.'

'Better than the instant stuff we have at Portishead.'

Pearce paused, then smiled to himself as he dropped into his high-backed chair. Leaning forward, he clasped his hands together on the desk.

'And how *are* things in sleepy old Portishead?' he grinned.

'Much the same,' Harland shrugged. Things had been quiet recently, and the job just seemed to be ticking over.

Pearce waited for a moment, as though expecting him to elaborate, then sat back in his chair. He opened his mouth, as if he was going to say something, but appeared to think better of it and smiled to himself instead.

'Fair enough,' he mused, adopting a more serious tone. 'Have you seen the paper today?'

Harland shook his head.

'I do my best to avoid it,' he said.

Pearce rolled his eyes.

'Wish I could,' he grumbled, picking up a newspaper. 'Listen to this public-spirited piece: "Despite vocal assurances that the Redland murder investigation has been given the highest priority, the uncomfortable truth is that eight weeks have passed without any sign of an arrest . . ." *blah blah* ". . . Following initial speculation surrounding the victim's husband, Phillip Vaughn, the police now seem to be casting their net ever wider in a desperate effort . . ."

*blah blah* ". . . The only thing worse than having no suspects is having one suspect who you know didn't do it . . .'"

Harland stiffened at the phrase, a prickling of suspicion dawning on him, but he said nothing as Pearce read on.

"'. . . Meanwhile, an official spokesman for Avon and Somerset reiterated their determination to bring the killer to justice, and appealed for anyone with information relevant to the case to call . . ." *Blah blah* fucking *blah.*'

Shaking his head, he folded the paper and let it fall onto his desk, then gave Harland a weary smile.

'Another helpful article from our old friend Peter Baraclough,' he sighed. 'But, contrary to what you may have read, the Redland investigation is ongoing.'

'Anything new?' Harland asked. 'Last I heard you were checking stations, looking for the cyclist.'

'That's right.' Pearce's face was grim now. 'The elusive cyclist.'

There was a tangible note of pride in the big man's voice as he described the effort his team had put in over recent days, tracing the passengers, gathering statements, patiently building up a picture of events. It now seemed certain that their suspect had still been on the train at Bath, but nobody from Bradford on Avon or any of the subsequent stations remembered him.

There was only one stop in between: Avoncliff.

'OK,' Harland mused. 'What about CCTV? Any indication where he went next?'

Pearce shook his head. 'Avoncliff is a quiet little stop in the middle of nowhere,' he sighed. 'It doesn't *have* any CCTV. Remember what Thompson said about him never looking up when there were cameras around?'

Harland nodded slowly. 'And he chooses to get off at the one station with no CCTV.'

'Exactly. Practically nobody lives round there, and it's right on the Kennet and Avon Canal – the towpath is crawling with cyclists.'

'Damn.' Harland slumped back into his chair, lifting a hand to massage the back of his neck. There it was, that same weary frustration he'd felt throughout his pursuit of the Severn Beach murderer the year before – one dead end after another. His thoughts turned to Naysmith, but they were different now, personal, clouded with images of Kim. And she'd been clear when he first asked her – Naysmith was stuck at home that day. Whatever else he'd done, he wasn't the Redland killer.

'The guy's a fucking ghost,' Pearce muttered. He let out a deep sigh, then sat forward and shot Harland a weary grin. 'Anyway, that's enough good news. Tell me how you're getting on in Portishead.'

*Portishead again.* Harland lowered his eyes and smiled to himself.

'It's all right, I suppose. One or two interesting cases.' He considered his daily routine since he'd been sent back from his period in Bristol. 'And of course, none of the poor misunderstood kids we round up ever get sent down, so that keeps us busy when they reoffend.'

'Blake treating you well?'

There was no correct answer to a question like that, so he gave a non-committal shrug.

Pearce eyed him thoughtfully.

'Ever thought about requesting a transfer?'

Harland looked up sharply. Was he suggesting a move to Bristol CID? A permanent move?

'I don't know,' he said, thrown a little by the question, wanting to make sure he hadn't misunderstood the meaning of it. 'Why, do you think I'd find a place somewhere else?'

Pearce gave him a knowing look.

'I reckon you'd be a top acquisition for any team,' he said carefully.

Harland sat back in his chair. He'd always expected to move over to Bristol eventually, but he hadn't really thought about it since Alice died. So much of his life had stopped then – now it seemed that some things were beginning to move again.

'Thanks,' he managed. 'I'm not sure what to say . . .'

Pearce smiled.

'Obviously, I can't go poaching from other stations,' he explained with a mischievous look. 'That's not on. I just wanted to make sure you were aware of your options.'

Harland nodded.

'I appreciate that,' he said. 'And I'll give it some thought.'

At least he now knew what today's meeting had really been about.

He was smiling as he made his way down the stairs, but as he reached the ground floor he paused and frowned. Turning left, he followed the corridor and pushed through the double doors that opened onto the canteen. There were a few people there – unfamiliar faces for the most part – but his eyes soon came to rest on the person he was looking for, and anger surged up through him.

Striding forward, he approached the solitary figure without a sound, dropping suddenly into the seat opposite him.

Pope looked up in surprise.

'Oh, hi, Graham—' he began, but Harland silenced him with a furious gesture and leaned across the table so that their faces were only inches apart.

'I know it was you,' he hissed. '*You're* the one who's been talking to the papers.'

'Eh?' Pope jerked back in his chair, his puffy face going red. 'What the hell are you talking about?'

Harland's hand shot forward, seizing Pope's elbow and dragging him close again.

'Don't fuck with me,' he snarled. 'I *know*.'

Pope gaped at him, flustered, blinking rapidly.

'What makes you think—' he stammered, then flinched as Harland leaned forward again.

'Because *you* read Phillip Vaughn's file before the rest of us – you even told me you'd spotted something interesting in there that should help wrap things up quickly – but by the time we saw it, Pearce had done some checking and effectively ruled him out.' Harland's eyes blazed with rage. 'That and the fact that you quoted me word for bloody word to your friend Peter Baraclough.'

Pope's bluster seemed to give way and his shoulders sagged.

'He's not my friend, but I didn't have any choice.'

'What do you mean?' Harland glared at him.

'He approached me a while back.' Pope looked up wretchedly. 'I'd dealt with him before – he actually helped me out a bit on the Shirehampton case – but then he came to me and said that his paper was going to be asking some serious questions about several Bristol CID cases.'

'So what?' Harland scowled.

'So I didn't want to see Pearce and the team take a kicking in the media,' Pope explained. 'I wanted this transfer for a long time, and when I got here I . . . well, I just wanted to do my bit to protect the department.'

Harland stared at him.

'*This* is how you try to protect the team?' he hissed. 'By betraying their confidence to a fucking hack?'

'He just wanted an inside view, so he could understand that we were making progress.'

'And so you gave him Phillip Vaughn.' Harland shook his head in disgust. 'So he could see we were *making progress.*'

Pope bowed his head.

'It was just a passing comment.' He spread his hands wide on the table. 'How was I supposed to know it was going to balloon up into the whole pervy-dentist thing?'

'Because it was *obvious!*' Harland slumped back in exasperation. 'You've been played like a bloody idiot!'

Pope glanced up, his expression fearful.

'Are you going to tell Pearce?' he whispered.

Harland looked at him for a long moment. He finally had the little shit right where he wanted him.

And yet, he felt certain that Pope hadn't been acting for any personal gain. It had simply been a colossal error of judgement – probably one of many – but a huge mistake nevertheless.

He leaned forward, his voice low.

'You've fucked up . . .' he growled.

*A huge mistake, like the one he was making with Kim.*

'Don't fuck up again.'

Abruptly, he got to his feet and pushed back his chair, then strode wordlessly from the room, leaving Pope to stare after him.

# 49

It had been raining all morning – sometimes a drizzle, some-times a downpour – with grey clouds rolling low over the Portishead rooftops. They sat in the cramped little office, Mendel sipping from a mug of tea while Harland leaned back in his chair, listening to the constant spatter of water leaking from the gutter to hit the window sill behind him.

'So.' Mendel leaned forward and put his drink on the desk. 'The trail ends at Avoncliff?'

'Looks that way.' Harland gave him a dejected nod. 'A little station in the middle of nowhere, with no CCTV. And right on a bloody cycle route where he'd blend straight in.'

'Clever,' Mendel muttered grudgingly.

'Very.'

Everything their suspect had done seemed calculated to make things impossible for them. Again, he felt the stirring of old memories, the uneasy echo of the Severn Beach case. But Mendel had warned him off that one already . . . and sleeping with someone's girlfriend didn't mean you could implicate them in every unsolved crime, however much you wanted to.

They sat in silence for a moment.

'So, *does* Pearce have anything else?' Mendel asked. 'From what you've said, it seems like he's not had much luck.'

'No, he hasn't,' Harland agreed. 'And with all that media exposure, he's under a lot of pressure to make an arrest . . .'

He hesitated, wondering how best to broach the subject. 'That wasn't really what he wanted to see me about though.'

'Oh?' Mendel looked up.

'He was fishing. To see if I had any interest in moving over to Bristol CID.'

'Well, well . . .' The big man's expression betrayed a momentary twinge of regret, but he covered it with a smile. 'Congratulations, Graham.'

'Thanks.' He felt awkward now. Whatever the ups and downs of the last few months, it had been great working with Mendel again. 'Told Pearce I'd give it some thought, but I'm not really sure how I feel about moving at the moment.'

'It'd be a hell of a commute for you – what is it, five minutes from your house?'

'Yeah.' Typical Mendel – always putting a brave face on things. A transfer to Bristol might get Harland's career moving again, but he would miss his old friend.

He turned and glanced up at the clock.

'What time have we got to be at the court?' Mendel asked.

'As long as we're there before one.' Harland pushed back his chair. 'Shall we get going?'

'Yeah, we wouldn't want to keep Leroy waiting.'

Harland picked up his jacket, checked he had his phone, then followed Mendel out into the corridor.

'Want me to drive?' the big man asked him.

'No, I'm fine,' Harland replied.

They made their way down the stairs.

'Hey, I've just thought of another silver lining for you.' Mendel grinned as they walked towards the door. 'You get to work with Pope again.'

Harland shot his friend a bleak look.

'You take the fun out of everything.'

The court was a large building, with white walls, marble floors and an oppressive civic hush that discouraged casual conversation. Harland and Mendel walked down the long corridor, their footsteps echoing out before them into the main waiting area, where scrubbed-up relatives and nervous witnesses glanced up expectantly before lowering their eyes and returning to their own concerns.

There weren't many free seats but Harland knew the place well enough – he peered through the glass door of a small side room, then opened it for Mendel and followed him inside.

'Reckon they're running on time?' the big man asked, wandering over to the window and glancing down at his watch.

'Don't know,' Harland said, turning to ease the door closed and looking back through the glass. 'Plenty of people in the waiting area, but they don't look like they're from Team Leroy.'

Mendel chuckled.

'Team Leroy . . .' He shook his head, smiling. 'They'll be too busy worrying about their *own* court dates to come and cheer *him* on.'

'I suppose so,' Harland mused. 'Don't see his mum out there. Thought she might have shown up.'

'She knows the score by now,' Mendel shrugged. 'Leroy's brother is a regular and his dad's inside.'

'Proud family tradition,' Harland muttered, and turned away from the door.

There were four chairs set against the far wall. Mendel lowered himself onto one of them and yawned.

'Think Leroy will go down for long?' he asked.

'Not long enough,' Harland sighed. 'But at least he gave us the rest of the gang.'

'I won't miss them,' Mendel nodded. 'Think we'll get less call-outs to the Long Cross area once they're banged up?'

'Yeah,' Harland joked, 'maybe we can all put our feet up.'

He moved across the room and sat down beside his friend.

Neither of them spoke for a while. It was Mendel who finally broke the silence.

'Still on for the comedy club next week?'

*Damn.*

'It completely slipped my mind,' Harland grimaced. 'Sorry.'

'What's the matter? Another candlelit meeting with Pearce?'

'It's not that . . .'

Mendel gave him a sly smile.

'Seeing your mystery woman again?' he asked.

Harland glanced across at him.

'Maybe.'

'Come on then,' Mendel pressed. 'Tell me about her.'

Harland sat forward in his chair and frowned. He had to say something – maybe just the basics for now. No need to elaborate just yet.

'Well, her name is Kim . . .' He pictured her in his mind, imagining all the things he'd like to say about her but couldn't. 'She's twenty-nine, and she's an accountant.'

Once again, he was struck by how little he knew about her. Perhaps that was what made this stage of a relationship so exciting – so much potential, no disappointments yet.

'And?' Mendel prompted him. 'Blonde? Brunette? White stick and a guide dog?'

'Very funny,' Harland sighed.

Mendel chuckled to himself.

'So have you been seeing her long?' he asked.

'A little while, yes.'

'Sounds like it could be serious.'

'I don't know,' Harland murmured. He found that he didn't want to think that far ahead. 'Wait and see, I suppose . . .'

'Uh-oh,' Mendel grinned, 'sounds like it *is* serious.'

Harland shrugged and said nothing. His eyes drifted to the door, wishing a court usher would come and interrupt them.

'So, where did you meet her?' Mendel asked, settling back and stretching his legs out.

Harland frowned. It was going to be impossible to talk around this and he really didn't want to deceive his friend.

'Look, if I tell you something . . .' he glanced across '. . . I don't want you to get all worked up about it, OK?'

Mendel shot him a puzzled frown. 'Go on then.'

Harland took a deep breath and exhaled with a sigh.

'You remember that woman who came to Portishead? The one with the story about the Severn Beach case?'

He paused, waiting for it to register. Mendel stared at him for a moment, then his face creased into a frown and he closed his eyes in despair.

'Oh no. Come on, Graham, not *her*?'

Harland stared at him, then looked down.

*Keep quiet for a moment, let him get his head around it.*

Mendel stiffened and got to his feet, pacing slowly across the room as the uncomfortable silence grew between them. Finally, he turned on his heel, arms folded as he glared back.

'What the hell are you doing, Graham?' he demanded. 'I mean *really*, what the hell?'

'I know—'

'She's a potential witness in a murder investigation.'

'I know—'

'And we've been ordered to keep well away from that case.'

Harland sagged in his chair.

'I'm not involved with the case,' he muttered. 'I passed all the information over to the Met—'

'Not involved?' Mendel spread his palms in exasperation. 'You could compromise the whole thing! This is a defence lawyer's wet dream.'

Harland put his hand across his eyes and rubbed them, conscious of where he was.

Mendel was right of course. No matter how he tried to excuse it, he knew he was involving himself with someone he shouldn't. Here he was, thinking about how Pearce's offer might revitalise his career, and at the same time he was digging himself deeper into a relationship that could ruin it.

He sighed and glanced up tentatively at his friend.

Mendel had been scowling at him, but his face softened and there was the hint of a wry smile as he shook his head slowly.

'I don't know, Graham . . .' He leaned against the far wall. 'You can't do anything the easy way, can you?'

Harland acknowledged him with a grateful nod.

'Thanks,' he said simply.

He checked his watch. It was only a quarter past one – they could be there for a while yet.

'So . . .' Mendel seemed to be regaining his usual calm. 'When are you seeing her next?'

For a brief moment, Harland thought about admitting that she was staying with him, but quickly decided not to. He had pushed things with Mendel enough today. There was no way of knowing how the big man would react to another revelation and, in truth, he wasn't really certain how it was going to work out with Kim. They'd been thrown together suddenly and now that things were settling down a bit, he wasn't sure what would happen. But he knew that there was something about her that affected him, that he had a peace he'd not felt for a long time. And he wanted that.

For now. For as long as it lasted.

'Not sure,' he replied. 'Tonight, probably.'

'Don't get me wrong.' Mendel's tone was more concerned than angry now. 'I want to see you happy with someone. But you've had a rough enough time and I don't want to see you get messed around . . .'

He tailed off, leaving the warning unspoken.

'I appreciate that,' Harland nodded thoughtfully. 'But I have to see where this goes, or I'll regret it. Do you understand?'

Mendel looked at him for a long time, then sighed and sat down on the chair beside him.

'Just watch yourself, OK?' he growled.

# 50

Kim frowned. Picking up the half-eaten packet of biscuits, she twisted the top closed, and walked over to put them away in the cupboard. Out of sight, out of mind.

It wasn't even five thirty yet, but she'd found herself hungry, and Graham wouldn't be back from work for a while yet. She wondered if he'd got the packet for her, or if she'd been eating something he'd bought for himself. He did seem to be keeping the cupboards more full than when she'd first arrived, but the last thing she needed now was to start comfort eating.

She turned and went back to her seat at the kitchen table. The local property paper was still open in front of her and she began to leaf through the pages again.

Hotwells. Kingsdown. St Pauls. She had no clear notion of where any of these areas were, or what they were like. Thus far, the prices had seemed high and she sighed as her eye scanned the page, taking in the tiny photographs and the big numbers.

She'd have to sell the house in Taunton. It had certainly shot up in value, and at least that would get her a reasonable deposit on somewhere in Bristol. She frowned, thinking about Sarah and Simon, but it *was* her house after all. Did they have any money put aside to buy her out? Even if they did, she might struggle to get a new mortgage until she'd been working for a while. There had been two very positive job interviews last week, and she was confident she'd be earning again soon, but for now her options were limited.

And then there was Graham.

She sat back in her chair, absently twirling a strand of hair around her index finger. He might not have the easy good looks that had always snared her in the past, but there was something about him. He certainly cared for her, and when he was with her she felt safe, secure . . .

But it was more than that.

There was something different in the way he treated her – as though it was all right to take the lead, to make her own decisions. A sense of freedom without the ache of loneliness . . .

She shook her head, and flipped forward through the pages until she came to the *Properties To Let* section.

Just in case.

The ringtone startled her, shattering the stillness of the house. Pushing her chair back from the table, she got up and walked across to the counter to retrieve her phone. Picking it up, she anxiously checked the name on the screen, then breathed a sigh of relief when she saw it was Sarah. She hit the answer button.

'Hello?'

'Hey, sis, how's it going?' Sarah sounded as if she was in a good mood.

'Fine thanks,' Kim replied. 'How are you and Simon?'

She walked back across to the table, sitting down and trying to find her place on the page again.

'Simon's away in Swansea or somewhere today,' Sarah was saying. 'I wasn't properly awake when he told me this morning – could be anywhere really – and we've been rushed off our feet at work this afternoon because that new guy got fired . . .'

Kim smiled and propped her head up with one elbow on the table while her other hand traced down a list of apartments in Bristol Central.

'. . . but that's not why I'm phoning you.'

'What is it then?'

'You'll never guess.' Sarah's voice was hushed now, as though she was savouring the news she was about to reveal. 'Rob called.'

Kim jerked upright in her chair.

'He phoned you?' she asked, her stomach tightening.

'Yeah,' Sarah replied. 'Seemed a bit down, poor thing.'

Kim sat frozen for a moment, then desperately gulped a breath of air.

'What did he want?' she stammered.

'Well . . .' Sarah paused for effect. 'He said he wanted me to let you know there're no hard feelings.'

'*What*?' Kim choked.

Another pause, and this time Sarah's tone contained a hint of reproach.

'He told me, you see. About the money you took.'

Kim's mind was reeling. She got shakily to her feet, pressing the phone hard against her ear.

'I think he's still carrying a torch for you,' Sarah continued, undaunted. 'I wasn't sure what to say to him really – it's not my place to start taking sides.'

*Taking sides?*

'What did you say to him?' Kim snapped. 'What did you tell him about me?'

'What *could* I tell him?' Sarah retorted. 'You've certainly been keeping *me* in the dark about what you're up to . . .'

Kim bent forward, bowing her head wearily.

'I just needed some time to think,' she explained. 'Is that so unreasonable?'

At the other end of the line, Sarah chuckled.

'I'm not stupid, you know.' There was an edge to her voice.

'What do you mean?'

'All this rubbish about Rob cheating, about you staying in a B & B.'

Kim shook her head.

'What are you saying?' she asked.

'I *know*, sis.' Sarah snapped at her. 'I know all about you, shacked up with your detective in Bristol . . .'

It was like a physical blow and Kim staggered backwards, one arm stretching out to steady herself against the table. Everything was wrong.

'How . . . ?' she stammered.

'Rob told me,' Sarah scolded. 'Poor thing, I think he's really missing you . . .'

*Rob told me.*

The hand holding the phone dropped to her side, and Kim heard nothing more.

*How? How could he possibly know?*

She put the phone on the table and stumbled over to the sink, bracing herself with both hands as she leaned over it, not sure if she was going to be sick.

*'Shacked up'. He must know where she was staying.*

She closed her eyes for a moment, trying to calm her breathing even as her pulse raced, thumping in her ears.

*He must know about this house.*

A sudden urge to run gripped her. She pushed herself away from the sink and dashed into the hall, grabbing her handbag as she approached the front door. Her fingers were almost on the handle when she froze, then changed her mind and hurriedly fumbled the security chain into place.

Backing away from the door, she turned and scurried upstairs, pacing urgently along the landing and into the front bedroom.

Very cautiously, she pulled the curtain open just a crack so that she could look out into the street without being seen. Her eyes traced along the line of cars – there was no sign of his.

Relaxing just a little, she sat down heavily on the bed, waiting for her breathing to settle down.

*Why? Why couldn't it just be over?*

She bowed her head, waiting for the tears, but none came. After a few moments, she got to her feet and went back to the window.

*She had to get out.*

# 51

She sat alone, squeezed into a corner at the back of the small café, well away from the windows. Her laptop was open in front of her, but the screen was dark as she peered out over the top at each new customer who came in, watching them walk over to the counter.

She hated feeling like this, hated the dread, the helpless waiting.

Reaching absently for her drink, her fingers found the tall china mug, but it had long since gone cold. She sighed, resting her palms on the polished wooden tabletop, and glanced back to the door.

It was all right. She'd been careful. There was no way he could find her in here . . . but hadn't she thought the same about Graham's house on Stackpool Road? Somehow Rob had known about that, tracked her down. Had he been following her all the time? Toying with her?

She shook her head, weary, annoyed. It didn't matter. Right now, all that mattered was how she was going to escape.

A movement caught her eye. Outside, a tall man in a suit approached, silhouetted in the doorway. She tensed, squinting against the light, then relaxed when she saw it was a stranger. Leaning forward, she allowed her head to rest in her hands, suddenly very tired.

★   ★   ★

She'd hardly slept last night. Lying there in the dark, staring across at the wall, listening as the sounds of the city outside grew quieter. Waiting until she was sure Graham was asleep, then slipping out of bed and creeping over to the window. Pulling back the curtain to gaze down on the street, still and silent . . . knowing he was out there somewhere.

This morning, she'd left the house right after Graham, hurrying down to Coronation Road, walking quickly across the iron footbridge and glancing behind her as she disappeared into town. She'd spent the day in cafés, feeling safer among other people, trying to think. She wanted to tell Graham, wanted to be honest with him, but she already knew what his response would be, and she'd tried it his way before.

*If only they were somewhere else, somewhere far away from all of this.*

And that was how she had got the idea. A single, clear thought – a glimmer of hope – that had carried her through the morning.

Now, wearily, she turned back to her blank laptop screen. She'd spent hours searching, thinking it all through. The only potential problem was Graham.

Sitting up, she pushed her hair back from her face, then reached into her bag and took out her phone. Searching through her recent calls, she found his number and dialled it, then closed her eyes and held the phone to her ear.

*Let him be OK about this . . .*

There was a click and Graham's voice said 'Hello?' There was a lot of background noise, as though he was outside somewhere.

'It's me,' she said, trying to speak lightly.

'Hey.' He sounded surprised to hear from her. 'Everything OK?'

'Yeah, I'm fine. I . . .' She hesitated, then decided to just get the words out as quickly as possible. 'Look, I was just wondering if you could maybe take a couple of days off?'

'Yes . . .' he said, a faint note of caution in his voice. 'I suppose so. When were you thinking?'

'Friday and Monday.' She tried to say it casually but her voice almost broke.

'*This* Friday?'

'Yes.'

There was a long pause before he replied.

'What were you wanting to do?'

She leaned forward, one hand pushed up under her hair, staring at the long shadow of her coffee cup on the table.

'Please, Graham, *can* you take the days off?'

'Er . . .' He hesitated then sighed. 'I suppose so . . . Are you going to tell me why?'

Her shoulders drooped and she breathed in relief.

'Tonight. I promise. Thanks, Graham.'

'Are you sure you're all right?' he pressed her.

'I'm fine. It's just . . .' She was at a loss. 'I'll explain tonight, OK?'

'OK,' he replied, still a little wary.

'I'll see you later.'

'Yeah. See you tonight.'

'Graham?' She spoke quickly, not wanting him to hang up. 'Yes?'

'Thank you.'

She ended the call and set the phone down carefully on the table. Her laptop had gone to sleep some time ago, but she tapped the power button to wake it and reconnected to the café's Wi-Fi. Bringing back her web browser, she checked the payment page one last time, then clicked to confirm her booking.

*Somewhere else, somewhere far away . . .*

Staring at the screen for a moment, she yawned, then leaned back in her chair and rubbed her eyes.

Stackpool Road was no good now. She couldn't even go back there until she knew Graham was on his way home. The situation was impossible – something had to change.

The noise of the street suddenly grew louder as the glass door swung inward; her eyes snapped open, but it was just a woman going outside. She took a breath, settling herself, as a couple of older men burst out laughing over some private joke up at the counter.

She was almost done. Her hand reached out to pick up the phone. There was just one more call to make. Leaning her weary head against the wall, she dialled Sarah's number and waited.

# 52

Harland knew something was wrong. Kim had been very subdued last night, and then there had been the strange phone call from her while he was at work today.

Now, when he came home, she opened the front door and threw her arms around him.

'Kim?' He untangled himself enough to gaze down into her large, frightened eyes. 'What's the matter?'

She smiled at him shyly, as though nothing was the matter, as though she could pretend and have him not notice.

'I'm just glad you're back.' She stood away from him a little, suddenly conscious of his concern. 'How was your day, Graham?'

'Same as usual,' he shrugged. 'What about you?'

'It was OK.' She turned away from him, and he wondered if it was to hide her expression. 'I spoke to the agency and they've got me two interviews for the tail end of next week.'

'That's great.'

He followed her down the hall and into the kitchen, slipping off his jacket and draping it over a chair before going to the fridge and taking out a beer.

She watched him as he closed the door and reached for the bottle opener.

'Kim?' He moved towards her, but she turned her body away from him slightly, her gaze going to the kitchen window. 'What's wrong?'

She stiffened a little, doing her best to speak lightly, but he could hear the edge in her voice.

'You took Friday and Monday off?'

'Yes,' he replied.

'Good.' She seemed almost relieved. 'I thought we might go away . . . a long weekend, somewhere quiet.'

He was about to ask her what had brought this on, but something warned him not to.

'OK.' He spoke carefully, watching her across the kitchen. 'Where were you thinking?'

'I found the perfect place,' she replied. Her body language was tight – an arm crossed over her chest, one hand in front of her mouth. 'And I got an amazing deal on it.'

'You booked it already?'

He caught a brief flicker of anguish in her expression, but she mastered it.

'It was a *really* good deal. And once I'm working again, we might not get the chance for a while.' Rational arguments, guarded speech – he recognised the effort she was making to persuade him.

'I . . .' He shook his head, unsure what to say to her. 'It's a bit last-minute, isn't it?'

She looked at the floor, her hair falling forward to hide her face.

'Yes,' she said quietly. Then, before he could speak, she added, 'Don't be angry with me.'

'I'm not angry. It's just . . .' His shoulders dropped and he sighed. 'It's OK. It'll be fine.'

She stared out at him through a gap in her hair.

'Was there a problem getting the time off?' she asked.

Normally, there might have been. Normally, he should have given at least a couple of weeks' notice.

He gazed at her, reading the urgency in her eyes. She

needed him, he realised. And it was a long time since he'd felt needed.

'Graham?'

Things were quiet at work just now. And he still hadn't taken all of his annual leave for last year.

'No problem,' he told her.

'Oh Graham, thank you!' She sprang forward and kissed him, her face a mixture of relief and excitement. 'You'll love it, I know you will.'

He rested his hands on her hips and gave her a thoughtful smile. His agreement seemed to mean so much to her . . . Was he missing something?

'So,' he asked casually. 'Where is this perfect place you've booked?'

'It's an amazing little cottage, down on the coast.' She dropped her gaze to his chest, but her eyes were staring at something far away. 'It has the most wonderful views looking out over the sea.'

'You've been there before?' he asked.

Just a trace of hesitation, but her smile hardly faltered.

'Yes,' she murmured. 'That's why I know it'll be perfect.'

She was restless that evening, busying herself around the house and adopting a determinedly cheerful smile whenever she felt his eyes on her. The following day was no better, but whenever he questioned her she shook her head and told him that everything was fine, that she was just excited about going away. He arrived home to find that she'd already packed a bag for him.

'I just got a few things together for you,' she explained awkwardly. 'I thought it would save you doing it. And then we can leave earlier in the morning and have more time down on the coast.'

He had a sudden disconcerting vision of her alone in the house, peering into his wardrobe, opening cupboards, searching through drawers.

'Great,' he told her.

He cooked pasta for them and they ate quietly at the kitchen table while Kim steered the conversation towards safe subjects over a glass of wine.

'I spoke to Sarah again yesterday,' she said as she moved her fork around the plate. 'She reckons I should take the job with Heasman's. Bigger company, more chance for progression.'

'She's probably right,' Harland nodded. 'A lot of senior positions aren't even advertised if they can find someone to promote.'

Kim smiled.

'You sound just like her,' she said.

'Then she must be a very charming and intelligent person,' he replied. Sitting back, he stretched, then got up and took the plates over to the sink. 'It'd be good to meet her some day. You could invite her up one weekend . . . if you want.'

Kim looked at him with a thoughtful smile.

'Some day,' she said quietly.

They drifted through to the front room and watched the tail end of one film and the beginning of another, with Kim curled up against him on the sofa like a cat. At eleven o'clock, she sat up sleepily and asked him if he wanted a drink before she went to bed.

He told her no and got to his feet, stretching slowly before making his way upstairs. The kitchen light was still on as he came out of the bathroom and walked to the bedroom, where he undressed wearily before turning back the duvet and dropping down onto the bed. Lying back, he closed his eyes and let his body relax, his head sinking into the pillow.

He heard her enter the room, her footsteps soft and tentative as she came round to the other side of the bed, felt the pull on the covers and the give in the mattress as she got in beside him. He opened his eyes, turning to say goodnight to her, but she was already leaning across to him, her hair tumbling forward over her shoulders as her face came close to his.

'Shh,' she murmured, with a quiet little smile, and he felt her thigh sliding across his as she eased herself over to climb on top of him.

Afterwards, she didn't say anything. Just a single kiss, and then she nestled down beside him with one slender arm across his chest. He lay awake for some time, calm in the afterglow, listening as her breathing settled and she slowly drifted away. Staring up into the darkness, he wondered what lay before him that he couldn't see, but he was still wondering as he slipped into a troubled sleep.

He woke up alone, and for one awful moment he was back where he'd been for so long – on his own, a single man in a double bed. His body stiffened, but as he turned over, his outstretched hand felt the enduring warmth on the sheets beside him, and he smelled her scent on the pillow. The tension left him and he sank back down in relief – like waking from a bad dream and realising it was only that. His doubts from last night seemed hazy as he sat up and leaned back against the headboard, phantom thoughts that fled in the morning sunlight. A few days away on the coast were just what they needed. And the change of scene might help Kim to open up and tell him what was on her mind.

He got to his feet and walked drowsily out onto the landing, smiling as he heard the clink of mugs coming from the kitchen. Yawning, he made his way downstairs.

'Hey,' he greeted her, moving close behind her and encircling her waist with his arms as she poured milk into the coffee.

'Hi,' she replied, wriggling her small frame around in his embrace and pulling herself free. 'Don't get yourself all distracted – just drink your coffee and get dressed before the morning's gone.'

Harland shrugged and let her go.

'Whatever you say,' he yawned.

The bags were waiting in the hallway when he came downstairs.

'Have you got everything?' she asked him brightly.

'I think so,' he nodded, patting his pockets and checking for his wallet. 'What's the hurry?'

'No hurry,' she replied, handing him his car keys. 'I just want to get on the road before the traffic gets bad. You know what it's like heading down to the West Country.'

He gave her a long look, then picked up the luggage and opened the front door.

Outside, Stackpool Road was quiet. Kim stared out at the street as he locked up, her expression quickly softening when their eyes met – something *was* troubling her, but there would be time enough for talking once they reached the cottage.

The car was parked a few yards further up the hill and he dragged the cases along behind him as they walked side by side along the narrow pavement. Somewhere just behind them, a dog started barking and they both looked round.

'That's one thing I won't miss.' Harland smiled at her. 'Come on.'

He unlocked the car and lifted the bags into the boot. It had been a long time since he'd been away and now that it came to it, he found he was really looking forward to the break.

Sliding into the driver's seat, he started the car, and pulled the steering wheel hard round to avoid the minivan that had almost boxed him in. Easing away from the kerb, they crept down the hill, past the house, and turned left onto Coronation Road.

As they pulled out into the traffic, Kim glanced back over her shoulder, then seemed to relax down into her seat.

'Thanks for this,' she said as she lay back against the headrest.

'You're paying,' he replied as they drove out towards the motorway. 'I should be the one thanking you.'

In his peripheral vision, he was aware that she had turned her head towards him, but when he glanced across at her she just smiled, then turned her eyes out to the road ahead.

The M5 was already busy, but at least the traffic was moving when they joined it at Portbury, and they made good time on the journey south. Kim was asleep before they reached Weston-super-Mare, her head lolling to one side, her lips parted as she dozed fitfully. Harland gazed across at her for a moment, taking in her delicate features, those wonderful dark lashes that seemed even longer when her eyes were closed, then returned his attention to the road. It was going to be a great few days.

After Exeter, there was no more motorway. The road climbed and they cut across the barren heights of Dartmoor before descending through a rolling green landscape as they approached the coast. They took smaller roads now – narrow lanes with occasional passing places, bordered on either side by high hedges or drystone walls, so they could only see where they were as they crested each new hill. Awake now,

Kim watched the satnav on her phone, reassuring him that they were on the right route when she spotted familiar landmarks until finally, at the summit of a long rise, the ground fell away before them and they glimpsed the sea.

'Wow,' Harland murmured, slowing the car as he gazed out across the shimmering blue to the broad horizon. 'That's quite a view.'

Kim smiled and put a small hand on his knee.

'I told you,' she said.

It was the sort of place that made Harland think of period dramas – a rugged coastline, unblemished by the clutter of modern buildings or the ruinous stain of caravan parks. Even the road was free of signs and markings as it angled down into a slight valley before turning back inland, then ahead of them the ground rose up towards a grassy headland with rocky cliffs visible in the distant haze.

At the foot of the hill, Kim indicated a break in the old stone wall and they turned aside, rattling across a cattle grid and onto a potholed track that wound like a muddy ribbon over the rough grass slope. Sheep watched as they made their ascent, and Harland had to drop the car into first before they crested the slope and finally saw their destination.

The track widened here and came to an end just short of a sturdy stone cottage with whitewashed walls, square chimneys and a dark slate roof. The gables, gutters and window sills were picked out in an old-fashioned shade of green and there was a good store of cut logs piled up against one of the side walls.

But Harland's eye was drawn to the lighthouse.

A faint path led round the side of the house and away towards it, leading up through the tufted grass and the gorse bushes of the headland. Like the cottage, the lighthouse was built of whitewashed stone, a squat turret on a high precipice with a smaller glass chamber above it, topped by a white metal dome. It stood a few hundred yards beyond the cottage, stark against the sky.

'So this is where the lighthouse-keepers used to live?' he asked her as he pulled up and switched off the engine.

'I think so,' she nodded. 'There's nothing else around here, so I suppose that must have been what it was built for.'

They got out, Harland stretching to release his muscles after the long drive before he walked a few paces away from the car to get a better view of the headland.

'Does it still work?' he asked, turning back to her. 'The lighthouse, I mean.'

'As far as I know,' she replied. 'I think it's automatic now, but I remember it came on at night the last time I was here.'

He gazed at her for a moment, then turned back to look along the coastline.

*The last time I was here.*

Something in the way she'd said it made him uneasy, and he wasn't sure if it was her being guarded about something, or him not wanting to think about her coming here with someone else. But either way, this wasn't the moment to discuss it.

His eyes followed the horizon, past the cottage and on along the rest of the coast, where a bank of darker clouds were gathering.

'Kim?' he said, walking round to the back of the car and opening the boot. 'Shall we dump the bags inside and go for a walk?'

'Don't you want to have a drink first?' she asked, joining him and lifting her bag out.

'I think we might want to go now,' he said. Then, seeing the question in her face, he pointed past the cottage to the distant sky. 'There may be a storm coming.'

# 53

Outside, the wind howled around the cottage, rattling the tiny kitchen window. Harland stirred the two mugs of hot chocolate and dropped the teaspoon into the sink.

'Listen to it,' he said, gazing out into the darkness as rain lashed against the glass. 'It's really coming down.'

He picked up the drinks and edged his way around the small, farmhouse table that occupied most of the room, sitting down opposite Kim.

'Thanks,' she murmured, warming her hands on the mug he'd placed before her.

'No problem.'

She looked thoughtful, preoccupied. They had spent the evening talking, trying to make sense of everything that had happened, but somehow her mind seemed elsewhere. He lifted his own drink and considered it for a moment, then decided to continue.

'So how long were you with him?'

She glanced up at him briefly, then lowered her eyes again, staring into the past.

'Almost three years.' Her finger traced a line down the side of the mug. 'It seems like a long time now, but I suppose that's all it was.'

'Were you happy?'

Another brief look, but she didn't answer him. It was a stupid question, and a selfish one. Annoyed with himself, he tried a different approach.

'When did you first suspect that things weren't right?'

'I always suspected him,' she said softly, then looked up. 'I don't mean—'

She broke off, a pained expression on her face.

'I thought he was cheating on me,' she explained. 'I was always . . . accusing him of stuff.'

'And was he? Cheating on you?'

'Probably,' she sighed. 'I don't know, maybe I pushed him into it.'

She shook her head and took a sip of her hot chocolate. Harland could feel the distance growing between them and tried to pull the conversation back around.

'What about the other stuff?' He reached across the table, gently touching her hand. 'What about Severn Beach? How long have you suspected what he was?'

She slowly wrapped her fingers around his.

'A few months . . . at least, that's when he first said anything.'

She looked up at him for a moment, her large eyes wary, vulnerable.

'We were staying here when he told me.'

Was she worried about past associations with the place? No, she probably felt a sense of guilt that she'd stayed with him. She knew what he was going to ask next.

'You didn't leave him though?' He said it gently, letting it hang in the air between them.

'No.' Her hand had tensed a little, but she didn't draw it away.

'Was that because you were frightened?'

'Yes.' She answered very quickly, then looked down at the table and reluctantly added, 'That was part of it.'

Harland waited, giving her time.

'I didn't want to drive him away,' she murmured.

'Drive him away?'

Her shoulders sagged and she bowed her head.

'I always seem to screw things up.' She broke off, drawing her hand away now, closing up a little before she continued. 'I don't know . . . I just didn't want to ruin another relationship.'

Harland sat back a little, studying her – those long lashes hiding her downcast eyes, her small hand touching the silver pendant that glistened at her neck.

'But he told you he had killed someone.'

*How could she think it was her fault?*

Kim leaned forward, absently hugging herself as she stared at her hot chocolate.

'I thought he loved me.' She seemed to be talking to herself.

The window rattled again as the storm raged on, and a chill seemed to slither through the room. She looked so small and sad now – they weren't getting anywhere tonight.

'Come on,' he told her with a weary smile. 'It's getting cold in here. Let's go through and I'll light the fire.'

He got to his feet and opened the door, stepping through into the passageway and waiting for her as she stood up slowly and followed him. The whole place felt cold now, but he'd noticed a few logs piled beside the fireplace when they arrived, and staring at the flames would be comforting for them both.

He opened the lounge door and approached the hearth. There was no kindling in the grate, but he thought he'd seen some bundled beside the logs—

Behind him, Kim let out a shriek.

He whirled round to see her framed in the doorway, frozen. Her eyes were wide and he turned further, following her terrified gaze to the opposite corner of the room.

It was Naysmith.

He stood there, a tall figure with a chillingly calm expression, looming up against the back wall of the room, dripping wet and glistening in the shadow. His dark hair was plastered down from the rain and he wore a grey sweatshirt under a slick black anorak, but it was the evil-looking machete that caught Harland's attention. Naysmith held it calmly, easily, the two-foot black blade pointing down, dripping water onto the floor.

Kim reacted first.

'Run, Graham!' she screamed, turning and bolting from the room as Harland stood reeling.

Naysmith gave an eerie smile.

'Yes. Run, Graham.'

He straightened, seeming to grow taller as he stepped towards the middle of the room, his movements agile as he began sweeping the blade around in easy, fluid arcs.

Harland stumbled backwards, turning and running after Kim. Bursting through the doorway, he raced down the hall and into the kitchen, where she was jerking open the back door. A sudden blast of cold air swirled into the room.

'Kim,' he called, 'wait!'

'No!' She looked back over her shoulder at him, eyes wide as she shook her head. 'Come on!'

And then she disappeared out into the howling gale and he was skidding around the damn table, cursing as he leapt after her. The wind and rain smothered him as he followed her into the storm stealing his breath and stinging his face, whipping the long grass into billowing waves.

She was going the wrong way!

Their best hope would have been to head inland, down the hill so they could make for the road, but she'd run straight ahead, sprinting along the cliff path that led up to the lighthouse. As he chased after her, he struggled with his pocket, trying to find his phone so he could call for help, but it wasn't there – he must have left it in the bedroom – *shit!*

'Kim!' he yelled. She was only ten yards ahead of him, but the gale threw his shout back in his teeth. He tore after her, his ears catching the deep crash of breakers rising from the rocks far below, mingling with the wind. They were close to the cliffs now. He could almost make out the crumbling edge on his left, where the last of the grass gave way to a sheer drop with rocky coves on either side of them.

'KIM!'

Finally, she looked back, glancing over her shoulder, slowing as she saw him, then looking past him at something in the darkness behind.

He flailed out a desperate hand to her, grabbing her arm as he turned to see what she had seen. Behind him, the path wound away into the gloom, leading back to the distant yellow lights of the cottage windows. And there, close enough that he could make it out through the rain, an advancing silhouette came after them, the long blade swinging at its side.

Harland looked round quickly. The headland came to an end at the precipice ahead of them, and there were sheer drops on either side. They were trapped.

He pulled Kim close to him, hands gripping her shoulders as he bent his face close to hers so she could hear him against the wind.

'Listen to me.' He spoke urgently, shaking her as she stared blankly at him. 'Listen! Stand behind me. Whatever happens, stand behind me and keep away from him, OK?'

She stood trembling, arms limp at her sides, her long hair a tangle of wet strands across her face.

'*OK?*'

She seemed to hear him and nodded slightly. Harland held

her gaze for a second to make sure, then gulped down a breath and turned round to face their pursuer.

Naysmith came towards them through the storm – a dark shape that grew steadily clearer as he walked calmly up the path. He stopped a few yards away from them, his body taut, the machete held in readiness, suddenly illuminated by the glow of the lighthouse as it lit up the rain.

Instinctively, Harland moved to stand in front of Kim, his arm reaching back as though to shield her.

Naysmith smiled and inclined his head briefly.

'Detective Harland. Kim.' His manner was calm – almost polite – as he called out to them across the wind. 'Quite a night for it.'

The storm swirled up around the headland as the two men stared at each other. Behind him, Harland felt Kim moving backwards, tensing as though about to run. Naysmith saw it too, and laughed in the darkness.

'Forget it, *sweetheart*,' he called to her. 'Ask your new boyfriend – he knows how fast I can move.'

Harland started, his mind recalling that night in Docklands when he'd chased a shadow and almost paid with his life.

'So that *was* you then?' he shouted across the wind.

Naysmith inclined his head once more, an oddly modest gesture that Harland found confusing. What was he so pleased about?

'Why didn't you kill me?' he called.

Naysmith seemed to relax just a little, the tip of the blade dipping for a moment.

'You weren't part of that game,' he replied, thinking for a moment, then adding, 'well . . . not a target anyway.'

Harland nodded grimly. It made a strange sort of sense.

'I have to know,' he said. 'What was the connection? How did you choose them?'

This seemed to amuse Naysmith.

'I didn't choose them,' he laughed. 'That would have been far too easy. No, they chose me.'

Harland frowned. What did he mean by that?

'Except for the last one,' Naysmith added suddenly. 'You remember, the woman in Redland?'

Harland took a step back.

'That *was* you as well?'

Illuminated again, Naysmith took a step forward, tracing lazy curves with the blade.

'You'd be surprised at how much I've done.' He paused, then fixed his eyes on Kim. 'But *I* didn't choose that one, did I?'

His tone was suddenly bitter, mocking. Harland whirled round to find Kim looking confused, fearful.

'Remember, Kim?' Naysmith continued. 'Remember that day when we were people-watching in Bristol?'

'What do you mean?' She shrank back, then seemed to freeze, her face showing a terrible realisation. 'Oh no, Rob. *No!*'

'Oh yes!' he snapped. 'In fact, I think you're wearing her necklace.'

Kim's hand went to her throat.

Naysmith laughed at her, then addressed Harland. 'Your poor little girlfriend picked out the Redland woman for me. *She* chose the target.'

Kim turned, clawing at Harland's arm, staring wildly up into his face.

'I didn't know!' she cried. 'I didn't know what he was going to do!'

Naysmith grinned, then shook his head in mock reproach.

'You knew enough,' he snapped, taking another step closer. 'You knew what I was. I was *honest* with you.'

He spat the word 'honest' with sudden venom, almost as though it pained him somehow. But Harland was reeling, unable to take it all in as Kim stared up at him, her face stricken.

Naysmith raised the machete and pointed it at them.

'More *honest* than you've been with your new *fucking* boyfriend,' he snarled.

Harland stared at him, his eyes following the blade, as Kim began to panic, tugging at his arm, trying to pull him away. He stumbled back, a little closer to the cliff edge as stinging sheets of rain billowed over them. Somewhere far below, a wave boomed on the rocks.

Naysmith's movements were fluid as he came closer, holding the machete confidently – familiar, comfortable with it. His face was serious now, and he seemed to be readying himself as he bowed his head briefly, then straightened.

'There's nowhere to run, Kim.' His voice was stern. 'Nowhere to go, but back to me.'

He stared past Harland, holding her gaze.

'Time to choose, my love.'

Harland backed away another step, his arm held out protectively as he turned to look at her, a small bedraggled figure, forlorn in the downpour. She stared up at him, pale skin bleached white by the glare of the lighthouse, blinking the rain – or the tears? – out of her large eyes, then bowing her head.

She murmured something he couldn't quite hear as the gale howled along the clifftop, then moved to one side. He tried to put his arm around her, but she shrugged it off, stepping out from behind him and picking her way unsteadily across the grass, drawing the sodden cardigan around herself against the wind.

Harland stared after her, then sagged as the despair came crashing in on him – it had all been for nothing.

A weight seemed to have lifted from Naysmith's shoulders. His eyes were alight, exultant, as he watched Kim walk through the billowing grass towards him.

*The bastard.*

Harland glared at him and felt the familiar flicker of hatred deep inside. Here, at the end, his anger was all that remained – all he had left. Glancing over his shoulder, he measured the distance to the precipice. Ten yards, maybe less. There was nowhere to run, but he knew now that he would go down fighting. He would go down hard, and maybe take this fucker over the edge with him.

Gritting his teeth, he stood up ready, defiant, watching as Naysmith held out a hand to Kim and she reached out and took it.

*Fuck them. Both of them.*

He was determined to make a good end, to show her that he wouldn't break, no matter what happened to him.

Taking Kim's hand, Naysmith smiled in triumph, drawing her close to him as the rain lashed down, staring past her at Harland. She hesitated for a second, then silently put her arm around him.

And there, as Harland glared at him, he seemed almost to stumble, though he had been standing still. Naysmith's features tightened suddenly in a mixture of pain and puzzlement and he made an odd sound that stabbed through the wind, like a gasp cut short. He tried to move away from Kim, but she held onto him tightly, swaying with him as he staggered and the machete dropped from his hand.

Harland's training kicked in and he launched himself forward, desperately trying to cover the ground between them before Naysmith could stoop to retrieve it.

But Naysmith didn't bother with it. Or him.

Leaning back, he choked out an unsettling laugh, then

struggled to peer down at Kim, who still had one arm around him as she gazed up unblinking into his eyes. And now, as the light flared again, Harland could see her other hand, the wet gleam of metal between her and Naysmith, the dark stain that bloomed out across both their clothing, and the trickle of red on the pale skin of her hand. And still Kim wouldn't let Naysmith go.

'Kim!' Harland cried, hesitating as he stooped for the machete. 'Oh God!'

'It's all right.' Her voice was calm, soothing almost. He wasn't sure if she was speaking to him or to Naysmith.

Harland took the long black blade from the grass, then stared at the two of them, locked in a bitter embrace. He suddenly felt terribly alone, like a stranger disturbing an intimate moment. They stood without words as the rain poured down until Naysmith tensed, bowing with great effort to plant a single kiss on Kim's upturned forehead. The light flared again. As he drew away, Harland could see the drops of blood his lips left behind, like red tears running down between her eyes.

And then, when she couldn't hold him up any more, he crumpled down to his knees, the handle of the kitchen knife still jutting out from between his ribs. Kim stood over him sadly, one arm red with blood.

The spell broken, Harland moved quickly to her side.

'Kim! Are you all right?'

He wasn't sure what to do, hesitating before awkwardly putting his arm around her shoulder. For a moment, she didn't move, then one small hand crept up to hold his wrist.

'What the hell happened?' Harland gasped. 'Where did you get the knife?'

She looked up at him, her face calm.

'I brought it from the house,' she said simply. Something

in the way she spoke bothered him, but what was one more
doubt when everything was wrong?

'OK.' He took a breath, trying to think straight. 'We need to
get back to the cottage, phone this in, get an ambulance—'

'No!' Suddenly she was alive, her voice urgent. 'Please,
Graham, don't!'

Harland stared at her, confused.

'But he'll bleed to death,' he told her.

She stared up at him and nodded sadly.

'Yes.'

And suddenly he knew what she was asking. Her steady
gaze suddenly seemed unsettling and he turned away from
her, looking back down the path to the waiting lights of the
cottage. How many relatives needed closure? How many
police investigations needed a result? Naysmith might be the
key to numerous unsolved cases . . .

He turned back, ready to argue, but as he did something
seemed to pass between the two figures before him, and
Naysmith raised his head slightly, a painful smile on his face.
Kim looked up mournfully.

'*Please*, Graham.'

And he understood. This was her chance to be free of him,
really free. No technicalities, no indecisive juries, no parole.
Really *free*. He took a tentative step forward, peering down
at Naysmith, noting the amount of blood that had soaked
out across his clothing, then stepped back and looked at Kim.
She held out a bloody hand and, after a moment, he took it.

'Thank you,' she said softly.

They stood there as the storm blew itself out. Naysmith spoke
very little, but did raise his head briefly and beckoned Kim
close to him as the wind dropped. She knelt beside him as
he struggled to speak.

'My car,' he told her. 'Parked on a farm track. On the right
. . . at the bottom of the hill.'

She watched as he took a difficult breath, then continued.
'Get rid of it.'

She stared at him for a moment, then her eyes filled with
tears as it dawned on her what he was saying.

'We'll find it,' she nodded gratefully.

Harland stood silently, staring down at them. *He was telling
her how to cover her tracks – how to get away with killing him.*

He realised that Naysmith was looking up at him, grinning.

As the clouds rolled on along the coast and stars winked out
against the clearing sky, Naysmith's breathing became ragged.
He was pale now, haggard-looking. Kim started to cry again,
but the sound seemed to rouse something in the dying man
and he opened his eyes.

'Well played,' he whispered, then fell silent.

Harland wondered who he'd said it to.

# 54

Harland stepped out of the small glass shower cubicle, gripping the bathmat with his toes as he felt the uneven lie of the floor. The air was cold on his skin after the spray of warm water and steam, but he didn't care about the cold. Not tonight.

He wrapped one towel about himself, tucking it in so it would stay up, then rubbed his hair dry with another. His muscles felt stiff now, tired after the exertions of the previous hours, and he stretched wearily before padding through to the bedroom.

They looked at each other for a moment, a brief flicker of eye contact, before Harland moved round to his side of the bed and sank down onto the duvet. He leaned forward for a moment, bowing his head as he rubbed his hair once more, then sat back to rest against the headboard, the towel round his shoulders.

Kim hesitated, then leaned across, one bare arm slipping out from under the covers to hold him. After a moment, she moved closer, resting her head on him, her hair still damp, cold against his chest.

And now, only now, in the quiet of dawn, his mind replayed the events of the night, trying to piece things together, to fill in the gaps. He stared unseeing at the far wall while his memory ran after her, following her out of the lounge and through to the kitchen, where she'd slipped around the table and wrenched open the back door . . .

When had she picked up that knife?

It had all happened so quickly. *Too* quickly.

He frowned for a moment, then looked down at the top of her head.

'Kim?'

She stirred slightly but didn't look up.

'Yes?'

He was going to ask her about the knife – the knife she'd never had time to pick up – but his mind had raced ahead and was already waiting with another, more important question.

'How did he find us?' He waited, listening as the silence yawned like a chasm between them. 'How did he know we were here?'

She remained still for a long time, then finally squirmed her body around so that she could turn and look up at him.

'I told Sarah.' She held his gaze, waiting for him to react, to register some surprise, but there was none. He'd just wanted to hear her say it. 'I knew they were talking, gossiping about me . . .'

'. . . and that she would tell him,' Harland finished. 'He would have suspected if you'd called him yourself.'

'It was the only way,' she murmured.

She had planned it. Not so much self-defence, more an execution. Premeditated. Murder.

'Why didn't you tell me?' he asked, a few moments later. Kim gave him a long, steady look, then turned away.

Stupid question. There was no way she could have told him. He'd never have gone along with it – he'd have wanted to go through the proper channels. And she'd tried it his way already, without success.

'No, I suppose you couldn't,' he mused. She'd done what she had to. And he'd played his unwitting part. 'You couldn't ask a police officer to help you kill someone, even someone like him.'

She turned to stare up at him again, biting her lip as a shadow of concern passed over her face.

'What are you going to do, Graham?' she asked after a moment.

He knew what he ought to do. Get out of bed, find his phone and call the whole thing in while he still could. He had to snap out of this honeymoon stupidity and get back to acting like a proper copper. But his thoughts returned to the car they'd found, tucked away down a lonely farm track, just as Naysmith had said. From long years of habit, he'd glanced at the tax disc, noting that it didn't match the registration on the front of the vehicle, and had crouched down to discover the fake plates fixed over the real ones. *Clever.* It explained how Naysmith had been able to drive to and from his victims without leaving a trail that could lead back to him. Nicely anonymous . . .

. . . unless the police should somehow discover the real owner of the car.

'Graham?' She'd turned her face away again, resting her head on his chest.

If he'd just pushed her harder about Naysmith when he'd had the chance, or pursued his original suspicions about the Redland murder – might he have prevented this, spared her from the terrible thing she'd done?

He stared at her for a long, serious moment, the killer in his arms, then held her tight and tenderly kissed her wet hair.

And gladly closed his eyes.

# EPILOGUE

*Tuesday, 7 October*

The main office at Portishead was quiet. The day shift had just started and Mendel was hunched over reading a report when Firth came across to stand by his desk.

'Morning,' she said, her voice expectant.

'All right, Sue.' He looked up at her and his broad face creased into a grin. 'What are you after?'

She returned his smile.

'Well, I was going to ask DI Harland, but he's on leave again . . .' She shook her head, ordering her thoughts. 'Josh says they may have a suspect on the Severn Beach case. You know, from last year?'

Mendel leaned back in his chair and nodded.

'That's right,' he said. 'Devon and Cornwall found an abandoned car with fake number plates. Nothing too exciting but someone logged it on the PNC and the computer found a match. Turns out that the fake registration was the same as a vehicle Hampshire Police were after for a murder in West Meon.'

'The one that you and Harland linked to the Severn Beach murder?'

'Yeah,' Mendel's expression grew more serious, 'and several others, including that stabbing in Redland.'

Firth raised her eyebrows.

'I hadn't heard that,' she said.

'It's not common knowledge yet, but Pope reckons they've found the Vaughn woman's necklace under the driver's seat.' The big man set the report down on his desk and rubbed his square jaw reflectively. 'Of course, that's coming from Pope, so it might be a load of old bollocks.'

Firth smiled.

'Do you know if they've picked up the owner of the car?' she asked.

Mendel scowled and shook his head.

'The owner's missing,' he explained. 'And the car was found on the coast, parked at a well-known local suicide spot.'

'You think he killed himself?' Firth asked, puzzled.

Mendel looked away for a moment, then shrugged.

'My guess is they'll never find him,' he said.

Firth considered this, inclining her head to one side.

'Who was he?' she asked.

Mendel sat forward in his chair and folded his arms.

'Robert Naysmith, some sales director bloke from Wiltshire.' He paused, then added, 'Funny thing is, the Met actually interviewed him a while back – Graham put them on to him.'

He frowned to himself.

'So Harland was right, then?' There was a note of pride in Firth's voice.

Mendel looked at her thoughtfully before answering.

'Yes, I suppose he was right . . . ' The big man appeared troubled by something, then shook his head and reached for a large mug on his desk. 'Fancy a cuppa?'

'OK,' Firth nodded.

'Come on then.' Mendel smiled as he got to his feet. 'I'm gonna make you the finest cup of tea you'll have all day.'

# ACKNOWLEDGEMENTS

Writing is meant to be a solitary pursuit, but at the end of this story I find that I have quite a few people to thank:

Andrew Sprunt, Julia Painter, Kate Ranger and Nick Day, for their valuable feedback on early drafts of the story, and their encouragement, which I value even more;

Chris Wild, for introducing me to the wonderful Les Mirabelles, where New Forest ponies really *do* walk past the window;

Andrea Popkess, who pointed out how easily cyclists can move through a city;

Imogen Heap, for the songs that became my audio mood board for Kim;

Andrew Oates, Christopher Hilldrup, Mark Langdon and Sandy Osborne, for taking the time to help me with my enquiries;

Caroline Johnson, for her fortitude in the face of numerous corrections;

Eve White, my excellent literary agent, plus Jack Ramm and the rest of the team, for looking after me so wonderfully well;

All the lovely people at Hodder & Stoughton, but especially my editor Francesca Best, for some epic brainstorming, great guidance and questionable orange iced tea;

And finally, Anna and Cameron, for their patience and belief. Thank you.

Now read on for the tantalising opening to the next DI
Harland crime mystery by


# FERGUS McNEILL


Out in hardback and ebook 2014

HODDER &
STOUGHTON

# CHAPTER ONE

Detective Inspector Graham Harland nosed the car into a cobbled alleyway and bumped the passenger-side wheels up over the kerb. Switching off the engine, he leaned forward, gazing up through the windscreen at the old, industrial building – three stories of sturdy Victorian brickwork, illuminated against the darkness by the steady flash of blue lights. The arched windows were bricked up and sealed beneath decades of masonry paint, while spiked iron railings and aluminium-cased security cameras crowned the upper floors. But it was the murals that held his attention.

Burning bright against the grime-blackened walls, a host of nightmarish images reared up – sinister, subjective, suggestive. Stencilled creatures stood ten feet tall above the cracked pavement, wreathed in slogans, while aerosol figures twisted themselves around the architecture of the upper stories, leering down out of the gloom – different styles and colours, yet somehow the characters danced together to form an unbroken skin, stretched out across the nightclub's walls.

Ahead of him, Harland could see a small crowd of ghouls – shuffling silhouettes pressed up against the gently twisting police tape, all eagerly staring towards the lights of the ambulance and the patrol cars.

*Waiting for the body to be brought out to them.*

He sighed and sank back into the seat, his watchful gaze flickering up to the reflection in the rear-view mirror. He looked tired. The strobing blue lights glinted cold in his eyes, casting shadows beneath the high cheekbones, picking out flecks of silver grey in his short, dark hair and in the stubble on his angular jaw.

'Shall we?'

Beside him, Detective Sergeant Russell Pope stared at him with small, expectant eyes, one pudgy hand on the door handle, eager and inquisitive to poke around the scene.

*Just like the bloody ghouls.*

'Might as well,' Harland shrugged. It was a narrow alley, and he watched Pope struggle to clamber out without banging the passenger door on the adjacent brick wall, then turned away and got out himself. Standing up and stretching his tall, lean frame, he briefly thought of lighting a cigarette, but the chill touch of a breeze that blew across the cobbles dissuaded him. Not now. He'd have one later. Afterwards, when he'd really need it.

Pope was staring up at the building, head back, his lips slightly parted as they always seemed to be when he was thinking.

'Know anything about this place?' Harland asked, slamming his door and walking over to his colleague. 'I've not been down here before.'

'Not much,' Pope shrugged, turning back towards him. 'A few drugs busts, the odd fight. Nothing out of the ordinary. Locals and students, I suppose.'

Harland glanced up at the mural, noting the eerie, psyche-delic nature of the figures. Above him, a painted octopus held two giant pills marked *Truth* and *Freedom*.

'Not my sort of place,' he mused.

They made their way along the alley, pushing between the milling on-lookers, and the snatches of murmured speculation. A uniformed officer stepped forward briskly to intercept them as Pope went to duck under the blue and white cordon tape, but relaxed as the shorter man flourished his warrant card.

'DS Pope and DI Harland, CID.' A little pompous, but Harland was too weary to make anything of it tonight.

'Evening sir,' the officer nodded, lifting the tape for them.

'All right Johnson,' Harland nodded as he stooped beneath it, then walked a few paces away from the ghouls. 'How's it going?'

'Fine thanks.' Johnson had been welcome backup during a difficult arrest on the Lawrence Weston estate last year. In the confines of the alleyway he seemed even taller than usual – an imposing figure, with broad shoulders and a square jaw. 'They got you working for central now?'

'That's right.' Harland maintained his deadpan expression. 'We solved all the crime in Portishead so I've come to help you sort Bristol out.'

As they talked, he let his gaze sweep the crowd of onlookers, noting the average age, the way people were dressed, looking for anything out of the ordinary . . . but it seemed to be just the usual bunch of misfits – faces painted pale, and eyes sunk in shadow from the streetlamps. The only one who caught his attention was a wasted-looking man in his thirties who appeared to be blatantly skinning-up a joint, despite all the blue flashing lights.

He sighed and turned back to Johnson.

'Everyone inside?'

'I think so, yes. DS Linwood was talking with the ambulance crew . . .' Johnson turned and pointed towards the club's main entrance – a vaulted archway lined with stencilled yellow teeth, and double doors painted like a lolling tongue. 'Just through there.'

'Thanks.' Harland glanced over at Pope, then gestured towards the building. 'Lead on.'

The double doors opened onto a small foyer, wallpapered with posters. One showed a girl with a rapturous expression on her upturned face, and blood running out of her ears, except the blood was blue. Harland paused to look at the image.

*Not a quiet place, then.*

Ahead of them, a long black-walled corridor led into the club, with recessed spots in the low ceiling casting pools of illumination onto the chequered lino floor. At the far end of it, a knot of people stood in the light, talking quietly. One of them looked round, excused himself from the group, and hurried over to meet them. He was a wiry man, with short brown hair and a suit that looked as though he slept in it.

'Evening sir, evening Russell.' He smiled – a bundle of nervous energy and quick movements.

'Evening.' Harland acknowledged him. He'd got to know DS Jack Linwood quite well in the first few weeks following his transfer to Bristol CID and, while he'd found his new colleague's relentless enthusiasm a little wearing, it was infinitely preferable to being teamed up with Pope. 'Who was first in on this one?'

'Ambulance crew beat us to it.' Linwood jerked his head towards the green and yellow clad paramedics he'd been talking to. 'They were here a few minutes before PC Burgess and Reed in the area car. Do you know them?'

Pope shrugged and shook his head.

'Not yet,' Harland replied, 'but I suppose we will before the night's out.'

Linwood smiled.

'Well,' he said, beckoning them to follow him, 'I reckon everyone will want a look at this one.'

'What are you on about?' Harland frowned.

'You don't know?'

'I know you're starting to annoy me.'

'All right, all right.' Linwood held his hands up. 'Just making conversation. Come on, you're going to like this.'

He led them down a wide set of steps that opened out onto the main dance-floor area – empty now, but still heavy with the smoky reek of dry ice and the sharp tang of sweat. Huge colourful shapes were suspended from the high ceiling, giant paper butterflies and vast canvas flowers twisting slowly in the gloom above. A brightly illuminated bar area ran along one wall, and several police officers were standing there, along with a couple of vacant-looking kids who, judging by the logos on their t-shirts, were members of staff.

Linwood led them across to the far side of the room, where another officer was pulling off a set of blue paper overalls beside a scuffed metal door marked *Men Only*.

'Suit up,' he said brightly. 'It's in there.'

The toilets smelled of bleach and liquid soap. A battered vending machine hung from the wall by the door, supplying the late night combo of breath mints and condoms, and glassy puddles meandered out across the tiled floor from beneath the urinals. A photographer, wearing white overalls, was crouched on one of several steel stepping-stone plates, training his lens into the furthest of the three graffiti-covered stalls. There was a soft click, and a glaring flash lit the walls.

Harland blinked and lowered his eyes, his own overalls rustling as he stepped carefully from one steel platform to the next. His shoes were wrapped in protective plastic coverings, but in here he was glad of any excuse to keep his feet from touching the floor.

The photographer studied the screen on the back of his camera, then glanced up.

'Want me to . . .?' He gestured towards the door.

'No, it's fine.' Harland shook his head. 'You carry on.'

He took another step towards the photographer, and another, then paused as the scene inside the toilet cubicle came into view.

It was the body of a man, slumped down in the corner at the side of the porcelain bowl, like a puppet with its strings cut – legs splayed wide, bald head slumped forward. The arms were stretched out horizontally – one along the back wall, one along the inside of the stall – palms shown outward as though in surrender.

Another click and the camera flash glared back from an ugly wet stain on the crotch of the dead man's jeans. His skin looked sallow, but he didn't appear to be that old. Brilliant white trainers, a slim red zipper top – expensive clothes that passed for stylish among the younger generation – and the dark shadow on his scalp suggested he was bald by choice rather than age.

Harland crouched down, wanting to see the victim's face, frowning as he leaned forward to–

*Flash.*

'Shit!' He stumbled back, putting a hand on the floor to steady himself, as he glared up at the photographer. '*Just* . . . just give me a second, okay?'

Wiping his fingers on the leg of the overalls, he realized that his pulse was racing.

*Breathe.*

Turning back, he leaned in closer, trying to discern something in the alien expression on the dead man's face. It looked almost foetal – eye squeezed shut, lips pressed together . . .

'Superglue.' Linwood's voice came from behind him. 'Or

some other sort of fast-bonding stuff. Someone sealed his eyes, nose and mouth. Even his ears.'

Harland recoiled slightly, as the awful expression before him suddenly made sense. Slowly, he turned to look at the man's outstretched arms.

'And glued his hands to the walls,' he murmured. 'Like posing the corpse for us.'

He started to get to his feet, glancing down to make sure he didn't misjudge his position on the stepping stones.

'Was this done to him post-mortem?' He hoped it had been, tried to stop his imagination careering into the claustrophobic horror of what it might have felt like to be conscious, aware.

'No,' Linwood said quietly. 'He was alive.'

And now, Harland noticed the small peels of bloody skin, an angry blemish on the tiled white wall behind the body.

'For fuck's sake.' He averted his eyes, staring up towards the merciless glare of the ceiling lights – anything to burn the image out of his mind – forcing himself to breathe steadily.

*Breathe.*

This poor bastard had been so desperate to breathe that he'd torn the skin off the back of his head, trying to thrash himself free himself before he suffocated.

'Sir?'

*Get a grip. Don't try and empathise with the victim.*

Turning away from the body, he waved for the photographer to continue, then picked his way stiffly back towards the door where Linwood was watching him.

'Told you,' the younger man shrugged.

Harland shook his head, composing himself. He couldn't let the Bristol team think he was squeamish.

'Do we know who he is?'

'That's the good news,' Linwood said. 'One of the bar staff knew him. Ever heard of The French Connection?'

'The film?' Harland asked, puzzled.

'No, a nasty piece of work called Arnaud Durand.' Linwood nodded towards the toilet cubicle. 'He's better known to his friends as The French Connection.'

'Let me guess . . . because he's French?'

'I suppose there's that too,' Linwood conceded, 'but mostly because he's your friendly local dealer.'

Harland pictured the miserable toilet cubicles, their doors covered in scrawled obscenities, imagining dull-eyed junkies slipping inside to score.

'Makes sense,' he said. 'What about the paramedics? Did they disturb anything?'

'I've spoken to both of them,' Linwood replied. 'He'd already been dead for some time when they got here – they went to check his airways, saw what had been done to him, and stepped back. They know the drill.'

Another flash lit the room. Harland turned to look back at the row of stalls. From here, the body was hidden but he could still see the man's face in his mind, yearning for air.

*Breathe.*

'Must have been subdued,' he scowled. 'You don't *let* that sort of thing happen to you.'

Linwood tapped his chin thoughtfully.

'The paramedics said there's a lot of trauma to the back of the skull, not just around where the glue was.' He gazed across the room towards the cubicles. 'I don't know . . . maybe somebody bashed his head in, knocked him out first. Then they'd be able to stick him to the wall, and finish off doing his eyes, nose, mouth.'

Harland looked at him and nodded slowly.

'And then the poor bastard woke up.' He shuddered. 'Come on, let's get out of here. I need some air.'

Have you read the first part of DI Harland and
Robert Naysmith's story?

# FERGUS MCNEILL
# EYE CONTACT

If you look him in the eye, you're dead.

From the outside, Robert Naysmith is a successful
businessman, handsome and charming. But for years
he's been playing a deadly game.

He doesn't choose his victims. Each is selected at random
– the first person to make eye contact after he begins 'the
game' will not have long to live. Their fate is sealed

When the body of a young woman is found on Severn Beach,
Detective Inspector Harland is assigned the case. It's only
when he links it to an unsolved murder in Oxford that the
police begin to guess at the awful scale of the crimes.

But how do you find a killer who strikes without motive?

Out now in paperback and ebook

HODDER

In the best books, the ending often comes as a shock.
Not just because of that one last twist in the tale,
but because you have been so absorbed in their world,
that coming back to the harsh light of reality is a jolt.

If that describes you now, then perhaps you should track down
some new leads, and find new suspense in other worlds.

Join us at www.hodder.co.uk, or follow us on
Twitter @hodderbooks, and you can tap in to a
community of fellow thrill-seekers.

Whether you want to find out more about this book,
or a particular author, watch trailers and interviews, have
the chance to win early limited editions, or simply browse
our expert readers' selection of the very best books,
we think you'll find what you're looking for.

And if you don't, that's the place to tell us what's missing.

**We love what we do, and we'd love you to be part of it.**

www.hodder.co.uk

@hodderbooks

HodderBooks

HodderBooks